The Ice Match

ALSO BY TRINITY LEMM

The Roommates Duet:

The Puck Arrangement

The Forever Series:

Forever Burn
Forever Frozen
Forever & Ever

Standalones:

Home

Poetry:

Fingerprints

Playlist

"Last Night" | Morgan Wallen

"All-American Bitch" | Olivia Rodrigo

"Dirty Little Secret" | The All-American Rejects

"boyfriend" | Ariana Grande, Social House

"Champagne & Sunshine" | PLVTINUM, Tarro

"Escapism" | RAYE, 070 Shake

"Ego" | Beyonce

"Into It" | Chase Atlantic

"She's so Mean" | Matchbox Twenty

"Cupid's Chokehold" | Gym Class Heroes

"Say It Ain't So" | Weezer

"Inside Out" | Eve 6

"Unholy" | Sam Smith, Kim Petras

"Dirty Thoughts" | Chloe Adams

"I'm Good (Blue)" | David Guetta, Bebe Rexha

"Seven Nation Army" | The White Stripes

"Under the Influence" | Chris Brown

"Holy Grail" | JAY-Z, Justin Timberlake

"Confidence" | Ocean Alley

"Nonsense" | Sabrina Carpenter

"Something in the Orange" | Zach Bryan

Cedar U Team Roster

#1 | Lane Avery

#4 | Keith Sunset

#5 | Sawyer Peterson

#7 | Matt Gallagher

#10 | Mason Makela

#11 | Brayden Thompson

#14 | Cody Holtz

#18 | Nicholas Crew

#20 | Nathan Bailey

#21 | Joseph Costa

#25 | Jett Jameson

#27 | Robert Shesky

#30 | TJ Douglas

#32 | Brody Moore

#39 | Ross Hughes

#42 | Jonah Morgan

#44 | Griffin Edwards

#50 | Riley Davis

#54 | Bryson Miller

#60 | Derek Wrigh

Trigger warnings:

This book contains content about topics such as absent parents and divorce, as well as the mentioning of the death of a family member and adoption.

This book is recommended for readers ages 18+ only.

Please read at your own discretion.

Friendly reminder to all my girlies:

Never let a man tell you what to do.

You're too beautiful and powerful for that bullsh*t.

<u>Chapter One</u>

Crew

I stood at the bar, TJ to my left and a hot blonde with blue streaks in her hair to my right.

The rest of the team was crowded around, taking up every inch of space at the bar, with the exception of a few younger players that were scattered throughout the room, laughing and flirting their drunken asses off with girls that they hoped they'd spend the night with.

Stallions was the most popular college bar in town, and although most people weren't back yet from summer break, it was still fairly packed tonight, which meant there were plenty of options for me to take home.

But my eyes were currently set on blondie-with-blue-streaks.

Clutching my beer in one hand, I had my other wrapped around her waist. I leaned in, content when my voice seemed to send a small shiver through her body. "What did you say your name was again?"

She gulped as she turned her head towards me, making us only a few inches apart. "Lucy."

"Lucy," I nodded with a flirtatious smirk. "I like it."

She gave a small smile, causing my eyes to land straight on her pink, glossy lips.

"I'm Cr—"

"I know who you are," she said.

"Really?" I asked nonchalantly, playing it cool.

It wasn't rare for girls to know who I was before I formally introduced myself, and like the egotistical son of a bitch I was, I liked it.

"Of course," she answered, her eyes dropping to *my* lips for a moment. "I pay attention around here."

"Ah," I gave a nod, sipping my beer. "So, you watch hockey then?"

"A bit," she shrugged lightly with her exposed shoulder.

Hmm, now she *was the one playing it cool.*

I was into it.

"Gonna come to our games this year?" I asked casually, leaning into the bar.

She tipped her head side to side, still grinning. "Probably."

"Well, I hope you do." I shot her my best, most inviting smirk, pulling out the big guns knowing damn well my dimples popped up with it.

Her eyes lit up, and by the way she took a deep breath while rubbing her hand tensely along her thigh, I could only infer that if we were alone right now, she'd be jumping straight onto me, begging me to rip her clothes off.

Not that there was much to rip off anyway.

Her gray top barely covered her boobs, and her jean shorts were so short that I could see the bottom of her ass falling out.

I wasn't complaining though.

Considering it was past midnight and Lane made me promise we wouldn't stay until closing, I knew my time was running out.

If I wanted blondie-with-blue-streaks in my bed at the end of the night, I needed to act fast.

My mind reeled for a moment, jumping back and forth between which line to pull out next. I had a few that I usually alternated between just to keep things interesting.

"You look gorgeous."

"I want to see you again."

"Do you have plans later?"

But before I had the chance to spit something out, there was a loud gasp coming from behind me, followed by what sounded like Lane's voice.

I turned, noticing that some of the guys were laughing, while others had their mouths in the shape of an *O*. Regardless of their reactions, they were all looking towards Lane.

I pushed one of our younger players over to get a glimpse of what the hell was going on. Right when my eyes landed on a short red-haired girl who looked like she was about to commit first-degree murder, I recoiled a bit myself. Her entire front-side was soaking wet, outlining her boobs. And considering she was wearing a tank top, the outline was pretty defined.

I sucked in a sharp breath, seemingly unable to look away from her chest until she shrieked in frustration and stomped off.

Lane let out a stressed sigh, turning towards me.

"What the hell was that?" I asked, motioning in the direction the girl scurried off in.

He seemed visibly shaken, a hint of guilt swimming in his eyes. "I spilled my drink on that girl."

"Damn," I said, mindlessly letting out a chuckle. "You're an ass."

"It was an accident!"

I patted him on the shoulder. "Don't worry, man. Everything's fine."

"I feel bad," he murmured. "I didn't even apologize."

Welp.

"Panicked?"

"That might be an understatement," he admitted, gazing off.

"It's alright," I assured him. "It's not that deep."

He leaned over the bar with a frown, trying to wave the bartender down to get a new drink.

I stayed beside him even though my dick was yelling for me to go back to Blondie. I ignored the temptation though. Afterall, it was *bros before hoes*. And even though I had a little brother of my own, I considered Lane as more blood than my actual family. If Lane needed me, even if it was for something as small as this, then I'd be there.

I'd had plenty of close friends throughout my life, most of which were met at the rink, but Lane was my chosen family. At eighteen, we played on the same team in the National Junior Hockey League before committing to Cedar University to play hockey here. In a short amount of time, we had gone from strangers to teammates to best friends to brothers. It felt like I'd known him my whole life even though we'd only been best friends for four years now.

I was already NHL bound after this season, signed by the Chicago Blackhawks, which I still couldn't believe. The NHL had always been my dream ever since I was a kid, and now I was less than a year away from living out that dream. In the meantime, I was studying sports management, a common major for athletes.

But Lane, on the other hand, still didn't know if he wanted to go pro or not, and I'd been trying for years to convince him to.

"Hey!" a shrill voice screamed, causing more than half of us to turn around. "Which one of you spilled all over my friend?"

The voice in question was coming from a small, dark-haired girl that was an Olivia Rodrigo look-alike. My brows shot up as she began interrogating the guys, sticking her tiny finger in their faces. Her friend, the poor red-haired girl that fell victim to Lane's beer, stood there sheepishly, attempting numerous times to tone her friend down but failing every time.

Lane stepped forward, hand raised, confessing to the crime. "It was me."

The outspoken one crossed her arms. "So, you poured your drink all over her and didn't apologize? What the hell!"

Lane's head tipped down as he blew out a breath. He turned to the redhead. "I'm sorry."

Typically the golden boy of Cedar U, Lane was hardly ever in a situation where he was the bad guy. This was a rare occurrence, which made it extremely hard for our teammates to look away.

The girl's shy eyes dropped as she nodded once, seemingly accepting his apology. Little Miss Fury, on the other hand, didn't seem fully content with it.

Before thinking twice about it, I stepped in. "Alright," I said, lightly raising my hands, "calm down. It was an accident."

Her eyes shot over to me and she jutted her chin out. "Haven't you ever heard that you should never tell a woman to calm down?"

My smirk grew, slightly amused. "There's a lot of fury in that tiny body."

She had daggers for eyes. I could feel her anger radiating off her body like campfire smoke as it hurdled your way. If she wasn't slightly taller than the munchkins from The Wizard of Oz, perhaps she'd be offered a spot on the team for probably having more aggression than anyone else on the ice.

"You haven't seen the half of it," she said, scorn dripping from her tone.

I kind of liked how feisty she was. It was annoying but also slightly entertaining because it was not what I was used to at all.

Usually, it was always batted eyelashes and flirty smirks, boring small talk and overly sweet compliments. But this girl seemed like a wild card.

"Alright, let's see it," I dared.

"Do *not* encourage her," Redhead blurted, gripping her friend's wrist and yanking her away.

Once they were out of earshot, Lane muttered, "Yikes."

"Yikes is right," I agreed. "Do you at least feel a little better now that you got to apologize?"

"A little."

"Good," I said. "Now please forgive me for leaving your ass to go make sure I'm getting laid tonight."

He rolled his eyes, but his frown slightly lifted. "Good luck."

"Thanks, buddy," I joked, nudging him before heading back over to where I last saw Blondie.

But when I got there, Blondie was gone.

Goddammit.

All my hard work was for nothing. The prize was gone. Poof. Vanished.

What a tragedy.

If I really wanted to get laid tonight, I still could. I had plenty of girl's numbers and Snapchats that would practically run to me if I invited them over. But I wasn't a big fan of hooking up with the same girl twice. It wasn't because I was intentionally trying to be an ass, but nine times out of ten, they expected something more than just sex the more you brought them around, and that wasn't something I could provide.

I sulked all the way back to Lane. "I'm ready to go when you are."

"That was fast. Abandoned mission?"

"Nope. Failed mission."

His eyes widened. "She denied you?"

"Yeah, right," I laughed out loud. "She wasn't there."

"Gotcha." He scanned the room. "There's no one else you want?"

My eyes followed his lead, glancing around at the options. "There are plenty I want," I confessed with a sly smile, "but I don't got any patience left for it tonight."

"Fair," he said. "In that case, let's go."

"Wait," I said, gripping his arm. "What about you?"

"Eh, not tonight."

I sighed, even though I wasn't surprised.

Lane was much less promiscuous than I was, which was sort of a shame considering he could probably pull twice the amount of girls as me if he wanted to.

We paid our tabs quickly then headed outside to wait for a few of the other guys.

Lane walked in front of me, and the second he opened the door, I noticed him stiffen in the slightest, but I didn't know why until I saw the two girls from earlier standing there.

I couldn't help but smirk. "Look. It's Little Miss Fury."

"Shut up, Crew," Lane grumbled.

I wasn't sure why this was all so amusing to me, but it was. Honestly, I was pretty sure it had to do more with Lane than with the girls. Any time Lane lost his cool, it was like some sort of sick pleasure for me. The guy was as cool as a cucumber twenty-four-seven.

When we were playing hockey together in juniors, we were down by three at the end of the second period in the championship game and Lane didn't even bat an eye while the rest of our team was practically pissing in their gear.

When I crashed my car last year and nearly tore off the front bumper while Lane was in the passenger seat, he was undaunted and acted like it was just a small scratch.

When he got into a small disagreement with his mom and she threatened to stop helping him pay his rent, I was pretty sure I was freaking out more than he was. It somehow turned into *him* comforting *me*.

I swore he was rarely fazed.

So right now, seeing him upset and rattled from accidentally spilling on this pretty little stranger had me a bit happier than it should've. I loved seeing him all worked up.

There was the lightest breeze, creating the perfect summer night. It was a refreshing difference to the hot, sticky air inside. No one was around besides us and the girls, a small array of cars driving by every few moments. I leaned against the brick building, getting comfortable as I eyed the feisty one. "What are you guys doing out here?"

"Waiting for an Uber," she answered, sounding bothered. "What are you doing out here?"

I threw a lazy thumb over my shoulder. "Waiting for our buddies."

"Good for you," she whirred, keeping her eyes on her phone.

"What's your name?" I asked.

Not paying me a single ounce of attention as she tapped away on her phone, her voice had an edge of agitation. "Kota."

"I'm Crew."

"I don't care," Kota mumbled. She looked up at her friend. "It's not working."

I sort of thought the feistiness thing was an act she was putting on inside to back up her friend. *Guess not.*

I pushed my hands into my pockets, glancing over at Lane who quite literally was kicking rocks.

The redhead let out a small groan, tilting her head towards her shoulder. "It's always hard getting an Uber on Saturdays. We might have to wait a bit."

For some reason, I felt the need to play hero. "Do you want us to walk you guys home?"

Little Miss Fury crossed her arms, her eyes burning into me. "Is that code for something?"

Goddamn, she was starting to push my buttons. I was just trying to be nice, but she was continuously rubbing me the wrong way. I was already in a shit mood knowing that I wasn't getting laid tonight, and even though she was standing in sky-high stilettos and a skin-tight dress, causing my dick to twitch, I was still growing more agitated by the second.

If she wanted to be a bitch, then I'd be a bitch back.

I leaned in. "Yeah, it's code for '*Do you want us to walk you home?*'"

Kota didn't even flinch, her voice remaining bothered. "No thanks. It's fine. We'll wait for an Uber."

"Fine. Didn't want to anyway."

She scoffed. "Yeah, okay."

My eyes narrowed, my foot tapping along the pavement. "What're you saying?"

"I'm saying," she spoke, motioning to me and then Lane, "you and Mr. Abercrombie over there are obviously just trying to get us to go home with you."

I choked back laughter. "You're not my type."

She lifted a brow, her eyes full of doubt. "Really?"

"Really."

"Then what's your type?"

"Anything besides bitch," I said confidently.

Mouth dropping open, her loud scoff gave the same deafening effect as nails on a chalkboard. "You're not so pleasant to be around either."

I snickered. "That's not what most other girls tell me."

"There's a difference between your dick and your personality, dude."

I could feel my wicked grin threatening to break my face in half. "Ah, so you wanna talk about my dick, huh?"

Kota gave a light sway. Her body language said innocent, but her devilish smirk and bold eyes said otherwise. "Sure," she paused, smirk growing as she looked me dead in the eyes. "I heard it's small."

What the fuck?

Either she was just making shit up to piss me off or there were some bitter girls spreading rumors about me because I stopped talking to them after hooking up.

My jaw immediately clenched, but I held my facial expression, refusing to show that she was getting to me.

I didn't even have a good comeback for that. I didn't want to deny it because then she'd know she was getting under my skin. But no way in hell was I going to confirm it because it wasn't true.

Thankfully, right then, I could overhear Redhead shitting on hockey, and I used it as my way out.

"Hey," I stepped forward, jokingly placing a hand over my chest, "my ego is hurt."

As if I were nothing but a target, Kota's eyes narrowed in on me. "It *would* be."

I rolled my eyes, lolling my head to the side to look at her. "Do you always have something to say about everything?"

"Pretty much."

I huffed, running a hand through my hair. "How adorably obnoxious."

She smiled with spite, tilting her head. "You think I'm adorable?"

This girl was kind of the worst. She was like a baby cobra— tiny but still able to spit enough venom to kill you. I was pretty certain I'd never been spoken to like this by a girl ever. Most girls tried to be overly nice to me to get my attention or simply get in my bed. Meanwhile, this one seemed disgusted by the thought.

Kota gave a small jump when her phone buzzed, and when she checked it, her face lit up. She grabbed the redhead's hand. "Uber's here. Let's go."

I sighed a breath of relief as they ran off. "Jesus," I muttered, stepping closer to Lane. But he stayed fairly quiet, his eyes following the girls until they got into their Uber. "Hello?" I said, waving a hand in front of his face. "Earth to Lane."

"Yeah, what?" he finally replied, snapping out of it.

My brows furrowed. "You good?"

"I'm fine." He glanced through the front window of the bar. "Where the hell is everybody?"

18

"Don't know, but it would've been nice if they showed up five fucking minutes ago. That was brutal."

"Don't be dramatic."

I scoffed, practically jumping backwards. "*Dramatic?* Did you hear that girl? She was like the devil in heels."

His eyes found the ground as he scratched the back of his neck. "Her friend wasn't bad."

Shaking my head, I attempted to throw off the frustration that was sticking to my skin.

The door swung open and just as I was about to turn around and give the guys shit for taking so long, my anger subsided a bit, and I was pleasantly surprised to see blondie-with-blue-streaks.

She didn't seem to notice me as she began walking off with her friends.

Fuck, what was her name? Lacey? Lainey? Lily?

Fuck, fuck, fuck.

Finally, my eyes widened in both realization and relief. "Lucy!" I called out, causing her to turn. "Hey," I smiled, jogging lightly over to her.

"Hey, Crew," she smiled back.

"What are you doing for the rest of the night?"

She gave a subtle shrug. "Not much, I don't think."

"Do you wanna come over?"

Her two friends were eyeing her excitedly, egging her on.

"Yeah, alright," she agreed.

"Cool. You guys can come too," I said, extending the invite. "We'll all just be hanging out at the house."

Her friends nodded rapidly, following me back over to Lane as the rest of the guys finally stepped outside.

TJ had a girl with him. Jett and Matt were alone. Cody left an hour ago with a girl already. And since Lane didn't want a hookup tonight, it looked like there were three guys and three girls. Perfect.

I shot Jett and Matt a mischievous grin, furtively gesturing to the girls. They shot a grin back.

They'd be thanking me in the morning.

Chapter Two

Kota

Bridget Bell was my best friend on the entire planet. Ever. Point, blank, period.

I'd do anything for that girl, including take down a team of hockey players at the bar on her behalf. She was much shier than me and far more soft-spoken. She'd always had trouble standing up for herself, ever since we were thrown together as roommates freshman year in the dorms.

Our hearts were so similar, but our personalities were opposites, and that somehow made our friendship work better.

After living together for two years in the dorms, we decided to get an apartment together. The mistake we made? Rooming with two girls we barely knew.

Claudia and Carolina were the epitome of hellish roommates. Don't get me wrong, my bitchy exterior definitely made me difficult to become friends with, but the second Bridget expressed that she had issues with them too, I knew I wasn't the only problem.

If they'd kept to themselves and respected other people's privacy, then we wouldn't have had so many issues. But Claudia was a fucking weirdo. In my opinion, it wasn't strange to hang-dry laundry, but it *was* strange to hang-dry thongs. She did it on a regular basis, acting as if it was the most normal thing in the world. One time, I brought a guy home and

20

the first thing he saw when he walked in was an array of g-strings hanging from a clothesline across the span of the living room.

Aside from the weird laundry "hacks," I was also convinced she was into some dark magic stuff. Her room looked like a vampire's, and sometimes, the music she blasted throughout the apartment didn't really sound like music at all. It sounded more like some creepy cult chanting.

As annoying as all that was, she still didn't piss me off more than Carolina, who acted as if everything in the apartment belonged to her.

She'd take everyone's belongings without asking, even self-care items that shouldn't be shared, which was gross. Hairbrushes. Shaving razors. Makeup. Clothes. You name it, and she took it.

The worst part? She'd take people's food too.

That sure as hell didn't fly with me. I was very protective of my snacks.

So, I was very relieved that Claudia and Carolina weren't home when Bridget and I got back from the bar. There was only one week left until our current lease ended and we would get to move into our new apartment, which was a two-bedroom. We'd never have to see either of them again or have to deal with any other roommates, and I couldn't fucking wait.

My phone buzzed, and when Bobby's name lit up the screen, I let out an irritated groan.

Bobby and I had been seeing each other for the past month. He happened to be at Stallions tonight, and we were chatting and flirting it up until the whole hockey-spill-fiasco.

I figured he would've stuck around until after I was done beating some sense into the hockey team, but when Bridget and I returned, he was nowhere to be found.

My hostility echoed through the phone. "Hello?"

"Hey," Bobby said softly. "I know you're probably pissed I left without saying anything..."

"Duh," I spat, hitting the speaker button and setting the phone down on my nightstand while I pulled the Modelo poster out of my purse that I took from the bar's bathroom. I unrolled it, a hint of a smile crossing my lips as I brought it up to a blank space on my bedroom wall and began taping it.

I loved liquor posters, and I'd been collecting them for the last year, ever since Bridget and I turned twenty-one and started going to the bars.

One side of my bedroom wall was covered in them; it was my own personal collection. The bar bathrooms always had liquor posters hung, and I was notorious for stealing them. I had posters about any and every liquor I'd come across.

As I slid the tape over my new poster, I knew I'd have to take it right back down in a few days considering we'd be moving, but I didn't care.

Our new place was in the brand-new apartment building that was just built next to Stallions. When we got a tour eight months ago of the two-bedrooms, I was absolutely enchanted. Everything was gray and black, giving it a modern feel. I was pretty sure I was talking about the gray marble countertops to Bridget for the entire week following our tour.

We signed our lease immediately after that.

The school year was right around the corner, and in a gorgeous new apartment with our futures slowly coming together, it was going to be *Hot Girl Senior Year* for us.

"I'm really sorry," Bobby said through the phone. "I was DD tonight and everyone kept badgering me to leave and I wasn't sure where you went, so I just said fuck it and left to drive them home."

I sighed. "It's whatever."

"Lemme make it up to you."

I grinned, plopping down on my bed. "How so?"

"I can come pick you up?"

"Hmm, and then what?" I flirted.

I could practically hear him smiling through the phone. "You know what."

"Fine," I gave in, playing with the corner of my comforter. "Let me change into some pajamas first."

"Oof," he said, sounding wounded. "You sure? That dress you had on earlier was making me feel some type of way."

I tapped my red nails along the edge of my mattress. "Fine, I'll wear it. As long as it means I get special treatment."

"All the special treatment in the world," he assured me. "Pick you up in twenty?"

"Sounds good," I said, ending the call.

Keeping the dress on was already a stretch, so there was definitely no way I was putting the heels back on. I swapped them for white sneakers instead.

My stomach rumbled in the slightest, so I headed into the kitchen to find a snack. Since I had twenty minutes, I toasted a bagel, then snagged my cream cheese out of the fridge. There wasn't much cream cheese left in the container, so I only used a little bit to make sure I had enough for the last bagel I had.

After eating, I tossed a piece of minty gum in my mouth, double checked my appearance in the front mirror, and headed out when Bobby texted that he was here.

***

The next morning, I did the walk of shame all the way back up to our apartment.

Bridget was on the couch with *Gossip Girl* on, sitting cross-legged as she ate avocado toast.

"Hey," I said.

"Hey," B said.

"I'm gonna go change real quick. I'll be right back."

"Kay," she nodded.

I threw on some sweats and a t-shirt, then made my way back out to where B was.

"That looks yum," I said, slumping beside her.

"It is," she mumbled. "You can use the other half of my avocado if you wanna make some."

"That's alright," I said. "I've got one bagel left that I'm gonna chow down on."

She spoke as I headed into the kitchen. "How was your night? I'm assuming you went to Bobby's."

"Nah. I actually went to that hockey player's house."

B's eyes bulged out of their sockets. She covered her full mouth with her hand, words coming out as a jumbled mess. "Excuse me?"

I let out a whoop of laughter. "Just joshing. That guy was the worst. But yes, I went to Bobby's."

She let out a deep exhale. "Geez, for a second I actually thought..."

"Hell no!" I said. "That guy sucked his own cock for a living."

Don't get me wrong, that guy was attractive. But the thing was, *he knew it*. And that immediately made him *un*attractive.

With a perfectly messy head of brown curls, a chiseled jawline, and huge, warm brown eyes, he looked like he was straight out of a magazine.

But he reeked of a gigantic ego and playboy personality, and I fucking hated guys like that.

B laughed, nearly choking on her toast. I smiled, opening the fridge and digging around for my cream cheese. "Have you seen my cream cheese?"

"No."

Brows drawing in, I immediately became suspicious. I roamed over to the trash can, stepping a little too hard on the foot pedal, which caused it to spring up and thud against the wall.

I clenched my teeth, feeling the heat of anger slither through my bloodstream, all the way up to my brain and exit as smoke through my ears. "Are you. Fucking. *Kidding me!*"

"What's wrong?" B asked.

I grabbed the empty container of cream cheese that was sitting atop the garbage and held it up. "This!" I shouted. "This is what's wrong!"

B recoiled in the slightest, probably fearing for our roommate's safety. "Uh oh."

"I'm gonna kill her," I fumed, breathing heavily. "I'm gonna fucking kill her!" I threw the container back in the trash, turning on my heels and making a beeline towards Carolina's room.

I'd never been very good at hiding my emotions—especially when I was angry.

I'd kill for the people I loved.

I'd also kill for my snacks.

"Kota!" B screeched, chasing after me. Right before I reached her room, B yanked me back. "Stop it!" she yelled as a whisper.

"I'm so tired of her stealing my shit and eating my food!"

B whipped me around to face her, keeping her hands firmly planted on my shoulders. "Six more days."

"Which means I only have six days left to *murder* her," I spewed.

"Kota," she warned.

It felt like everything had been slowly building up over the last year of all of us living together, and even though Carolina and I had gotten into plenty of arguments before, usually all about her taking my stuff, it was next to impossible to keep my chill anymore.

I wouldn't say I was the most confrontational person, but I was when I needed to be. More so, I was a realist. And if someone was doing something wrong or disrespectful or hurtful, whether that be towards me or my loved ones, then I'd speak up.

I inhaled deeply, shutting my eyes. I nodded, "Okay. I'm calm."

"Are you sure..."

"Yeah," I murmured. "Yeah, I'm good."

"Okay..." she said doubtfully, dropping her hands.

The second she no longer had a grip on me, I lunged for Carolina's door, banging on it repeatedly. "Open the fuck up!"

"Kota," B whined, tossing her head back.

"Sorry I had to deceive you, B. But this has to happen."

The door swung open to reveal a yawning Carolina, her hair tied back in a messy knot. "What?"

"Oh, don't act like you just woke up," I accused.

She pretended to be taken aback. "Um?"

"Did you just so happen to have some cream cheese this morning?"

Carolina crossed her arms, her face scrunching as if the accusation couldn't have been falser. "No. Why?"

I took a deep breath, my hands drawing into fists. "Alright," I said calmly. "Let's try this again. Did you eat cream cheese at any point between one a.m. last night and now?"

She cocked a brow, slightly leaning in as if she was trying to intimidate me. "No."

I matched her. "You are the worst fucking liar on the planet." Pointing to the half-eaten bagel on her nightstand, I screamed, "There's evidence right there!"

"I used my own cream cheese for that."

With a deceitful smile, I blinked rapidly at her, crossing my arms. "Is that so?"

"Yeah," Carolina huffed.

"You're so fucking lucky we're moving out in a week," I said through clenched teeth. Sliding past her and into her room, I snagged the other half of her bagel that hadn't yet been touched.

"What the hell are you doing?"

"I'm takin' this fuckin' bagel," I shot at her, trudging right back out to the living room, just in time for her to slam her door shut.

Bridget's face was scrunched, and she gave a slight cringe, staring at the bagel in my hands. "Are you really gonna eat that?"

I scoffed, revolted by the idea. "Hell no," I said, tossing it straight in the trash.

B's sugary laughter filled the air, until Claudia's voice echoed from her room.

"Hey, can you guys keep it down please? I'm trying to do something!"

Immediately, music that sounded like it was meant to be at the beginning of a horror movie blasted throughout the apartment. I sighed to myself.

Get me the fuck out of here.

Chapter Three

Crew

When my eyes peeled open, I saw a mess of blue streaks on the pillow beside me, questionably close to me.

When she started stirring, gradually moving towards me, I rolled over so that my back was facing her. I secretly felt around for my phone, moving at a snail's pace in hopes that she wouldn't realize I was awake.

The second my phone was in my hand, I shot Lane a text.

Me: The girl from last night is still here

Lane: Okay. And?

I froze when I felt the mattress move beneath me, followed by the small of her hand on my back. My eyes widened, and I remained as still as possible while responding to Lane.

Me: She's trying to cuddle

Lane: Hahah cuddle with her then

Me: Um, no?

"Good morning," Lucy said.

I squeezed my eyes shut, sighing underneath my breath before shifting onto my back. "Good morning."

"Have you been up long?"

"Nah, just woke up. You?"

"Yeah, I haven't been up long," she said, dropping her head onto my shoulder. "Kinda hungry though. Would you want to go get breakfast?"

Lord, help me.

I gulped. I needed an excuse. Any excuse.

I slyly pulled my phone out by my side where she couldn't see, typing with my free hand. "Uh, I'm not really ready to get up yet," I said casually.

"That's fair. We can lay down for a bit longer."

Me: Oh gosh, now she's asking if I wanna go get breakfast with her. Help me

Lane: How do you expect me to do that?

Me: Knock on my door and pretend we have practice or something

Lane: No

Me: No?! Why the hell not?

Lane: Because you're a child

I could feel a growl get stuck in my throat and I choked it down, pulling up Cody's contact instead.

If anyone in this house understood shit like this, it was Cody Holtz.

Me: Help me

Cody: What's wrong?

Me: Level 10 clinger. Come bang on my door

28

Cody: On my way

Within sixty seconds, there was a loud fist pounding against the door.

"What?" I shouted, pretending to be clueless.

"Get your ass up! We've got practice in thirty!" Cody yelled.

"Oh shit," I mumbled, running a hand over my eyes. "I'm sorry. I totally forgot we have practice."

Lucy's brows knitted slightly. "You have practice on Sundays?"

"Uh, yeah," I lied.

"Damn, that must suck," she said.

"It does." My conscience was shunning me, but I was trying to brush the remorse off.

We did have to go lifting today, so I guess it wasn't a total lie.

"Well..." she muttered with disappointment, sitting up. "I guess I'll head out then."

"I'm sorry," I said again. But I did mean it. Just not for the reason she thought.

"No worries."

I bit my bottom lip as I watched her get dressed. Fucking dammit. If I wasn't practically kicking her out right now, I'd be pulling her on top of me.

Instead, I swung my legs over the side of the bed and grabbed the closest pair of pants there was.

Once Lucy was entirely dressed, she turned to me. "Can I... get your number?"

"Yeah, of course," I said. She handed her phone over and after I typed my number in and handed it back, I walked her out, giving her a friendly hug beforehand.

Cody was sitting back against the couch, a smug smile on his face. I joined him.

"You're welcome," he said.

"Thanks. You're a lifesaver," I replied genuinely. "What happened to the girl you were with?"

He sat forward. "Get this," he tapped me with a shrewd smirk. "Took her back from Stallions last night, fucked, laid there for a bit, fucked *again*, and then she just got up and left!"

My mouth fell open. "You didn't even have to ask her?"

"Nope," he shook his head. "I passed out right after the second time and when I woke up in the middle of the night to piss, she was gone."

I fell back against the couch. "That sounds so nice. Those are rare. Only happened to me once."

Cody Holtz was one of the best goalies in the NCAA. He was just as good of a playboy as he was a goalie. With the infamous "hockey player haircut", he was rocking the flow, which I could never pull off. But with Cody, girls flocked to him, always complimenting his hair.

It was hardly ten a.m., and I wasn't surprised that the rest of the guys were still asleep. I also wasn't surprised that the house looked like it had been ransacked.

Dirty dishes littered the tables, and random shit was all over the floor— blankets, backpacks, snack wrappers, red solo cups.

Nine times out of ten, the house was a mess. Lane usually dedicated time every few days to cleaning, and he'd make us help most of the time, but sometimes he'd tell us we were messing stuff up and would send us to go do something else.

One time, Lane asked TJ to wipe down the countertops in the kitchen and gave him the all-purpose cleaner for it.

Instead, TJ tried using straight bleach and spilled it all over the floor. The house reeked and was almost unbearable to be in for a whole day.

Slumped against the couch, I watched Lane appear from the kitchen with a glass of water, plopping down on the recliner in the corner. Face scrunching together as he glanced around, he didn't say anything, but it looked like he was about to gag.

Don't get me wrong, I wasn't the biggest fan of the house always looking like this. But Lane? It absolutely disgusted him. So much so, that he insisted we moved. As his best friend, I couldn't say no. He was going to move either way, whether I went with him or not, and we'd lived together for years now, so the thought of living without Lane was a bit jarring.

Our new apartment was only two blocks away from the hockey house, so luckily, we could come hangout whenever we wanted. It was also right across the street from Stallions, which was extremely convenient since our team could be found there all throughout the season. It would be nice in the winter, because our freezing cold walks would be much shorter.

I narrowed my eyes at him, remembering how unhelpful he was this morning. "You're a dick," I muttered to him.

He smirked. "Why? Because I didn't help you solve the problem that *you* created for yourself?"

"Yes," I said sharply. "Brothers are supposed to help clean up each other's messes, regardless of how dumb they are."

His face dropped and his voice fell with it. "C'mon, bro. Don't hit me with that."

I took in his sullen expression, knowing exactly what was on his mind. "You're right. I'm sorry."

My brother was a whole decade younger than me, same with my sister. I didn't know what it was like to have a sibling I was close with, to grow up with them, to share a *womb* with them.

And ultimately, to lose them.

I'd probably go insane if I lost either of my siblings, and half the time, I didn't even like them.

He responded with his head down. "It's alright. I know what you meant." Everyone was silent for a few moments until Lane spoke again. "We need to pack."

"Ugh," I groaned, tipping my head back. "Why today? We've got all week."

"Because I know your ass won't do shit during the week and you'll wait until the last minute."

Cody stood. "I'm leaving this conversation because it makes me depressed."

I rolled my eyes.

All the guys in the house had been giving us shit for moving out, and honestly, I didn't blame them. If it wasn't for Lane wanting to move, I probably wouldn't have been moving.

I genuinely enjoyed living in the house, and I knew Lane did too, but he was so much more mature and smarter than everyone else that I was pretty sure it was just hard for him to live with five idiots.

At least this way, he'd only have to deal with one idiot— *me*.

"Alright," I sighed. "Let's hit the gym first and then pack after."

"Deal," Lane agreed.

Chapter Four

Kota

I usually hated moving. Typically, it was a pain in the ass to me.

But today, I was freaking ecstatic to move.

If I'd been in our previous apartment for a fraction of a second longer, one of our roommates was bound to end up strangled.

Bridget and I agreed that it would be quickest to bring everything into the apartment first and then move them into our individual rooms afterward, so that we could just grab and go.

We'd already brought a few boxes of kitchen stuff inside and were on our third trip back up to the apartment.

One of my favorite things about this apartment? It was right across the street from Stallions and only a ten-minute walk from campus. I loved walking to class in the fall when the leaves were changing to an assortment of colors, or in the spring when everything was coming back to life. Winter was a whole other beast, but since we were so close, our drive to class wouldn't be as far or treacherous as it was from our old apartment, which was more than twice the distance.

The apartment building had no affiliation with Cedar U, but we knew it was going to be full of students anyway, which brought a sense of comfort and community.

"My arms already feel like they're about to fall off and we just started," B said, huffing and puffing.

"I know," I agreed. "We need to go down to the office and get one of those rolling cart things."

"Let's do it on the way down?"

"Please."

I spotted two guys down the far end of the hall by our apartment. They were too far away to tell who it was, but as we got closer, my idiot radar started going off.

"Oh no," I muttered.

"What?" B asked.

"I hope that's not who I think it is."

The closer we got, the more identifiable they were, and the clearer it was to see that they were standing at our apartment door. When the curly haired asshole looked over, mirroring the disgust in my expression, I shouted. "Hey, dickwads! Why the hell are you trying to get into our apartment?"

"*Your* apartment?" Crew challenged.

"Yeah," I nodded as we came to a stop in front of them. "*Our* apartment."

Bridget readjusted her box in her hands, her voice coming out civilly. "We've already brought some boxes in there."

Lane's eyes bounced back and forth between Bridget and me, his mouth set in a hard line. "Okay... Maybe they gave us the wrong apartment number or something?"

With a tiny shrug, Bridget said, "Maybe."

"Just try the key," Crew said.

Lane shot him an aggravated side eye, and it was satisfying to know that even *he* got annoyed by his friend sometimes.

When he shoved his key into the lock, my mouth nearly hit the floor as the door opened. How could the leasing office give them keys to our apartment? Wasn't that like, highly illegal?

"Um, why the fuck did they give you keys to our apartment?" I said aloud.

"Because it's *our* apartment," Crew hissed as we all wandered inside.

"No, it's not," I said firmly.

"Have you guys walked around yet?" Lane asked over his shoulder, strolling through the kitchen.

"No," B said. "We just brought a few boxes in so far."

The kitchen area was right as you walked in, and the living room was straight ahead. A hallway spanned out from each side of the living room, but B and I hadn't decided yet which room we'd each have.

Lane wandered around as we set our boxes down, and I let out a small huff of repulsion as I looked over at Crew. He was just standing there with his hands in his pockets, seemingly doing everything possible not to look at us. I hated that he was standing in our apartment right now, contaminating it.

Reappearing with a crease in his forehead, Lane eyed Crew as if to say *Uh, oh.*

"What?" Crew asked.

"This is a four-bedroom."

I turned my ear towards him, convinced I'd heard him wrong. "Excusez-moi?"

"That can't be right," B said with a light shake of her head. I followed her as she walked down the side halls.

I could admit, Lane knew how to count. There were definitely four bedrooms and two bathrooms.

Which was not what we signed a lease for.

What the hell was happening here?

"We're gonna have to go down to the leasing office and see what's going on," B said, and Lane nodded in agreement, taking a stressed breath.

Crew sighed. "Alright, let's go now then. Cause I'd rather not bring all my shit in here and then have to move it somewhere else."

Shooting him a grin of animosity, I said, "Wow! Your first good idea!"

Crew's jaw shifted beneath his skin, eyes narrowing at me.

But to my surprise, he kept his pretty little mouth shut.

Chapter Five

Crew

After the lady at the leasing office pretty much told us we were doomed, Lane and I took it upon ourselves to go to my dad's house with the hope that he could find a loophole in our lease since he was a contract lawyer.

Lane pulled the lease up on his phone and read through it on the way. "I can't believe none of us read this."

"I read some of it."

His eyes narrowed, calling my bluff. "No, you didn't."

I bobbed my head. "Alright," I admitted. "I didn't."

He rolled his eyes. "Shocker."

"My dad better find us a way out of this."

"I'm sure he will," Lane said casually.

I shot him a look of annoyance as I pulled into my dad's driveway. "How are you so chill right now?"

He shrugged, undoing his seatbelt. "I don't know."

"I don't get why you're not freaking out. You do realize that if we end up having to live with those two, Kota will probably cut off our balls while we're asleep and feed them to her pet snakes."

"Nobody said anything about pet snakes."

"Wouldn't put it past her," I mumbled, hopping out of my jeep. "She's a snake herself."

Lane and I walked inside, and I came to a sudden halt as my younger brother zipped past me, full of energy. I sighed under my breath.

Nate was in the sixth grade, and according to everyone, he was my younger twin. With the same curly brown hair and similar facial features, I couldn't deny the resemblance between us. However, it was weird having someone look so much like you when you weren't close with them at all.

"Dad?" I called out.

No answer.

As my brother ran past us again, I grabbed the back of his shirt, pulling him backwards. "Where's dad?"

"I dunno," Nate fumed, fighting my grip on his shirt. "Probably on the back patio."

I finally let him go, making my way out back with Lane on my heels.

There my dad was, sitting casually on the back porch, soaking in the sun beside my stepmom, Georgia.

It was absolutely beautiful outside, which was ironic considering this was such a horrible, dreary day to me.

Between the large stone patio and the in-ground pool, the backyard was always my favorite part of my dad's house. For the last few years since I started attending Cedar U, I had a pool party each summer, and the whole team would come over. It was the perfect spot since my dad's house was only twenty minutes from campus.

"Nick!" Georgia exclaimed. "What a pleasant surprise."

"Hey," I acknowledged her.

"Hi, Lane," she smirked.

"Hi, Mrs. Crew," Lane said.

I had this weird, messed up theory that she had a thing for Lane. She had always been a friendly woman, but she was extra friendly and smiley whenever Lane was around. It wasn't a longshot of a theory either considering she was only in her early thirties. My father was nearly a decade older than her, and she was a little more than a decade older than Lane and me.

Lane thought I was crazy though.

With her caramel-colored hair that always rested in perfect waves and her fragile features, Georgia was very pretty.

So much so, that some of the guys made comments about her when she wasn't around. I gagged every time. Real mom or not, it was still gross.

My dad was in his late forties, but he looked much younger than his age. It was only a few years ago that his gray hair started coming in. Some people had said before that he looked like Patrick Dempsey, which always made me roll my eyes because I personally didn't see a strong resemblance. On the other hand, my dad embraced the hell out of it; I guess I couldn't really blame him though. If I'd been compared to Patrick Dempsey, my ego would be knocked up a few notches too.

"Hey, son," my dad said before his brows suddenly came in. "Aren't you guys supposed to be moving into your new apartment right now?"

"Yeah... about that..." I said, scratching the back of my neck. I didn't want to be the one to break the news. Nervously, I licked my lips. "Lane?"

His head was lolled towards me as he eyed me with hostility. "Really?"

"Fine," I sighed, turning towards my dad. "We need your help."

"What's wrong?"

I looked at Lane again and he shook his head at me, denying my silent plea for him to be the one to explain.

"Apparently there was some change to our lease and now we're supposedly stuck living with two girls."

My dad's brows lifted as Georgia's mouth fell open.

"Oh yeah," I added, "and the girls hate us. Like a lot."

My dad blinked in confusion. "How the hell did that happen?"

"Well, Lane spilled his drink on one and then—"

"Not that," Lane finally spoke. "He probably means what the hell happened with our lease."

"Precisely," my dad said.

"Oh, Lane," Georgia said, sounding heartbroken, "you spilled your drink on a girl?"

Wincing, he replied, "It was an accident."

Her voice came out smooth. "I'm sure," she said, her eye wiggling.

I did a double take. Did her eye twitch or did she just wink at Lane?

"Nicholas," my father pushed.

I hated that he still called me that.

I started going by Crew during my freshman year of high school. My coach at the time, Coach Riddleman, didn't care a single bit about our first names. He referred to everyone as their last name only. To him, our first names seemingly didn't exist. So, after being called Crew for the entire year, it stuck, and I started introducing myself as Crew to everyone I met from that point on.

To this day, only my parents and Coach Palmer called me Nicholas. I think Coach Palmer only called me Nicholas though because he knew it pissed me off. Freshman year, I tried correcting him once, and he told me to shut my smartass up before making me do extra drills after everyone else got off the ice. After that day, whenever he called me Nicholas, which was always, I just rolled with it.

My father's harsh glare forced me out of my thoughts. Goddamn, was I the only one that noticed that weird interaction from Georgia?

I sighed, shaking it off. "The lady at the leasing office said they sent out an email back in February explaining that they messed up the amount of two-bedrooms they had available and that they changed our lease to a four-bedroom. But none of us got the email."

"Well, did you read through the lease before signing it?"

I exhaled deeply out my nose, rocking back and forth on my heels. The freaking office lady asked us this same question and it made me feel even dumber hearing it the second time around.

"I'll take that as a no," Dad said, not sounding surprised. But then he shook his head with a small sigh. "Nicholas, I hate to say it, but this is kind of your fault then. You're twenty-two. You're an adult. And I'd like to think I've taught you better than to sign contracts without reading through them first. This was a dumb move."

I let out a huff as my dad turned towards Lane.

"And what about you, Lane? Did you read the lease?"

Now Lane seemed uneasy being the one in the hotseat. "I..." he trailed off.

"Lane," my dad groaned. "How could you stoop down to Nick's level? You're supposed to be the responsible one!"

"Hey," I interrupted. "What's wrong with my level?"

"A lot of things," my dad replied before looking back to Lane. "You're the smart one. C'mon, now."

Sighing, Lane stood with his head down. "I know."

Immediately, Georgia scolded my father. "Oh, honey. Leave Lane alone."

My dad and I both rolled our eyes, but for very different reasons.

"Well, do you have a copy of the lease with you?" he asked.

"I do on my phone," I answered.

"Let me see it."

I pulled my phone out of my pocket and brought the lease up.

He began reading through it but was interrupted when my phone buzzed in his hand from a text. His brows came in. "Who's Marla?"

"I dunno," I shrugged. "Some chick."

Dad let out a scoff, shaking his head as he began reading again.

Like he was one to talk.

He was the reason I didn't do relationships. Well, correction— both him *and* my mom were the reason I didn't do relationships.

I was only ten when their marriage fell apart. Dad was cheating on Mom and Mom was cheating on Dad. Yet they were somehow pissed at each other even though they were both having affairs at the same time.

Yeah. Riddle me that.

After a very messy and bitter divorce, they both ended up getting remarried within the same year and both had another kid shortly after. Just like that, I went from being an only child to having two new siblings.

I didn't get much attention after that from either of my parents, considering I was entering my teen years and my siblings were both toddlers.

It created a lot of distance between my parents and me, and all the separation did was give me the space to think about how unpredictable relationships were, which was why I steered clear from them.

My dad suddenly winced.

"What is it?" Lane asked.

"Doesn't look like there's much you guys can do," he said, handing the phone back.

"What!" I panicked. "I thought you'd be able to find us a way out of this!"

"Your only way out is if you had a solid, legal reason."

"Such as?" I asked.

He exhaled, thinking. "Some examples would be if your landlord violates the lease or the apartment is unsafe or you're the victim of domestic violence, etcetera."

"So theoretically," I tipped my head, "let's say one of the girls cuts off our balls in the middle of the night and—"

"Crew," Lane chided.

"What?" I shot back. "It's a very big possibility."

"God, you're so dramatic," he huffed, shaking his head.

With a seemingly careless shrug, my dad said, "Sorry, boys. Let this be a good life lesson to read your damn contracts from now on."

Lane sighed, shoving his hands in his pockets. "Alright, well I guess let's head back."

"You know, it's not too late for us to leave the country."

"Lane's right," my dad announced. "You are dramatic."

"Whatever," I mumbled. "Let's go."

"Bye boys!" Georgia called with a smile as we walked out, her eyes on Lane. "Good luck!"

I stayed silent as we got into the car. Not that it was Lane's fault, but this wouldn't have happened if we'd just renewed our lease at the hockey house. I wasn't mad at Lane for the unfortunate series of events that had just occurred, but I was a bit irritated that he wasn't bothered by it at all.

Pretty much what I was gathering was that he was more affected from spilling his drink on a girl than he was by us being forced to live with her and her demon friend.

As I started driving, he pulled a classic Lane and hit me with the same line I'd heard from him dozens of times before.

"Everything's gonna be fine."

"This is a fucking disaster," I replied.

"I'm sure it won't be that bad."

"Yes, it will. This is a fucking disaster." I bit my bottom lip so hard that I was surprised it didn't start spurring blood. "I'm locking my door at night."

"So dramatic," he repeated, looking out his window.

"No, I'm not," I said surely. "This is a fucking disaster."

***

After nice guy Lane made me help him bring some of the girl's stuff into the apartment, I wanted nothing more than to just sit the fuck down.

Preferably, I'd go take a nap or something, but now was the time for us to have our "group discussion." And to be honest, even if we weren't having this talk right now, I'd probably go to the hockey house to nap instead of my own damn bed. Being around the girls, particularly Kota, for this long was disrupting my sanity.

I was pretty sure the only girls I'd been around consciously for longer than a few hours at a time were my mom and little sister.

I gave a small sigh as I stepped into the living room, and when I saw Kota and Bridget sitting on the only couch in the room, I gave another.

"We should get another couch," I muttered, grabbing a stool and spinning it around, resting my arms on the backrest as I sat.

"You could just sit on here with us, you know," Kota said. "We don't have cooties."

"Debatable." Not to mention that the only way I'd fit on that couch was if I was smushed between them.

As Bridget spoke, I could tell she was trying her best to be assertive. You didn't need to study her hard to know she was fairly shy and reserved. It seemed like her feisty side only came out on rare occasions. Like when she had beer poured all over her. I held back a snicker at the thought. Poor Lane.

"Look, if we're stuck living together, then all we can do is try to get along and lay down some basic ground rules," Bridget said.

"Such as?" Lane asked.

Kota and Bridget traded a glance before she spoke again, using her fingers to list things off. "Stay out of each other's way. Clean up after yourself. Don't eat each other's food."

Lane nodded, "Fair enough."

I took it upon myself to add the obvious. "No hooking up with each other."

Kota scoffed as if the idea of touching Lane or me was disgusting. "Yeah, as if that would happen anyway."

"You two are gonna have to try to get along," Lane said sharply.

Pointing at Kota, I whined, "She always starts it."

Defensively, she leaned forward. "Do not!"

Bridget waved her hands through the air in annoyance, her voice a rippling groan. "Geez, I feel like we're your fucking parents. Both of you, shut up!"

I snapped my mouth shut, certainly feeling like a child from the tone of her voice. I gave Kota another scowl when she wasn't looking before hastily standing. "Alright, fine. We'll try to get along. Are we done now?"

Bridget gave a small shrug, seemingly returning to her shy side. "I guess so."

"Cool," I grumbled, pushing the chair back to the kitchen island. I gave Lane a desperate look. "I'm going to the house for a while."

I didn't bother asking if he was coming before I left.

Chapter Six

Crew

I busted through the door, slamming it shut behind me. Matt's head snapped over to look at me, a smug smile coming over his face.

He sank back against the couch. "Back already?"

"Shut up, Gallagher," I shot at him, plopping down on the opposite side of the couch.

He looked offended yet amused, one corner of his mouth ticking upwards. "Damn, what's got your panties in a twist?"

My jaw tightened, eyes remaining forward. All I could do was shake my head. It was as if saying the words aloud would only solidify that this entire situation was real. But even more so, I knew Matt would get a kick out of the whole thing, and I wasn't ready for all the *"It's your fault for moving out"* bullshit.

"Alright then," he said.

It fell silent between us for a moment other than the sound of the TV until I finally decided to spit it out.

"It's the fucking girls."

"What girls?" Matt sat forward, intrigued, before his face twisted with hilarity. "Are more girls making up rumors about you?"

"No," I shot at him sharply.

"You sure?" he smirked, laughing through his words. "Cause I remember how angry you got when rumor went around that you only got onto the team because you were having a secret love affair with Coach."

"Shut the fuck up. I'm not mad about a rumor."

Unless the whole "small dick" comment that Kota shot at me *was* actually a rumor. In that case, I'd be a bit ticked off, but we had bigger problems at the moment.

"Then what the hell are you crying about?" Matt said.

"First of all, I'm not crying."

"Well, you look like you're about to."

"I don't cry," I hissed through gritted teeth.

"Stop avoiding the subject."

My voice raised, "Fine! You wanna know what the damn problem is? Lane and I are stuck living with two fucking girls!"

His eyes narrowed to slits, studying me with utter confusion. "What?"

"Remember when Lane spilled his drink on that girl last weekend?"

"Yeah..."

I turned towards him, talking with my hands. "Yeah, well, apparently the leasing office fucked up hardcore and gave us a four-bedroom apartment, and now we're stuck living with her and the other girl she was with. Imagine that."

It sounded even crazier saying it aloud. I'd been hoping that this whole day was some deranged, unbelievable nightmare. And as I had been driving over to the hockey house, the only thing going through my head was, *Wake up, Crew. This is just some fucked up dream.*

Yet here I was now. Still stuck in whatever cruel hallucination I'd been placed in.

Matt eyed me in silence for a moment before letting out a howl of laughter so loud that it made TJ stroll into the room with curiosity.

"What's so funny?"

Matt's face was turning red, unable to catch his own breath through the laughter. I sat there like a statue, jaw ticking while I had visions of reaching forward and wrapping my hands around his neck.

"That girl..." Matt spoke between spurs of laughter, "hated... your guts."

"I fucking know," I said. "She's pure evil in walking form." More laughter. "Can you stop fucking laughing?"

He shook his head frantically. "This is... too funny!"

"I'm so confused," TJ said. No shocker there. TJ was always confused.

Matt waved him off, physically unable to explain. He was laughing so hard that he bent forward, falling off the couch and onto the floor.

"Matt," I seethed, "if you don't stop laughing, I swear to God."

It took a few more minutes before his laughter finally toned down, becoming bearable enough for him to speak. He motioned to me, "Idiot One and Idiot Two are living with chicks."

TJ gave a proud smile, holding his fist out for me to bump. "Nice, man!"

That sent Matt into another laughing frenzy.

I looked at TJ as if he just said two plus two was five. "No! Not nice!"

He dropped his fist, his smile falling with it. "Why not? I'd be stoked to be living with two pairs of tits."

"I mean," Matt spoke, holding his stomach, which I could only assume was hurting after laughing so damn hard, "it doesn't sound like it'd be that bad. Easy hookup access."

"Are you fucking crazy? Kota would probably fuck an animal before she fucked me."

"That's called bestiality, bro," TJ said.

"Isn't that shit like, illegal?" Matt laughed.

"It was just a fucking example!" I shouted.

Matt took a few steps down the adjacent hall. "Yo!" he shouted. "Cody, Jett, get your asses in here now!"

I rolled my eyes. Fucking great. *Here comes the teasing.*

I should've known better than to come here to rant about the problem at hand, but then again, it was still better than being stuck in that apartment with Kota and Bridget right now.

Speaking of which, where the hell was Lane?

Jett and Cody sauntered in, both looking slightly confused but pleased to see me.

"Long time, no see," Cody teased.

"Missed us already?" Jett said.

I didn't even have the chance to respond before Matt beat me to it, chuckling through his words. "Nah, he just came over to escape the panty party."

He thought he was so fucking clever, didn't he? My teeth gritted together as I took a shallow breath. "Nobody said anything about panty parties."

"I wanna go to a panty party," TJ sulked.

Cody scoffed, butting in. "Yeah, where the hell was my invite?"

I tipped my head at TJ, my glare filled with frustration. "You know, if you're so happy by the thought of being stuck with the she-devil and her little sidekick, why don't you switch living arrangements with me?"

He casually leaned back into his seat and crossed his arms over his chest, not looking affected in the slightest. "No, thanks. I'm much more amused by your reaction than I would be to be under the same roof as chicks every day." He let out a snort. "Hell, I'm under the same roof as chicks every day already."

My spine was splitting with resentment and jealousy. Frowning, I took in all the guys, seeing how relaxed and nonchalant they were, whereas I was currently overthrown by every negative emotion in the book.

If I had a time machine, I'd go back and force Lane to stay here with me.

When we agreed to move out, I already knew I'd be losing a lot. Our casual hangouts in the living room. Last minute group outings. Random girls in and out all the time. Carpooling to practice together.

And now, in addition to all that, I was losing my fucking sanity too.

"Can someone please explain what we're talking about?" Jett insisted with his arms out.

I shot Matt a glare, knowing he'd be more than happy to explain for me. He took the opportunity without a second thought.

"Crew and Lane got fucked real hard and—"

"Fucked real hard, eh?" Cody snidely interrupted with a chuckle.

I rolled my eyes while everyone else ignored him.

"Long story short, they're stuck living with two girls that hate them," Matt finished.

Jett leaned forward, smiling wide. "Two girls that hate *you*? Damn, did you already hook up with them and never call them again?"

Eyes narrowing to slits, I responded, "I haven't hooked up with either of them actually. Thank you."

"Impressive," TJ said.

"Is that why you're mad?" Cody joked through a laugh.

I shot up, finally having had enough. "Can you guys please stop joking around? I'm fucking pissed. Lane doesn't seem to care, and—"

"Of course not," Jett said, shrugging. "It's Lane. Nothing bothers him."

With a light snort, Cody added, "Except last weekend when he almost cried after pouring his beer on that girl."

Matt's laughter echoed throughout the room again. At this point, the sound of his laughter was enough to make me wish I was deaf.

"That's the best part!" he shouted with enthusiasm. "They're living with that same girl!"

There was only one brief moment of silence before the entire room was filled with laughter and knee slaps.

Just fucking kill me now.

"The bottom line is—" I stopped, knowing they couldn't hear me. When I spoke again, I was practically shouting. "The bottom line is that I want to move back here!"

"Dude," Cody said, "you know that's like impossible. Keith and Jonah are moving in here tomorrow."

"Well, tell them they can't," I said.

He eyed me like I was speaking a different language. "They signed a lease! We can't just tell them they can't."

Letting out a stressful huff, I ran a hand over the light stubble on my jaw. "This is fucking stupid."

A casual shrug was all Jett had to offer. "It's your fault for moving out."

And there it was.

I was on the brink of exploding. I could physically feel my blood heating as it coursed through my veins, its speed accelerating.

"So, what? I'm just supposed to deal with it?" I blurted out.

Everyone responded at the same time; I couldn't even make out who was saying what.

"Yep."

"Pretty much."

"Sorry, dude."

"This is just..." I trailed off, shaking my head at the floor.

Jett placed a comforting hand on my shoulder. "If it makes you feel better, you're welcome to come over any time."

"Yeah," I mumbled, "I was fucking planning on it."

Chapter Seven

Kota

When we were first told that there was no way out of our leasing fiasco, Bridget and I had a complete meltdown—after the boys had left, of course.

We'd tried everything to fix the situation.

After speaking to nearly every person in the leasing office, they all told us the same thing. Unless we were okay being financially penalized or subleasing our apartment, there was nothing they could do.

Subleasing seemed like our best option, so we contacted every apartment complex in the area, but none of them had any available two-bedrooms left, so that option was ruled out.

Bridget and I even tried scaring the boys out by hanging up our community period calendar. It did bother the shit out of Crew, but Lane wasn't affected in the slightest.

I'd truly thought that this had to be some messed up karma for something we'd done. My mind even went as far as to think Claudia used some dark magic to curse us somehow.

It had only been a week since moving in, but I'd admit, living with the boys wasn't that bad so far.

But that was probably because I was staying away from them as much as possible.

After all, rule number one was set in place for a reason.

50

I carried my full laundry basket to the washer and began throwing my dirty clothes in. When I grabbed my laundry detergent that was on the shelf above the washer and dryer, my brows knitted.

There was a small stream of detergent that had dried along the side.

First of all, this detergent had been brand-new.

Second of all, I never let it spill on the side because I hated when it got sticky.

I set my basket on top of the dryer and stomped into the living room.

Crew was lying shirtless on the couch, one arm draped behind his head. "Sup?" he said when he noticed me.

"Did you use my laundry detergent?"

He shrugged against the couch. "I thought it was mine."

I held up the bottle. "It has a giant K written on it."

He shrugged again, his eyes back on the TV. "Sorry."

"Ugh," I groaned, marching away. I could hear Crew let out a quiet giggle, causing me to backtrack. "I heard that."

"Okay?" he said with no regret, fighting a devious smile.

Was he trying to fucking test me? Because if so, I'd make sure he knew I wasn't joking.

"It's not funny!"

"Okay," he repeated.

"I mean it. Knock it off. I know where you live."

He raised a brow, amused. "What're you gonna do? Chop my balls off in the middle of the night?"

I stepped forward, my jaw tight. "Don't tempt me."

Crew's smile disappeared and he gulped so hard that I could see his Adam's apple bob.

Good. He was scared.

I tipped my chin up as I strutted out of the living room, much more content knowing that Crew was sitting there worrying about keeping his precious balls intact.

After starting the washer, I began getting ready. It was a Saturday morning, and my mom and I usually met up for lunch twice a month. Today would be the first time I'd see her since before we moved in.

My mom and I had lived in a small town called Millstone for my entire life. It was only an hour away from Cedar, but my mom and I usually met halfway at a diner called Betty's. She'd been taking me there ever since I was little, so it was our own special place.

I knocked on B's door as I placed the strap of my black purse over my shoulder.

"Hey," I smiled as B appeared in the doorway.

"Hey," she smiled back. "Heading to lunch?"

"Yep! Can you do me a favor though?"

"That depends..." she said curiously. "Is it anything dangerous or illegal?"

Jokingly, I rolled my eyes. "No. I was just going to ask if you could switch my laundry into the dryer when it's done."

Her smile returned. "Oh! Sure, I can do that."

"Thanks," I said. "What are you up to today?"

She sighed, leaning her head against the doorframe. "Oh, you know. More research."

I was raised by a single mom who had been my superhero. When she was in college, she and my dad, who I typically referred to as "The Sperm Donor", had only been dating for a few months when my mom got pregnant. He tried convincing her to get rid of me, and although she was pro-choice, her choice was to keep me. The Sperm Donor disappeared long before I was born. I never met him. And at this point, I wouldn't want to.

On the other hand, Bridget had been given up for adoption when she was born. She had never met her biological parents, and although her adoptive parents were loving and accepting, she was on a mission to find her real parents, or at least her mom. She'd been doing research since she was still in high school, and her research led her all the way to a town near Cedar, which was why she decided to come here in the first place.

I gave her a subtle smile of encouragement. "Find anything new?"

She shrugged unenthusiastically. "Not really."

"You're so close, B," I assured her. "Don't give up."

She gave a faint smile. "I won't."

"Good," I said. "Now, I'll be back in a few hours."

"Kay," she nodded. "Drive safe!"

***

"Oh! There's my Kota girl!" my mom yelped, drawing me in for a bear hug.

"Hi, Mom," I smiled as I squeezed her back.

We sat down at a booth and within minutes, Stella, our waitress, was standing in front of us. She turned to my mom, "Coffee?"

"Yes, please."

"Orange juice?" she asked me.

I nodded. "Yes, please."

Betty's was a small diner, consisting of a small staff. My mom and I had been coming here so often for so long that all the waitresses knew our names and our usual orders. Hell, I was pretty sure they knew us on a personal level too.

Not only had they overheard dozens and dozens of our conversations over the years, but they sometimes joined in, and we'd chat about our lives, both the good parts and the bad ones.

Once Stella pranced off to get our beverages, my mom placed her elbows on the table, resting her chin in her hands.

Her beauty always amazed me. With tan skin, a perfect smile, and kind, brown eyes, her presence captivated everyone she met.

My mom was of Filipino heritage. Her parents, my grandparents, were born in the Philippines, and they both emigrated to America with their own families at young ages. Attending the same college, they met and fell in love, getting married right after graduation and having my mom shortly after. Their love story had always been my favorite; I never got tired of hearing them tell the story again and again.

Even though our roots were Filipino, our family didn't practice a lot of Filipino customs other than traditional cuisines at family gatherings.

Since I never met my dad, I had no idea growing up what ethnicities I'd inherited from him, but a few years ago, I actually took a DNA test because I was interested to find out. Apparently, I had some Irish and German genes in me as well.

"How's the new apartment?" my mother asked.

I internally cringed. I still hadn't told her about the boys.

"Oh yeah," I said, slightly nervous to drop the bomb. "It's... interesting."

"Why?" Her brows creased with worry. "Is everything okay between you and Bridget?"

I was quick to assure her. "Yeah! Everything's fine with B, but..."

"But?"

I sighed, spitting the words out as fast as a speeding bullet. "But we're living with two boys."

She eyed me in silence for a moment, blinking repeatedly. "Excuse me, what?"

As Stella brought our drinks out, I explained what happened with our lease and my mom seemingly relaxed a bit, falling back against the booth cushion.

"Okay," was all she said.

"Okay?"

"I'm just relieved this wasn't something you two orchestrated and kept as a secret from me."

"No, no. Of course not."

"Well, are these boys at least clean?"

"For the most part," I replied, sipping on my OJ. "One of them is cleaner than the other." *Lane, of course.* "And I've caught him cleaning up after the messy one a few times." *Crew, of course.*

"Are they nice?"

All I could do was laugh.

She raised a brow, concerned. "Kota?"

I lightly smacked a hand on the table, still laughing.

"Kota," she repeated, sharper this time.

"Sorry," I said. "Um, one of them is alright, I guess. I don't mind him too much. The other one though really knows how to aggravate me."

My mom peered at me over her cup of coffee. "Does it happen to be the same one that's messy?"

"Of course, it is."

"Ugh," she groaned, "men."

"You're tellin' me, Ma."

"Have you put him in his place?"

"Many times," I said confidently.

"Good," she smiled proudly. "You know better than to ever let a man tell you what to do."

"I know," I grinned. "Just like my mama."

The smile she gave held so much pride. "Exactly."

After lunch with my mom, I headed straight home. Bridget and I were planning on going out later, which meant that I needed to get some homework done beforehand in case I was cursed with a hangover tomorrow.

The moment I stepped through the door, my mouth smacked open, and my keys made a loud clatter against the floor. I let out a distressed scream as if I'd forgotten we had neighbors.

Crew was still shirtless on the couch, but this time, he wasn't alone. A pretty, tan girl with dark hair was straddling his lap, their mouths going at it.

It was like they hadn't heard me scream the first time. "What the hell!" I shouted.

Their lips finally parted, eyes sliding over to me. Crew looked unaffected, indifferent. But the girl's brows wiggled around in confusion.

Her head snapped back to Crew, eyeing him like he was a three-headed monster. "You have a girlfriend?" she roared.

Hands remaining steadily on her hips, his brows drew in. "What? No—"

"Yes, he does," I butted in. "We've been dating for a year and a half, so I suggest you leave before things get ugly."

She scoffed in disgust, peeling his hands off her and grabbing her belongings off the floor. "You're a whore!" she shot at Crew.

I covered my mouth with the back of my hand, attempting to hide the massive smile on my face.

"Alysha, wait!" he stood, shouting after her as she rushed past me and ran out.

The second the door shut behind her, I burst out laughing.

Crew's jaw twitched, his eyes glazing over with hatred. "Really?"

I shook my head, my rage returning. "What do you mean *really*? What the fuck is wrong with you?"

Crew threw his hands up in frustration, looking like a large toddler having a temper tantrum. "She's probably gonna go run around campus telling everyone I have a girlfriend. No girl is gonna touch me now!"

I knew Crew was the biggest playboy on the hockey team but hooking up with a girl in the middle of our living room was too much, even for him.

It was a sign of complete disrespect to everyone else in this apartment. Not to mention it was gross. I mean, we all sat right there, *every day*.

His dirty dishes in the sink and the disarray of his belongings around the common areas was already enough. But this? No way in hell was I dealing with this. I didn't want to be scared to see naked bodies every time I walked into my own apartment.

Leaning forward, I grew more agitated by his lack of self-awareness and maturity. It felt like he was feeding me a grenade of bullshit and it was about to make me explode any second. "*That's* what you're concerned about right now?!"

Crew squinted his eyes at me. "You don't have *anything* to be concerned about right now."

I laughed once without humor. "What about the bodily fluids that are probably on our couch?"

Rolling his eyes like I was an idiot, he said, "There are no bodily fluids. We didn't get that far."

I wished my gaze was lethal enough to kill him right then and there. I motioned to his bare legs. "You're standing there in boxers!"

"So? Have you never seen a dude in boxers before?"

A deep growl rippled out of my mouth. "The bottom line is that you have a bedroom for a reason!"

"I didn't wanna take her in there."

"Why?"

"Because, well..." He shifted around, almost sheepishly. "I just washed my sheets, and I didn't wanna have to wash them again."

My teeth clenched together, hands drawing into fists at my sides. Voice climbing, I screeched, "You mean with *my* laundry detergent?" But Crew just let out a quiet huff, sounding bored. "And what," I added, "so you were just gonna fuck her on the couch?"

He bobbed his head side to side.

This kid was unbelievable. It felt like he was practically daring me to step forward and punch him straight in the face.

"You're fucking disgusting," I spat, stalking towards my room. I turned over my shoulder. "You better lock your door tonight!"

"Why?"

"Because I'm cutting your balls off and selling them on Ebay!" I screamed, slamming my door.

I puffed out a breath and I was pretty sure I could see smoke come out with it.

Goddamn. This was going to be a long year.

Chapter Eight

Kota

"**T**his show is probably fake," Lane said, seated on the other side of the couch from me.

My forehead creased as I shot him a look. "No, it's not."

"Oh, come on, Kota," he said with a friendly smile, "you can't possibly believe any of this shit is real. It's *The Bachelor.*"

"Whatever," I rolled my eyes. "Your opinion is wrong."

It was strange to think we'd already been living here for almost a month. *One month down, eleven to go.*

Lane and I had surprisingly been getting along pretty well. He always made sure to clean up after himself and to occasionally clean up after Crew when necessary. He didn't annoy the piss out of me, and he also didn't eat my food, which was pretty much all I could ask for.

We'd been spending a decent amount of time together over the past two weeks for a few different reasons. For starters, he was my freaking roommate so hanging out was convenient. But more so, Bridget had been hanging out with a guy named Mitch that she met at a party a few weeks ago at the hockey house, so she hadn't been around as much.

I hadn't officially met Mitch yet, but Bridget seemed happy every time she talked about him, so if that meant I'd be seeing her a bit less, I was fine with it.

"Put something else on," Lane complained.

"No."

"Fine," he sighed after putting up the weakest fight ever.

I laughed. "See, that's the thing. I know you secretly like it."

"Nah."

When I shot him a look of doubt, he crumbled in the slightest.

"It's entertaining. I'll give you that," he admitted.

I shrugged nonchalantly. "Good enough for me." A few more minutes of girls screaming at each other on the TV passed before I turned to Lane again. "And just as a reminder, what are we not gonna do?"

Blowing out a long exhale, he responded, "We're not gonna tell Bridget we watched *The Bachelor* without her."

I smiled, content. "Good."

But the content faded when Crew walked into the apartment.

The second we made eye contact, his face matched mine, showing nothing but disgust.

"Hey, Lane," he nodded once.

"Hey," Lane replied as Crew strolled down the hall and into his room.

Of course, he was acting like I didn't exist. I was pretty sure we'd said a total of ten words to each other since last week when I walked in on him and whatever the hell that girl's name was.

My eyes narrowed at nothing in particular. "I hate him."

Lane nodded with a tight jaw. "I know."

"He sucks."

"Not always, but yeah, sometimes."

"Always," I corrected him.

He shifted around on the couch, seemingly drawing in a sharp breath as he quickly changed the subject. "So, where's Bridget at?"

"Out with Mitch."

"Again?"

I eyed him curiously. "Yes..."

Lane gave a slow nod, keeping his eyes glued to the TV.

"Why?"

He avoided eye contact with me as he spoke, giving a light shrug. "Just curious."

"Okay..."

I would've pushed him further on the subject if Crew hadn't walked back into the living room. As he took a seat on our new, small couch adjacent to the one we were sitting on, I cringed, standing.

I didn't hesitate to walk out of the room without saying anything. I just hated breathing the same air as him. He was such an idiot that I was convinced I got dumber every time I was near him.

Since Bridget was out with Mitch, I decided to shoot Bobby a text.

Me: You busy?

Bobby: Never too busy for u

Me: Good answer. Come pick me up?

Bobby: Sure

Thank God.

I waited outside in the parking lot because the farther away from Crew, the better.

I'd already told Bobby about our unfortunate new living arrangement, but that didn't stop me from taking the entire car ride to Starbucks to rant to him about Crew.

Truthfully, there wasn't really anything to rant about when it came to Lane.

But after unwillingly holding onto every detail of each occurrence where Crew bothered the piss out of me, it all came soaring out like a rocket taking off.

60

He was the only one that left his dirty dishes in the sink instead of just putting them straight in the dishwasher and he left other random shit everywhere too.

Lane had to wake him up every morning for practice because he was nowhere near responsible enough to wake up his damn self at the age of twenty-two.

He was a complete fucking airhead.

He'd already had an array of girls in and out of the apartment like a drive-thru window.

He was rude, inconsiderate, disrespectful, and egotistical.

The list went on and on. By the time the flames radiating off me had simmered, we'd already found our way back to the apartment.

Chapter Nine

Kota

I was both in awe and impressed, my mouth wide open as Bridget filled me in on her morning, where she caught Lane letting a girl out of the apartment.

Did I mention that he was apparently shirtless?

This was kind of exciting, not going to lie. Crew had been so promiscuous from the moment we met him that he made Lane look like the Virgin Mary.

"So, you're sure this girl spent the night?" I asked B.

After a long night out with Mitch, she came home last night sloshed. I had no idea what they'd been drinking all night, but whatever it was must've been loaded with sugar because it looked like she'd been hit by a small bus.

Bridget's strawberry blonde hair was up in a messy bun, a small bag underneath each eye. But regardless, she was still gorgeous, as always.

She clutched onto her bottle of Pedialyte that she'd been chugging all morning, her brows drawing inwards. "I mean... yeah? I wouldn't imagine she came over this morning."

I nodded with a sly grin. "Wow. This is awesome."

B gave a slight eye roll, readjusting herself as if she were uncomfortable.

"Oh c'mon, B!" I spoke. "I have Bobby. You have Mitch. Crew has all his conquests. And now Lane can finally have someone too! This is a good thing."

Her mouth formed a hard line. "Is it?" she said rather quietly.

I sucked in a sharp breath to ramble on an answer but held it back as Lane strutted into the kitchen.

Bridget and I sat back on the couch, pretending like we hadn't just spent the past fifteen minutes talking about him. I watched him out of the corner of my eye as he grabbed his usual ingredients for a protein shake.

His mouth was in a long frown, and he was moving rather sluggish. Not quite the type of behavior I expected from him today.

I shifted towards Bridget, leaning in. "You know," I whispered, "for someone who just got laid last night, he looks kinda sad."

"A little," she whispered back.

Of course, I took it upon myself to figure out what was up. "Hey," I called out to Lane.

He dumped protein powder into his shake, his gaze down. "Hey."

"Heard you got laid last night," I said.

B hit me on the shoulder with the back of her hand. "Kota," she scolded me quietly.

Lane's voice echoed throughout the room, his tone just as dull as the rest of him. He still didn't bother to look up at us. "Where'd you hear that?"

I glanced at B briefly, taking in her pleading expression. B had never been good with being thrust into the spotlight. She gave a wince, not wanting to be mentioned, and I wouldn't go against her wishes.

"Crew," I blurted out.

That got Lane's attention. His head popped up, two sapphire blue eyes narrowed in on us, filled with doubt. "Crew?"

"Yep," I gave a tense nod.

"You're telling me that you and Crew had a conversation?"

Considering Crew and I had still been avoiding each other at all costs, Lane's doubt came with no surprise.

"Yes..." I slowly let out, trying to keep a straight face, but I could feel my expression skewing.

Lane pressed his hands into the countertop. "I don't buy it."

There was a beat of silence as his harsh expression melted. But I didn't initiate this conversation to find out what he did or didn't buy. I wanted him to tell me about his damn night.

"So, is it true?" I asked.

Lane's eyes dropped back down to his shake. "Yeah," he murmured, a hint of shame lingering behind the words, "it's true."

"Then why do you seem so damn pouty?"

His eyes narrowed. "I'm not pouty."

I gave him a playful grin, tipping my head. "Dude, you're pouty."

"No, I'm not," he denied sharply.

"Well, you're not smiley," I said.

All he did was sigh.

"Was it bad?"

He seemed to be getting tenser with each question I asked. "No. Not at all."

"Then what's the problem?" I shrugged.

"Nothing." Lane avoided looking at us as he put stuff away and picked up his shake. "I've gotta go to the gym. I'll see you guys later." He grabbed his keys off the key holder near the door, speaking over his shoulder. "Can you guys tell Crew to meet me there when he wakes up?"

We didn't even have the chance to respond before he was gone.

My brows knitted as I collapsed back into the couch. "That was weird," I thought aloud.

"Very," was all B said.

"I wonder what's up with him."

"Yeah."

My head swiveled over to look at her. What was up with the sudden weird mood and short answers?

"Why do *you* seem all gloomy now?" I asked.

With a tiny smile, she replied, "I'm fine. Just hungover, remember?"

I pursed my lips out. "Oh yeah."

64

The second I saw Crew slump down the hall out of the corner of my eye, I could feel a small ball of fire forming in my center, and not the kind you got when you liked someone.

The kind you got when you wanted to *punch* someone.

Bridget gave him a small nod of acknowledgement. "Hey."

"Hey," he said back, grabbing a glass of water.

"Lane wants you to meet him at the gym."

"Yeah," he said, "he'll have to wait a bit. I need to piss and get dressed."

I let out a sigh of relief when he left the room, feeling like I could relax again.

But within less than a minute, there was a high-pitched scream coming from the boy's bathroom.

B and I traded glances with wide eyes when Crew reappeared, seemingly pale and a bit out of breath. He made it a point to stop five feet away like he was scared to come closer. "What... the fuck... is in... our bathroom?"

B and I exchanged another clueless glance. Maybe Lane left a mess? *Highly unlikely.* Was there a spider he needed me to kill since he was too pussy to do it himself? *Sounded more accurate.*

I spoke impatiently. "What are you talking about?"

He fidgeted around, looking uncomfortable in his own skin as he continued struggling to speak. "There's a, uh... *thing* in the trash."

I raised a brow, jutting my chin out. "A what?"

"A girl thing," he spit out with disgust.

"Oh, Jesus," I said, rolling my eyes to the maximum possible. I leaned forward with annoyance. "A tampon. Say the word, Crew. *Tampon.*"

His expression looked like a strange mixture of revulsion, anger, and fear, but he remained quiet, standing there in shock.

B twisted to look at me.

"What?" I shot at her with a shrug. "I had to change it this morning while you were in the shower, and you wouldn't let me in."

She sank back into the couch, looking embarrassed. "I was shaving my legs."

Giving another meaningless shrug, I turned back towards Crew. "So, I went into your guy's bathroom to change it. Big deal."

"Big deal?" he heaved. "Why didn't you flush it down the toilet?"

"You're not supposed to," Bridget and I said in unison.

He raised a brow, leaning forward slightly as if he wasn't sure if he heard us correctly. "Excuse me, what?"

"Yeah, it could clog the pipes," B explained.

Crew buried his head into his hands.

Every moment this conversation carried on made me more irritated. "Oh my gosh," I bellowed, "don't cry about it. It was wrapped in toilet paper anyway. You couldn't even see it. The most you probably saw was the damn wrapper of the new one."

Crew eyed me with disgust, his mouth propped open as if it were stuck there. He gagged through his words. "You wrapped your used tampon in toilet paper and threw it into our trash can?"

Without hesitation, I confirmed, "Yes."

He placed his hands behind his head, shifting his weight around as he blew out a long, stressful breath.

"You live in an apartment with two girls," I said. "It's bound to happen."

Crew spoke through malice, muscles becoming taut. "Well, it can happen in your bathroom. Not ours."

"You're a child," I spat at him.

"Shut up," he retaliated, letting out a huff as he turned on his heels and stomped away. He was back minutes later wearing a muscle tee and gym shorts, still huffing and puffing as he trampled out of the apartment.

I stared at the door as if Crew had just tainted it by walking through it. My evil mind was brewing.

He pissed me off, sure. But I'd be lying if I said pissing *him* off wasn't entertaining.

My eyes slowly trailed from the door across the room, ultimately landing on Bridget. She gave a small sigh, recognizing the devious gleam in my eye.

"What?" she asked.

"I just got an awesome idea."

"Oh God," she tipped her head back, her bun bobbing as she did so. "No."

Lightly frowning, I said, "You haven't even heard it yet!"

"I don't need to hear it to know it's probably not a good idea."

She knew me too well.

"C'mon," I pleaded, desperately grabbing her hand. "I just need your help."

"Ugh," she groaned. "What is it?"

My smirk inevitably grew.

This was going to be far too much fun.

Chapter Ten

Kota

"Next," I said, holding my hand out as I stood steadily on a chair, Bridget on the floor beside me.

Bridget let out a small sigh as she handed me another tampon. "You know he's gonna wanna kill you, right?"

I smiled. "He already wants to kill me."

I'd seen people online pull this prank on their friends where they taped hotdogs to their ceiling.

The only differences here were that Crew was *not* my friend and that we were substituting hotdogs with tampons.

After I got the idea, I asked Bridget to run to the store with me to get two big boxes of tampons. She was more than hesitant, so it took quite a bit of convincing, but after twenty minutes of giving her my best puppy dog expression, she gave in.

"Have you ever thought that maybe you take things a little too far sometimes?" she asked.

"All the time," I admitted.

"Yet you never stop and think, '*Hey, maybe I shouldn't do that?*'"

I gave a light sneer. "What's the fun in that?"

Shaking her head, she handed me another tampon with a piece of tape attached to the end of the string.

"I could've done much worse," I said. "I could've filled them with fake blood or some shit."

B kept her voice flat, sarcastic. "Wow, how sweet of you to not do that."

"Just think of it this way— I'm teaching Crew how to be more comfortable living with us."

"And what happens if he tries getting you back?"

I glanced at her, the thought immediately making my blood boil. "Then I'll get him back harder."

"Oh geez," she muttered. "If this turns into a full-on war, I'm staying out of it."

"That's fine," I shrugged, attaching the tape to the ceiling and sliding my hand across it to make sure it stuck. "Even if Crew convinced Lane to be on his side and help him— which he won't because Lane is too much of a little angel— *but* if he did, they still wouldn't be able to beat me."

"You don't think so?" she asked. "Not even if it were two on one?"

"Nah," I said confidently. "They're not smart enough."

B's voice became a bit sharper. "Lane's pretty smart."

"Yeah," I admitted. "He is." I hopped off the chair and looked around the room. Tampons lined the ceiling, looking like some strange room décor.

This was going to be awesome. I couldn't wait to see the look on Crew's face and brand the sight into my memory forever.

"Can we be done now? There are hardly any tampons left."

"We haven't done above his bed."

Bridget let out a groan, gesturing towards it. "Be my guest then."

I stared at Crew's unmade bed, my face twisting into disgust when I remembered how many girls he's already brought home after only a month of living here. "Actually, pass. I don't wanna have to stand on that bed. Who knows what's been done on that thing?"

Bridget picked up the remaining tampon wrappers off the floor while I pushed the chair back into Crew's desk.

When the apartment door opened, followed by heavy feet against the kitchen floor, Bridget's and my head zipped towards the bedroom door and then to each other.

Without saying anything, we both scrambled out of the room and tiptoed down the hall. I led the way, stopping at the corner and peeking my head around it.

I breathed a sigh of relief. "It's just Lane," I said aloud, emerging into the common area fearlessly.

His eyes shot over to us, brows inwards. "Why were you guys down our hall?"

"Where's Crew?" Bridget asked, brushing over his question.

Lane flicked a thumb over his shoulder, studying us suspiciously. "Right behind me. He should be walking in any second."

Bridget and I traded another glance, then rushed over to the couch and practically dove onto it, trying too hard to situate ourselves so that we looked normal.

"You guys are being weird," Lane said.

"Shouldn't you go shower or something?" I whirred.

He raised a single brow, unamused.

"What?" I shot at him, hands up. "You just got back from the gym. Aren't you all gross?"

"Yeah," he confessed. "But Crew already called dibs on showering first, so I'm gonna have to wait."

Speaking of the devil, there he was, strutting in like he owned the place.

He tossed his keys on the counter. *Typical Crew move, throwing his shit wherever.*

We had a key holder hanging by the door for a reason.

But I kept my mouth shut, same with Bridget, our eyes glued painfully to the TV.

Crew stopped just short of the boy's hall. His curly hair was a mess, and he was glistening— quite literally— the remnants of sweat lingering all over his body.

His eyes narrowed, taking in our stiff and awkward positioning. "Why do you guys look like that?"

Bridget's small voice shook in the slightest as she responded. "Like what?"

Crew's eyes darted over to me, growing wary.

I sat up straighter. "What are you looking at?" I spewed.

Jaw shifting for a moment, he slowly turned and headed down the hall.

We stayed quiet as Lane studied us, seemingly on edge just as much as Crew. Out of the corner of my eye, I could see him open his mouth and inhale as if he were about to make another comment, but he was cut off by a deep yell.

"What the fuck?!"

My hand shot up to my mouth, covering my giggle while Bridget sank deeper into the couch beside me, shielding her entire face minus her eyes with a blanket.

"What did you guys do?" Lane asked with irritation, just in time for Crew to appear from down the hall, his face red hot.

"What the hell is all over my room?" he spat.

I gave him a casual shrug through my laughter. "You tell me."

Bridget lowered her blanket for a moment as she spoke. "I told you he'd be really mad."

"I know," I laughed. "This is like Christmas!"

Crew pointed at me with a taut finger. "I know this was *your* idea."

"Of course, it was!" I said proudly, still laughing.

Lane threw his hands up. "I'm fucking lost."

"Go take a look," Bridget said to him.

Letting out a long exhale, Lane lightly bumped into Crew's shoulder on his way down the hall. Crew remained steady, eyes angrily on the floor, jaw still twitching beneath his skin.

An entertained holler echoed through the apartment and Lane reappeared, bending over in laughter. "Are those tampons?"

I could tell his reaction was pissing Crew off more from the way his fists drew in at his sides. "This isn't fucking funny," Crew muttered.

Tapping him on the shoulder, Lane said, "Bro, c'mon."

With an insidious smirk, I asked, "You don't like it?"

"No," his voice raised. "No, I do not like the tampon mistletoe in my goddamn room!"

Bridget shyly raised her hand like a young child in a classroom.

"What?" Crew snapped.

"I just want to make it clear that this was not my idea, and I was coerced into participating," she said before hiding behind her blanket again.

He sighed, shaking his head before turning all his attention *and anger* solely onto me. "Clean it up now," he demanded.

"Too scared to clean it up yourself?" I teased.

"Kota," he pushed.

"Ugh," I groaned, giving a slight eye roll. "I just sat down. Give me a few minutes."

He took a step backwards, eyes still targeted at me. "I'm gonna take a shower. It better be gone by the time I get out."

I held in another giggle as he began walking away, and when he turned over his shoulder, I raised a brow. "And I hope you know I'm gonna get you back," he promised.

I smirked in amusement. "Good luck."

Chapter Eleven

Crew

I couldn't stop thinking about my revenge.

I was practically fantasizing about it throughout the day, trying to decide what the best way to get Kota back would be.

It had been a few days since she pulled her "genius" prank and I wanted to wait a few more until I got her back, solely so that she wouldn't know when it was coming. I was sort of hoping she'd just reach a point where she thought she was in the clear, that I'd forgotten all about her little shenanigans.

But if that was a thought of hers, she was way off.

I wanted to think of something that was a bit personal, something that would really set her off. The only thing I could think of messing with of hers was her snacks. But I felt like my options with that were a bit more limited. It wasn't like I could poison her. For starters, I wasn't trying to *hurt* her. I wasn't a psychopath— yet sometimes I wondered if *she* was. I just simply wanted to get under her skin.

But for the time being, I needed to forget about my revenge. Because we had a game to play tonight.

The first game of the season was always an important one, because however you played was going to set the tone for the rest of the season. And when the first game was a home game, the pressure went up, because your entire school was watching you, prepared to either kneel at your feet or give you some harsh words depending on what the scoreboard looked like at the end of the third period.

I felt pretty prepared to step onto the ice later. Meanwhile, I could feel Lane's nerves radiating off him from beside me.

It was his first game as captain, which meant he'd be the biggest target if things went south during this game. It was already a lot of pressure having the entire school looking at you, but to have the entire team looking at you as well? That'd be way too much for me to handle.

There wasn't another player that could lead the team as well as him though.

Lane and I finished up gelling our hair in the bathroom. I whistled as I washed my hands, waiting until Lane was done doing the same.

We stood side by side, glancing at ourselves in the mirror.

Suiting up to head to the arena was a hockey tradition, and at Cedar U, we made sure it was upheld. We took pride in looking sharp, every single one of us. Even Cody and TJ always dressed to the nines, and they were some of the laziest motherfuckers I knew when it came to off-ice time.

Lane was in a cobalt blue suit with brown dress shoes. He looked like he was ready to walk onto the red carpet.

My black suit and dark purple tie matched perfectly, and I pulled down on my suit jacket, making sure it was as crisp as possible.

Lane smiled. "We look good."

I held my fist out and he bumped it. "We always do."

"Are you ready to win this fucking game?"

"Ready as hell," I replied, following him out of the bathroom. I could hear the girls talking in the kitchen and when we stepped into the common area, both of their attention drew to us.

I watched Kota's sandwich stop halfway to her mouth. She stayed there for a moment, frozen like a strange statue before she blinked rapidly, wrestling her gaze away from me.

74

When I glanced at Bridget, her expression matched Kota's. She seemed not to be as concerned with hiding it though.

I could feel the imperceptible smirk that danced across my lips as I fixed the cuff of my suit. "Well, don't drool over us."

Kota let out a quick rush of air, sounding flustered. "We're not drooling."

"Yeah, okay," I said, feeling a divergent sense of satisfaction that I'd never felt before.

Don't get me wrong, my ego always went up when girls looked at me this way, but it was completely different when it was coming from my arch nemesis.

It made me feel a sense of triumph. I hadn't gotten her back yet, but this was a pretty damn good start to me. Because even though I wasn't pulling a prank on her, I could physically see that I was affecting her.

Kota usually never had a problem looking someone in the eye, but she was struggling to do so at the moment. I spoke again just to challenge her. "Are you guys coming to our game?"

She was aimlessly poking at anything and everything on the kitchen island, pretending to be occupied for the sake of not looking in our direction.

But she gave herself away further by her distraught tone. "Why would we do that? We spend enough fucking time under the same roof as you two."

Because Bridget didn't have a single mean bone in her body, she gave a friendly smile, acting like her best friend didn't just insult us. "We'll be there."

"Cool," Lane said.

Taking one last look at Kota, I soaked in the snapshot because I knew damn well that I'd probably never see it in real life again.

"See ya," I said as we slung our hockey bags over our shoulders and headed out.

***

The air was electric. The entire team was vivacious. And I was ready to beat some ass on the ice.

Hours and hours of practice had led us to this game. There was a lot of pressure on our starting line since we were all veterans and everyone looked up to us, and I hoped I delivered tonight.

When it was time to warm up, we hit the ice. My favorite part about home games was observing the sea of black and silver, our school colors, that filled the student section.

Even though my parents hated each other and of course never sat closer than two sections away from one another, they both tried to come to all our games, especially my dad. He played hockey growing up and fell in love with the sport, encouraging me to get into it at a young age.

Although it was always special having my family in the crowd, there was something so meaningful about having our peers there to cheer us on.

As a college student myself, I understood how busy life could get. Everyone had their own things going on— homework, sports, parties, or things in their personal lives, which was why it meant that much more knowing people took time out of their day to come watch us play.

North Dakota skated around full force on their half, warming up. They played well last year, making it into the tournament and winning the first game. But they fell short in the second, losing in overtime to Minnesota State.

It was a similar situation to us. We too lost in the second round of the tournament last year during overtime to Western Michigan. It was a brutal loss, one that still haunts each and every one of our team members to this day.

We had been up for the entire game, up until the third period. That was the worst part. Everything went to shit right towards the end, right when it all mattered the most. That was the thing about hockey— everything could change in an instant.

Whenever I thought hard about that loss, the feelings and memories came rushing back.

The heartbreak of being within reach of everything you'd ever wanted, only for all of it to be ripped away.

The exhaustion of playing at such a high and intense level for so long, only for it to not be enough.

76

The time and energy you'd put towards the dream, day in and day out, only for it to be worth nothing in the end.

I never wanted to feel that way again.

Now, North Dakota was said to have come back stronger, and experts had deemed them to be a lethal force this year.

With it being the first game, along with how good our opponents were said to be, I was nervous; I refused to show it though. I knew winning this game wouldn't fill the void that our tournament loss left, but it would definitely ease the burn and give us some motivation going into the season.

I wanted to win. Not in overtime. Not by just one goal. But by a fucking landslide.

After getting some stretches in and taking shots at Cody to help him warm up as our starting goalie, my eyes scanned the silver jerseys for *1*, Lane's number.

We usually found each other before every game, having our own moment to hype each other up before we headed back to the locker room for some words of encouragement from both Coach Palmer and Lane.

When I noticed him facing the glass, standing still, my brows knitted together. Lane never stood still during warmup. Ever. He was usually the one who was swerving in and out of everyone like a psychopath, not wasting a single second of warmup time.

Skating carefully through Jett and Matt as they passed a puck back and forth, I headed over, catching a familiar sight through the glass.

Mouth agape, I was no longer paying attention to where I was going, crashing right into Lane. He gave my shoulder a light push, but I ignored it.

Kota's smug, fiery grin reminded me of a cartoon villain, all picturesque and wicked as she stood there so confidently in something she had no fucking business wearing.

I recognized my jersey when I saw it. The number. The colors. The custom stitching of a stallion on the shoulder. But even though it was right in front of my face, I was still in denial.

"Are those our fucking jerseys?" I growled to Lane, unable to take my eyes away from the catastrophe in front of me.

Bridget was dressed in Lane's jersey, and it didn't seem to bother him in the slightest. As casually as ever, he mumbled, "Looks like it."

I could feel my jaw come unhinged. For how cold this arena was, it couldn't ease the inferno growing inside my body. The corners of Kota's eyes crinkled with delight as she studied me, wondering if I was going to snap and knowing a thick divider of tempered glass sat between us.

I didn't hesitate to bang my fist against it. "Take my fucking jersey off, Kota!"

That malevolent gleam in her eye only brightened at my reaction. Blowing a perfect bubble of pink bubblegum, she brought up both middle fingers and held them there.

God fucking dammit. This girl is going to be the death of me.

Blood boiling in my veins, I wanted to break my own hockey stick over my knee.

Not only had she beaten me down with bitchy comments and used my discomforts against me, but now she was taking my stuff? Stuff that actually meant something to me? Stuff I worked my ass off to earn?

My spot on this team was not guaranteed; it was earned. And now, my least favorite person was exploiting that for her own entertainment.

I knew she was only wearing it to get a rise out of me, and I hated that I was giving her what she wanted, but I couldn't help myself.

And what pissed me off the most? She looked kind of good in it.

Her dark hair cascaded smoothly over the thick fabric, and the light blush she had swiped over her cheeks was the perfect contrast to the dark material.

I didn't want people around us to get the wrong idea though. I'd never had a girl wear my jersey. And for this to come so soon after she told my recent conquest that we'd been dating, it brought this nightmare to a whole new level.

Lane was cracking up beside me. "This isn't funny!" I shouted at him. "She's gonna get her germs all over it!"

With a light shake of his head, I caught his eyes jumping across the arena for a moment at our opponents. He closed the small gap between us, leaning in. "Look, we can deal with this later. Right now, we have a game to play."

Eyes trailing upwards, I took in North Dakota once again. And just like earlier, that same, competitive spark carried through me.

I didn't bother giving Kota another glance as I nodded to Lane with a tight jaw and skated away.

Chapter Twelve

Kota

The boys were up three-to-one by the start of the third period. Bridget and I were enjoying the game, getting rowdy alongside the rest of the student section.

But honestly, I was starting to have a hard time focusing.

The group of girls sitting behind us, which I could only assume were freshman by the way they were dressed like they were heading to a party and by their juvenile conversations, wouldn't shut their fucking mouths about the players.

"I want number one," one of the girls said.

"Ooo!" another responded. "He's captain, right?"

Bridget and I traded equally annoyed glances.

I could've sworn they'd almost gone through the entire roster, rating all the guys and calling dibs on the ones they wanted. It had been easier zoning them out when they weren't talking about our roommates though.

"Well, I want number eighteen," the last one said.

"I already called dibs on him, Katie."

"I don't care. I want him."

I raised a brow, facing the rink as I listened in on what they were saying about Crew.

No fucking wonder why the dude had such a big ego. Girls that he didn't even know were drooling over him left and right. I wished more than ever that I really could chop his balls off and sell them on Ebay. I'd bet these freshmen would pay big bucks for them.

Bridget leaned closer to me. "I wish they would shut up."

"Do you want me to make them shut up?"

Normally Bridget didn't condone my impolite behavior, but this time, she gave a supporting smile, along with a shrug. "Kinda."

"Done." I spun around. "Hey," I said, looking over the freshmen. They were even more dolled up than I originally thought. Who the hell put on so much makeup and minimal clothes to come sit in a cold hockey arena? Weren't they freezing? They looked like they were on their way to a damn club and just decided to stop here out of convenience.

"Why do you guys want number eighteen anyway? He sucks," I said.

Two of the girls quietly sunk back as if they had a mute button that I just hit.

The last girl shot me a dirty look. "Then why are you wearing his jersey?"

Narrowing my eyes at her, I was prepared to spit fire. "None of your damn business."

"Then stay out of *our* business," she spat.

I leaned forward. "You make that a little damn difficult to do when you're practically shouting it in the middle of a hockey game."

Slightly, she retreated. "Whatever," she muttered, looking back to the ice.

I turned back around with a smirk, giving Bridget a subtle fist bump as she let out a giggle.

"Sometimes I like when you're a bitch," she whispered.

I smiled wider, eyes back on the game. I watched as Crew sent a North Dakota player into the boards with a clean hit, immediately causing my smile to drop and my jaw to become tense.

It wasn't that I necessarily wanted Crew to be the one getting hurt but every time he made a good move, I could feel a pulsing coming from my core and I couldn't help but think about him wearing that goddamn suit.

I didn't drop my game face often— if at all— but I'd be lying if I said I was entirely composed earlier. The worst part? *He could tell.*

I was trying to be at ease though. For all he knew, I was only acting that way to make him think he was getting to me. Either way, it seemed like he'd forgotten all about my hot and bothered encounter when he saw me wearing his jersey.

He still hadn't gotten me back from my tampon mistletoe prank. And after today, I was sure he was extra fired up.

He may have been out for blood on the ice right now, but I knew damn well he was going to be out for blood at home too.

I smirked at the thought of a challenge.
Bring it on, Crew.

Chapter Thirteen

Crew

After a clean sweep this weekend, the guys were throwing a celebratory hockey party after our game on Saturday night.

Usually, I'd be there all night, drinking and flirting and eventually hooking up with some girl I'd probably never see again, but tonight was different.

Tonight, I had better things to do.

Once I was sure there was no one currently at our apartment, I left the hockey party early when no one was paying attention.

When I got home, I double checked to make sure I was the only one there before tossing my shit in my room so that I could get to work.

I took a glance at my away jersey that was hanging up in my closet, the one Kota wore to our first game yesterday. I narrowed my eyes at it.

The nerve of that girl. I still couldn't believe she had the guts to walk through the arena with my name and number on her back. The jersey seemed tainted with her bitchiness. I'd never wanted to burn one of my jerseys before until now.

Focus, Crew, I reminded myself. *Stick to the task at hand.*

It wasn't until late last night that I came up with this idea, but the second I did, I knew I had to do it.

Rushing into the bathroom, I snagged the bag of toothpaste that I bought for the occasion from where I'd hidden it underneath the sink.

I had no idea how long I had before someone would come home, so I worked as if I only had minutes.

Once I got all my supplies situated, taking up most of the kitchen island, I got to work, carefully untwisting every Oreo cookie and using a butter knife to scrape the cream off. I squeezed a glob of toothpaste onto each wafer before pressing its other half against it to create a perfect Oreo with toothpaste filling.

A menacing smirk, so strong that it physically hurt, sat on my face. I felt kind of evil for what I was doing. For a second, I wondered if I should just scratch this whole prank, be the bigger person and try not to let Kota get to me.

Until I waved the thought off.

No way in hell was I going to let her think she won. And let's face it. My lack of retaliation probably wouldn't stop her from pulling some more shit on me anyway.

She'd gotten me twice now— once with the tampons and once with my jersey. But I felt like messing with her snacks was personal enough to even the score.

And I couldn't fucking wait.

I finished just in time for Lane to trudge through the door, all sullen eyed with saggy shoulders.

When his gaze left the floor just long enough to notice me sitting on the couch, he looked almost disappointed to see me. "Why are you home so early?"

"I had a migraine," I lied, expecting him to catch it, but even if he did, he didn't seem to care, giving what was hardly a nod. "How about you?"

"It's almost midnight."

"Oh," I let out underneath my breath, glancing at the clock on the stove. "Yeah, it is... I'm assuming I won't really see you tomorrow?"

I could hear the pain laced into his voice. With a sigh, he said, "Probably not."

He sounded tired, run-down, as if he'd just had the most exhausting day of his life.

"You want me to bring you food throughout the day?"

"Yeah," Lane sighed again. "Thanks." As he walked off and hid in his bedroom, my stomach started to hurt.

In twenty minutes, it would officially be Lane's birthday, his least favorite day of the year.

Lane lost his twin brother a few years before we met, and for as long as I'd known him, he hated his birthday. The first few years I knew him, I tried getting him out and about on his birthday to celebrate. One time, I even threw him a party. It turned into everyone else celebrating while he locked himself away in his room with a fifth of vodka.

I usually stayed up late on the weekends, but since Lane was an early riser and I needed to make sure I was awake to cook him breakfast, I decided to crash.

The second my head hit the pillow, my mind was filled with fantasies of what Kota's reaction may be when she tasted her new Oreos.

A mischievous grin settled on my face, and I wouldn't have been surprised if it stayed there all throughout the night.

Chapter Fourteen

Kota

After the boys won their second game of the weekend last night, I was the only one in the apartment who didn't make an appearance at the hockey house.

Bridget went for a while with Mitch; Lane and Crew were obviously there. But I preferred to go grab dinner and drinks with Bobby, because I didn't need to spend any extra time around Crew, or the rest of the hockey team for that matter.

Bridget and I had already recapped our nights to each other, and now, we were fixing breakfast for ourselves, knee deep in *The Bachelor* gossip.

This was exactly the kind of Sunday mornings I had envisioned when Bridget and I signed our lease to what we thought was a two bedroom. I had imagined us making breakfast together, chatting about one of our favorite shows and listening to the faint echo of Taylor Swift playing in the background.

It would've been perfect if there wasn't a dumb hockey player sprawled out on our couch.

When Crew didn't politely ask, but instead, *insisted* that we turned our music down, I turned it up just to spite him.

Of course, he turned the tv up as a result, which made me turn the music up more.

We'd been playing this petty game for fifteen minutes. Both things were so loud at this point that I was surprised it hadn't woken Lane.

I caught Bridget glancing at the clock a few times, and when eleven o'clock came rolling around, her brows furrowed. "Hey," she said towards the living room, "where's Lane at? He's usually up by now and I haven't seen him since last night."

"Yeah, um," Crew answered so quietly that I had to pause *cardigan* just to hear him, "you probably won't be seeing him today."

Trading glances with B, she asked, "Why?"

Crew's chest expanded with a heavy breath. "Well..."

He was starting to freak me out a little. My first thought was that maybe Lane got hurt bad at their game last night, but he went to the hockey house afterwards, so I doubted he had any injury serious enough to keep him in bed all morning.

"Crew?" B pushed, and we both scooted closer.

Crew roamed into the kitchen, leaning across the island. His voice dropped from quiet to a full-on whisper. "Don't make a big deal about it or say anything, okay? Trust me."

It was hard not to notice that he was practically only looking at Bridget as he spoke. A sassy comment was itching in my throat, but I was worried about Lane, and that overtook all the annoyance that was sitting in my bones.

"Is he alright?" I warily let out.

Eyes acknowledging me for half a second, Crew then peered down the boy's hall. With a slight gulp, he said, "It's his birthday—"

"It's his *birthday?*" B practically shouted, hands slamming down on the kitchen island.

"Shh!" Crew hushed. "Keep it down."

"Why?" I wondered, a bite in my tone.

"Just trust me."

"Why would we trust *you?*"

Crew rolled his eyes before going back to pretending like I didn't exist. His attention turned solely onto Bridget. "Trust me. Just let him be today."

A striking contrast to my venomous tone, B's sounded sweet like Strawberry Shortcake. She even had the hair to match. "But if it's his birthday, we should do something nice for him."

"Oh!" I squealed, my face lighting up. "Let's bake him a cake."

Crew's frustration was becoming tangible, traveling like smoke throughout the air. I couldn't tell if I loved it or hated it. "That's a horrible idea. That's the complete of what I just told you to do, and he doesn't like cake anyway."

My face scrunched. "Who doesn't like cake?"

"Just fucking listen to me," he hissed, eyes shut. "I've known him for years. He wants to be left alone."

B tipped her head innocently, and once again, it was just another startling moment of an angel and devil standing next to each other. "But why?" B asked. "Why doesn't he like his birthday?"

Sighing, Crew pushed away from the island. "He just doesn't, okay? Trust me," he repeated before sauntering into his room.

Concern and curiosity were searing into my skin, and I wished that Crew had given us more information. Clearly, whatever the problem was had to be super personal to Lane, and I respected that, but all Crew did was leave us with questions.

After a few moments of silence, I ran a hand through my hair. "Alright."

"Alright what?" Bridget asked.

"We're baking him a freaking cake."

***

It's the thought that counts.
The cake didn't turn out as pretty as I wanted.

I'd had a picture in my mind of a cute birthday cake with blue frosting along the sides and *happy birthday* written on top.

But unfortunately, we overestimated our baking skills, and instead of presenting Lane with a cake that he couldn't refuse, we presented him with one that had *happy birth* slathered across the top because I ran out of room halfway through doing the frosting.

I'd been hoping that regardless of the horrendous delivery, the cake would still be delicious enough that Lane would love it and I'd have bragging rights to tell Crew he was wrong.

But that didn't happen either.

Lane hated the cake.

Bridget and I could tell he was trying to force feed it to himself before we finally told him to stop because it was painful to watch.

After listening to Crew say *I told you so* on repeat for ten minutes, he finally shut the hell up a while ago, letting me clean up the kitchen in peace.

Even though Lane didn't like the cake, the gesture was enough to lure him out of his room. Bridget and I still hadn't asked questions. There were a few times I had to bite my own tongue just to keep myself from doing so. I'd always been known for being nosy.

"You know," Lane finally said, seated beside Bridget on the kitchen stools, "today hasn't been that bad so far."

"And why is that?" Bridget asked.

He nodded to Crew and me, "Because those two have gone a full hour in the same room without trying to kill each other."

Had it really been that long since Crew had been blaming me for ruining Lane's birthday with a shitty cake? A lightning-fast glance at the clock above the stove verified it, and I whipped my head towards Crew, immediately sickened when I saw him already glaring at me, eyes narrowed.

Jaw shifting beneath my skin, my eyes thinned to slits. "I can stir up something good if you want."

"No thanks," Bridget and Lane said in unison.

Crew looked like he had a million and one rude thoughts right now, his eyes hardening to stone. More than anything, I wanted to dare him to speak his mind, to even say *one* of those virulent thoughts and start a fight, just so that I could say I didn't start it this time. I was itching for an argument; the peace was overrated.

But I was also trying to prove a point. That I had self-control. That I was mature— sorta. And that I wasn't always the one starting shit.

So, instead of egging Crew on, I gave him a cold shoulder, going straight for my Oreos in the pantry. Hearing a strange giggle coming from my arch nemesis, I instinctively spewed, "Shut up. I hate when you make noise."

So much for not starting shit.

Surprisingly, he didn't give a snarky response. All he did was shrug and sit there quietly with a questionable smirk.

He kept giggling under his breath as I shoved a cookie into my mouth, and the more I chewed, the more repulsed I got. Were these cookies bad? They were relatively new, so they should've been fine. Plus, they weren't stale; they just tasted like a freshly cleaned foot.

Gagging, I swung around myself and dove straight for the sink, spitting it out. "Why the fuck do these taste like ass!"

Crew spoke steadily, unwavering confidence soaring out. "Maybe because I replaced the filling with toothpaste."

Vision blurring red, I shot him a glare so sharp and deadly that it could've cut glass. My body shook through anger, and heavily, I breathed out, "You what?"

He shrugged again, nonchalantly. "I told you I was gonna get you back."

"Apparently, I spoke too soon," Lane said.

I could hear Lane and Bridget exchanging responses, but I couldn't tear my eyes away from Crew, as if there was some unsaid hope that staring harshly at him long enough would kill him right then and there.

With each passing millisecond, my chest expanded with deeper, more ragged breaths. I couldn't believe he fucked with my snacks. "You have no idea what you just started."

Leaning across the kitchen island, Crew grinned. "Oh, but I do."

"I'm going to make your life a living hell."

"Good luck," he challenged. "This is war."

As if it were planned, we both glanced at our friends at the same time. They shook their heads, frowns galore.

"Don't look at us," Bridget announced.

"Yeah," Lane added, "we both already said before we don't wanna be involved."

Huffing, Crew looked like he'd just been punched in the gut, and my interpretation of that was that he wasn't confident he could take me on alone.

"Fine," he said firmly, but I still wasn't convinced. "One-on-one then."

Mr. Ego had absolutely no idea what was in store for him. He just signed himself up for a life of misery. If he thought there was any chance in hell that this was all going to end his way, with him victorious, he had a rude awakening coming.

I couldn't control the criminal smirk that touched my lips and I stared at him, smothering him with my tenacity and hoping he'd crumble to dust from the feeling. "Fine," I grinned bigger.

Chapter Fifteen

Crew

There was a small get-together going on at the hockey house tonight, so I woke up after a short nap and got dressed. When I stepped into the living room, Lane was on the couch, wearing the same clothes he wore to class.

"Dude?" I spoke. "Aren't you gonna change?"

He glanced back and forth between the TV and me. "Uh, nah."

"Um, okay," I said. "Well, are you ready to go then?"

His mouth formed a hard line. "I don't really think I'm gonna go."

My brows drew in, arms raised. "Why the hell not?"

He tipped his side to side.

I gave a sigh, glancing away. "Don't tell me."

"Don't tell you what?"

"I'm afraid to ask."

He eyed me in silence, waiting for me to either drop it or spit it out.

So, I spat it out. "Is this about Bridget?"

Lane opened his mouth slightly before clamping it shut.

"Lane," I said firmly, "you cannot keep doing this to yourself."

I knew shortly after we moved in that Lane had a thing for Bridget. I didn't think it was anything significant. I figured it was a little crush he'd get over in a week, but his feelings had clearly progressed, given that he'd been spending every night on the couch for the past week, waiting for Bridget to come home whenever she went out with Mitch.

It was becoming painful to watch.

Over the last few days, I'd caught him numerous times creepily glancing at the door, waiting for her to walk through it. He even made me text her one night asking what time she'd be home, which was extra fucking awkward because Bridget and I rarely ever texted.

Lane was usually always down to hangout, usually always in a good mood. But instead, he'd been spending all his free time sulking. And now he was skipping out on a get-together? This was all completely unlike him.

I'd never seen him like this before and I was hating every second of it. Lane had never been as promiscuous as most of the hockey team, but he'd never really been one that actually fell for girls either.

"C'mon," I encouraged him. "Don't waste your night sitting here and basking in your misery."

"I'm not miserable," he replied. But I wasn't convinced. He motioned around to all his things. "I've got a movie on. I've got snacks. I've got a beer. I'm just chilling."

I rolled my eyes. "You're seriously not going to come to the house? Everyone's gonna be asking where you're at."

He shrugged nonchalantly. "Tell them I'm busy."

Shaking my head at the floor, I responded, "Well, if you're really not coming, then can you at least invite someone over so that you're not by yourself?"

Lane eyed me like the idea was absurd. "Like who?"

"Anybody," I said desperately. I thought for a moment, trying to come up with someone who could get his mind off Bridget. The first person that popped into my head was the girl I practically peer-pressured him into talking to last week that he ended up spending the night with. "What about that girl from last week at the bar? Ally?"

His brow lifted. "Ava?" he corrected.

"Yeah!" I said. "Invite her over. You said you liked her, right?"

"Bro, I'm fine," he insisted.

"Lane," I urged through my teeth.

"Will you feel better if I tell you that I'll think about it?"

"That depends," I said. "Are you telling me that so that I shut up or are you telling me that because you mean it?"

"A little of both," he admitted.

I groaned, tipping my head back. "Do you want me to stay here with you?"

"No," he immediately said.

I was sort of relieved to hear that, considering that I definitely didn't want to sit on the couch all night while Lane moped beside me. *Again.*

My concern didn't ease though.

"Just go," he insisted casually. "I'm literally fine."

I blew out a stressed breath as I turned towards the door. "You're not fine," I muttered to myself before glancing over my shoulder. "Text me if you need anything, alright?"

"I will."

***

I had my eye on a smoking hot dirty blonde that kept glancing at me from across the room. Luckily, I had already called silent dibs on her tonight before any of the other guys could.

I'd never seen her here before, but it wasn't rocket science to figure out that one of the girls in her friend group had been invited tonight, which in girl terms meant the whole friend group got to go.

I wasn't complaining though.

This was typically how it went under this roof.

All it took was for one person in the house to invite one girl and an entire army showed up.

Goddamn, I missed living here.

There were no girly decorations hung up in the common areas. No arguing over the TV when a new episode of *The Bachelor* was on. No evil witch hiding around the corner, patiently waiting to gauge my eyes out.

The only reason I still had my sanity was because of Lane.

Speaking of Lane, I should probably check on him.

I reluctantly took my eyes off the blonde, digging my phone out of my pocket.

Me: You good?

Lane: Better than ever

I rolled my eyes. Could he just admit how he was feeling?

Don't get me wrong, I wasn't good at handling emotions or giving advice, but this was Lane we were talking about. My brother by choice. And to see him so miserable, whether he admitted it or not, was like getting punched in the gut myself.

Me: Did you invite anyone over?

Lane: I don't feel like entertaining someone

Me: Then let them entertain u (;

Lane: I'm not like you

Me: Clearly

When he didn't respond, I groaned, putting my phone away.

My eyes made their way back to the blonde, looking her over. She'd been standing in the same spot for at least ten minutes, a perfect path to my line of sight. Was she waiting for me to come talk to her?

Only one way to find out.

I began striding across the room but came to an abrupt stop when I saw a blur of red walk through the door. I tensed for a moment, unsure if what I was seeing was real or if someone had somehow slipped something into my drink and I was hallucinating.

As if forgetting about the blonde, I darted towards the person who stole my attention.

I lightly grabbed her hand and swung her around, my brows drawing inwards. "Bridget?"

"Hey, Crew!" she smiled.

"What the hell are you doing here?" I asked, fearfully glancing around to see where Kota was.

"I was with Mitch, and he got invited," she said. I followed her gaze over to Mitch, who was casually greeting a few of the guys.

"So, Kota's not with you?" I asked, relief laced into my voice.

She gave a small laugh, as if she knew what I was thinking. "No."

Breathing a sigh of relief, my shoulders lightly dropped as I relaxed. "Good."

Lifting a brow, Bridget spoke, "You really should just forfeit though."

I tensed up again. "Why? Do you know what she's planning?"

"No," she shook her head. "But whatever it is, it's probably bad."

I sighed. "I wish Lane would at least help me."

"Sorry, buddy. This is between you and Kota." She glanced around, her tone aiming for casual but landing closer to disappointment instead. "Speaking of Lane, where is he?"

I shut my mouth so tight that it hurt my jaw.

At home, waiting for you.

"He's not here actually," I said.

She shoved her hands into the back pockets of her jeans with a faint frown, shoulders dropping. "Really? Why not?"

"Um," I stuttered, glancing towards the ceiling in thought. "He, um, wasn't feeling good."

Her shoulders slumped further. "Aw, poor Lane. I should text him to make sure he's okay."

Frantically, I held my hands up as she slid her phone out. "No, no, no!"

Bridget hesitated, eyeing me in wariness. "Why not?"

"Because..." I stumbled.

She raised a brow, her wariness turning to suspicion.

"Because he's probably asleep and you don't wanna wake him up by texting him, right?"

She glanced at the time on her phone. "It's hardly ten o'clock."

I inhaled deeply, prepared to spew some more bullshit, but luckily, Mitch appeared at just the right moment.

"Hey," he smiled at Bridget, handing her a drink.

"Hey, thanks," she smiled back.

Mitch gave me a friendly nod. "Crew."

"Mitch," I nodded back indifferently.

When Bridget shoved her phone back into her pocket, I eased up. The last thing Lane needed was to receive a text from Bridget, get confused, realize she was with me, and then either mope even harder for the rest of the night or show up here and get his jealousy knocked up ten notches.

I leaned towards Bridget in the slightest. "Are you sure you don't know what Kota's planning?"

"Crew," she laughed, "I literally have no idea. She hasn't told me much since the first prank."

Narrowing my eyes at the memory, I spoke through clenched teeth. "Tampon mistletoe."

She made a face. "Yeah... Sorry 'bout that one again."

I sighed. "It's fine. I know you were conned into participating."

"That, I was."

"Well," I sighed again, "if you really have no information for me, then please excuse me while I go talk to a hottie."

Bridget fist bumped me. "Go get her."

Thankfully, the blonde was right where I saw her last. She had a pouty frown plastered on her face, and as we made eye contact from over her friend's shoulder, her frown flipped.

I smirked, knowing she'd been waiting for me. And as I neared, she shot her friend a look that screamed *Love you but go the fuck away now*.

I stopped just before them and as her friend turned and spotted me, the same bright shade as pink cotton candy swirled throughout her cheeks before she dropped her head and wandered off.

Lightly biting my bottom lip, I turned my attention to the blonde. "Hi."

"Hi," she said.

I shook her hand. "Crew."

"Tori."

"How are you doing tonight, Tori?" The moment her name left my lips, I could see her chest expand with a deep breath. Either she was nervous or hearing me say her name was turning her on. Either way, I liked it.

"I'm good," she nodded, clutching onto her White Claw. "How are you?"

"A lot better now that I've finally got the chance to talk to you."

Tori raised a brow, trying to hold back a smirk, but failing.

I smiled. "That one was bad, wasn't it?"

She let out a sweet laugh as she nodded. "A bit, yeah."

"Damn," I said through a smile, dropping my head for a moment. "Did I blow it?"

She shook her head. "Not at all."

I pretended to blow out a stressed breath, my shoulders rising and falling with it. "Thank God."

Tori laughed again, this time a light blush accompanying it. The next fifteen minutes were filled with small talk, flirting, and another drink before I popped the question and asked her if she wanted to go back to my place.

With sparkling eyes and a captivating smirk, she agreed, and I led her out the door.

***

Tori seemingly took in every inch of the apartment as I led her inside.

"Is that Lane Avery?" she whispered, pointing towards the couch.

Lane had an arm slung over the side of the couch, his mouth wide open as he let out a light snore.

"Yeah," I whispered back, draping my jacket over the back of one of the kitchen stools.

"My friend was really hoping he'd be there tonight."

"Ah, really?" I asked casually. "Who's your friend?"

"Her name's Nya."

Never heard of her. Didn't think I would've anyway, but I felt obligated to ask.

"I don't think I know her," I said.

Tori nodded, then eyed me quietly, waiting for me to make the next move. I cocked my head down the hall, signaling for her to follow.

The second I closed my bedroom door behind us, I didn't even have time to turn on a light before she grabbed my hand and yanked me towards her, throwing her lips onto mine.

Right to the point, I see.

I didn't hesitate to dig my fingers into the skin between her jeans and crop top, pulling her backwards with me until I met the bed and took a seat.

She straddled my lap, pushing herself against my growing dick before moaning into my mouth, the vibration flowing through me.

My hands explored the skin underneath her shirt, more than prepared to rip the fabric off.

But before I got the chance, Tori pulled away, slightly out of breath as she studied the wall behind me.

"What's wrong?" I asked.

There was one stream of light flowing through the window from the streetlamps outside, just enough to make out the look on her face. She looked almost... disturbed?

"Um," she paused, still looking past my shoulder. Her head tipped, "Is that..."

Was this girl on drugs or something? Was there a fucking ghost behind me? What the hell was she looking at?

I narrowed my eyes in confusion as she stiffened to stone on my lap.

"What's what?" I finally asked, a little snappier than intended.

"Your wall..."

With a troubled breath, I carefully moved her off my lap and reached for my bedside lamp, tugging on the string.

I could've sworn you could hear my jaw hitting the floor when I could finally see what she'd been staring at. We ate silence for a minute, shock and rage and embarrassment coursing through my veins.

"Um," she finally spoke distastefully, grabbing her purse off the floor, "I'm gonna head out."

All I could do was give her a tight-lipped nod. Because how the hell do you come up with an excuse for why you have a One Direction shrine hanging above your bed? There was no bouncing back from this. I was not getting laid tonight.

I watched in utter silence as Tori practically ran out of the apartment.

Well fucking played, Kota. Well fucking played.

Chapter Sixteen

Kota

I told Bridget to keep an eye on my things while I wasn't home, so hopefully she'd drop this whole Switzerland thing she had going on for the day and be on my side.

I was still on a high from hearing the story of Crew's failed hookup this week. I almost wished I'd been home so that I could've seen the poor girl running out of the apartment.

I knew Crew was fired up and that he'd retaliate, but anything he came up with wouldn't have anything on me.

Because the thing about Crew was that he was too predictable.

If he was gone in the morning, he was at practice.

If he was gone during the day, that meant he was either at class or at the gym.

If he was gone at night, he was fucking around. And if he was fucking around, that meant he probably wouldn't be coming home alone.

That's where the real opportunities were at.

I was pretty proud of this one. After all, tampon mistletoe was a spin-off of something else I saw online, but this prank was all me. An original masterpiece by Dakota Darling. I should've signed my name on the wall next to Harry Styles.

I already had a multitude of ideas of the best ways to torture him further, but for the moment, those fun thoughts had to be put on the backburner. Because I was currently on my way to see my mom.

We were planning on doing some shopping and grabbing lunch. My mom had some fundraiser gala thing that she'd be attending next week, so she requested that I helped her find a dress.

Ironically, I was jamming out to some One Direction when I parked in the parking garage that led inside to the mall. I smirked as I shut the car off, letting out a small giggle.

My mom was waiting at the entrance for me, her arms extended out with an ample smile on her face.

I accepted the gesture, squeezing my arms around her. "Hi, Mama!"

"Hi, honey. How are you?"

"Good. How are you doing?"

"I'm alright. Minus all this stuff," she gestured around. "You know shopping stresses me out."

"I know," I smiled. "Don't worry! We're gonna find you a hot dress."

She let me take the lead, trudging behind me as I examined the window of each store, deciding if it would be worth our time or not.

I stopped outside one that had mannequins wearing prom dresses in the window. "How bout this one?"

Mom raised a brow, skeptical. "Those dresses look a bit too glittery for my liking."

"Mom," I rolled my eyes, "they probably have other dresses inside." I grabbed her hand, dragging her along. "Plus, you'd look great in a bedazzled dress."

"I don't wanna draw too much attention to myself," she countered.

I let out a quiet sigh. This was where my mom and I differed. We had the same feisty personality and sense of independence, but when it came to being the center of attention, she wasn't a fan. Whereas I would gladly fuck up a sparkly dress on the dance floor, she'd rather hide in the corner with it. She didn't like an immense number of eyes on her, although I wasn't sure why. Since Mom had me while she was in college, she was still pretty young, only in her early forties. She looked like she was ten years younger though, still as beautiful and lively as she had been in photos I'd seen of her from decades ago.

But since she refused to wear any fun dresses, I picked out some simpler dresses for her to try on.

She spoke as I waited outside her dressing room door. "How are things at the apartment?"

I smirked, holding in laughter. "Great."

"That didn't sound too convincing."

"Don't worry, Mom. I'm not even being sarcastic." The door opened, and I could see my eyes light up in the mirror behind my mother. "Wow! Mom, you look so pretty."

"You think so?" she asked, glancing in the mirror.

The dress was an elegant floor length, fire red, a striking contrast to her dark hair.

"Yes," I nodded firmly. "I love it."

"Okay, okay," she said, giving a small spin. "Let me try the other ones on just to be sure."

"I agree."

As Mom shut the door behind her again, the silence didn't last long. She jumped right back into our previous conversation.

"So, are things better with your boy roommates?"

I gave a light snort at her awkward wording. "Yep. I've got everything under control."

"Oh, God," she said. "What's that mean?"

"It means I'm adjusting well."

"Um, yeah, that's not very reassuring."

"Oh, c'mon, Mom," I said. "Don't you know me at all?"

"Yes," she replied confidently. "That's why I'm concerned." All I could do was respond with a wily laugh. "What did you do to those poor boys?"

Now, I was scoffing. "Poor boys?" I practically shouted. "Mother, they are devious little monsters. Well," I corrected myself, "one of them is."

The door opened again, revealing my disapproving mother in a sky-blue dress that had a slit down one leg.

"I like this one a lot, actually," I said.

"Don't change the subject," she insisted. "But for the record," she glimpsed in the mirror, "so do I."

My mouth stayed clamped shut, my only response being the mindless nod I gave, eyes glued to the dress.

"Kota?"

"Mhm?"

Impatience clouded over her eyes as she raised a brow at me.

"Mom! This isn't about me. We're finding you a dress."

She gave a light sneer, and it was like looking in a mirror. "Dakota Lyn," she shook her head, scolding me.

"Alright, well can we change the subject, for real? Because I need your advice," I said.

I hadn't been planning on asking my mom for her opinion on my current situation with Bobby, so I wasn't quite sure why I felt the need to bring it up in the moment, but if it was going to skew the conversation away from the boys, I guess it was worth it.

My mom gave a small sigh, but her eyes lit up with both fascination and concern. "What is it?"

"You know the guy I've been seeing? Bobby?"

"You mean the one I still haven't met?" she said, giving me another look of disapproval. *Seems like she was full of disapproval today.* "Yes."

I rolled my eyes. "Mom, I told you that you could meet him once we officially start dating," I explained. "Which is sort of the problem. We're still not an official couple."

"Hm," she nodded along, still studying herself in the mirror.

Silence followed, and I could tell she was deep in thought about her dress fiasco, causing me to sigh.

The delicate blue hanging off her skin perfectly matched her aura— compassionate, yet resilient. Even though my mom and I looked so much alike, I didn't think I'd be able to pull that dress off. It was far too soft of a color for someone so full of rage and stubbornness.

I allowed the silence to saturate the air for another moment before I cleared my throat. My mom gave a slight jump, snapping her attention back to me. "Sorry, honey," she murmured.

"So... do you have any advice?"

Watching me in the mirror, she said, "Just give him a tiny bit more time. Maybe he's trying to take things slow."

I didn't hesitate to tip my head with a look that said *Really?*

"Maybe he just wants to get to know you better first."

"Um," I lightly cringed, "yeah I don't think that's it."

With a huff, she studied me harder in the mirror. It was like her gaze was shooting straight into my brain, reading every thought I'd ever had.

"Oh goodness, Kota. I don't like that look you're giving me. I know exactly what it means."

My mom and I were close, and we told each other a lot, but there were certain details of our lives that we most definitely never disclosed.

Our sex lives was one of them.

"You better be being safe," she added.

Heat was rushing to my cheeks, and I knew red was blossoming over my warm skin complexion. I was afraid to look at my reflection in the mirror; my eyes skimmed the floor. Regardless of the sudden embarrassment flooding over me, my voice remained strong and secure. "I am, Mom. I'm smart. Don't you think so?"

The stiffness in her shoulders relaxed, but she clutched onto the side of the dress. "Of course, I do. But still..." her voice lowered, "things happen."

I knew she didn't want to use the word "accident" or "mistake", granted that *I* was the accident.

"Yeah," I nodded softly, "I know." Neither of us said anything else for a few minutes, the only sound being the rustling and chatter of people out in the store area. "Did you decide, Mom?" I finally asked.

"Yeah," she grinned lightly. "I think I'm gonna go with the blue."

Well, I could've guessed that.

Chapter Seventeen

Crew

I'd been waiting rather impatiently to get Kota back. It had been almost a week since she embarrassed me so bad that I was still scared to show my face on campus. I was just waiting for some random girls to come up to me and ask about my One Direction obsession.

We had a game against our rivals, St. Cloud State, next weekend, which meant that Coach Palmer was going to make this upcoming week brutal for all of us.

Which was why we usually called this week Hell Week.

It usually consisted of non-stop, hardcore drills with little to no breaks, Coach being a complete, unwarranted dick, and a handful of guys either puking or fainting at one point or another from how intense our practices were.

Our rivalry with St. Cloud went back decades before any of us were even born. No one knew why it started; all we knew was that our job was to beat them.

When Lane and I were freshman, we defeated St. Cloud State in the regular season, but they ended up beating us out for the conference title.

Last year, we were lucky enough to take the title back.

But it only meant that coach was going to put more pressure on us to keep that title.

106

The game we had against them next week was a regular season game, but that didn't mean the stakes weren't high enough already. Plus, the game was at their school, which meant they had the home advantage. Luckily, their student section was nothing compared to ours, so we didn't have to worry as much about thousands of people screaming at us to go fuck ourselves.

Since we were about to hate our lives for the next seven days though, why not go into it with a little bang?

We were having a team dinner and grabbing some casual drinks. I had Matt on one side of me and Lane on the other, fully content with the plate of buffalo wings in front of me.

"You know they have things called napkins, right?" Lane ridiculed, popping a fry into his mouth.

I shot him a glare, my mouth full of food. He looked smug from my irritation as I plucked a napkin out of the dispenser in the center of the table and wiped my face.

"Thanks, Captain. Didn't know these existed," I mumbled, tossing the napkin beside my plate.

He grinned lightly as he took a bite of his burger, swatting Matt's hand away when he tried reaching across me to steal a fry.

"Get your own," Lane said after swallowing.

"Just give me one," Matt cried.

"Knowing you, one means five, so no," Lane grimaced.

I sat back as they leaned over me to face each other. "Ladies," I grumbled, unamused, "no need to fight."

Matt leaned forward more, blocking the pathway to my plate. "Well, Lane's being unreasonable."

"And now, you're in my way." I brought my hand to his shoulder and subtly pushed him back into his seat.

With a sigh, Matt gave up, clutching onto his beer. "Whatever."

I stopped mid-bite as everything on the table began vibrating, the table buzzing beneath us. For a second, I thought there was an earthquake or some shit before Matt wiped off his hands on his own lap and picked his ringing phone up.

"Ah, it's El," he announced, accepting the FaceTime call.

El, whose full name was Eleanor, was one of Matt's best friends from back home. I didn't know the full story, but from what I did know, their parents had been friends since high school, so they'd known each other for years.

El had visited a couple times while Lane and I lived in the house, so we knew her pretty well.

"Yes?" Matt answered.

"Hey, I need guy advice."

His face scrunched together like he'd just smelled something rotten. "I don't wanna hear about all the guys you've been fucking."

I could see her glossy lips curl upwards on the screen, a delighted twinkle in her eye. "Why? Cause you're jealous?"

I leaned over Matt's shoulder so that the camera caught the corner of my face. "Yeah, he is!"

"He moans your name in his sleep!" Cody shouted across the table.

"Not surprised," she said. "I always knew you wanted me."

Matt shook his head, scoffing, but I caught the light red glow that came across his cheeks. "Oh, shut up," he stood, exiting the room.

Cody choked on a laugh. "He's so in love with her."

"Obviously," I agreed.

She was practically the only girl that he genuinely respected from head to toe. I'd never heard him speak badly of her ever, and I had no doubt that if someone had some nasty things to say about her, he'd defend her honor over his own.

Not to mention that any time she came to visit, he gave up his bed for her to sleep in and slept on the couch with no complaints.

I wasn't going to lie, she was hot as fucking hell and all the guys wanted her. Including me.

But Matt instilled a hands-off rule long before the first time she ever came to visit and threatened the whole team that they'd become best friends with his fist if anyone ever made a move on her. And considering Matt Gallagher was one of the best defensemen in the country and could fight dirty both on and off the ice, no one was looking to pick a fight with him.

I finished the last of my wings before running to the bathroom to wash the sauce off my hands. Pulling some cash out on my way back to the table, I handed it to Lane.

"Use this to cover mine, will ya?"

Unsurely, Lane used two fingers to pluck it away from me. "Why can't you pay yourself?"

"I, uh... gotta go run some errands."

He stared me down with judgement behind his eyes. "Dude."

"Yeah?" I asked, sounding as clueless and naive as possible.

"Just give it up already."

Goddamnit. I hated how he always saw through me. How he saw through everyone.

This was just one of the many moments that solidified how much smarter Lane was than everyone else.

Instead of starting an argument, I decided to continue playing stupid. "Dunno what you're talking about."

Giving me an apathetic glance over, he said, "Sure, let's just pretend like I'm dumb."

"Sounds good to me." With a placid smile, I left the conversation at that. After saying goodbye to the other guys and hearing their groans when I said, *"See you at practice,"* I headed straight to the store.

There was one thing and one thing only that I needed to get.

I rubbed my hands together, taking a look at all the options of tinfoil they had.

One by one, I shoved package after package under my arm.

Goddamn, why didn't I grab a cart?

Letting out a frustrated expletive under my breath, I walked back to the front of the store and chucked all the packages I already had into a cart before heading back to the same aisle.

By the time I was on my way to the register, there were only a few boxes of tinfoil left on the shelf.

In all honesty, I had no idea how much tinfoil I would actually need, but considering I spent over fifty dollars, I figured I had enough.

I overheard Kota telling Bridget this morning that she was spending the day with her mom, which meant I had the whole day to create something magnificent.

Bridget was putting her groceries away in the kitchen, singing along to "Save Your Tears" by The Weeknd.

"Good song," I declared my arrival.

"Oh, hey," she smiled.

I moved all the bags I had into one hand, using my now free hand to reach for a strawberry out of the bowl of fruit Bridget was snacking on, but she slid the bowl away from me.

"Get your own fruit," she chided. "Don't you have some in one of those five-thousand bags you're holding?"

My chin fell towards my chest sheepishly. "No."

Eyes trailing down to the bags in my hands, Bridget took in the packs of tinfoil peeking out of the top. "Do I even wanna know?"

Striding past her, all I said was, "Nope."

"Ah, geez," she said, shutting the fridge. "I was told to stop you if you tried to pull anything."

I aimed a crooked smile at her, testing her. "Are you gonna?"

She inhaled deeply with one hand on her hip, staring off in thought. "Guess not."

My playful smile grew as I pointed at her. "That's why you're my favorite roommate."

Rolling her eyes, Bridget gave a little tsk noise with her tongue. "Don't even. Lane will always be your favorite."

"Alright, alright. Well, you're my favorite roommate with a vagina."

"Wow, I'm honored," she joked with a hand on her chest.

A lighthearted laugh echoed down the girl's hall as I pranced down it, and I broke into a malicious grin as I reached for Kota's door handle and pushed it open.

Chapter Eighteen

Kota

"**Y**es, Mom, I made it home safely," I walked inside, locking the door behind me.

"Alright, sweetie. Just wanted to call and make sure."

"Okay, well I hope you have fun at your gala next week. You're gonna turn heads in your dress."

She chuckled through the phone. "Thanks, honey. I'm gonna get started on dinner. I'll talk to you soon, okay?"

"Okay. Love you!"

"Love you too, Kota girl!"

I set my phone and the few shopping bags I had on the counter. Bridget and I had a double date with Mitch and Bobby tonight. We didn't realize until recently that they had a class together and knew each other, so we decided it was time to plan something fun for all of us.

There was a fun entertainment place in town called Rave 'N' Roll that had bowling, an arcade, and a bunch of other things to do. They also had some fun drinks, which was a huge plus.

I took a frozen pizza out of the freezer and tossed it on the counter before turning the oven on to preheat. Rave 'N' Roll had really good appetizers, but they didn't have much actual food to order from, so Bridget and I agreed earlier that we'd eat something before heading there.

I grabbed my shopping bags and phone, heading towards my room to start getting ready while the oven heated up.

The second I opened my bedroom door, my mouth was on the floor— along with everything I'd been carrying.

There was a blur of silver that spanned across the entire room, not a trace of any other color.

Cautiously, I stepped inside, and every pulse of blood going through my veins was raising my blood pressure.

That. Fucking. *Dumbass.*

Each square inch of the room was covered in tinfoil. From my vanity to my nightstand to my bedside lamp. Every single item on my desk. The fucking walls. My fucking *bed.*

My cheeks flushed with anger as I let out a fiery, raspy screech. Stomping around the room, I ripped the tinfoil off everything I could, crumbling it up and tossing it into a pile on the floor.

There was some shit that I couldn't even reach though, no matter how hard I tried, which only made me more enraged.

Fuck this.

I muttered to myself, cursing Crew all the way to his room. I didn't bother knocking, basically busting down the door.

Crew was practically dead to the world, sound asleep with his mouth hanging wide open and his limbs stretched all over the place.

I didn't hesitate to stomp over to his bed and lean over, screaming in his face. "Wake the fuck up!"

Slowly, his eyes peeled open, and an annoyingly pompous smirk appeared at the sight of my livid face.

"Oh, hey," he casually said, voice sounding gravelly.

"My *entire* room? Really?" I fumed.

Crew shrugged against the mattress. "Did you like it?"

"Did I li—" I cut myself off, stepping away from the bed to stop myself from jumping onto it and suffocating him with a pillow. When I let out a scornful shriek, he barely batted an eyelash at the sound.

Crew looked way too pleased with himself right now. I hated that I was contributing to him feeling that way, but I couldn't contain my fucking irritation. It felt like my body was on fire from the rage.

"Are you forfeiting?" he asked, looking hopeful.

"Absolutely the fuck not." I stepped forward, disdain dripping from my tone. "I'm not forfeiting until you're on your knees, begging for mercy."

His dark eyes were overly content, resting an arm underneath his head and staring up at me like my reaction was the best thing he'd ever seen.

"I don't get on my knees for any girl," he smugly said.

My voice didn't waver in the slightest as I spoke. "Well, you're about to fucking start."

"Mhm," he grinned, "we'll see."

***

I wasn't at all surprised when Lane forced Crew to take down the rest of the tinfoil.

This was exactly why Lane was the better one.

And now, I was already thinking of what to do to Crew next.

I wasn't exaggerating when I said I wouldn't stop until he was begging on his knees. I refused to lose *anything* to a man, especially one as egotistical and ludicrous as Nicholas Crew.

"You're so damn tense," Bridget whispered as we walked behind the boys into Rave 'N' Roll.

"Yeah, well," I muttered.

She sighed, "Stop thinking about Crew."

"I can't. He's under my skin."

"Clearly," she murmured, hooking her arm onto mine.

After Bridget confessed and apologized that she slyly let Crew go through with his evil plot, I couldn't even be mad at her.

She said from the get-go that she didn't want to be involved, so I shouldn't have tried to force her to be. This war was between Crew and me, no one else.

After two games of bowling and Bridget coming dead last in both, she suggested we switched gears and grab a table to order some drinks and appetizers.

Bridget and I shared a drink menu, skimming over all the fun drinks they had. I ended up ordering a Peach Punch and Bridget ordered something called a Blue Magic because she thought the name was cool.

The best thing about their drinks was also the worst thing about their drinks— they were strong as fuck.

Which meant it only took one to get you pretty tipsy, but they also tasted like straight up alcohol.

Luckily, the four of us Ubered so that we could all get hammered.

I was having fun. Really, I was. But that little devil on my shoulder was loud, contaminating my night with heinous thoughts and playing my earlier confrontation with Crew on repeat like a scratched disc.

Before I knew it, the night was over, and I was angrier than I was when the night started.

He'd gotten me twice now. And he had no idea that he'd just walked straight into a hurricane.

Chapter Nineteen

Crew

Other than my ever-growing, crippling anxiety, there hadn't been much going on other than when the girls came home from the bar with a fucking cat.

I was still very confused about how this even happened. According to them, some drugged up woman in the parking lot conned them into giving her thirty bucks in exchange for a tiny gray kitten that they stumbled back into the apartment with.

I'd be lying if I said the kitten wasn't cute as hell though.

The girls drunkenly named her Kim K, and when it was me who realized that Kim K had a ballsack, I refused to be the one to break the news to Kota.

I made Lane and Bridget do it instead, and Kim K officially became Rob K.

Unfortunately, though, they let my name slip during the conversation, and Kota reacted like I was somehow to blame for the cat anatomy, as if I magically gave him a ballsack just to piss her off.

Out of hatred, she had cursed my name at the top of her lungs as she stomped throughout the apartment, leaving me more unsettled than I had already been.

I was on edge.

Alright, I was a little more than on edge— I was fucking frantic.

It'd been nearly two weeks since my tinfoil prank, and Kota hadn't retaliated yet. Emphasis on the word *yet*.

I'd been expecting her comeback to come quickly after she pretty much told me she was going to make me hate my life and beg for mercy, but there had been nothing.

After the first few days of silence, I started anticipating it, expecting my room to be trashed every time I walked into it or to get attacked when I rounded every corner.

When it'd been over a week, the anxiety was killing me. I hated knowing she was waiting and plotting, enjoying watching me squirm with trepidation more and more as the days passed.

Finally, I'd had enough and decided to stay at the hockey house for a few days, making my own make-shift bedroom out of the living room.

The guys didn't mind, practically encouraging me to do so. Ever since moving out, I knew I missed them, but I didn't realize just how much I missed them until I'd been staying here.

I was going to stop at the apartment last night and grab some more clean clothes, but after realizing Kota was at home, I decided to stay at the house and play Xbox with the guys instead.

Since we had practice this morning, I figured I'd swing by the apartment beforehand. I made sure to text Lane first to ensure the coast was clear.

Me: Is Kota home?

Lane: Yeah but she's asleep

Me: Are u sure?

Lane: It's hardly 7 a.m. so yeah, I'm pretty sure lol

Gathering up my dirty clothes, I stuffed them into a drawstring bag so that I could toss them in my hamper at home. As I was walking to my car, my phone buzzed again.

Lane: Stop being a pussy and just come home

Me: Respectfully, fuck u <3

I tossed my phone onto the passenger seat, ignoring it for the five-minute drive when it buzzed again.

Kota usually didn't wake up until closer to eight every day, but the plan was still to get in and out as quickly as possible.

I entered the apartment as quietly as a two-hundred-pound man could, intending to head straight to my room and straight out.

"Hey."

"Shit!" I yelped, catching my breath as I turned to see Lane leaning casually against the kitchen counter, smothering a grin behind his morning cup of coffee.

"What're you doing man?"

"Grabbing some clothes," I explained in a low voice.

Lane took another sip. "What I really meant to ask is when are you coming home?"

I blew out a breath, running a hand down the back of my neck. "Just... give me a few more days."

He saw right through me, reading my mind as if it were his own. "You're gonna try to wait until break, aren't you?"

Damn right, I am.

If I waited until Thanksgiving break, Kota would head home, and I'd be able to successfully dodge whatever she had planned. Well, for a few days at least.

"It's not that far away," I said.

He drowned his disapproving look with another sip of coffee, eyeing me like a disappointed father. "Crew, that's in two weeks. You've already been gone for four days." I opened my mouth to defend myself, but he brought his hand up, signaling for me to shut it. *Such a dad move.*

"She's probably forgotten about it all by now," he claimed.

I always said that Lane was one of the smartest guys I knew, but that right there was the dumbest shit he's ever said. "You know that's not true."

He sighed, not bothering to fight me on it as he set his mug down. "Well, you can't avoid her forever."

"Trust me, I'll find a way."

"You know, this could all be over in a split second if you just surrender."

"Hell no! I'm not letting her win."

His mouth twitched, fighting a menacing smirk. God, I wished I could read *his* mind for once. I bit the inside of my cheek, watching him, my eyes narrowing.

He didn't break eye contact with me, but he did look a bit sketchier as the seconds ticked by, shifting his weight unsteadily.

I nodded at him. "What do you know?"

By the way he reached for his mug again, attempting to use it as a shield to hide his suspicious expression, he'd easily just given himself away.

"I don't know anything."

"Lane," I hissed, "you know something. What is it?"

"I don't know anything," he repeated with a shrug.

A sense of betrayal ripped through me. "Whose side are you on?!"

Voice remaining as calm as ever, he said, "I told you from the beginning that I'm on no one's side."

"This is bullshit," I fumed, continuously cussing under my breath as I spun around and flounced into my room.

I reached for the light switch, but when I flicked it up, nothing happened. "What the hell?" I quietly huffed, fighting with the switch.

Guess I needed to change the lightbulbs.

That task was going to have to wait though.

After letting my eyes adjust to the darkness, the contents of my drawstring bag were dumped into my hamper. I went through each drawer in my dresser, grabbing an abundance of things.

T-shirts, check. Pants, check. Socks, check. Boxers, check.

I stuffed a few more things in the bag from my closet before making a beeline for the front door.

***

Practice wasn't too bad.

For the upperclassmen, at least.

Apparently, some of the freshman decided it would be a bright idea to have a get together last night and stroll into practice twenty minutes late and hungover.

Coach Palmer wasn't very happy obviously and told them if they thought solely alcohol could make them puke, they had another thing coming.

Every single one puked by the time the last whistle was blown.

Cody and I learned the hard way ourselves freshman year that Coach was never fucking around when it came to our time on the ice. We too thought it would be a good idea to drink before practice one night. A couple beers and half a fifth later, we were fucked up. And it didn't take a fucking genius to tell by our half-dead appearances the next morning that we spent our night jacking off bottles.

I threw up five times during that practice, and never drank that much the night before hockey ever again.

After a quick shower at the hockey house, I went to get dressed, quickly realizing I left my bag in the living room.

Tying a towel around my waist, I trudged out to grab some clothes.

Cody was lying on the couch watching TV, the remote resting in the center of his chest. He had one arm slung behind his head, a stupid, smug grin rising as he saw me.

"Wow, Crew. No wonder why your roommate loves you so much. Who wouldn't when you walk around looking like *that*?" he said sarcastically.

"Fuck off," I quietly muttered, digging through my bag.

The look in his eyes was quite mischievous, matching his smirk. "You sure you haven't fucked her?"

I groaned, shaking my head. "For the thousandth time, no, I haven't fucked her."

He shrugged against the couch. "Just wondering. I mean, it would explain why she's plotting your death."

"Well, good thing she can't kill me when I'm not there."

His smirk turned a bit serious, yet playful all the same. At this point, he seemed to be talking to himself, uttering some bullshit nonsense that I hardly had the mental capacity to listen to. "Hey, from what we know about her, she seems pretty smart. Definitely smarter than you. She's probably fully capable of hatching a plan to kill you even if you're not there. Hell, maybe she even hired a hitman."

Goddamn, I was wishing I put these clothes in the bag nicer. Everything was tangled together like a knot. I only had a t-shirt and some joggers picked out so far, and considering I had to leave for class soon, I needed to hurry my ass up.

"Or do you think she'd rather kill you herself so that she gets the full satisfaction?" Cody added.

I dropped the bag for a moment so that I had a full view of him. "I need you to shut up."

There had been a lot on my mind the last few days, but the only thing I was trying to focus on right now was getting to class on time.

It was my sports marketing class, one of my few classes where they took attendance before the lecture began, and I definitely didn't want to miss the attendance points since I didn't do well on our last homework assignment. I was relying on the attendance points to help cushion my overall grade.

"You're feisty today," Cody said.

Found socks. Fabulous. Now I just needed boxers.

"Are you sexually frustrated?"

That one I couldn't ignore.

My head snapped up, annoyance climbing up my spine. "What the hell are you talking about?"

Cody smiled deviously at the edge in my voice, looking like he was having a ball. "I mean, you haven't gotten laid in days. Unless you've been sneaking girls in and fucking them on the couch?"

I stared at him with a blank expression, causing him to let out a spurt of laughter.

"How many days has it been? Four? Five? Are you having withdrawals?"

"You're an ass," I murmured through clenched teeth, refusing to look at him anymore. The worst part was that he might've been a little bit right. I wouldn't say I was having quote on quote *withdrawals,* but this was definitely the longest I'd gone without sex in a while.

He let out another laugh as I caught sight of what looked to be an article of clothing whose color did not match the rest in the slightest.

My brows furrowed, thumb and forefinger pinching the fabric and slowly pulling it out.

I held it away from my face, staring in disbelief.

They were my boxers, definitely my boxers. But they were *hot fucking pink.*

Cody's voice cracked through laughter like he was going through puberty and his balls were in the midst of dropping. "What the *fuck* are *those*?"

I just stared at them, my mouth agape. I wanted to scream, but I kept it inside. All I could feel was the heat of anger blooming across my body.

Cody was laughing so hard that I could hardly understand him as he spoke. "Is this her work?"

I gave a tight nod, staring at the mess of pink between my fingers. I couldn't fucking believe what I was seeing.

Every time Kota retaliated, it seemed to be worse than the time before. I wasn't even sure how she thought of shit like this. It really verified how evil and twisted her mind worked.

Cody still hadn't stopped laughing, but now he was also clapping like he was at a goddamn show. "Mad respect. This girl is my new idol!"

Considering I had less than five minutes to leave or else I'd be late for class, I swallowed my pride and put the hot pink boxers on.

Chapter Twenty

Crew

Everyone was spread out around the living room, pitching prank ideas to me like they were goddamn salesmen.

The only person missing from our starting lineup was Lane.

I hated getting all soft and sappy, but I kind of missed him. We'd lived together for so many years now that it felt strange not seeing him every day.

He admitted that him and Bridget had caught Kota dying my gray boxers pink the other day and then saw her switching off the power to my room in the apartment's breaker box so that I couldn't see what I was grabbing.

Even though I was holding a tiny grudge against him for not being on my side, it still felt strange staying at the house without him here. It was making me a little sentimental.

Matt tapped me on the shoulder. "Are you still wearing the boxers?" He slipped his phone out of his pocket, pulling up his camera. "Can you drop your pants so I can take a picture?"

"Oh, fuck off," I spewed. "Someone fucking help me before I lose my mind, please."

"You can put a bunch of fake spiders in her room," TJ pitched. "Or a snake."

"Lame," Cody blurted dully, uninterested as he tapped away at his phone.

I had to agree with him. That was hardly a prank. Kota would immediately realize everything was fake and then laugh in my face.

"What about real spiders or a snake?" TJ said, looking complacent like the idea was brilliant.

I shook my head, scrolling through more ideas on the internet. "Lane would kill me."

"Draw on her face while she's sleeping," Matt suggested.

"Also lame," Cody said.

Jett crossed his arms, using his feet to push himself further into the couch adjacent from me. "Why don't you get her a porn package?"

I grumbled, "What?"

"Yeah, you've never seen those? You can get like a subscription where they send you a bunch of weird sex toys. Anal beads, wacky dildos, all kinds of shit."

TJ blinked at him. "That sounds more like a gift than a punishment."

My eyes jumped over to TJ, a little concerned. "Anal beads sound like a gift to you?"

"Well, for a girl!" he shot at me before snapping his mouth shut and sitting back in his seat.

"You're gonna get her a box of dildos?" Matt asked. "That's like something you'd get a girl when you're trying to apologize."

Cody's phone plopped into his lap, his mouth tugging upwards, finally caring to join in on the conversation. "Is that what you got Carly last year when you accidentally fucked her friend?"

"It was Halloween, you dick! I was hammered!" Matt sank back a little as if it was still a sore subject. "And no, actually. I got her flowers."

"Yeah, like a normal fucking person would," I said, growing agitated. We'd been sitting here for nearly an hour and still hadn't come up with anything good. "Who the hell would get a girl a dildo as an apology gift?"

Clearing his throat, Jett inched his finger back and forth in TJ's direction.

"Please tell me you have not done that," I said to TJ.

"No, I haven't." He pursed his lips, pouting as he stared off at the empty corner of the room. Folding his arms across his chest, he admitted, "But I did think about it once."

For Christ's sake.

"Wow, we're learning so much about you tonight, TJ!" Matt laughed.

We were still hardly getting anywhere. It felt like I was getting pulled closer and closer to having to forfeit. Ever since we met, Kota had made comment after comment about my huge, disgraceful ego, and now, it seemed like she was aiming to destroy my ego.

I would be lying if I said being in a lecture hall with over one hundred people while I was worrying every second about making sure my hot pink boxers weren't sticking out didn't knock my ego down a few notches.

But what she didn't know was that I was probably one of the only people on the planet that was as stubborn as she was.

My ego was too big to lose this war. I refused to forfeit. Even if she hammered the nails into my coffin and buried me alive.

"Well, the packages come with more than just dildos, you fuckheads," Jett said. "There's all kinds of shit. Fucked up stickers. Socks with dicks on them. Bondage gear. Strap-ons."

I nodded along, envisioning what Kota's reaction would be receiving dick socks in the mail. I didn't think she'd be very pleased.

"I'll put it on the list," I said, writing it down in my notes app.

Matt's phone buzzed on the couch between us. I glanced over his shoulder as he picked it up.

He gave a not-so-convincing sigh. "El again."

"Answer it," I said, trading wicked grins with Cody.

The moment the call connected, she was immediately spitting fire through the phone. "Your stupid fucking advice backfired."

I was surprised she didn't seem to catch the underlying satisfaction in Matt's voice as he muttered, "Sorry."

Leaning over, I hit the mute button so that she couldn't hear us. "Did you give her bad advice on purpose?"

"No."

"Mhm, alright." I unmuted it and tilted my head to share the camera with Matt. "Hey, sorry that dumbass over here screwed you, but do you wanna help us out?"

"Define 'us.'"

"Me," I said. "Do you wanna help *me* out?"

El pulled her sexy mouth over to the side. "As long as it doesn't include Matt. I'm mad at him right now."

Scoffing, Matt went, "It's not my fault that you go for guys that suck."

Cody shouted across the room much louder than necessary. "What he really means is that he wants you to date him instead!"

"Awe, is that true Mattie?" she teased.

"No," he groaned, his face turning a light shade of pink as he tossed the phone in my lap. I stifled a laugh, bringing the phone up to my face.

Goddamn. I didn't blame him for wanting her. She was gorgeous. Her light brown hair was tied in a perfectly messy knot atop her head, two thin strands of hair framing her face. It was dark wherever she was, but I could still make out her clear skin and almond-shaped eyes.

"When are you coming to visit again?" I blurted out.

El smiled at the flirtation in my voice. "Why? Are you trying to make a move?"

"Yeah, Crew," Matt growled beside me. "*Are* you trying to make a move?"

I took my bottom lip between my teeth, trying to shield my grin, but failing.

"You know I'll fucking kill you, right?" Matt said.

I believed him. He'd probably fight Kota on who would get the chance to drive the knife in. He couldn't stand the thought of one of his best friends touching El before he ever got the chance to himself.

"Anyway..." I awkwardly shifted, "I'm trying to pull a prank on my roommate, and we can't come up with anything good. Got any ideas?"

"I gave you a fucking good one," Jett stated.

"Yeah!" TJ yelled. "Do the dildo one!"

El ignored the boys in the background, her brows drawing in. "Lane?"

"No, no, no. Her name's Kota," I said.

"You're living with a girl?"

"Two, actually."

She pulled back. "Uh, I don't think I can help you."

"What? Why not?"

"Because," she snorted, "that's so against girl code."

"Ugh," I whined. "You two would probably be best fucking friends, honestly."

A leery note entered her voice. "What's her name again?"

"Dakota," Matt said over my shoulder.

"Last name?" El insisted.

Just as I was about to tell her to screw off because I didn't like where this was going, Matt, AKA the one that's been whipped for her since he was probably five years old, spoke again. "Darling."

"Well, good luck with your little prank, Crew," El smirked. "I'll text you next time I'm gonna visit."

Matt snatched the phone out of my hands. "You better not."

She gave a little seductive, "Bye, Mattie," right before hanging up.

Chapter Twenty-One

Kota

I'd never been happier than right now. This was the type of happiness that people probably felt on their wedding day.

I was lying in bed, aimlessly scrolling through social media when Matt sent me a photo of Crew, pants around his ankles, hot pink boxers hiding his junk, and a miserable expression on his face.

This was gold.

This may have been my favorite prank yet.

Don't get me wrong, I loved the shrine prank, but Crew ripped down all the posters before anyone else could see them. But with this prank, I now had physical evidence that I could use to force him into hiding forever.

You know what they say— a photo lasts a lifetime.

I sent the photo to Bridget, and not even thirty seconds after the message was delivered, I could hear her cackling through the wall we shared.

Bridget: You're evil.

Me: Not all villains are bad.

Bridget: Name one

Me: Myself

Bridget: Doesn't count

Me: Count Dracula

Bridget: Wtf?

Me: He was in love with that one chick. Wasn't he?

**Bridget: I don't know. I don't remember anything from
that movie except for his big ass head
Me: HAH!**

Bridget: The 90's movie, obvi. Not the original

Me: Obvi

When Bridget left the conversation at that, I started
scrolling through Instagram some more, which was part of my
usual nighttime routine before bed.

I had a DM request notification from someone named
Eleanor Burkeley. Usually, I ignored DMs from random people,
but judging by how normal, *and pretty*, she looked in her tiny
profile picture, I decided to take a peek.

**Eleanor: Crew told me that you and I would make the best
of friends. He said it with a look of disgust, if that means
anything to you.**

The corners of my mouth tugged up in the slightest, but
before I was going to respond, I needed to see who the hell this
girl was.

How did she know Crew? It was easy to speculate that
she was just some girl he'd hooked up with, but considering I'd
never met a girl that he continued talking to after the fact, that
theory was unlikely.

I clicked on her profile, pleased to see that it was
public. At first glance, I could tell she didn't go to Cedar. She

looked like she was in college though; I just wasn't sure where at.

It took me less than a minute to find a multitude of photos of her and Matt, along with a photo of her and some of the other Cedar hockey boys.

Me: I love when he's disgusted

Eleanor: You and me both.
I may know a clue of what he's plotting against you

Me: I'm listening

Eleanor: Something about dildos

My face twisted. What the fuck could he possibly be planning that had to do with dildos?

Me: What

Eleanor: Yeah, I'm not sure where he's going with that either

Me: I'll smack him with a dildo

Eleanor: Right across the face?

Me: Right across it.

Eleanor: *laughing emoji*
Props to you, by the way. Pink is definitely not his color

Me: You saw the photo?

Eleanor: Mattie sent it to me.

Judging by the way she called him "Mattie," I wasn't sure if it was being used as a term of endearment or an embarrassing nickname she'd given him.

My nosy ass decided to jump right to it.

Me: R u dating Matt?

Eleanor: Nooooo, we're best friends

Me: Interesting
So, are you saying we're going to be friends?

Eleanor: I'd say so

Me: I'd say so too

Chapter Twenty-Two

Crew

To everyone's surprise, I'd survived a full twenty-four hours at the apartment.

As much as I didn't want to be there, and as much as I preferred the hockey house, there was one thing that was missing.

Lane.

It sounded pathetic and probably dramatic, and there was no way in hell I'd admit it aloud, but I missed the dude too much to stay away any longer.

The only reason why I felt alright being here was because I knew the ball was in my court. Kota wouldn't— at least, *hopefully* wouldn't— pull any shenanigans when it was my turn to, right? Then again, she didn't appear to play by the rules, so I really couldn't be sure of anything.

After a long night out with the guys last night, Lane and I were still nursing off hangovers, lounging around as if we had the day to waste.

Rob K was snuggled up beside me, and I'd be lying if I said this little guy hadn't clawed his way into my heart over the past month.

My phone lit up on the coffee table, and I didn't bother glancing in its direction, having a good idea of who it was.

"Your mom's calling," Lane said.

"Just leave it," I grumbled, letting it ring all the way through.

Twenty minutes later, sure shit enough, it was ringing again.

I ignored it a second time, breathing deeply, but refusing to take my eyes away from the TV.

"It's your dad this time," Lane said.

Of course, it was. Ever since splitting up over *a decade* ago, my parents still held a grudge against each other, and the one way to get under each other's skin was by using the only denominator they still shared.

Me.

So, every year when my birthday was around the corner, they'd turn it into a competition.

Who could be the better parent? Who got the best gift? Who did I enjoy spending more time with? Blah, fucking blah.

They'd each been trying to reach me for days now and I'd been ignoring every call and every text. I knew I couldn't avoid them forever, but damn was the idea tempting.

"Just toss me the phone," I finally mumbled. Catching it with one hand, I reluctantly brought it up to my ear. "Hey, Dad."

"Hey, Nick. You doing alright? I haven't heard from you in a couple days."

"Yeah, I'm fine."

"Alright," he said, sounding content with my half-ass answer. "Well, since your birthday is coming up, I was hoping you'd come over for dinner."

I blew out a breath. If only I could pretend we had a game or something that day, but my dad knew our game schedule by heart. Not to mention my birthday was on a Wednesday this year and we only had games over the weekends.

"Can we do dinner on a different night?" I asked.

"Oh, c'mon, son! You don't have to stay long. We'd like to see you for a bit, though."

I ran a hand over my face. "Dad..."

"Nick," he pushed.

132

I sighed, accepting defeat. *Just one hour*, I assured myself. *I could sit through dinner for one hour without it ruining my birthday.*

"Fine," I agreed.

"Great! How's five o'clock sound?"

"Sounds fine."

"Georgia said she's gonna cook all your favorites."

Great. "Tell her I said thank you."

"Will do," he said. "Well, I'll let you go now. Tell Lane we said hello!"

"Mhm," I hung up.

The second my phone hit the couch cushion beside me, it was ringing again.

My mom.

"Hello?" I said sharply, before regretting my tone at the sound of my mother's sweet voice.

"Hi, honey, just checking in. How are you?"

I closed my eyes, inhaling enough air for ten people. "I'm alright, Mom. How are you? How's Kayla?"

"I'm good! Your sister's doing well, but she misses you. Asks about you all the time."

I swear to God, if this is her introduction to guilt tripping me into coming over on my birthday, I'm gonna flip the fu—

"Do you have plans on your birthday already?"

And there it was.

"Uh, I'm supposed to stop by Dad's for a little."

I could hear the hostility in her voice, replacing the sweetness. "Oh. Well, do you want to stop over here as well?"

Not really, I wanted to say.

"Um..." I stuttered, "could we do another day?"

She gave a light tsk. "Crew, we'd love to see you on your birthday. You haven't stopped over in so long, and Kayla and I already wrapped some of your presents."

I shot Lane a look and he glanced back with sympathy, knowing exactly what was happening.

"Sure, yeah, alright."

"Yay! Your sister's gonna be so excited."

"Mhm, I'm sure."

"Well, we love you, honey! See you next week!" she squealed, hanging up.

Just fuck me, I guess.

***

I was feeling ballsy. Wasn't sure why, but I was.

With my birthday coming up and the impending disaster that it was bound to be hopping back and forth between my parent's houses, I figured that maybe some of my stress would lessen if I didn't have to worry about World War 3 going on with Kota.

If I caught her at a good time, maybe I could just civilly approach her. I still refused to forfeit, but I guess I was hoping I could convince her to call a truce. Maybe that way, I wouldn't have to order this stupid porn box I'd been staring at on my computer for twenty minutes like a fucking freak.

When she rolled into the common area with her hair in a low, messy bun, wearing pajamas and fuzzy slippers whose front was shaped like a puppy's face, I felt unprepared.

I gulped as Kota gave a yawn. She plopped down on the opposite couch, snatching the TV remote off the coffee table and changing the channel like I hadn't been in the middle of a movie.

"Hey," I said, a slight waver in my voice.

Finally, she glanced in my direction, looking indifferent. "Hey?"

I was sure she could tell I was nervous, and even though she wasn't giving that infamous, wicked grin of hers to prove it, I could see a pleased glimmer in her eye, watching me like a python before it attacked an injured antelope.

I cleared my throat. "I have a question."

Now, she leaned back a bit, seemingly wary. "What?"

I wasn't even sure what I wanted to ask. I couldn't ask *Can we call a truce?* That would just sound like I was forfeiting.

"Why do you hate me so much?" I blurted out instead. Silently, she stared at me, as if trying to figure out if this was

134

part of a prank. "Ever since we moved in, you've had it out for me. You don't act this way towards Lane." The idea hit me the second the words left my mouth, and I couldn't help but voice it aloud. "Do you have a thing for him or something?"

She broke into a disgusted grimace. "Ew, no! I do not have a thing for Lane!"

"Then what is it?"

Her eyes turned dark, and as she leaned forward in the slightest, I didn't realize until now just how much we got along like gasoline on a flame.

"You wanna know why I hate you?" she dared.

"Please," I insisted.

"I hate you because you're an egotistical jock that uses girls whenever he pleases and thinks he can do whatever the hell he wants. And I *hate* men who think they're better than everyone else and that they're too good to deal with their own responsibilities!" With that, she stood. "Men suck!" she yelled, stalking off.

I stared off in silence, unsure of what the hell just happened. Was I missing something here?

Only half of that response sounded like it was about me. Did she just hate men in general?

I tried to be nice the first time we met. I even offered for Lane and me to walk the girls home and she pretty much pissed all over my offer. Maybe we would've gotten along had she not come out swinging that night.

I jerked my computer back open and hit the order button.

Chapter Twenty-Three

Kota

I was walking through campus to my bio lab, clutching my jacket tighter around me when my phone vibrated deep in my pocket. I refused to take my gloves off to check, so I ignored it for the time being.

Stress was currently my biggest enemy. Thanksgiving break was coming up, which meant finals would be following a few weeks later, and I'd never felt so unprepared.

I always thought junior year of college would be the heaviest academically, but first semester of senior year was kicking my ass just as hard.

Biology was a tricky thing to be studying, and I was lucky that I hadn't failed any of my classes throughout college, considering how many of my peers did each semester.

I'd rather not start now though.

I'd already begun studying for finals, which was eating my time and energy like a beast. I hardly even had time to *think* about pranking Crew again. I was becoming kind of exhausted from it, not going to lie. As much as I loved bothering him, it was time consuming to plan my devious schemes. I was sort of hoping he'd give up soon.

I could feel the cold stinging my ears, my eyes watering as I finally stepped into the building for my lab. I caught my breath from the hike, dreading how much worse it'd be when we got the first snowfall of the year, which was already overdue for Minnesota.

Our professor wasn't there yet since I arrived early. Figuring it would be the only time I'd be able to check my phone for the next two hours, I ripped my gloves off and shoved my hands into my coat, digging for my phone.

Lane: You got a package

Me: ???
I didn't order anything

Lane: Well, your name is on it
Me: Weird

Something didn't seem right here. And I'd bet money it had to do with Crew.

***

I was in a shit mood. Apparently, my golden-retriever-looking partner and I got a C on our last lab report, and considering I was already sitting at a mid-B, I was worried it would make my grade drop further.

Not to mention our bitch of a professor assigned us another fucking essay that's due next week.

Four pages on an individual type of bacteria. How the fuck was I supposed to come up with that much information about a single-cell organism?

I hoped for Crew's sake that this mystery package had nothing to do with him. Because if he tried pulling some shit right now, all hell was bound to break loose.

I slammed the apartment door behind me. "Fucking fuck!"

"Well, hello to you too," Lane said. His homework was scattered around the living room coffee table while he typed away at his computer, Rob K sleeping in a ball beside him on the couch.

"Where's this stupid package?"

He pointed to the kitchen counter.

The package wasn't big, only a foot or so wide. "Where'd this come from?"

Lane spoke slowly, his brows pulling in like I was an idiot that needed things spelled out. "Um, the mail room?"

"Who grabbed it?"

"I grabbed everyone's mail when I was coming up."

"So, Crew hasn't touched this?" I gestured to it, still too cautious to pick it up.

"No," Lane insisted, slightly irritated.

"Just making sure. Who knows, it might explode or something when I open it."

Lane didn't respond, probably too annoyed to continue engaging, but he was too nice to say so.

I could tell him and Bridget were getting closer and closer to the edge, completely over Crew's and my bullshit. Bridget even told me herself a couple days ago that her and Lane were talking about sitting us down to have an intervention. They both thought things had been going on for too long and were going too far.

When I ripped the box open, my face distorted.

"What the *fuck?!*"

There was a small promotional poster that read *The All Things Butt Box* in big, purple letters. Beneath it, there was a heart shaped butt-plug, fire red anal beads that were at least six inches long, and a small box that said *Three-Piece Mini Anal Kit* on the front.

"What is it?" Lane asked from across the room.

This might have been worse than something that would explode in my face.

On a different day, I might've laughed. But given how my day had been going so far, I was not in the mood to be messed with.

And obviously, I didn't order this. Which left one person who would've.

I was taking deep, ragged breaths, my face inevitably flushing with anger. "Is Crew home?" I asked through clenched teeth.

"He's in his room, I think."

I was about to stomp over and bang on his door, but instead, I decided to pretend like this never happened. I stuffed everything back into the box and dropped the entire thing in the trash.

If Crew couldn't see my reaction, he couldn't possibly be satisfied. If he didn't know I even saw this stupid box, maybe he'd think his plan failed.

All I knew was one thing and one thing only— the next prank I pulled on him was sure to be the last.

Chapter Twenty-Four

Crew

I didn't get to see Kota open her package, but I did hear about it from Lane.

He had no idea what was inside or why she was so pissed until he demanded I told him what I'd done.

So, I told him.

Blaming part of it on Jett, of course, for giving me the idea.

I was a little bummed that I didn't get to see her reaction. I fantasized about what she probably looked like at that moment. Lane had described her as a pissed off little strawberry, all red in the face.

Good thing I got the bi-weekly subscription so that I had the chance to catch her reaction next time.

I'd been swinging by the mail room every day for the past few days, hoping I could snatch the package and make sure to be there when she opened it this time.

To my delight, the next package had arrived, and I snagged it on my way up as I got back from grabbing some lunch.

Also, to my delight, Kota wasn't home yet, which meant I could sit on the couch, snuggled up with Rob K and pretending to be an oblivious bystander as I waited for her.

I didn't know her weekly schedule, because why the hell would I? And after nearly an hour of waiting with no idea still of when she was coming back, I was getting antsy like a kid waiting for his parents to take him to the park.

Lane and I were planning on heading to the gym when he got home, which should've been any minute now. I was already dressed and ready to go, prepared to blow off some steam before my debacle of a birthday tomorrow.

I was about to knock on Bridget's door and ask her when Kota would be home, but I didn't want to seem sketchy.

Lane and Bridget had been making it evident that they were tired of our shit. Every other day, Lane was trying to talk me into forfeiting.

The truth was, I was getting a little tired of it all too. It was just becoming exhausting to plan and execute while watching my own back.

But I'd never been one to back down. Plus, I sort of attempted to end the war the other day, but that mission went south. It was starting to feel like D-Day was slowly and inevitably approaching.

I held back a groan when Lane was the first one to prance through the door instead of Kota. He nodded at me and went to his room, reappearing a minute later in a t-shirt and gym shorts.

"Ready?" he asked.

That angel and devil that I'd become so familiar with over the last few months danced around on each shoulder, both whispering in my ears.

Tell him the truth. Tell him you're waiting for Kota.

Lie. Make up an excuse as to why we can't go yet.

My mouth opened and closed with words that weren't coming, making Lane eye me warily as if he needed to come over and check my pulse.

Finally, I gulped and stood, ignoring both the angel's and devil's requests. Following Lane out, an overwhelming sense of disappointment hit me with the force of a bus.

Guess I wouldn't get to see her reaction after all.

Chapter Twenty-Five

Crew

"Are you sure you don't want me to come with
you?" Lane asked as I buttoned up my white dress shirt.

"Yeah," I sighed. "The both of us don't have to go
through pain if it's unnecessary."

There was a buzz against my mattress, and I assumed it
was Lane's phone when he went to pick it up, until he read the
text aloud.

Dad: Georgia asked if Lane is coming with you?

I tipped my head back laughing, finishing up the last
button.

It was almost painful, not to mention sad, how
oblivious my father was and how in denial Lane was that
Georgia had a thing for him.

"That's another reason you shouldn't come," I said.
"Not sure if I feel like watching Georgia eye-fuck you
throughout dinner."

"Crew," he complained.

"You know I'm right."

"I really don't think so," he said, laying back and
propping himself up using his elbows at the end of my bed.

"Then why's she asking about you?"

He shrugged nonchalantly. "Maybe she just wants to make sure they made enough food."

"No, no, *nooo*," I yelped towards the ceiling. "You know what?" I turned, "Come with me then. But only *if...*" I paused, emphasizing the word.

"If?"

"If you flirt with her."

He let out a humorless laugh that echoed around the room like he was laughing loudly into a well. "What?" he shrieked.

"I'm being serious," I assured him.

Burying his head into his hands for a moment, he tried to wrap his mind around the idea. "You want me... to flirt... with your stepmom?"

"Yes."

"Why the hell would I do that?"

"So, you can finally see what I'm talking about." I tipped my chin back, spraying the small of my exposed skin with my Burberry cologne. "If she engages back in flirting, *which she will*, then you can't deny it anymore."

"She doesn't have a thing for me, bro."

"Then prove it to me," I dared.

Lane used the tips of his fingers to rub the bridge of his nose, squeezing his eyes shut in pain like he'd just taken a nasty hit on the ice.

"Consider it my birthday present," I snickered.

"I already got you a birthday present!"

That, he did. He got me a pretty damn good present actually— the newest Apple Watch that recently came out, serving as a replacement for my old one, which I desperately needed after we went skating for fun over the summer and like an idiot, I forgot to take it off beforehand. It fell off mid-game and TJ skated right over it.

"That is true," I said, "but this would be a nice, fun addition to the present."

"You're unbelievable," Lane shook his head, "and ungrateful."

"Hey!" I snapped at him. "I'm extremely grateful. You want me to show you how grateful I am with a nice hug and a smooch on the cheek?" I stepped towards him with my arms out, and I didn't think I'd ever seen Lane skirt away so quickly.

"Get outta here," he muttered, hopping across the bed.

Letting out a chuckle, I watched him shift around uncomfortably. "But seriously, if you do it and nothing happens, I won't mention anything about Georgia wanting to fuck you ever again."

Lane eyed me intently, the gears in his mind turning. Just as I thought he was about to take the offer, he threw another objection my way. "Dude, your dad's gonna be there."

"So? I see you subtly flirt with Bridget all the time, and no one ever catches it." His eyes narrowed, becoming thin slits. "If they do, they never say anything at least."

"And what happens if your dad asks why the hell I'm flirting with his wife?"

"He won't," I shrugged. "He's oblivious."

Lane stared up at the ceiling as if he were silently asking God for advice. His eyes dropped back to me, voice nowhere near enthusiastic. "I'll go get dressed."

***

"I'm pumped," I announced, turning down my father's street.

"You're *pumped*?" Lane heaved. "You went from being miserable about this dinner to being pumped?"

"Yes," I pulled into the drive, then turned to Lane as I undid my seatbelt. "Now we gotta make sure we pay attention to the time. One hour. In and out. Then one hour at my mom's." He nodded along tightly as I spoke, glaring at me like I'd threatened to beat him with a hockey stick if he hadn't come along. "The only goal is to survive."

"No shit," Lane grunted, reaching for the door handle, but stopping and turning back to me as I spoke again. He looked more bothered than he did sixty seconds prior.

"And then we stop at the liquor store on the way back, head to the house, and get obliterated because it's my fucking birthday."

"Fantastic," he murmured, following me in.

"Hello!" I yelled, announcing our arrival.

"Nick!" My father appeared with a blazing smile, Georgia right on his heels. I had a clear view past his shoulder, seeing Georgia's face brighten as she caught sight of Lane.

I grinned into my dad's shoulder as he hugged me, noticing Georgia head straight to Lane to hug him first. We switched, hugging the other for a moment.

Tipping his head towards the staircase, my dad yelled, "Nathan! Come down!"

My little brother appeared a minute later, trudging down the stairs. "Happy birthday."

I ruffled his hair, amused as he fought with my arm. "Thanks, kid," I said.

"It smells really good," Lane said beside me.

"Thanks, Lane," Georgia smirked, gesturing for us to follow her into the kitchen. The counter was filled from end to end with food, and at first glance, I could tell she truly did make all my favorites like promised. "Go ahead and grab some plates and start digging in, guys."

Lane nudged me, "Birthday boy first."

"Don't mind if I do," I muttered, grin disappearing as Nate ran ahead of me. "Really?"

He gave a shrug, picking up a plate.

"Nathan," my dad chided.

I gripped him by the back of the shirt and tugged him behind me. "Yeah, *Nathan*."

Georgia gave him a light smack on the shoulder with the back of her hand. "Be polite. Let the boys go first." Her eyes jumped directly to Lane as she smiled, and I stifled a laugh, biting the inside of my cheek.

Everyone filled their plates and took a seat at the table, and the first few minutes were quiet other than the sound of silverware clattering. This was one of the many moments why I was so grateful for Lane. How many other people would voluntarily sit through an awkward dinner for me with no questions asked?

"How are things at the apartment?" my dad asked, shoveling pasta into his mouth.

I shot Lane a look, trying to send him a mind message to keep his mouth shut about Kota. He raised a single brow at me as he chewed but seemed to get the memo.

"Things are fine," I said. Lane was still eyeing me, his mouth slowly and inevitably tugging upwards. I gritted my teeth together, wiping my mouth with a napkin. There I was, saying how grateful I was for him one second then throwing him under the bus the next. "Lane's been seeing someone. She's nice, name's Ava."

My eyes scanned the table, taking in everyone's expressions. Nate's and my dad's focus were on their food, mindlessly glancing up every few seconds. Lane was shooting daggers at me, and when my mouth lifted lightly, the daggers got sharper.

When I looked over at Georgia, I noticed how tense her movements had become, how her jaw seemed to tighten as she brought her drink up and took a sip.

Georgia's eyes dipped to Lane before falling back to her plate. "Oh, that's nice. Is she pretty?"

I was trying to shield my growing smirk with the back of my hand, but it didn't seem to be working as Lane's eyes zeroed in on it. "Oh, yeah. She's real pretty," I answered, fighting a laugh. "Real, real pretty."

C'mon, Lane. Flirt with her a wee bit. She's waiting.

His mouth pulled up, the gleam in his eye fading from angry to impish. "Actually, ah, I ended things with Ava a few days ago."

I stopped chewing, blinking at him. Was he for real right now? I wasn't sure if he was being serious or if he was just saying shit to make my plan implode. Then again, Lane wasn't a great liar, and he looked awfully candid right now.

"What?!" I screeched. "And you didn't bother to tell me?"

Lane's shoulders fell up and down with a shrug, head falling with it as he looked at his plate, digging around with his fork. "I've been busy," he murmured nonchalantly.

"With Bridget?"

His fierce blue eyes shot back up, daggers reappearing with it and sharper than ever.

"Who's Bridget?" Georgia asked.

146

"Yeah, Lane," I egged him on. "Who's Bridget?"

His award-winning, kind expression came through as he turned to Georgia. "She's our roommate." Unfortunately for me, the kind version of Lane was going towards everyone besides me tonight. I could feel karma circling through the air as he looked back at me smugly. It was the moment I realized I fucked up— that mentioning Bridget made the conversation do a u-turn, bringing us right back to the apartment. "We have another roommate," was all he said.

My dad spoke between bites. "Do they both still hate you guys?"

"Neither of them hates me. Bridget doesn't seem to hate Crew either. Then again, she's too nice to hate anyone," Lane said, a small smile flickering over his face as he spoke of her, making me roll my eyes.

Don't get me wrong, at this point, I genuinely liked Bridget. She was sweet and easy to be around, smart and considerate. But Lane was still in denial about his feelings.

Or was he just keeping them quiet from me?

I'd been so caught up in everything going on with Kota that I hadn't been paying as much attention to Lane, or Lane *and* Bridget together for that matter. Not to mention the few days I was practically living at the hockey house.

My dad nodded. "What about the other one?"

Maybe if I just played dumb, I could save myself the embarrassment and coming lecture and get out of this conversation.

"What other one?"

Lane let out a deep chuckle, covering his mouth with a napkin.

I smiled at him, taking a glance at the clock on the oven's control panel. It'd already been twenty minutes, which meant we were a third of the way through.

"How's hockey going, Nate?" I asked.

Him and my dad both seemed to take the bait, and the next fifteen minutes were filled with solely hockey talk. My dad drilled me once again about when I'd take Nate to the rink and help him practice before asking us for every detail about our season so far and how we thought the rest of the season would go. And after my dad subtly dropped some comments about the draft, Lane excused himself from the table to go get seconds.

I wasn't sure if he actually wanted seconds or not though.

In all honesty, Lane should not have been playing NCAA hockey. If he declared himself eligible for the draft years ago, he would've gotten drafted right out of high school. He had his own personal reasons for not going into the draft, and like the selfish prick I was, I was thankful he hadn't. Because if he had, we never would've met.

But after my time in juniors, I was the twelfth pick in the opening round of the draft, chosen by the Blackhawks.

The drafting process was complicated with a lot of rules, but I made the age cutoff at the perfect time to participate in the entry draft. Lane however, no longer did. If he decided he wanted to go to the NHL, which it would've been a shame if he didn't, he'd have to get signed as a free agent. In my opinion, it wasn't a bad option since it gave him the opportunity to talk to as many teams as he liked. Since he truly was one of the best players in the country, he could easily choose whichever team he wanted. And man, oh man, would it be fucking awesome if we played on the Blackhawks together.

It was already November, so I had about five months until I was Chicago bound.

Which also meant Lane had about five months to make up his mind.

Georgia pushed her chair back. "I'm gonna... go grab the dessert."

My brows shot up. "There's dessert too?" Jesus. I knew Lane and I always ate a lot, but this was practically a pre-Thanksgiving feast.

I hoped my mom didn't make a bunch of food, because I would not be able to fit a single bite in my stomach after leaving this house.

My mind aimlessly wandered, foot tapping against the floor as my dad started asking Nate more hockey questions. From my seat at the table, I had a perfect view of the kitchen, whereas my dad and Nate had their backs to it.

I couldn't tell if Lane was actually putting more food on his plate or not. He was standing at the counter, shuffling around but not facing me.

Georgia murmured something to him with an alluring smile, swaying beside him with a dish in her hands. His mouth tugged upwards in response, shiny white teeth bright on display, his head tipped in the slightest.

Even from afar, I could see those dark blue eyes of his pulling her in like a sinking anchor in the middle of the sea.

He was flirting with her.

This was such a Lane move. The subtle flirting.

Was it kind of fucked up that I asked him to do this? Yeah. On so many levels, yeah.

But instead of stopping it, I leaned forward as much as the table in front of me would allow, watching intently as they interacted. God, I wished I could hear what they were saying.

Georgia grabbed candles out of a nearby drawer and began shoving them into the dessert, which I was assuming was a cake.

When the very last candle was hammered in, Georgia shot him what looked to be a wink, and just as I thought the exchange was done and over with, her hand swiftly smacked Lane's ass, causing his entire body to become stiff like stone.

She grabbed the cake and before she could even turn around all the way, I was done for.

My rambunctious laughter was the only thing that could be heard throughout the room, along with my fist hitting the table. My body shook through the laughter, and although my eyes were closed, I was absolutely certain everyone in the room was staring at me.

I forced myself to stand, pushing away from the table. "I'm sorry," I held my hand up, chortling. "I need a minute." I cackled the whole way to the bathroom.

After spending the next five minutes attempting to muffle the sounds of my own laughter, I finally made it back to the table.

"Sorry," I muttered, biting the inside of my cheek as I sat and scooted my chair back in. I could feel Lane's eyes piercing through me, and as much as I wanted to catch a glance,

I restricted myself. Because I knew damn well that I'd lose my shit again if I did.

"What's your deal?" my dad grumbled at me.

"Nothing, nothing," I waved him off, fending off laughter. "I'm ready for cake."

After everyone sang *Happy Birthday* and started digging into their slice of homemade chocolate cake, I gestured to Lane and myself. "We're gonna have to head out shortly."

"Got plans with the boys?" Dad asked.

"Later, yeah, but we're gonna stop at Mom's for a while."

Dad's spine stiffened against his chair. His jaw hardened a little, such a subtle change that if I hadn't been seeing it happen for the past decade of my life, I probably wouldn't have noticed.

"Ah," he nodded. "How's she?"

As if he cared.

"Good," I answered, leaving it at that.

I should've just lied and said we were going straight to the hockey house. But I fucked up, thinking for whatever reason that my dad would've reacted like a goddamn adult instead of the bitter and childish man he was.

For fifteen minutes straight, he sat there and talked shit about my mom.

"Did I ever tell you about the time your mom said blah, blah, blah to me?"

"She never even brought you to your hockey practices. It was always me that did it."

"You were probably too young to remember but one time, she cussed me out in front of a whole group of people for no reason."

"I did everything for her, and she still had the audacity to cheat on me."

He wouldn't fucking stop. It was like I'd hit some sort of on button. I zoned out after the first minute, becoming numb. I should've said something, should've put him in his place, but this was all like déjà vu for me. I'd been dealing with it since I was a kid, and as a result, I still responded to it the same way now that I did then.

By saying nothing. By zoning out. By numbing it.

150

My anger flared, and I pushed myself back from the table so hard that my chair toppled over, slamming against the wooden floor. "We have to go."

I didn't even bother picking it up or hugging my family goodbye before I was storming out of the house. I peered over my shoulder just long enough to catch Lane carefully pushing my chair back into place and shaking my dad's hand before jogging after me.

The autumn air was crisp and cold, washing out my lungs. I could feel the storm brewing inside me, chest heavy, and I stood beside my car for a moment, circling aimlessly around myself while trying to let the fall breeze calm me down.

"Hey, man," Lane said. "You alright?"

"No," I admitted.

Lane's voice was smooth, almost angelic, honestly. "Don't let him ruin your day. Let's just stop by your mom's really fast so that we can go celebrate you, okay?"

Lane had a way of soothing people with his presence like some sort of tranquility god. He put people at ease, whereas I usually did the opposite.

Resting my hands on my hips, I stared at the pavement, trying to regulate my breathing. The first breath came out shaky. The second one was drawn out, lingering throughout the autumn air the same way that orange and red leaves caught the breeze on their way to the ground.

By my last exhale, I felt a bit better, calmer.

Yeah, there was no way in hell I could've done this alone.

Lane and I made our way over to my mom's, and the second we arrived, my sister was running out the door to greet us.

"Nick! Happy birthday!"

Kayla looked like she grew a foot compared to the last time I saw her.

Her toffee brown hair was pulled into a low ponytail, and she was repping a Cedar U sweater with black leggings to match.

"Thanks," I said.

Barefoot, Kayla bulldozed into me with the force of a linebacker. I grunted, taking a step backwards. I'd never really viewed my sister and me as being close, granted we didn't talk much outside of the little time we spent together, but I was her only sibling, and I think that made her cling to me in a way she didn't cling to anyone else.

It was a strange dynamic, considering that I was technically Nate's only sibling too, but it seemed like the only thing he and I had in common was hockey. If we weren't talking about hockey, then we usually weren't talking at all. I wondered if that would change when he got older. The age gap between us was a lifetime apart, so maybe things would be different once we had more things to talk about.

When Kayla greeted Lane with a hug, it looked like pink cherry blossoms were swirling around in her cheeks. I'd always been convinced she had a crush on Lane ever since she was little.

Everyone was just obsessed with Lane, I guess.

I couldn't even blame them. Lane was a fucking catch.

Unlike Georgia's borderline creepy fascination with him that Lane could no longer deny, I think he always knew Kayla had a little crush on him. He never outright said it, but I think he thought it was sweet.

I made a mental note to make sure I teased him later for the ass slapping. I'd been so amped up on the car ride over that I didn't get the chance to rub it in his face that for the first time ever, I was right.

Within five steps through the door, I saw my mom's smile fall when her eyes met mine. She squeezed me tightly, muttering in my ear, "You look tense. Why do you seem tense?"

"I'm fine, Mom."

Hands gripping my shoulders to keep me in place, she held me there, studying me. "You know I can read you like a book. You don't seem fine. Lane, is he fine?"

"Uh, yeah," Lane fibbed, "he's fine."

"Alright... Well, let's eat!"

Fuck.

"Uh, Mom, did you make a lot of food? We just ate a lot at... Dad's..." I trailed off as I witnessed the buffet set up in the kitchen.

Double fuck.

My mom told me the other day that my stepfather, Al, was away on a business trip. He was a regional sales manager for some auto parts company, and he had to travel to different shop locations in his region a few times a year to check in and do reports and shit.

Which meant all this food was just for us four.

Exchanging painful glances with Lane, we both gulped.

"Oh," my mom's voice turned sharp, "you already ate?"

"Yeah, I told you we were stopping at Dad's."

"Is that why you seem tense? Did your Dad say something to stress you out?"

Oh no. Here it comes.

Avoiding her heated gaze, I plodded passed her. "Mom, just—"

She cut me off, shaking her head and handing each person a plate. "I'm really tired of him ruining everything."

You both ruin everything.

I didn't even respond, too afraid to feed the fire.

Lane and I filled our plates, *again*, with as much food as our stomachs could handle after everything we just ate an hour ago. The silence as everyone took the table was peaceful, but it seemed as though I got too comfortable in it.

"Did your father say anything about me?" Mom asked.

Jaw tensing as I chewed, all I did was stare at the shiny mahogany tabletop in front of me.

Call it brother's intuition or just another case of Lane being in tune with everyone else's feelings, he picked up on my vibe. Trying to jump to the rescue, he kept his tone respectful and lush. "Dinner went just fine, Mrs. Lancaster. We weren't there long."

That wasn't a good enough answer for her. She started going off in the same manner that my father did, rambling on for what seemed like an eternity.

"Your father is one of the most selfish people I've ever met."

"He'll never learn how to mind his own business."

"I feel bad for his new wife for having to deal with all his bullshit."

153

"Ever since we got divorced, your dad has never been able to keep my name out of his damn mouth."

This was my life. Time and time again.

Every family gathering. Every holiday. Every birthday. It all turned into a hate fest.

I was a firm believer that everyone should feel special and appreciated on their birthday, but truthfully, I couldn't remember the last time that happened for me. Every birthday that I could remember was never really about me at all. They always made it about themselves.

For the first few birthdays after their divorce, they tried to co-parent and have joint parties for me. All our guests would awkwardly scramble out because my parents would end up screaming at each other by the end of it.

Once I was able to drive, I started splitting up my birthday between them, but that just slowly led us to where we were now.

After suffering through the rest of dinner and practically vacuuming up my food to be done faster, Lane and I sped out of the house.

Within minutes of leaving, both of my parents were texting me, complaining. Then apologizing. Then wishing me a happy birthday. And then going back to complaining. Then apologizing. Then telling me they loved me.

It was just a vicious cycle.

And the texts didn't stop until far into the next morning.

Chapter Twenty-Six

Kota

This was it. The day it was all going to end.

A special thank you to El for helping me plot it out.

It was a little embarrassing how much time I spent on this prank, considering how many other productive things I could've been doing, like cleaning my messy room or writing my stupid bio essay.

But I kept telling myself this was necessary, even though it most definitely wasn't.

There was an inflatable pool filled with ice cold water that had replaced Crew's mattress. His comforter was carefully covering the top of it, hiding it in plain sight like camouflage.

Crew's birthday was yesterday, and after seeing the pictures and videos of the wild party the hockey boys threw for him last night, I wasn't surprised that it was already noon and he still wasn't home.

I'd been checking Lane's location occasionally, waiting to see it move to know when they were on their way back.

I was growing impatient, considering I had class in an hour and a half, and I wanted to be here when Crew got home.

The minutes were ticking by, slowly and painfully, and my patience was shrinking with it. I could hear husky voices down the apartment hall, growing louder and louder. And to my delight, the two idiots in question finally burst through the door.

"I don't fucking understand," Crew fumed, clutching tightly onto his phone as if he was about to crush it in his hand. "This has been going on for years and they won't fucking stop. They wreck my birthday every goddamn year, and quite honestly, every other holiday for that matter. I'm fucking tired of it!"

Lane remained quiet, peacefully closing the door. His mouth formed a hard line as he looked at me, his eyes shooting me a loud, strained warning to stay quiet.

My throat went dry, the type of dry where you tried to swallow a knot of uncertainty and it wouldn't go down.

I had not a single clue of what was going on, but when Crew's ice-cold glare hit everything in the room, including Lane, I knew I might've been in trouble.

"This is fucking bullshit!" Crew screamed, slamming his phone on the countertop and stalking towards his room.

Uh oh.

Panic latched onto me, inviting regret to join it. I'd seen Crew pissed, annoyed, confused, the list went on and on, but I'd never seen him... hurt?

Sure, his angry outbursts weren't foreign to me, but this felt different. There was pain behind his words, a deeper reason for the sudden eruption than just being mad on a surface-level.

Within a millisecond of Crew rounding the corner, I shot off the couch and tiptoed over, screaming in a whisper. *"Lane!"*

He shook his jacket off, shooting me a look that said *You don't even know the half of it.*

"Lane," I hushed again, sounding more urgent.

He spoke quietly, my face becoming hot from distress as he explained. "His parents practically ruined his birthday... again."

"You're not understanding!" I yelled in a whisper.

Looking at me in a daze, Lane finally registered what I meant. His eyes widened, practically popping out of their sockets. "What did you do?"

I scratched my head, grinding my teeth together. "Um, I—"

"Are you fucking kidding me?!" Crew roared.

Lane's eyes snapped shut, his head falling backwards like a disappointed dad that was about to ground his children. "Kota," he scolded, his tone eerily calm.

Small droplets of water trailed behind Crew as he stomped towards me. His clothes were soaked, his hair wet and messy like a dog with damp, shaggy fur. He had almost the same look on his face that he had when he got rammed by an opponent during a hockey game— eyes on fire, jaw unhinged, muscles tensing one by one.

And suddenly, this prank was no longer amusing.

"Are you kidding me? Are you fucking kidding me right now, Kota?" he spewed, running a large hand through his dripping hair. "You know what? You win! You fucking win! I'm over this stupid war. I forfeit, alright?" he yelled, his arms wide. "Is that what you wanted to hear today?"

Well, it originally was.

Now I wasn't so sure.

Clearly, I hit a wrong nerve with the timing of this prank, and although I got what I originally wanted, my regret was only growing.

Every breath leaving Crew's lungs was like a puff of smoke rushing out of his mouth. Staring directly at me, he was probably waiting for a snarky comment, or really, anything at all.

But I stood there, silent and expressionless.

He shook his head at me with enough hatred to burn down our apartment building. "Fuck this," he seethed, swiping his hand through his hair and flicking water onto the floor before twisting around and stomping off.

My eyes fell, staring at one of the many small puddles of water that I was now responsible for cleaning up.

Frozen beside me, Lane's lips were so tight that it looked like they were glued together.

By no means was I expecting Crew to be in a good mood when he got home, but I was more so just expecting a rough hangover and some exhaustion. Obviously, I knew the prank would piss him off, and I'd been preparing for him to civilly surrender, but I was not at all expecting that explosion. I didn't think Lane was expecting it either.

Maybe I took it too far this time.

***

I didn't see or speak to Crew for the rest of that day, other than when I cleaned up his room and put his mattress back. But even then, he left the room while I did it, refusing to be within five feet of me.

I wasn't good at expressing my feelings, and I especially wasn't good with apologies, so I'd kind of just been hoping this whole thing would blow over as the days went by.

But it seemed like each passing day made the air in the apartment staler, and all four of us were reluctantly breathing it in.

It was no secret that Crew and I never got along. We'd been playing games this entire time, testing each other, waiting to see who the first to crack would be.

But it felt like we'd— or rather, *I'd*— crossed a line.

And now we were all paying the price.

Both Lane and Bridget were upset. They kept saying it had less to do with me and more to do with the situation. I knew the timing of the prank was shitty, but in my defense, I didn't know the timing was going to be shitty. I still wasn't entirely sure what Crew's relationship was like with his parents, and by the sound of it, it didn't seem like a great one to me, but I did feel bad for making his already-bad-birthday a little bit worse.

After talking more about it with Bridget, I decided to swallow my pride and try to apologize.

My steps were slow and reluctant, like gravity was trying to drag me further and further away from Crew's bedroom door.

Standing there quietly like I was lost, I stared at his door for minutes on end as I tried to gather up the courage to knock.

Just get it over with, Kota.

My fist clenched and unclenched various times as I raised it, blowing out a strained breath. I gave three solid knocks, tapping my foot against the floor in anticipation.

When the door swung open, a dissatisfied Crew stood in its wake, eyeing me with the intimidation of a great white shark.

"What?" he greeted me with.

I ignored his gaze as I spoke, feeling a swirl of embarrassment. "I know you don't wanna talk to me right now, but I just wanted to say that maybe I took it too far and..." my voice dropped to a quiet mutter, "I'm sorry."

His harsh gaze branded me for a moment, and when he finally decided that I was being genuine, his stance softened. "I'm sorry too."

Blinking at him, my mouth parted. That was definitely not the reaction I expected him to have. I'd pretty much been expecting him to slam the door in my face.

"For what?" I questioned.

He shrugged against the doorframe. "Maybe I overreacted a little bit."

Head bobbing awkwardly, I stood uncomfortable. We'd never had an interaction that wasn't filled with annoyance, disgust, or malice, so I wasn't quite sure how to act at the moment.

Crew sighed subtly. "Alright... can we agree to pretend like neither of us apologized to each other?"

With eyes widened in gratitude, I nodded. "Agreed."

He gave a tight-lipped nod. "Cool."

"Cool."

Chapter Twenty-Seven

Kota

My patience with Bobby was thinning. It had been months and he still hadn't tied the knot.

Not the marriage knot, of course, but the relationship knot.

He had just picked me up from class and we were supposed to hang out for a bit before he had poker night with his friends.

"Do you mind if I stop at the liquor store to grab some beer for later?" he asked from the driver's seat.

I shook my head lightly. "I don't mind."

"Cool," he smiled before turning into the parking lot. "I'll be right back," he said, hopping out of the car and rushing inside.

I tapped my feet against each other, anxiety starting to prick my skin. I needed to just have this conversation with him. It'd been on my mind constantly for days now, and the thoughts weren't slowing down.

Obviously, I didn't want to be played. But I also didn't want to waste my time. And after months of this we're-dating-but-not-actually-dating behavior, I was ready for a clear-cut answer.

I waited rather impatiently for Bobby to finish up inside, letting out a sigh that was cut short when his phone buzzed on the center console beside me.

I'd never been one to peek at people's phones, but there was something gnawing at me, a strange feeling growing in my gut that was demanding I just simply looked. Not to mention, it was a little damn hard not to when it was practically in my face.

I didn't even have to touch the phone, all I had to do was glance at it.

Kimmie: Are you still coming over tonight?

My jaw tightened. *Poker night, my ass.*

I knew Bobby well enough to know that he didn't have a sister, or even a very close cousin for that matter. He'd never mentioned any friends that were girls either.

Heat was creeping up the back of my neck, and as Bobby reappeared with a case of beer in one hand and a four-pack of seltzers in the other, I let out a fucking laugh.

I'd been around his friends long enough to know that none of them drank fucking seltzers.

Do it now, Kota. Catch him in the lie.

I somehow kept my temper from flaring as Bobby placed the alcohol in the backseat and climbed into the front. I even managed to plaster on a fake grin as if nothing had happened.

"Ready?" I spoke.

"Yep," he said.

I cleared my throat as he began driving. "So, um, I have a question."

He glanced back and forth between the road and me. "What's up?"

I kept my ice-cold glare ahead of me to make sure he couldn't catch it. "Well, we've been talking for a few months now."

"Mhm," he nodded along.

"So, I was just wondering," I paused, inhaling deeply, "where is this going?"

He let out what sounded like a quiet sigh. "I knew this question was coming," he said, a trace of reluctance in his voice. "I mean... honestly, I like how things are between us. This semester has been crazy busy and I'm starting my new job in a few weeks, so it's only going to get busier. But you know I like you," his voice softened, "and I do want to keep seeing you."

In other words— *You're cool, and we should keep fucking, but I don't wanna commit myself to you.*

There was an ache in my core, but I refused to show it. Clearly, Bobby didn't want to be with me, and there was no reason for me to try to convince him to.

I gave a careless shrug. "Okay."

He shot me a look that was full of surprise, as if he'd been expecting me to put up a fight. Had he wanted me to put up a fight? To beg for him to commit to me? If that was what he wanted, or what he was waiting for, it was never coming.

I would never give a man that kind of power or satisfaction. My self-respect outweighed my feelings for Bobby, and I'd rather lose him than to lose myself.

But even though I was trying to stay strong and make the right decision for myself, it still hurt.

"Okay?" he asked.

I shrugged again. "Okay," I repeated.

"Okay," he murmured.

Bobby put on his turn signal, but before we reached the light, I pointed straight. "Actually, can you drop me off? I've got a killer migraine."

He shifted out of the turn lane, growing wary. "You don't want to hang out anymore?"

"Not tonight," I shook my head.

Once again, he said, "Okay," muttering it even quieter than the last time. It seemed like he was in his own head now, thrown off by my reaction, or lack of reaction, I should say.

Inhaling a stressed breath, my eyes began stinging in the slightest. *One more minute,* I told myself, *then you can cry all you want.*

That remaining minute was full of awkward silence, Bobby's discomfort lingering through the air like cigarette smoke.

He pulled up to the front of the apartment building, quietly shifting into park and glancing over at me as if waiting for me to say something.

But I didn't.

I climbed out of the car silently, prompting him to speak right before I could shut the door.

"Am I still going to see you tomorrow night?"

I gave him a wicked smile. "I don't think so," I said, slamming the door. I kept my chin up as I walked inside the building, refusing to let him see my confidence waver in the slightest.

Gosh, I fucking hated this feeling. The feeling of a heavy chest, a mushy brain, an aching throat as if little splinters of ice were stuck in there.

All I wanted was my bed. And Bridget. But I had no idea if she was even home right now.

I fished my key out of my purse, growing agitated with it as I fought with the lock, glossy eyes blurring my vision. I let out a strained, painful breath as I pushed through the door.

Immediately, Crew's brows came in with both concern and curiosity. He eyed me as if he were seeing a unicorn in real life. His words came out slowly, warily. "Are you okay?"

"Fine," I said, tossing my purse on the counter.

"Are you sure?" he asked. "You don't look fine."

I shot him a look, and even though it didn't feel very fierce with tears in my eyes, apparently, it still got the job done, because Crew recoiled a bit.

"I'm. Fine," I insisted, even though we both knew it wasn't the truth. My voice fell, and I looked away from him, beginning to sulk towards my room. "Just ended things with Bobby."

"Oh..."

"When Bridget comes home, have her come to my room please," I requested, shutting my door and collapsing into bed.

This was exactly why I was always hesitant to get involved with guys. I grew up having trust issues with men, and every guy that I ever let walk into my life only proved why those trust issues still existed.

I wasn't sure why I had trusted Bobby not to screw me over.

If my own father couldn't even love me, why would I trust another man to?

It was times like these that reminded me of the three most important things my mother taught me growing up.

One, how to be independent and take care of myself.

Two, how to be confident in my own skin.

And three, how to not deal with men's bullshit.

I was currently sitting in bed, hugging my knees to my chest and burying my head into them. Squeezing my eyes shut, a single tear escaped as I did so, trailing all the way down to my lips.

But all it took was that one tear for dozens to follow its lead. It was like the first drip of water that fell from the sky before an entire storm rushed down.

Then, I did what I always did.

I gave myself ten minutes, setting a timer on my phone.

For those ten minutes, I'd allow myself to be sad and cry it out, and once that time was up, I'd brush it off and continue my day.

Chapter Twenty-Eight

Crew

Was I supposed to try to comfort her? I didn't think I'd ever felt so awkward than I did when she walked in earlier on the verge of tears.

I had no idea what Bobby did, but it must've been hurtful enough if it made Dakota Darling cry.

I'd been starting to think that girl had no emotions besides pleasure in other people's pain and just straight up rage.

She came home over an hour ago, and I'd been awkwardly and impatiently waiting for Bridget to get home so that I could send her to Kota's room immediately.

I heard her crying for a few minutes before an alarm went off, and since then, there'd only been silence coming from her room.

There had been a few times where I almost knocked on her door to check on her before reminding myself that even though we'd been coexisting lately, that I was still her least favorite person on the planet and probably the last person she wanted to see right now.

Where the hell was Bridget? Also, where the fuck was Lane?

The realization made me stiffen for a moment like a sandcastle before it crumbled.

They were probably together. Actually, fuck that. They were definitely *together.*

Fan-fucking-tastic. Who knew when they were coming home?

I was about to snatch my phone off the table and send Lane a frustrated text when there was a light bang on the door. I stared at it with confusion before trekking over.

The second I had the door opened, I stiffened once again.

Bobby looked up at me with hopeful eyes, almost relieved that I'd been the one to answer the door. "Hey, is Kota here?"

I leaned against the door frame, arms crossed. "Why?"

Stress was flickering in his eyes as he shifted his weight back and forth. He gulped. "I need to talk to her."

I stared at him intently, my gaze hitting him like a dart landing on a bullseye. I was assuming he had come here to fix whatever shitty mistake he'd made, and I wasn't sure how Kota felt or if she actually did want to talk to him, but either way, I wasn't a fan of how he made her feel earlier. The thought of anyone messing with her besides me didn't sit right with me.

"No," I said.

His expression turned dazed, looking like a puzzle piece out of place. "She's not here?"

"No, she is," I casually said.

His tone grew sharper. "Then can I talk to her?"

"No," I repeated.

Bobby sighed, dropping his head. When he glanced back up at me, it was with softer eyes, an almost hurt gleam swimming behind them. "Look, I really need to fix things, and—"

"Fuck off, Bobby," I said, slamming the door in his face.

Chapter Twenty-Nine

Kota

"**W**as that Bobby?" I quietly asked, peeking my head around the corner of the hall.

Crew spun around, seemingly jolted by my presence. "Uh, yeah," he said rather sheepishly.

"What did he want?"

"He asked to talk to you."

"Oh," I uttered, probably inaudible from across the room. "And you..."

Crew's eyes found the floor as he shrugged. "I told him to fuck off." When he looked back up at me, his expression turned cautious. "Unless you wanted to talk to him?"

"No," I immediately said. "I don't... so... thank you."

His mouth formed a hard line as he gave me a cordial nod and walked off down the boy's hall.

I stood there quietly by myself, as if my feet were nailed to the floor.

Why would Crew help me? We'd been getting along a bit better after the whole awkward apology thing, but I didn't think we were at the point where we'd consider ourselves "friends," so I wasn't sure what Crew's intentions were right now.

Unless he didn't realize he was helping me when he did it. Maybe he thought I actually wanted to talk to Bobby and scared him off just so that I wouldn't get the chance to.

Whatever the reason was, I'd be lying if I said I wasn't grateful for it.

Instead of continuing to overanalyze it all, I retreated to my room. I wanted more than anything to crash into bed with some ice cream and a sad movie on, but I refused to give in to the heartache. I had my ten minutes to let it out, and those ten minutes had passed, so that was that.

While I sat at my desk, I avoided looking into my mirror. I was too afraid to see the woe that was probably covering my face.

So, I took out my bio notes and began making flashcards since Thanksgiving break was coming up and I had a mid-term right beforehand. Luckily, I got an A on my bacteria essay, which saved my grade from plummeting and put me in a pretty good spot going into finals.

But after ten or so minutes, it became harder and harder to focus.

Because my phone was blowing up.

I had two missed calls from Bridget and six from Bobby, along with a multitude of texts.

Bobby: Hey can we talk?
Please?
I know what it seems like, but I want to explain
I tried stopping by, but Crew wouldn't let me in
Can I come over? Or u can come stop by here if u want
Kota
Please don't do this

With one click of a button, I put my phone on do not disturb and tossed it behind me, onto my bed.

Nearly twenty flashcards later, Bridget burst into my room.

"Hey, um, what the hell?" she squealed with her arms up.

"Hey," I casually said, glancing up at her briefly and back down at my notes.

168

The strawberry blonde knot on top of her head bobbed as she tumbled onto my bed. "You can't just text me that and then ignore my calls!"

"Sorry," I murmured. "I got distracted."

B sighed, letting it go. Her voice softened. "Are you okay?"

"Perfectly fine."

"Hey," she said, "you don't have to lie. It's just me."

"I'm not lying."

"Kota," she pressed.

I sighed, swiveling around to face her. "I already had my ten minutes."

She rolled her eyes, letting out a small grunt of frustration. "Kota. It's okay to have feelings, you know. You don't need to bundle them up and lock them away after ten minutes."

"Yes, I do."

"No, you don't," she insisted, leaning forward.

I eyed her quietly for a moment, before ultimately turning back around. "Well, it's too late," I muttered. "They're already locked away."

"You didn't even explain what happened. All you texted me was *Just ended things with Bobby. Woohoooooo!* With a bunch of smiley faces."

I shrugged tenderly with one shoulder, pretending to be occupied by the blank notecards in front of me. "How do you know I didn't mean the enthusiasm? Maybe I did."

"Because I know you."

A loud sigh escaped my lips and I looked up at B in the mirror, whose gaze was already stuck on me. Catching the sight of the leftover redness in my eyes, I nearly winced. "He was planning on seeing another girl tonight. And when I asked where things were going between us, he pretty much said he didn't want to date me."

B spoke with her hands, utterly confused. "Hold on. Back up. He was going to see *another girl* tonight?"

"Yep."

"How do you know?"

"I saw his phone."

She gasped. "Kota! You snooped?"

I rolled my eyes. "First of all, I did not *snoop*. He had the goddamn phone practically on display. All I did was glance at it when it went off. Second of all, are you brushing over what I said? B," I said sharply, "he's entertaining other girls."

"Well, did you confront him about it?"

"No."

"Are you gonna?"

I brought my feet onto the desk chair, hugging my knees to my chest. "Apparently he tried stopping by to talk."

"Okay... So did you talk to him at all?"

"No," I shook my head. "He didn't make it past the door." Bridget leaned back into her hands, waiting for me to explain. A small smile appeared on my face as I spoke, growing like a balloon as it inflated. "Crew wouldn't let him in and told him to fuck off."

Bridget's brows lifted, a tiny chuckle escaping. "Interesting."

"I know."

"Did you ask him to do that?"

"Nope."

"Hmm," she hummed.

"Hmm is right," I said. "But anyway... enough about Bobby. Let's change the subject."

Chapter Thirty

Crew

It was _finally_ Thanksgiving break. And I wasn't saying that because I was excited to eat food or see my family. I was solely excited to not have class or hockey for a few days.

I was still pissed at my parents for how my birthday went, and I made the executive decision to skip out on Thanksgiving with both of them this year.

I lied and told each of them that I'd be spending Thanksgiving at the other's house, and that I'd spend all of Christmas at theirs to make up for it, even though that was a lie. I'd split the day like I had every other year, but that was a later problem to figure out.

At first, both of my parents put up a small fight but eventually accepted.

Lane had offered to let me go home with him to spend Thanksgiving with his family, but I turned him down too. Quite honestly, I was just looking forward to some peace and quiet by myself.

I'd never spent a holiday alone, so who knows? Maybe I'd hate it. But it would probably still be better than another shit show holiday with my parents.

Bridget left to go home on Tuesday and Lane left last night. Now, it was Thanksgiving morning, and Kota left before

I even got out of bed, taking Rob K with her, which meant I had the apartment to myself for the next three days.

Halle-fucking-lujah.

I spent most of the day playing video games and napping. Around five, I ordered a pizza. They had the entire *Fast & Furious* franchise on Netflix, so I decided to have a movie marathon.

I busted out a few beers from the fridge, slumping back against the couch.

This was the greatest decision of my fucking life, I thought to myself.

Now that I thought about it, I couldn't remember the last time I had quality time alone. I always heard Bridget talk about how important "self-care" was and that everyone should make time for themselves.

Most of my free time was spent with Lane. And if I wasn't with Lane, I was with the guys. It was hard having alone time when you lived with numerous other people. The only alone time you got was when you hid in your own room or had a few minutes to yourself when no one was home.

After my disastrous birthday, this was exactly what I needed to relieve some of the built-up tension and irritability from the last few weeks.

Nothing could ruin my night.

Chapter Thirty-One

Kota

"**M**om, really, it's okay," I said into the phone as I walked down the hall to our apartment. I had the phone tucked between my ear and my shoulder, my bag slung over my opposite shoulder while I clutched onto Rob K.

"Are you sure you're okay with this? I feel like I'm ditching you."

"You're not ditching me," I laughed.

I'd gone over to my moms to spend Thanksgiving with her. I was originally going to stay for the weekend, but when she got a call from the new guy she'd been seeing, asking if she wanted to go to his cabin with him for the weekend, I convinced her to take the offer.

The truth was, my mom had a lot of men in line for her while I was growing up, but nothing ever came out of any of those relationships. Not because they didn't have the potential to, but more so because of me.

I was one menace of a kid, that's for sure. Either I was purposefully such a brat to the men that they couldn't stand me, or I told my mom I didn't like them.

To this day, I wasn't entirely sure why I did it. But I assumed it was probably a mixture of my trust issues with men and being jealous of someone else taking my mother's attention.

Now that I was older and was able to see how shitty it was of me to do that to my mom, I encouraged her to talk to men and go on dates as much as possible. My mom was my favorite person on the planet, and I wanted her to have the most fulfilling, enjoyable life possible.

Even if that did mean sharing her on Thanksgiving.

"Do you promise you're okay with this?" my mom asked again.

"I promise," I assured. "How many times are you gonna ask?"

"As many times as possible before you hang up."

I chuckled, struggling to pull my key out of my purse as I approached our door. "In that case, I'm gonna hang up now."

She sighed. "Alright. Well, you have a good night, sweetie. Call or text me if you change your mind and I'll come home right away."

"Not gonna happen," I said with a smile. "Love you, Mama. Have fun!"

"Love you too, Kota girl."

I pushed the door open, grappling with everything in my hands. I immediately set Rob K down and watched him scurry off. When I stood back up, realizing that there was noise surrounding me, I could feel my spine stiffen to stone as the blood drained from my face.

Crew was sitting on the couch, his eyes glued to me, mouth slightly parted.

"What are you doing here?" I spit out, letting my bag fall off my shoulder and plop onto the floor.

"Uh," his brows came in, "what are *you* doing here?"

"I thought you were going to your parents?" I accused.

He raised a brow, challenging me. "I thought you were staying at your moms?"

My jaw tensed in the slightest. "Change of plans."

"Same here," he said.

I rocked back and forth on my heels awkwardly. "Are you... gonna be here all weekend then?"

"Yep."

Shit.

"Alriiight," I dragged, glancing around. "In that case... I'll be in my room." I could feel Crew's eyes on me as I hurried towards the hall, and just before I managed to reach it, Crew spoke again, causing me to come to a sudden halt.

"Hey."

I stood silently, the intensity of his stare burning into my skin. His shoulders weren't tense with animosity like I'd seen them hundreds of times before. They were relaxed, along with every muscle in his body. He leaned forward, resting his forearms casually on his knees.

"Are you alright?" he suddenly asked.

My brows furrowed for a moment. "I'm fine, yeah... What do you mean?"

"I mean, after last week."

All of a sudden, awkwardness hit me like a truck. We hadn't really spoken about the whole Bobby thing since he showed up at our apartment and was impolitely greeted by Crew.

"Yeah," I blew out with a deep breath. "I'm fine. Thanks."

He gave a single nod as I turned and dashed to my room.

***

I stayed in my room for most of the next day, pleased to do absolutely nothing.

I gave myself the day off from studying or doing anything around the house, even though my room was a mess and could use some elbow grease.

After watching a movie, scrolling through social media, and reading one of the slutty books I borrowed from Bridget, I figured it was time to make some food. I'd only been snacking throughout the day, and since I didn't cook often during the week because I was normally so busy, I figured tonight would be a good time to make one of the many recipes that Lane and Bridget had been recommending.

I forced myself to get out of bed, bribing myself with the thought of food. I tiptoed down the hall, peeking around carefully to make sure Crew wasn't in the common areas.

I hadn't seen him a single time today, which was fine with me. He'd been so much more civil ever since his birthday. It wasn't that I was mad about it; I just felt kind of awkward.

Quite honestly, I wasn't sure how to act around him. I was so used to arguing with him, showing him the worst versions of myself, and shooting irate glares every time we were in the same vicinity. Now that we were being decent to each other, I felt like I was in a foreign country whenever I was near him.

With a deep sigh, I rolled up my sleeves and got to work cooking. I wasn't totally sure what I was even making; I was just following the recipe.

After fifteen or so minutes of prepping, I finally stuck the chicken in the oven and set a timer before toppling onto the couch.

My eyes slowly fluttered to a close, and the next thing I knew, I was being jolted awake by the sound of the timer going off.

I rushed into the kitchen and took the chicken out, and I'd be damned if I said it didn't smell like Heaven. I couldn't get some on a plate fast enough, cutting it into tiny pieces so that it would cool off quicker.

"What's that?"

An ear-ringing screech left my mouth as I jumped, seeing Crew standing behind me, glancing over my shoulder. My hand found its way to my chest in a poor attempt to ease my hammering heart. "What the hell!"

"What?"

"Don't scare me like that!"

"Sorry," he shrugged nonchalantly. "What's that?"

I sighed, stepping away from him. "Some recipe Lane and Bridget gave me."

"Mmm," he hummed with a nod. "It's probably good then."

"Probably," I agreed, giving him a side eye.

He gave out a casual whistle, glancing around like he was waiting for me to offer him some. I watched him quietly, wanting to set him on fire more and more as the seconds ticked by. I was trying to hold back a smartass retort, because after all, he did help me out last week. But it was hard to be nice to him when he was being impossibly annoying.

Not to mention, being stuck *alone* with him for the weekend while he was being impossibly annoying.

Finally, I let out a sigh, the words leaving my mouth as if they were getting reluctantly ripped out. "Do you want some?"

He showed off a dimple as he gave a charming smile, and if I was any woman other than myself, my panties probably would've been on the floor.

"Sure. How nice of you to offer," he joked.

I rolled my eyes, grabbing my plate and taking a seat at the kitchen island. Crew shoveled the biggest piece of chicken there was onto a plate, then took it to the couch.

We didn't speak after that.

That was enough interaction between us to last the rest of the night.

Chapter Thirty-Two

Crew

"**S**top ignoring me," Jett said when I picked up his call.

"I'm not," I grumbled, half-asleep.

"Are you still fucking sleeping? It's almost one," he chastised.

Running a hand over my eyes, I tossed around in bed. "Fuck off. We're on break. I'll sleep as much as I want."

"Well, TJ and I are going out tonight. And you're coming with."

I groaned.

Jett and TJ were both from Canada, so they usually didn't go home unless our breaks were longer. Thanksgiving break was only five days, so it was too much traveling to be there for such a short amount of time.

"Why the hell don't you wanna hang out with us?" Jett whined.

"It's not that I don't wanna hang out. I just... feel like doing nothing, honestly."

His voice was sharp. "What?"

"I'm just feeling lazy," I explained.

"You're always lazy."

"Hey," I chided. "Not always."

"We'll pick you up at ten." He hung up, giving me no chance to rebut.

A cross between a whine and a sigh left my mouth, making me sound like a deep-voiced, babbling baby.

Guess I was going out tonight.

***

I got dressed around nine and made my way out to the kitchen to make something small to eat before the guys got here.

Kota and I hadn't spoken since she unwillingly shared her dinner with me last night. But when I walked out of my room and saw her bundled up in her snuggie on the couch, piling heaps of ice cream into her mouth while she sat teary-eyed with *The Notebook* on, there was a small pain in my gut.

I knew how hard it probably had been for her to swallow her pride and apologize to me after turning my bed into a damn pool. Before then, I didn't think the word *Sorry* was part of her vocabulary.

Then, it happened again last night when she shared with me. It was blatantly obvious that she didn't want to, but she offered anyway, and even though she had spoken like there was a gun pointed at her, it was still a nice gesture.

Clearly, that had all been her version of trying to be the bigger person and call a truce, and it felt like I needed to suck it up and do the same.

Before thinking better of it, my mouth started moving. "I'm going out tonight."

She didn't respond, just looked at me with an expression that read *Why the fuck would I care?*

The natural edge in my voice when I usually spoke to her came back, and I was fucking grateful for it. Because for the first time in over a week, it felt like the closest thing to normal. "You can come if you want. Since you know, you have no other friends besides Bridget."

Her eyes immediately narrowed, jaw tightening like steel. "Fuck you. I have other friends."

"Name one."

Her mouth twitched before she answered. "Patricia."

A sinister grin crept over my face. "You just made that up."

Kota reached forward and placed her ice cream on the coffee table before crossing her arms. "No, I didn't."

She was trying to smother me with that insidious glare of hers and I was trying not to laugh. Ultimately, I failed, letting out a soft chuckle. "Are you gonna come or not?"

The venom in her eyes faded away, but her grouchy tone stayed. "Yeah, fine. Give me a bit to get ready."

I watched her stalk off to her room. I could tell she was trying to seem careless and badass, but it was hard to do that while wearing an oversized snuggie.

After a few minutes rustling around in the kitchen, looking for food, I halted with realization.

What the fuck did I just get myself into?

***

The inside of my fist met Kota's door, banging heavily on it. "Are you done yet? The guys are gonna be here any second."

"Give me a goddamn minute!"

I let out a huff, checking my watch for the fifth time in the past ten minutes. Impatience pricked up my spine as I waited around in the living room, anticipating for the guys to text me that they were here.

Finally, Kota appeared from her room, and if she were anyone else, I probably would've whistled.

Big brown eyes illuminated by smoky eyeshadow, and lips so glossy they looked like they were wet, I nearly choked on my own saliva.

Kota had practically been drooling when I walked into the kitchen months ago suited up for our first game, and now, I was the one trying not to drool. Forcing myself to remain expressionless, I said, "You know we're just going to Stallions and not a freaking club, right?"

180

She slid her black Steve Madden purse over her shoulder, her brown eyes seemingly getting darker as she glared at me. "I'm aware of the venue, thank you."

"So, what's with the dress?" It was taking everything in me to keep my eyes on her face. All my gaze wanted to do was linger. Her black dress was short and *tight as hell*, clinging to every curve of her body. Not to mention that I never realized how great her fucking legs were. Tan, slender, long, and—

"Maybe I just like it," Kota shot at me, but when I lifted a brow in disbelief, she sighed. "Bobby might be there."

I allowed my smirk to finally show. "Ah, I see. Trying to get a little revenge."

Pushing past me, she headed for the door. "It'll be revenge when he's begging for forgiveness."

I tipped my head in agreement and followed her out.

Chapter Thirty-Three

Kota

Good thing I wore this fucking dress.

Bobby was sitting at a table across the room with his friends, his eyes trailing over to me every few minutes.

It was taking a lot of focus to not walk over and smack him across the face. Gladly, Jett and TJ were a great distraction.

"I'm disappointed in you, Jett." I could feel my high ponytail sway as I shook my head. "A porn box? Really? That's the best you could do?"

"Hey! It was better than everyone else's ideas. This one right here," he said, tapping TJ, "had the worst of all."

TJ let out a small scoff, raising his beer. "My ideas were good!"

"They were not good at all," Crew said, seated beside me.

I turned the opposite way as I chuckled lightly, refusing to face him as I did so. "It's three against one then, TJ."

"Um," he challenged, "you weren't even there. So, really, it's two against one."

"That's not much better," Crew said.

Other than a few occupied tables, with Bobby and his friends being one of them, the bar was practically empty. Everyone else was gone for the weekend, home for

182

Thanksgiving break. Since Bobby was a local, I'd assumed he would still be in the area, which had also led me to assume he may be out tonight. In other words, I was glad I came prepared.

It was kind of nice to be at Stallions when it wasn't packed with people. There was space to walk around freely, no wait at the bar, and we didn't have to scream over music and people just to hear each other.

Jett tipped his head back with a laugh, turning to TJ. "You know you're the dumbest one out of our friend group, right?"

TJ's eyes narrowed. "That's bullshit. Matt's the dumbest."

Crew smirked with amusement, and I'd be lying if I said he wasn't at least a little enjoyable to be around when we weren't at each other's throats. "That's debatable," Crew said.

We hadn't fought once all night. The closest thing we had to an argument was the little attitude he'd given me back at our apartment.

It might've all been in my head, but I think he was checking me out earlier?

The image had popped in and out of my mind throughout the night, taunting me. His eyes had seemingly glazed over, darkening while they lingered on my legs for a moment too long. He'd wrestled his gaze away from me as if looking at me in a way that wasn't filled with hatred was a crime.

And I sure as hell was feeling like a criminal for liking the feeling.

TJ leaned forward into the table. "It's not debatable at all. How many times has that fucker gotten his hand stuck in a goddamn Pringle's can? How fucking dumb do you have to be to do that once, let alone numerous times?"

An explosion of laughter took over our table, and although I had no idea what they were talking about, I still had a goofy smile on my face as if I did.

I would never admit it aloud, but I was thankful Crew invited me out tonight. If he hadn't, I would've spent the rest of the night with my ice cream and Nicholas Sparks movies, wallowing in all my negative feelings.

But right now, I felt like a bad bitch in my hot dress, sipping on a beer while my almost-ex was eyeing me from across the room.

"Speaking of Matt," I butted in, "what's up with him and El?"

That earned another explosion of laughter, along with some fists hitting the table.

El and I had been talking a lot lately, and I truly really liked her. If I had just seen her Instagram profile without ever talking to her over direct message, I probably would've thought she was just a preppy rich girl. Her profile gave off that vibe based on her aesthetic photos, trendy clothes, and traveling habits. Not to mention that she was studying to become a lawyer. But to my surprise, she was really cool and relatable. Based on some of the stories she'd told me, she seemed to have a little bit of a bite to her when it came to guys, so we were similar in that way.

She told me the other day that if the guys made it to the NCAA tournament this year, then she'd come visit for one of the games. I hoped that was the case because I really wanted to meet her in person.

"Absolutely nothing," Crew shook his head through laughter.

"Matt wishes," TJ said.

Jett's piercing blue eyes looked like ice cubes, shifting back and forth between the boys. "Remember that one time he had a girl over and accidentally called her El in front of everyone?"

Crew twisted to the side, doubling over in laughter.

Shoulders bobbing up and down with a chuckle, TJ added, "Let's be real though. What do we think the odds are of him accidentally saying her name during sex?"

"High," Jett said with confidence.

"Extremely high!" Crew agreed with a bright smile.

I raised a delighted brow. "So, you guys think he's in love with her?"

Jett brought his beer up to his mouth, speaking right before it touched his lips. "Um, we don't think; we *know*."

"Oh, I'm *so* telling her," I said with a devious smirk.

"No need," Crew waved me off. "She already knows."

"Yeah," Jett agreed. "Sometimes we think she feels the same way. Other times, it's hard to tell. I don't know. They've got some weird thing going on."

"They're probably gonna end up married," Crew said.

TJ pointed at him with his beer. "I'd put money on that."

"Interesting," I nodded along.

"I'm grabbing another beer," TJ mumbled, seemingly to himself as he wandered off.

"Wait up!" Jett called out, jogging after him.

"Kota!" a high-pitched voice called. I swiveled around as a small, brunette girl hurdled towards me with an eager grin.

"Oh hey!" I grinned back as she approached. Pivoting towards Crew, my grin turned satisfied and cocky. "Crew, this is—"

"Patricia," she finished for me, extending her hand past me and into Crew's face.

The corners of his mouth tugged upwards as he shook her hand, his eyes shifting over to me with an *I can't even fucking believe it* look.

I'd be lying if I said Patricia was a close friend. She was just someone that Bridget and I met freshman year while we were out. We used to hang out with her a lot that year, going to parties together and drinking in the dorms. Now, the only times we usually hung out with her were when we ran into her somewhere. Other than that, we didn't talk much.

But when Crew put me on blast earlier for Bridget being my only friend, I couldn't let him know he was sort of right. I had a decent number of friends, but none of which I really hung out with outside of class or seeing them at the bars. Sometimes I told myself it was because I was such a bitch that no one liked me. Other times, I told myself it was because I never let anyone into my circle.

They were both probably a little bit right.

Patricia tugged on my hand, yanking me out of my seat. "Come hang out with us for a bit!"

"Who'd you come with?" I asked, pulling my dress down.

She started listing off her friends, some of which I knew, as she dragged me along. I let her, but when I quickly glanced behind me, a knot of anxiety started forming in my core.

Bobby's strides were purposeful, seemingly heavy with anger as he headed towards our table, his dark eyes fixed on Crew.

Chapter Thirty-Four

Crew

And just like that, I was alone at the table.

It didn't last more than thirty seconds though when Bobby slid into the seat that Kota had accompanied before.

He stared at me like he was trying to crush me with his glare— eyes on fire, jaw tight, mouth pushed into a hard line. But unfortunately for him, I wasn't going to shrink away like a wilting flower.

He sat in silence for a moment longer until I raised a brow, challenging him to speak.

"What kind of game are you playing?" he finally spit out.

"Excuse me?"

Bobby leaned towards me, but I didn't move away. If this was his way of trying to intimidate me, it wasn't working in the slightest. If I wasn't afraid of two-hundred-pound men hurdling towards me on the ice, hoping to draw blood, I wasn't fucking afraid of Bobby.

He spoke in a condescending tone, tapping a knuckle against the table in an uneven rhythm. "I mean, I thought you hated her. Then all of a sudden, you won't let me into the apartment and now you two show up here together?"

My hand fell against the table as if to say *So what?*

Bobby dropped his chin slightly, that glare of his still going strong. "Are you hooking up with her?"

Now, *my* jaw was tightening. Lines creased my forehead as my brows came inwards. "Not that it's any of your business," I spewed, "but no."

Bobby gestured across the bar to where Kota stood, laughing loudly with some guy that I was assuming was friends with Patricia. "Is she fucking *him*?"

Why the fuck did he think he had the right to know? As far as I knew, Kota hadn't been with anyone this school year besides Bobby, so the fact that he was insinuating that she was sleeping around so soon after their breakup didn't sit right with me. And even if she was, so what? Not to mention, from what I heard through the grapevine, AKA Lane and Bridget, Bobby was the unfaithful one.

Had he not given a fuck about her at all? Is he only seeming to give a fuck now that he doesn't have her?

Kota was still one of my least favorite people, but she'd been decent tonight; I was feeling some sort of obligation to defend her.

I didn't hesitate to lean forward, but unlike when Bobby did it, I wasn't afraid to get up close and personal. I didn't stop until I was inches from his face. If he wanted me to show him what real intimidation was, I'd gladly give him a lesson.

Tension stretched between us like a rubber band, but I could feel it about to snap on his end. He seemed to shy away a bit, his sharp, strained features reluctantly softening.

I spoke with a steady hiss. "What she does is none of your concern. So, I suggest you do what I said last time and fuck off."

Bobby's grim eyes kept boring into me, but he didn't say anything. Where the hell were TJ and Matt? Or even Kota? I needed someone to get here before I beat the shit out of this guy. We all knew Kota pushed my buttons repeatedly, but this guy was testing my patience beyond repair. I wasn't sure why that was. It might've been his absolute lack of respect for women or boundaries.

And sure, who the hell was I to talk about respect for women? But in my defense, I didn't prance around possessively, acting like I owned them. If a woman wanted to sleep around, that was her choice. And even more so, if a woman just simply didn't want to talk to me because I fucked her over, then she had every right to act that way.

After another minute, Bobby seemed to make the smart decision. His shoulders rose and fell as he exhaled deeply through his nose, sitting back for a second before standing, angrily pushing his chair away, and stomping off.

I waited another minute for someone to come back to the table, and when no one did, I chugged the rest of my beer, set it on the table, and started walking away.

Without thinking, I went straight up to Kota. "I'm ready to go when you are."

Her dark irises held me in a trap, trying to read my expression. "Are you alright?"

"Perfectly fine," I muttered, shifting around.

She shot me a look, and like thousands of times leading up to now, I recognized it. There was a sassy comment heading my way, maybe even the start of a fight.

But to my surprise, Kota seemed to choke it back. She turned towards her friends and murmured something to them before stepping closer to me. "Okay. I'm ready," she said, adjusting her purse over her shoulder.

I nodded, leading the way towards the exit. I made sure to tell the guys we were leaving before we walked out. Settling into step beside each other, Kota asked what happened with Bobby.

I summarized, and surprisingly, she didn't push the topic more even though she had every right to. She seemed to be deep in thought. For someone who had expressed many times how much she hated my fucking face, I found it odd how often I'd caught her staring at me on the way home.

She was unusually quiet until we walked through the door.

"Crew."

I fell onto the couch. "What?"

She hung her purse on the hook next to the door, speaking as she did so. "Have I ever told you how attractive you are?"

My body went rigid, lips parted in utter confusion. "Are you on drugs right now?"

"No," she shrugged.

"Okay..." I responded warily, analyzing her every move. "How drunk are you?" Was she trying to see if I fell for it? Or if I'd compliment her back?

But when she answered, there was no venom in her voice, or in her facial expression for that matter. She seemed more than relaxed, her eyes blazing with a glaze that I couldn't quite decipher.

"I'm not that drunk," she said casually.

"Not that drunk," I repeated.

"I mean it. You're attractive."

A gust of laughter flew out of my mouth. "Stop that."

"Stop what?" she said, resting a hand low on her hip.

I sat back against the couch, trying to act composed even though I was anything but. "Stop acting like you don't think I'm the most vile thing in the world."

Kota smirked, full of mischief and seduction, a complicated mixture. In one swift motion, she kicked off her black stilettos before strutting over to me, her hips swaying precisely in her dress.

My lips remained glued together, not protesting as she slung one leg over me, followed by the other so that she was straddling me. I gulped, hoping she didn't catch it. My hands remained at my sides as if touching her any more than I technically already was would get me killed.

"Does it look like I think you're vile?" she hummed.

Time slowed for a second, my brain trying to catch up with what was happening. "You're only doing this to get a rise out of me."

Her eyes glowed, and when I finally recognized what was behind them— lust— I couldn't fucking believe it. It made no sense that one week ago she wanted to murder me and right now, she was straddling me, her bare ass threatening to fall onto my lap.

Was this what she had been thinking of on the way home?

"Am I?" she challenged. "Are you sure?"

Apparently, my brain didn't work right, because instead of thinking like a clear, rational human being and shifting her off me, my tongue darted out, moistening my bottom lip as I fell further into whatever trance she was putting me in. "Let's find out," I called her bluff. Slowly, I brought my hand onto her knee, and immediately, she shivered under my touch. My voice came out quiet and raspy. "Just tell me when to stop."

Gradually, my fingertips trailed upwards, and when I reached her thigh, I hesitated, looking for a sign from her to stop. But all I saw was the increase in her breathing, her chest rising and falling more rapidly.

The temperature in the room was becoming hotter, the air getting thicker. My fingers continued lingering, and right before I got to her pussy, Kota grabbed me by the back of the neck and pulled me to her, smashing her lips onto mine.

She kissed me like she was hungry, and as much as I wanted to pull away just to ask what the fuck was going on, I let her shut me up.

When minutes had passed and her moans grew louder, vibrating into my mouth, I hummed back, allowing my hands to explore her backside like all the ways I was thinking about earlier in the night.

She rolled her hips against me, riding along the rock in my pants.

There was an internal war happening within me, a battle between reason and instinct.

Fuck it.

Kota's arms tightened around my neck while my hands found their way underneath her, clutching onto her ass as I stood. Her lips left mine for a brief moment just to gasp for air and then they were on mine again.

Kicking my bedroom door shut, I set Kota carefully onto my bed. I was waiting for her to push me away any second, to laugh in my face and give me some shit about me falling for it or announcing that this was her ultimate prank.

But instead, she impatiently reached for my belt buckle.

Out of breath, I pulled away, attempting to swallow, but my mouth was so dry that I couldn't get anything down. "Are you sure we should..."

She shook her head swiftly against my mattress. "Just fuck me," she insisted, pulling me back onto her.

Alright then.

In minutes, all clothes were off. Without looking, I fished a condom out of my nightstand and slipped it on with one hand.

When I finally brought my thumb across her clit, I nearly gasped at how wet she was. I didn't think it was possible for someone that hated me to be this wet from my touch.

Wasting no time, I slid inside her, pleased to hear her breath hitch as I filled her completely. Her eyes were clamped shut, and I wasn't sure if it was because it felt good for her or if she just didn't want to see my fucking face.

"Look at me," I demanded in a low growl. "Now."

Brown eyes fluttering open, there was a weird tremble in my core when her irises locked on me.

Steadying myself with one hand, I brought my thumb up to my mouth and licked it before reaching down and tenderly rubbing her most sensitive spot.

Kota's desperate moans filled the room, and when I drilled into her harder and faster, she began breathlessly muttering, *"Crew."*

There was something oddly satisfying about making your enemy moan your name.

Small hands latching onto my biceps, she buried her head into the crook of my neck. I could feel her hot breath skating along my skin, sending goosebumps down my spine.

I watched Kota's teeth sink into her bottom lip, humming the sweetest sound as I sunk myself deeper into her. Feeling how her pussy tightened so fiercely around me and how her acrylic nails were digging shamelessly into my back, I almost forgot all about the games we'd been playing. How much we despised each other. How far we'd both gone to ruin the other's life.

Physical pleasure wasn't new to me, but there was an unusual, emotional fulfillment overtaking me that I'd never experienced before. I was on a power trip, and I wasn't going to stop until her moans had turned to screams.

Pulling myself onto my knees, I propped her legs on my shoulders and pounded into her so deeply that I could feel the end of her. I held onto both her legs tightly, right on her upper thighs to keep her in place.

Trembling and writhing beneath me, Kota looked like she was having a goddamn exorcism, and when my face started to hurt, I realized I'd been smiling like a fucking maniac.

I brought a hand to her throat, squeezing gingerly as she gasped for air, her hair fanning out perfectly along the white pillows around her.

She was still squirming, her legs shaking, sending a vibration through my shoulders. But I held her throat, keeping her head locked there so that she had no choice but to look at me, her enemy, as I fucked her.

Kota's mouth was hanging open, the smallest winces repeatedly rushing out. Seizing the opportunity, I loosened my grip on her neck and brushed a finger along her bottom lip before slipping it into her warm mouth.

I pushed my finger down her throat and carefully watched her reaction. There was a small knit between her brows, but she took it like a champ, sucking so good that I quickened my thrusts, working harder, faster, deeper.

Kota's bare chest popped up and down as her breathing accelerated, causing her tits to lightly bounce. Ripping my finger out of her mouth, I brought it right back to her clit, rubbing back and forth as fast as possible.

Arms flying above her head, she clutched onto the bottom of my headboard and let out the loudest, most satisfied cry I'd ever heard.

"Crew," her voice shook, eyes rolling to the back of her head.

I wasn't sure what the hell came over me that made me turn into a feral animal, but the next thing I knew, my dick was out, the condom was off, and I was sliding into her mouth.

Her hands gripped the bottom of the headboard and mine clutched the top, sending the whole bedframe ramming into the wall and sounding like firecrackers as I fucked her mouth.

And she fucking took it.

"God, Kota," I sighed. My words came out so raspy that I didn't even recognize my own voice. "You're taking it so fucking good."

Kota's mouth felt like a vacuum, and I made sure to be careful all while feeling out this insane frenzy I was in. My mind was swirling with pleasure, and when her tongue brushed along the side of my cock, I lost it, shooting come straight down her throat.

And she swallowed every fucking drop like it was water.

When I pulled out of her, I caught my breath, letting my legs settle from shaking and my brain come down from the mind-blowing high.

I'd never done anything like that with someone before. I wasn't sure what made me do it; it almost felt like an instinct.

Maybe that bold and rude mouth of hers just needed to be cleaned out.

I may have been done, but I wasn't done with her.

She laid there, her limbs like deadweight while her lungs struggled to catch up.

Adjusting myself, I scooted down until her pussy was in my face. Her skin was soft as my tongue chased along her knee to her inner thigh, leaving a trail of wetness in its wake.

With the slightest jump, I could tell she hadn't been expecting more, but the second her hands found their way into my hair, I dove straight for her clit, tongue darting out to brush it softly.

Her come tasted sweet like fruity candy, and I couldn't get enough of it. I planted a hand firmly around her waist, putting some pressure there as I licked and sucked until she eventually came again, right on the tip of my tongue.

When I finally collapsed beside her, both of us sweating and out of breath, it was silent.

And it stayed that way until we were both passed out.

Chapter Thirty-Five

Kota

I was extraordinarily warm as my eyes flickered open. They began closing slowly again before snapping back open with realization.

I was not in my own bed.

There was the lightest of snores coming from behind me, and although I already knew who it was, there was some thought, or *prayer*, deep in my mind that maybe I was somehow wrong.

Bit by bit, I turned, peeking over my shoulder.

Fuck.

Crew was fast asleep, his brown curls draped carefully over his forehead.

I sat up as slowly as possible, holding my breath as if breathing would cause him to wake up. Shifting out from underneath the covers, I grabbed my dress and underwear off the floor before scurrying out of Crew's room.

When I got to mine, the door crashed shut behind me, and I pushed my back against it, blowing out a breath in disbelief.

I hadn't been lying last night when I told Crew that I wasn't that drunk. Truly, I wasn't. I knew exactly what I was doing; I just didn't know why I did it. Based on the way Crew had been looking at me earlier in the night, and then how he stood up for me to Bobby, it all made him look desirable in the moment.

Crew was attractive. I'd always thought that. But his ego and lengthy hostility took that away. After last night, I probably fed that ego. I was probably the only girl on the planet that didn't jump his bones on sight, and now he could add me to the list of girls who had.

I threw my dirty clothes into the hamper and practically dove into the shower, attempting to scrub off all the memories from last night.

Not that it was bad. Because it sure as hell wasn't.

I'd never had a guy make me finish more than once until now, and even once was pushing it for most. No wonder why girls wanted a second round with Crew.

No way in fucking hell was I going to say that aloud though. Ever.

I was quietly cursing myself in the shower for finally allowing his charm to get to me. And even more so, I was quietly cursing *him* for making it so goddamn difficult to forget about what happened last night.

His hands applying pressure in all the right spots across my body, his tongue grazing along my inner thigh, his dick as he—

Stop, Kota, I demanded myself.

I could feel the insides of my thighs tingling just from the thought.

I swallowed a lump of annoyance. I needed to go back to bed for a few hours or something. At least that way, I wouldn't be fighting the urge to keep remembering it. Or worse, fighting the urge to touch myself to the thought of Crew.

After drying off, I headed straight to my bed, bundling up in my blankets. My eyes drew to a close, and the harder it became to clear my head, the more my body seemed to tense rather than relax.

It took a while, but eventually, I drifted back to sleep.

***

My nap was not productive at all.

Instead of dreaming about quite literally anything else, I dreamt of Crew.

I didn't remember the specifics of the dream. All I remembered was that he was there and that clothes were *not*.

Bridget and Lane were supposed to be coming back today, but neither of them would be home for a few more hours. To pass some time and distract myself, I grabbed the book I had sitting on my nightstand. But when I opened it to where I'd left off, the first thing my eyes landed on was a sex scene.

Not a good idea right now.

I tossed the book beside me in frustration, letting out a measly groan.

There was a light tap on my door, causing me to stare at it for a moment.

Was Bridget home already?

I wandered over, trying to look nonchalant as if I hadn't slept in our roommate's bed last night.

But when I opened the door, there Crew stood, nervously rubbing his hands together.

"Hey," he said.

I lifted my chin, focusing too hard on keeping my voice steady, even though all I was doing on the inside was screaming. "Hi."

His gaze flitted around; he looked lost. "Can we talk about last night?"

It took nearly three months of living here for the stone wall between us to crack and begin the process of crumbling. Now, it felt like the wall was repairing itself.

"Nope," I answered, trying not to let the uncertainty or awkwardness I was feeling shine through. "Nothing happened."

Crew's chin tipped towards his chest. I couldn't tell if the look in his eyes was relief or disappointment. "Nothing happened?"

"Nothing happened," I repeated.

His chin raised, and as it did, his brown eyes became a portal into his thoughts. It wasn't relief *or* disappointment he was feeling. It was bitterness, a small seed of resentment being dropped and planted at our feet.

"Alright," he gritted through his teeth reluctantly. "Nothing happened." With that, he turned and walked away, and honestly, I'd never felt more confused.

Shouldn't he feel relieved that he wouldn't have to worry about me telling Bridget, who would obviously tell Lane?

Unless he himself was planning on telling Lane...

I doubted it though. After all, Crew was the one that made the *No hooking up* rule.

It would just be easiest to forget about this whole thing, act like it never happened and go back to hating each other. And by the look on Crew's face as he had walked away from my door, I didn't think the hating each other part was going to be very hard to restore.

After two more hours filled with distractions, Bridget finally knocked on my door. "Hey," I said as I let her in.

"Hey," she smiled, "how was your moms?"

Oh, right. I hadn't even told Bridget that I didn't end up staying there. I opened my mouth to tell her that I was actually here for the weekend, but then thought better of it. Being at my mom's place was the perfect alibi.

"Good," I lied, a twinge of guilt tightening in my chest as I climbed back into bed. "How was home?"

"Good, nothing too exciting. It was Bianca's birthday last night, so of course she made my parents throw her a big sweet sixteen." B rolled her eyes.

"Sounds fun," I said sarcastically.

She sighed and shrugged. "It was alright. Nice to see my parents."

I gave a small, quiet nod in agreement, causing B's eyes to zero in on me in suspicion. "Everything okay? You're acting strange," she said.

"I'm fine," I fidgeted, propping myself up with my elbows on the bed. "How am I acting strange?"

"You've got that look on your face like you've done something you shouldn't have."

Oh, no. She's onto me. She knows.

B's hand found its way onto her hip, and she leaned into it, studying me like it would allow her to read my mind. "You texted Bobby, didn't you?"

Holding my breath, my mind reeled. *Yeah, sure. I texted Bobby. Let's go with that.*

I sighed as convincingly as possible, my head dropping. "Yeah."

B gave a light tsk with her tongue, shaking her head. "It was bound to happen." She raised a finger at me, a bright blue nail pointing in my direction. "As long as you don't give into his shit."

"No problem," I smiled at her as she left my room.

No problem at all.

Because the only problem that I currently had was the fact that I had sex with my roommate last night.

And why the hell did I kind of want to do it again?

Chapter Thirty-Six

Kota

I wasn't sure what Crew was trying to accomplish by walking around shirtless every chance he got.

I would though, be lying if I said it didn't have any effect on me.

Before our rueful hookup, seeing him shirtless didn't bother me in the slightest. Had I always thought he was attractive? Especially shirtless? Well, yeah. But after actually having the bare skin of his chest rubbing against me and running my hand over the prominent ridges on his stomach, the view was a bit more arousing than it used to be.

For the first two or so days after we hooked up, I could tell he was mad at me. Why, I still wasn't sure. He practically went back to ignoring me like he used to. Leaving the room whenever I walked into it. Refusing to look at me. Pretty much taking my request a bit more literally than I'd meant for him to. We were right back to square one.

After those first few days passed of him ignoring me, he began acting similarly to how he had been right before we hooked up. Being civil. Not acting like my presence was a curse. Sometimes even making conversation.

Finals were right around the corner, and I had a neurobiology study guide to finish. After my classes, I went home and took a power nap. Then, I moved my school stuff

200

into the kitchen because I kept getting distracted in my own room. I could've gone to the library or Starbucks, and honestly, I probably would've been more productive there, but I was rocking my panda bear pajama pants and a soft long sleeve, and I was far too comfortable to change to go out in public.

The first page of the study guide was a piece of cake, being mostly definitions and true or false questions. The last two pages were all short essay questions, which I hated most. I thought about saying screw it and turning it in how it was, considering it was for extra credit, but I needed the points to cushion my grade.

I'd been able to maintain a high B throughout the semester, but this final would probably be one of the hardest I'd ever have to take, so I wasn't trying to play it risky.

Although this would be my hardest final, the others wouldn't be far behind in terms of difficulty. Aside from a final in neurobiology, I also had biology of sensory systems, bioethics, pathology, and developmental genetics.

In other words— not a good time.

Sometimes I regretted choosing my major, and wondered how much easier my student life would've been had I done something less demanding or confusing like business or journalism.

Then, I would've been able to have a job during the school year. Instead, I spent numerous hours six out of seven days a week doing schoolwork, and spending almost every waking second over the summer working, just to save enough money to not have to work during the semester.

I was trying to divide my time this week between each of my classes to ensure I was prepared for all of them.

It was becoming harder to do that though when I kept getting distracted.

For what seemed to be the hundredth time since I sat down at the kitchen island today, Crew strolled in whistling. Of course, with no shirt on. But this time, he wasn't wearing pants either. Only boxers.

Each time he'd come in earlier, he seemed to do something quickly and leave. Grabbing a cup of water. Making a protein shake. Bringing his dishes back and putting them in the dishwasher.

But this time, he headed straight to the fridge, and when he started pulling out ingredients for scrambled eggs and toast, I knew I might've been fucked.

Because it meant he'd be here for a while.

He cracked a breathtaking smile at me, pretending like what was happening was normal. "Hey."

I kept my eyes down. "Hey."

"Studying?"

"Yep."

The last time I saw Crew wandering around the apartment in just boxers was shortly after we moved in and I walked in on him and that girl.

I hated him then.

I hated him now.

But I think this time, he'd somehow managed to land himself higher up on my hitlist.

When he had his back turned towards me, the weaker side of me gave in and I peeked.

It seemed like every square inch of his body was just pure muscle, and every time he shifted, making even the slightest of movements, some muscle on his body seemed to flex. Not to mention how phenomenal his ass was. Having him as my roommate was like dangling a treat in front of a dog.

I was relieved that lust wasn't tangible, because if it was, he'd be able to see mine growing by the second.

The reason within me was trying to remind me that I was drooling over *Crew*. And even though we'd hooked up, we still weren't friends.

Yet at the same time, the human part of me, AKA my biological instincts, were telling me to go tackle him and take him right here in the kitchen.

Flashbacks of the night in question raced through my mind, glimpses and noises all coming back to me.

The deep, sexy moans rolling out of his muscular chest as he buried himself inside me, barely fitting. My lips buzzing as he slowly ran his tongue over them. The shivers left in his hand's wake as they slid all over my body. The satisfied cries leaving my overwhelmed, breathless lungs.

Maybe the lust swimming through me *was* tangible. Because I wasn't sure what look was on my face as he turned back around, but whatever it was, it was enough for him to give a criminal smirk.

He was playing a game.

And for the first time, I wasn't trying to play.

The look in his eyes was mischievous, but somehow serious all the same.

My head dropped back down to my work. I could feel all the blood in my body rushing to my face. I hated that I'd been caught.

Either way, it was too late. I'd seen too much of him to calm my body down with just self-talk.

There was a throbbing, aching feeling low in my core, a tingling between my thighs. I could feel my body temperature spiking upwards, too stimulated by the thoughts.

With a huff, I scrambled to gather all my schoolwork, not wasting time to shove it into my bag before speed-walking away.

I could practically hear his satisfied smile. "Bye, I guess."

I threw a middle finger over my shoulder before disappearing down the hall.

The next twenty minutes were spent relieving my body, and unfortunately, I hated to admit it, but Crew's face was in my mind the whole time.

After that, I threw on actual clothes, grabbed my schoolwork, and headed to fucking Starbucks.

Chapter Thirty-Seven

Crew

I'd never hooked up with a girl who ended up regretting it.

Until now.

Did I ever think prior to that night that I'd end up hooking up with Kota? Absolutely the fuck not.

She caught me off guard with making a move and I caught myself off guard even more by letting her.

But was it some of the best sex I'd ever had? Yep.

I wasn't sure why that was. I assumed it was because there was so much fucking tension between us that it all just came out physically, creating one hell of a night.

There was no way it would be that good a second time around though, right?

I wanted to find out.

Ever since it happened, I'd been having weird fucking fantasies every day and it was driving me nuts.

Whenever Kota was casually on the couch, wearing quite literally *anything*, including her pajamas that made her look like a grown toddler, I envisioned ripping them off and taking her on the couch.

Whenever I walked through the door, I imagined she'd be waiting for me, ready to drag me into one of our rooms.

Whenever she had her hair in a ponytail, I thought about yanking it backwards and bringing my lips to the exposed skin on her neck.

Whenever I could hear her humming a song in the shower, I pictured walking in and joining her.

It was becoming too much.

I didn't know what I was expecting when I knocked on her door the next morning, but I wasn't expecting her to be so... *regretful.*

I could read it in her demeanor, see it all over her face. She may have made the first move, but she wished she hadn't.

The entire time she'd known me, she'd been trying to demolish my ego.

And now, she finally had.

At first, I was self-conscious, thinking it was my performance or something, but after replaying that night over and over in my head, remembering how she was shuddering beneath me and practically screaming, I decided that couldn't be it.

Now, I had no doubt that it wasn't the sex she was regretting. She just regretted that it was with me.

And that made me want her more.

I'd never been in a situation where I wanted someone that I couldn't have. And in this case, it was for more than one reason.

If I couldn't have her now, then I needed to make her want me.

And what better way to do that than with some teasing?

She'd been all over my upper body that night, clawing at my chest desperately, digging her nails into my back, clutching onto my arms like it was the edge of a cliff she was about to fall off.

So, I started walking around shirtless a little more often.

She seemed to get bothered every time I did, but she hadn't made any snarky *or* sexual comments. She hadn't made a move either, hadn't let that stone wall of hers break down. I'd always known she was stubborn, but I was more than ever determined to make her crack.

Ever since I caught her eye-fucking me in my boxers the other day while she was studying in the kitchen, she'd been doing her best to dodge me— practically running at the sight of me with a vibrant pool of red in her cheeks.

Which meant I was getting to her.

Like the many showers I'd taken over the past few days, I spent my time under the water envisioning Kota in there with me while we did R-rated things to each other.

When I got out, I tied a towel around my waist, my wet hair steadily dripping. The second I opened the door and stepped out, I was greeted with a bump in the shoulder.

Kota took a step back. Her initial reaction looked sheepish but as she swallowed, that wall of hers came up, and the ice in her eyes that I knew all too well appeared.

"What are you doing down our hall?" I asked.

"I had to ask Lane something."

"Lane's not here."

"Oh," she replied.

I raised a brow at her, waiting for her to run off, but she stood her ground.

"You know," she said scornfully, "if you're gonna walk around in a towel or boxers, you might as well just walk around naked."

"Okay," I shrugged, letting the towel fall to the floor.
Nothing she hasn't seen before.

Kota let out a screech, her hand flying over her eyes. Turning, she finally ran away like I'd expected her to in the first place.

A dry smile sat comfortably on my face. "Sorry!" I called after her, unapologetically. Picking up the towel off the floor, I walked into my room, feeling foolishly content.

Chapter Thirty-Eight

Crew

I was sure Kota was relieved that Lane and I were gone for the weekend for an away game.

We were playing Denver, and although Coach wasn't as hard on us this week as he was when we played St. Cloud, he was still pretty damn harsh.

I was almost completely sure every guy had been called out at some point this week besides Lane, who Coach considered to be a saint. In Lane's defense, it was very, *very* rare that he fucked up on the ice, whether that be in practice or during a game.

We were rocking an almost perfect season so far, with one loss to Minnesota Duluth, which pretty much got washed when we beat them in the second game of the weekend series.

Lane seemed to be more on edge than Coach was, although I wasn't sure why. I had a feeling it was because he finally decided to go pro after this year, even though he should've done it years ago.

The entire team knew his decision now, and although everyone was extremely happy for him, it seemed like everyone was also a little bummed that we would both be leaving. No one wanted to lose their captain, and everyone understood why they were going to, but Lane was so talented that I think everyone was afraid of what the team would become without him.

Although he was young and still had a lot to learn, Keith would take my place as right-wing starter.

We still weren't sure who would replace Lane, but everyone assumed it would be Jonah. Lane was next to impossible to replace though. And now, Lane felt this overwhelming pressure to make it Cedar's best season ever.

My stick was already taped and resting on the rack in the corner. I had my headphones in, stretching in the locker room before we hit the ice for our actual warm up. Every few minutes, I glanced over at the rack, checking on my stick.

A lot of the guys had superstitions when it came to game days. Mine was that no one could touch my stick before a game besides me.

Everyone knew better than to break my superstition. They all stayed away from my stick game after game, but for some reason, I still felt the need to check on it.

There was one specific game back in high school that started this frantic ritual.

It was the state championship game, and my teammate, Brody, moved my stick over to grab his. At that point in time, with my stats, I averaged 1.34 goals per game. I'd been able to sink at least one goal per game ever since I was in middle school, but during this game in particular, I couldn't sink a single one. I couldn't even get an assist either. I played sloppy all night, and during the last minute of the game, after we had busted our balls all of third period trying to tie it up, my stick broke. And the loss of a player on the ice, even for that short amount of time, was enough to allow our opponents to score at the last minute. We lost the state championship.

Rationally speaking, there'd probably been a time before that where someone touched my stick before a game, but it was that one game alone that haunted me. On that night, the superstition was born.

I was getting into my headspace, focusing and dialing in to the game we were about to play, and the rest of the guys were doing the same. The locker room was always loud and rowdy at first, but once we got closer and closer to actual warmup, the volume always died down, because everyone was starting to focus.

We were currently ranked third in the country, the other two teams above us being teams we hadn't played yet—Quinnipiac and University of Michigan.

Denver was currently ranked fifth, and they had a star captain of their own that we had to look out for.

It was anyone's game.

Warmup flew by, and after Coach Palmer announced the lineup, everyone continued moving to make sure we stayed warm.

With three minutes before we hit the ice, Lane stepped forward, his silent cue that he was about to give a few words. As usual, a few of the guys sat on the bench, while others took a knee and some remained standing towards the back of the room.

There was never a time where anyone looked at or spoke to Lane with less than respect, but these were one of the many moments that we looked at him with the utmost respect possible.

Lane was the calmest person that I knew outside of the rink, but when it came moments like these, all bets were off. To outsiders, he'd sound a little overdramatic, but to us, his speeches were what we needed to light a fire under our asses. We couldn't help but get pulled in by his essence.

Standing with his helmet resting on his hip, Lane let out a long breath before beginning to slowly walk side to side, head down as he spoke. "Third," he announced. "Third in the nation, and we're halfway through the season. Our schedule isn't getting easier, but we are getting better." With a pause, he looked up. "Denver's good, and I have a feeling this won't be an easy game, but we have sixty minutes to go out there and beat them on their own turf. Every drop of sweat, every sore muscle, every hit, every goal, *every single thing...* from this past week and this season so far has led us to this upcoming sixty minutes. It all comes down to the current sixty." His eyes scanned over every face in the room, hovering over mine for a second longer than everyone else. "Got it?"

"Got it, Captain!"

He flaunted a proud smile. "Good," he said. "Now let's win this fucking game."

                                    ***

     We absolutely dominated in the first period, making
the score 2-0 right off the bat. The first goal was scored by Lane
and the second was scored by Jett, with an assist from Lane. Go
figure.
     I wasn't sure where our energy or our heads were at in
the second period, because we fell flat, allowing Denver to
catch up and tie it.
     Lane wasn't happy at the end of the second. He'd
practically set up shot after shot for each of us and we missed
every one.
     But him being him, he didn't say anything. He just
choked down his frustration and put his game face back on.
     Coach barely said anything either, quickly pointing out
our biggest mistakes before letting us be. He knew what kind of
players we were. We didn't need to be screamed at in order to
play harder, better.
     The locker room was quiet, even quieter than it had
been before the game started. Everyone was focused, staying
warm, talking themselves through what needed to be done
during this next period.
     And when we got back out on the ice, the focus didn't
cease in the slightest.
     Repeatedly, Lane was getting double teamed,
sometimes even triple teamed, stuck against the boards in the
corner of the arena with the puck as Denver tried their best to
contain him.
     Even though there were a few times where they
succeeded in snatching the puck from him, most of the time,
Lane was able to fight his way out and send the puck off to Jett
or me immediately to keep the red jersey pricks at bay.
     There was a scoring drought for the first sixteen
minutes of the last period. After a lot of close goals but no
sound of the buzzer, I could tell we were losing it a bit. Our
stamina was wearing thin, and every time I collapsed on the
bench between line changes, I found myself not itching to be
back on the ice. I would've been perfectly fine taking a nap on

210

the sidelines. I wasn't sure if it was from playing on level ten for the first forty, or if it was the monstrous hits I took, but either way, I was feeling the exhaustion seeping into my bones.

I refused to show it though.

Squeezing my water bottle, a stream of water shot through my cage and into my mouth. The arena was freezing, and my water was ice cold, but I currently felt like a furnace sitting on full blast in the middle of the Sahara Desert, so the frigid water seemed like the best thing to ever happen to me.

Heaving, I dropped my head back, hoping I didn't miss anything important in the game.

When I straightened, I saw my line hopping onto the ice one by one. Letting out a small groan, I followed, determined to end this game now.

No fucking way did I want to head into OT.

We had four minutes left to clinch the win.

Denver's captain, Hodges, had been hogging the puck all night, so it wasn't difficult to pinpoint where the puck would be when it was in Denver's control.

That was another thing that made Lane an incredible captain— he was selfless.

As long as the puck went into the goal, he didn't give a fuck whose stick was shooting it in.

I kept my eye on the puck, using my peripherals to gauge my surroundings. Charging full force, I rammed into Hodges with a clean hit, knocking him off track with just enough time to seize the puck for a steal.

A sea of silver jerseys flocked to the opposite side of the ice when they realized the puck was currently mine. Finding Jett as he zigzagged through a trio of raging red players, I passed him the puck and he flew off, setting up shop on the left.

It was a play that Lane, Jett, and I had done dozens of times, both during practices and during games.

Lane positioned himself in the center with me on the right, and Jett wasted no time sending the puck to Lane who sent it to me.

The second it touched my stick, it was gone again, sailing over to Jett. I didn't even have time to blink before the puck was in Lane's possession for half a second, hurdling through red skates and sticks to make itself home in the net.

The buzzer screeched, and our whole line met Lane on center ice for a group hug.

With two minutes left in the game, half of it was on the bench and the other half was on the ice, holding off Denver to add another win to our belt for the season.

Chapter Thirty-Nine

Crew

I was hating my life. Every fucking second of it.

I'd been hesitant to leave home and go out with the group on New Year's Eve, but I hadn't spent a New Year's without Lane since we met, and I didn't want to start now.

Kota was strutting around Stallion's in a tight red dress, her dark hair resting in light curls past her shoulders. It was like trying not to stare at a shiny diamond in a pile of rocks.

I felt like I was putting on a show. To everyone else, I thought she was the enemy, and trust me, she still kind of was, but most people didn't want to bang their enemy.

And even less people already had.

I figured maybe if I drank more, it would be easier to ignore her— and her nice ass fucking legs. But the more I drank, the more I seemed to zone in on her.

I knew I'd been subtly trying to seduce her, but right now, it seemed like the tables were turning.

Even though it was winter break, tons of people came back to spend their New Year's Eve at Cedar. Stallions was busy, and usually, my eyes would be wandering around the bar, checking out every pretty girl.

But tonight, I seemingly only had eyes for one.

It was infuriating that Kota looked *that fucking good*. It was almost unfair. I couldn't stop staring at her, yet I couldn't have her either.

"Here, man," TJ said, appearing next to me with a shot.

Unlike the one I took earlier from Jett, I didn't bother asking what it was before shooting it back. "Thanks," I muttered, handing the empty glass back. He set it on the table beside him, along with the countless other empty glasses that had been piled onto it throughout the night.

"So, uh," TJ started, causing me to stiffen from whatever dumb shit he was about to say, "hear me out."

"What?"

"I know you hate her, but... she's hot," he said, his eyes flicking over Kota. "Do you mind if I get with her?" My jaw tightened, and I refused to look at him. I was growing so agitated from this entire night that it felt like smoke was starting to radiate off me. TJ spoke again, "Judging by the look on your face, I'm assuming you don't like that idea."

I couldn't tell what was bothering me more. The fact that he was asking, or the fact that I didn't have the right to be mad at him for it.

"No," I finally replied. "I don't. At all."

TJ nodded. "Noted."

"Trust me," I said, "you don't wanna try anyway. I can almost guarantee she'd laugh in your face and then bite your head off."

TJ raised a brow, his smirk growing playful. I still wasn't looking at him, but I could feel his eyes on me, and I hoped he didn't see right through me.

"You sound like you speak from experience," he said.

The lie came out easier than breathing. "No, I haven't tried with her, if that's what you're assuming."

He shrugged, accepting my answer. "Wouldn't blame ya if ya did."

Just knowing that my friends were eyeing her made me want her even more. I was losing my patience with the whole subtly thing. And every time I glanced at her, my patience weakened more and more, thinning like ice.

The type of ice you fell straight through.

Jett appeared. "Are you coming over after this?"

"Probably."

"Cool," he said before tapping TJ. "You wanna head back soon and get things ready before people show up?"

TJ nodded with his beer to his mouth, downing the rest of it before setting it on the table. He wiped his mouth with the back of his hand. "I'm gonna go talk to Lane and make sure he's coming."

He was gone before anyone could respond, and I watched as he questioned Lane to ensure he'd be attending the party. When Lane glanced at me, I gave him a quick nod.

TJ and Jett disappeared through the crowd of people and I wandered back to where Cody and Matt were in the middle of a useless argument.

"What now?" I asked.

Cody turned to me, his eyes ablaze. "Matt doesn't believe in the Lochness Monster."

"Are you fucking kidding me?" I mumbled to myself, rolling my eyes. I swore these two fought over the dumbest shit. Half the time, I wasn't even sure how these topics came up in a conversation in the first place.

"Well, you don't believe in Bigfoot," Matt shot back.

"That's because there's no actual evidence that Bigfoot exists," Cody snapped.

"Same goes for the Lochness Monster then."

Cody shook his head rapidly. "Hell no. Do you have any idea how big that lake is? It could easily be hiding in the water."

With my buzz, it was hard to gauge how hammered they both actually were, but for their sakes, I hoped they were fucking obliterated. Any level of sobriety in this argument would've been embarrassing.

"Lake?" Matt practically yelled, slamming his beer on the nearby table. "It's not even in the ocean? It's totally fake then. How the hell would no one have found it by now if it's just in a fucking lake?"

"It's a big lake!"

I was getting the feeling that this fight had already been going on for quite some time.

I butted in. "They're both fake. Now both of you, shut up. Let's go."

Both of their heads turned to me with record speed, eyeing me in disbelief.

"What?" Cody said.

"Let's. Go," I said sharply, leaning forward. But unlike when I got in Bobby's face, my teammates weren't quite as intimidated.

Matt raised a brow at me, his eyes slightly narrowed. "You don't believe in either of them? What about aliens?"

"The Chupacabra?" Cody added, arms crossed.

Shaking his head, Matt turned back to Cody. "What the *fuck* is the Chupacabra?"

"Oh my God," I muttered, seemingly to myself. I ran a hand over my face. "Are you guys coming to the house right now or not?"

"Not now!" they both shouted at me.

"Jesus," I said, turning on my heels.

Lane nodded at me as if he'd been looking for me. "Hey," he casually tapped me on the shoulder. "Bridget and I are gonna stop at our place before the party. You got her?" he asked, motioning towards Kota.

I stole another glimpse of her, the same way I had been all night. This time, she was standing beside Cody and Matt with her hands on her hips. I couldn't tell if she was part of the argument at this point or if she was just listening for entertainment.

"Yeah," I sighed. "I got her."

"See you at the house," Lane said, guiding Bridget out of the bar.

Part of me hoped that Kota didn't want to stop at home before we went to the hockey house. I wasn't sure if it was because I didn't feel like making the pit-stop, or if I was just simply afraid to be alone with her.

Let's be real though. It was definitely the latter.

It was ironic how I'd been eyeing her all night, secretly wishing we were alone, and now, I was scared to be alone with her. But I told Lane I had her, so I needed to suck it up and do what I promised.

Warily, I made my way over, and without acknowledging Cody or Matt, who were both still very invested in their debate, I lightly gripped onto Kota's elbow to make my presence known.

She nearly jumped, but seemed to relax *slightly* when she saw me.

"Are you ready to go?" I asked.

Her eyes darted past me, skimming across the bar. "Where are Lane and Bridget?"

"They left. They wanted to stop at our place before going to the house."

"Oh," she said, sighing. "Alright, yeah. Let's go then. I need to stop at home too though."

Fuck.

I knew it was inevitable that I was about to do something fucking dumb.

Chapter Forty

Kota

Note to self: never drink rumple minze around Crew ever again.

When Jett handed me the shot earlier, I thought it would be a good idea. Wasn't sure why.

I hadn't drank rumple minze since high school, when my friend and I finished the last half of her parent's bottle while they were out of town.

Within twenty minutes of downing it, we were forced to split up because we couldn't fit both of our heads in the same toilet. She took the upstairs bathroom and I took the downstairs one.

I wasn't currently feeling sick or anything, but I did indeed forget how strong that shit was. The one-hundred proof liquor that was circling through my veins was heightening my arousal every time I looked at Crew, and I was making a conscious effort to stand a solid three feet away from him on our walk home.

For the most part, we were both quiet on the walk, and I let Crew lead the way through the apartment complex parking lot.

As we were passing his car, he stopped mid-step, causing me to nearly run into him. When he turned, I immediately spotted the gleaming need in his eyes, lit by a single streetlamp nearby.

The longer he looked at me, the longer I knew the look in my eyes mirrored his.

And suddenly, everything, including logic, was wiped from my mind.

Crew's voice was a mixture of a demand and a plea. "Kota."

"Yes?" I said quietly.

His eyes scanned the length of me, and I was glad it was dark, because it felt like my skin was getting lit on fire, and I didn't want him to catch the flush.

It was cold out, freezing honestly, but between the liquor in my system and the heat that Crew's gaze was igniting all over my body, I couldn't feel a morsel of the cold air.

Crew stiffened, his spine straightening. He stepped closer, and there was the lightest breeze that blew by, sending his cologne wafting towards me.

Sandalwood.

His voice came out scratchy. "Say the word and I won't touch you." His eyes dropped to my lower half, his thumb and forefinger lightly pinching the hem of my red dress. "But I want to rip this dress off," he admitted. "Immediately."

Gosh fucking dammit.

It was hard not to get turned on when he said shit like *that.*

I hated repeating mistakes, but it felt like this one was bound to happen.

My greed came out as sass. "Here in the parking lot?" I questioned, but I didn't doubt he caught the breathy note in it.

His head snapped towards our apartment building, and I assumed he probably had the same thought as me.

It was too risky.

Crew planted a hand on my hip, giving it a light squeeze as he used his other hand to fish his keys out of his pocket.

His car gave a light beep when he hit the button on his key fob, and as if he'd done this hundreds of times before, he had the backseat down in seconds.

A hot shiver rolled through me as he helped guide me inside his car.

For a moment I considered stopping this. From talking myself *and my body* out of it. But I didn't have that kind of time. Or the motivation to do so.

Crew hit the button on the car door, and just like that, I was locked in. I scooted backwards to allow him some space, before leaning back on my elbows.

It didn't seem like he'd been having the same second thoughts as I had just moments prior, or if he did, he didn't seem to show it.

Because there was no hesitation as his mouth settled on mine and his hand snaked underneath my dress. His fingers found their way into the space between my panties and my clit, and I could feel him smile against my mouth in appreciation of how wet I already was.

Thumb hooking atop my panties, Crew gradually pulled them down, exposing me. He flicked them away, and they disappeared into the darkness of the car.

Keeping the promise about my dress, his mouth left mine, and he pulled away just enough to grab the bottom hem of the red fabric with both hands and yank it over my head.

In the blink of an eye, I was entirely bare, waiting and wanting the same way I'd been daydreaming about for weeks now.

After Crew slipped out of his own clothes, his large hand gripped my thigh, big enough to practically wrap all the way around me. He seemingly pulled a condom out of thin air; I had no idea where it came from, but I didn't care enough to ask. I was too eager to feel him.

Fingertips digging into my skin, Crew calmly guided my legs open.

I was already wet enough for him to effortlessly slide inside me, a sigh escaping my lips as he filled me. After weeks of thinking about our last hookup, it felt like more than just pleasure right now— it was also relief, greed, and lust rolled into one.

By no means was the car big, but we managed, Crew rocking *into* me as if we had all the room in the world.

A deep, dark groan saturated the air, sounding like music to my ears. I wasn't sure why it was so satisfying to hear Crew moan while he was inside me. Given our track record, I should've hopped out of the car and hurled, but instead, the harmony punctured my core, turning me on more.

I could smell the liquor on his breath, and I wondered if he'd only made a move as a result of it, similarly to when I did.

But as quickly as all the thoughts were coming, they managed to vanish even quicker. With how good he felt, there wasn't much room left in my brain to be thinking about anything else.

Crew's mouth found mine in the darkness, kissing me hard, giving me the chance to taste the leftover rumple minze that tainted his lips.

His teeth latched lightly onto my lower lip and pulled, not too hard, not too soft. It was just enough pressure to make me moan against him. In return, his hot breath fanned across my face, and he drilled into me harder.

When his thrusts tilted to a different angle, I bit my lip, trying to hold back from yelping, but the sounds still managed to slip through.

Suddenly, Crew paused inside me, and instinctively, I let out a whimper in protest. He didn't resume, and just as I was about to let out a loud cry, Crew's hand shot up over my mouth as if he knew it was coming.

"Shh," he hushed.

Our eyes locked, and the silence made it all the more sensual.

It wasn't until I heard Lane and Bridget's voices passing by the car did I realize why he'd stopped.

Once they were out of earshot, he began pumping into me again, starting at a slow pace and gradually quickening like a car accelerating.

The windows were fogged, the air thick and humid like desert air. I was practically panting, my heart hammering dangerously against my ribcage.

As his hand found its way back to my vulnerable area and began rubbing tenderly, a desperate moan escaped my lips and echoed throughout the car.

My insides were tightening, and by the groan he let out, I could tell he felt it as well.

When his mouth grazed past my ear, my white-tipped nails dug into his back. "Come," he demanded.

His voice penetrated through me and as if on cue, my entire body shuddered beneath his and I rode the high until every muscle within me relaxed.

"Mmm," I hummed, closing my eyes.

He didn't seem like he was close to being done though. His tempo hardly slowed, and he started thrusting deeper. At this point, *my* lungs were on fire; I was impressed that he was still going.

Perks of being an athlete, I guess.

With how wet I'd become, he felt even better. Pinching my nipple, he rubbed it between his fingers, sending a jolt throughout my body.

Every time I closed my eyes, I could've sworn I could hear a growl rippling out of his throat, demanding for me to open them.

I wasn't going to lie— he was the greatest fucking sight right now.

Sweat dripping off his body. Brown eyes on fire. Focus and hunger creasing his features as he fucked me with all the hatred in the world.

Naturally, I wanted to look at him. Of course, I did.

But I didn't want him to know how much he had me held in the palm of his hand right now while he was buried deep inside me.

"I'm..." I reluctantly let out, eyes threatening to roll back again.

"Finish," Crew snarled. "Be fucking good and finish twice for me."

As if he just hit an on button, my body released, hands latching onto Crew's biceps like he was my lifeline. If anyone was anywhere near the car, they most definitely heard my shrieks as I soaked in the moment of pleasure, feeling it roll through my whole body.

With a grunt, Crew's body twitched inside me, his head tipping towards the ceiling of the car. "Fuck," he muttered, giving a few slow rocks as he came.

222

Crew collapsed beside me, and I could feel the thin layer of his sweat glide across my arm.

Heavy breathing filled the car, along with the scent of sex and sandalwood.

We both stared at the ceiling, allowing our bodies to come down from the mind-blowing high.

Once our panting slowed, a long, awkward moment of silence treaded between us.

"I still hate you," I finally said.

"That's fine," he responded, looking at the ceiling. "I still hate you too."

Chapter Forty-One

Crew

It was hard to continuously hide a boner from your roommates, especially when one of your roommates was the *reason* for the boner.

Sometimes it was when she was walking around in a sports bra and shorts. Other times, it was just literally on sight.

It was like she had some weird control over my fucking dick or something. As if she had a voodoo doll of me and was making it do naughty things.

It had only been a few days since New Year's Eve, but it felt like it had been way too long. I was like a drug addict, needing my next fix.

But this time, I wasn't going to make the move. If she initiated something, I'd happily oblige, but until she did, I would suffer with my boners in silence.

The girls were going on some trip to Chicago with Kota's mom and would be gone for the next few days, which meant I was both cursed and in the clear.

There had never been a single person in the world that made me more infuriated than Dakota Darling did. So, tell me why it was becoming harder to stop thinking about her?

Believe it or not, I'd never had sex in my car before the other night, and goddamn was it hot.

224

There was also something about sneaking around that made this game all the more fun.

As far as I knew, Lane and Bridget were absolutely clueless. To them, Kota and I were the last people that they'd envision hooking up together.

They didn't even seem suspicious when we showed up late to the New Year's party.

Since Lane and I had the place to ourselves for a few days with no hockey because we were still on break, we decided to take the day to plan out our annual snowboarding and skiing trip.

We'd gone to Colorado for a weekend every year for the past five years. At this point, it was tradition. I always called it our "bromance trip," which Lane would always respond to by telling me to shut the fuck up.

"Alright," he said with his computer open on his lap. "When are we thinking?"

"We always go right after the season ends."

"Okay, yes," he said sharply like that part was obvious, "but if we're both going to be leaving shortly after the season ends..."

"We'll have a week or two."

He sighed, typing dates in. "Alright. *Where* are we thinking?"

I eyed him like *What?* "Oh, I don't know," I said sarcastically. "Maybe the same place we've gone to for the past five years straight?"

Lane's hands tensed over the keyboard. "I don't appreciate the sarcasm."

A shadow of a playful smirk danced across my lips. "Then stop asking dumb questions."

He let out a small huff before becoming silent, and I wasn't sure if it was the silence or the sexual frustration inside me that caused my thoughts to linger.

I replayed some of my favorite moments from the other night with Kota, the details stamped into my brain like cattle getting branded.

Her skin was so soft, especially her legs. I was fucking obsessed with her legs. Under me. Over me. Next to me. Walking away from me after the fact.

The way it felt being inside of her too—*fuck.*

Not to mention the only times I ever saw her perfect poker face unravel were when I was touching her. I think that was the most exhilarating part of it all. She was usually so deadly that it was intoxicating to turn her from deadly to delicate with just my fingertips.

"Ew, man!" Lane screeched, tossing a pillow at me. "Gross! Put that thing away!"

"Hmm?" I snapped out of it, glancing down at my lap.

Boner central.

Ah, geez.

I grabbed the pillow and covered myself.

"What the fuck is wrong with you!" Lane howled.

"Sorry... I was just... thinking..."

"Thinking about what?" he shrieked. "You're sitting next to *me*!"

Too embarrassed to look him in the eye, I stood. "I'm gonna, um, go take care of this." I scurried off to my bedroom and took care of the issue as quickly as possible. When I walked back out to the bedroom, I'd never seen Lane look so appalled in his life.

"You're disgusting," he said.

"Sorry," I muttered awkwardly.

He sighed, changing the subject, probably trying to forget about the trauma I just caused him. "I'm a little worried."

"Why?"

"Because if we take this trip right after the season ends, we might be cutting it close."

I blew a heavy breath out my nose, collapsing on the couch. Leave it to Lane to overthink every detail.

"Too bad we can't just go during break," I murmured.

Lane peered over at me, looking like those gears in his head were turning at a hasty pace.

"What?" I asked.

Ignoring me, all his focus went back to his laptop. I rolled my eyes, resting my feet on the coffee table as I checked my phone.

A few girls had texted, asking me to hangout, but just like I'd been doing the past few days, I ignored every one.

There was only one person I was currently interested in fucking.

Speaking of which, I somehow ended up on her contact, staring at it like she was about to text me something any second, even though the last message I received from her was over a month ago and it was just a middle finger emoji.

So unfortunately, I knew that she wasn't about to text a single word or an emoji for that matter. She'd expressed her indefinite hatred for me, and I definitely still didn't like her either, but the fact that I was kind of wanting her attention was starting to drive me up a wall.

Lane placed his laptop beside him and stood. "Alright."

"What?"

"Pack your bags," he said. As my brows scrunched, the corner of his mouth soared upwards. "We leave in the morning."

Chapter Forty-Two

Crew

When Lane woke me up at seven in the goddamn morning, I nearly lost my shit. He didn't mention last night that he booked an early flight for us.

I mean, most people probably wouldn't consider nine-thirty to be an early flight, but I'd been waking up at nine all break, so I'd be lying if I said I wasn't a crab-ass on the way to the airport. And while going through security. And while getting on the plane. And during the first half of the plane ride.

But, by the second half of the plane ride, I'd fallen asleep, and when I woke up from my nap during landing, I felt way better.

In previous years, Lane and I had shared a hotel room, but last year, I brought a girl home one night, and Lane wasn't very pleased with having to wait in the lobby for nearly two hours for the girl to leave.

So, this year, we rented an Airbnb with two bedrooms.

Once we got checked in and situated, we didn't waste any time hitting the slopes for a few hours, and by the time early evening rolled around, we were starved.

There was a bar and grill in the downtown area that we always wound up at at some point during our trip each year. We'd been coming here for so long that it still felt weird being in the bar legally, given we spent the first three trips using fake IDs to buy drinks.

Neither of us needed more than two minutes to look at the menu, already set on our typical, annual order.

"So," I smirked at Lane.

"So?"

"Have you looked into any teams yet?"

Lane sat back in his chair, extending his feet straight until they bumped into mine. He rubbed his lips together, his focus drifting past me as if uninterested in the conversation.

"A few."

"Do any of them happen to be close to Lake Michigan?" I asked, leaning forward with anticipation. "Just out of curiosity."

His body stayed perfectly still, his eyes being the only thing to move like a creepy painting whose gaze followed you as you walked away.

Glaring back at me, he responded, "I've looked into the Blackhawks, yes."

I pushed away from the table, leaning back in my chair to match Lane. "Yeah? What're you thinking?"

"I'm thinking," he said, shifting his silverware around, "that I don't feel like talking about this right now."

My lips thinned, enclosing the thwarted huff that was stuck in my throat. It had taken so much to push Lane towards the decision of going pro, and when he finally shared his choice with me, he seemed excited about it. He even had a private meeting with our coach to share the news. But getting him to talk about the topic was still a challenge, yet I wasn't sure why.

"Alright," I grumbled with a tight jaw.

Our smiling waitress came back with two beers. "Here are those drinks for you guys."

"Thanks," we said in unison.

Instinctively, my eyes landed on her ass as she walked away. There seemed to be a small jolt within me, turning me on. It seemed like the first time I'd gotten somewhat turned on for someone other than Kota in a while.

I needed to do something about this.

"Let's go out tonight," I said.

Lane's brows shot up behind his bottle. "Why?"

I nearly choked on my beer. "What do you mean *why?*"

He sighed, a gravelly, pissed off kind of sigh. "You gotta be like this on night one? Really?"

"You don't get it."

Lane dropped his hands on the table. "What don't I get?"

I fucked our roommate and now I can't stop thinking about her and I need to fuck someone else so that I can get over whatever the hell is happening to me.

"I just..." I said, lying straight through my teeth, "need to."

All he did was stare at me, his eyes narrowing further by the second. "When's the last time you got laid?"

What the hell did this have to do with going out tonight?

I almost said, *"New Year's Eve,"* but I caught myself, unsure if Lane would put the puzzle pieces together or not. "Few days," I finally answered.

There he was again, staring at me, leaving nothing but silence at our table, accompanied with "Under the Influence," by Chris Brown playing over the speakers.

Lane's fingers curled around his beer bottle, bringing it back up to his mouth for a solid chug.

Meanwhile, I sat there, listening to Chris Brown sing about bodies and riding it and if I heard one more word, my mind was going to wander right back to the one place I didn't want it.

"Do you have a... problem?" Lane finally asked.

"Hmm?"

Lane's cheekbones sharpened lightly, waiting for me to catch on. I blinked at him rapidly, unsure if he was asking what I thought he was.

"Are you asking me if I'm addicted to sex?"

Sheepishly, he answered, "Yes."

Was I addicted to sex? Nah, I didn't think so.

Maybe I was just addicted to it when it came to *her.*

"No," I nearly growled.

His hands came up defensively. "Only asking because I care."

I gave an "Mhm," and crossed my arms.

Lane was bobbing his knee, and I knew it because the table was shaking. I should've told him to knock it the fuck off, because I was a little put off— or I was at least *trying* to be.

It was nearly impossible to stay mad at Lane.

"Alright," he sighed as our waitress headed our way with two plates of appetizers.

"What?" I simmered.

"We'll go out tonight."

Chapter Forty-Three

Kota

You know what sucked? Not being able to tell your best friend about some of the best sex you ever had.

You know what sucked even more? Spending seventy-two hours straight with your best friend while you struggled to stop *thinking* about some of the best sex you ever had.

I was currently in that boat.

We were in Chicago, surrounded by beautiful buildings, tourist attractions, and shopping, yet my mind was currently back at Cedar.

Well, it was specifically back in Crew's car.

Every time I finally got myself to stop thinking about him, within an hour or two, he somehow managed to invade my thoughts again like an army of termites in a rotting cabin.

"This is cute, right?" Bridget asked, holding up a baby-blue sundress.

I glanced up from the rack of crop tops I'd been looking through. "Yeah, cute," I said. "What would you wear it for?"

A light, pink glow encompassed her cheeks as her gaze dropped to the dress. "I don't know."

Seemed like she did know.

I was about to press her on it until a silky red top grazed over my fingertips, the same color as the dress that Crew ripped off me.

Motherfucker.

Bridget had mentioned the boys decided to take a last-minute trip to Colorado. I assumed they'd be going out at some point, which led me to also assume Crew wouldn't be going home alone.

But why did that thought kind of sting a little bit?

Within seconds, my phone was in my hand, and my fingers were angrily typing away.

Me: I hate you.

But the second I hit send, I wasn't sure if I was texting that to him to remind him or to try to remind myself.

Crew: Thanks for enlightening me. Again.

Me: You're welcome.

Crew: Having fun in Chi?

I squinted at the phone. Was he trying to be nice and conversational or was this some sort of trap?

Me: Yup

Crew: I wish you weren't. I want you to have a terrible time

"Why're you smiling at your phone like that?"

My head shot up. "What?"

Bridget stepped towards me vigilantly, blue dress still in hand. The corners of her lips were puckered like she was trying to fight a smile. "Are you texting a boy?"

I dropped my phone by my side. "Ew, no! You know I hate boys!"

Her mischievous glare bore into me, studying my every feature to read me as well as possible, causing my heart to palpitate.

This better not be the moment she finds out.

Bridget slightly jumped, reaching into her back pocket to retrieve her own phone, the roses in her cheeks getting brighter with each passing second.

Swiftly, I turned my back to her and separated myself with a few steps.

She was acting just as strange as I was, but digging would cause her to do the same, and with the ugly truth I was hiding, I couldn't afford that.

Me: You're an asshole

Crew: I don't remember you calling me that the other night

Me: Shut your mouth

Crew: You should learn how to shut yours. You know you get real loud?

Was he referring to my rambunctious personality or to having sex with me?

Considering sex was one of the few topics associated with Nicholas Crew, ranked right alongside hockey, I assumed it was the latter.

Me: Are you trying to flirt with me right now?

Crew: Hell no

**Me: Good
Because I hate you**

When I didn't get another lightning-fast response, I slid my phone back into my purse and pretended like it didn't bother me.

Chapter Forty-Four

Crew

I was holding out as long as possible for Lane's sake.

We were at a club called *Drink!* and apparently, I was stronger than I thought, because even with the amount of girls in this building right now, I'd managed not to stare too long or wander off and introduce myself to any.

"You look like you're in pain," Lane said.

"I'm fine," I insisted, drowning the lie with the remainder of my beer. "Are you having fun?"

"Not really."

"Why not?"

"Because I've spent the past twenty minutes watching you look like you're in pain."

We were standing at a table upstairs that overlooked the dance floor, and every few minutes, I'd been getting glimpses of the curvature of girl's asses swaying.

I guess I hadn't realized it'd been causing me to look like I was in pain for the last twenty minutes.

The music had been pretty mellow, consisting of throwbacks like "Party in the U.S.A" and some old Kesha songs.

But now "No Hands" by Waka Flocka Flame was blaring, and I swore every girl dropped their ass to the floor at once like a group of synchronized swimmers in a pool.

Ah, geez. Ripping my eyes away, I rubbed the back of my head.

I wasn't usually this... I wasn't even sure how to describe it. Sexually frustrated? Was that what I was?

I was well aware that I was acting like a high-school-aged, horny virgin, and I was pretty sure I hated it just as much as Lane did. If not, I hated it *more.*

Lane fucking amazed me. The fact that his eyes hadn't wandered all night seemed like some weird hidden talent. I didn't know anyone that had the same self-discipline as him, and not going to lie, I was a bit jealous of it.

"I need another beer," I said, tipping my empty glass side to side.

"Same," he agreed. "To the bar, we go."

Relief encompassed me as we stepped away from the railing of the second floor, and when we got our beers, I made sure to pick a new table that wasn't anywhere close to the old one.

A trio of girls walked by, and if it weren't for one with the same tan skin and similar features as Kota, I probably wouldn't have been hyper focused on them.

Every muscle in my body was tensing, getting more and more frustrated with myself.

Lightly and out of habit, I licked my lips, and I could've sworn that for a second, I could taste Kota's mouth on mine. Her sticky, glossy lips that tasted like cherry.

"Let's play a game," Lane blurted out.

Yes, fucking please.

I had no idea what game he was referring to, but anything to get my mind out of the gutter it was currently in was a good idea.

"What kind of game?"

He tipped his drink towards me. "Go around and see how many numbers you can get."

I took another glance around as if I hadn't done so thirty times prior tonight. "Is this a competition? Are we gonna see who can get more?"

236

Because if that was the case, I was more than intrigued. This was the type of shit I'd do with Cody or TJ. Lane had never been as promiscuous as the rest of us, and the craziest part was, if he had been, he'd probably blow all of us out of the water.

I didn't want to hype him up too hard since I wasn't some girl with a crush on him, but Lane was a handsome dude. Not only that, but he was an actual gentleman to women *and* had a great personality. With a future NHL contract floating around. What more could you ask for?

Lane let out a sarcastic laugh. "Definitely not."

"Why?" I threw at him.

"I'm not as smooth as you."

Bullshit.

"You underestimate yourself. You'd definitely give me a run for my money."

Firmly, he shook his head, lips tight. "We'll change the game."

"To?"

Lane's chin lifted, spine straightening in that captain-like stance he always gave. "I get to pick out a girl for you."

My eyes met his with curiosity. There was something about the idea of all this that was so intriguing. I wanted to see Lane be a little wild for once.

"Do I get to do the same?" I asked.

He let out another laugh like I was insane. "No."

"Then no."

His chin dropped, head tipping as his voice lowered an octave as if he was my parent about to tell me some devasting news like my pet died or something.

"I'm not bringing a girl home tonight, Crew," he said.

I sighed, shaking my head. "You continuously disappoint me."

"I'm just not really into hookups," he shrugged. "You know that."

"Yeah, I do know that," I sternly agreed. "What I don't know is *why*."

"I could ask the same thing about you." He rested his elbows on the table, casually leaning forward while his hand had a death grip on his drink. "Why do you like hookups?"

I scoffed, forcing my line of sight to stay on Lane and only Lane. "Keeps things interesting," I said. When my response didn't seem to satisfy him and he only raised a brow at me, I added, "And no strings attached."

Did a string just include a relationship, or did it also include the mental chaos I was currently having?

Whether my response was enough this time or not, Lane didn't seem to care. He ignored everything I'd said, dropping his empty hand on the table. "Do you wanna play the game or not?"

Even though he couldn't hear it over the music, I let out a light groan. "Alright, sure, whatever."

Lane took a small step back as his eyes zipped around the vicinity, taking in every girl within a twenty-foot radius, which might not have seemed like a lot, but with how packed this place was tonight, the opportunities were sort of endless.

Meanwhile, I waited rather patiently, hoping Lane had good taste for me tonight.

"Her," he declared, his beer raising discreetly in the direction of a small group of girls. I stared at the group, unsure of which one he was referring to. Not all of them were facing me, but from the back, they didn't seem bad. "The one in the black top, blue jeans."

That one was facing me.

My head lulled, circling all the way back to Lane. "You *would* pick out the red head."

The lightest trace of his jaw flexing caught my eye as he rolled his. "This isn't about Bridget."

"Sure. Keep tellin' yourself that," I muttered as I headed towards my target.

She was watching me as I approached, and the closer I got, the more confused she seemed to get, looking around at her friends like a lost puppy.

All of them were seemingly occupied though, either with each other or with guys of their own. I stopped shy of a few feet from her, keeping a safe distance. She looked like a deer in headlights as she stared at me, and I took the moment to get a good look at her.

She was definitely pretty, with long red hair that went down to her mid-back. Although with the harsh lighting, I

238

wasn't sure if it was her natural hair color or not. Strutting around in a small black top and blue jeans, I wouldn't have admitted it aloud, but Lane didn't do me wrong with this pick.

"Hello," I said.

"Hi."

I held out a hand. "I'm Crew."

"Rachelle," she said, full of distrust as she glared at my hand, slowly bringing hers up for a shake.

"How's your night, Rachelle?"

"Good... How's yours?"

"Not too bad," I said, giving the most delicate smirk known to man.

She gave an awkward nod.

Usually, I knew what to say based on a girl's vibe, but this one seemed so shy and closed off that it was hard to get any kind of read on her. I wasn't sure what approach to take, and I especially wasn't sure how I was going to get her to go from nervous to shaking my hand to willing to give me her number or anything beyond that.

I didn't usually go for shy girls. Now that I thought about it, I seemingly only went for girls who were a little more extroverted like me. I probably wouldn't have picked Rachelle out myself had the circumstances been different, but here I was, which meant I needed to see it through.

"Are you from around here?" I asked.

"Kingston," she said, expecting me to know where that was.

I lifted a brow lightly. "Is that... around here?"

She gave a light chuckle. "You're not from here, are you?"

I shook my head. "I play hockey in Minnesota."

Now, she was lifting a brow, a light smirk trudging across her lips. "Is that supposed to impress me?"

This, I could go along with.

"I mean," I grinned, "hopefully."

I could see the large intake of breath she took to respond. Too bad I'd never know what she was about to say.

"Rachelle!" one of her friends shouted. "We're going back now!" With a tug, she was whisked away, not bothering to look back once.

Great.

I stood there in my defeat for a minute, not only disappointed but also embarrassed knowing that Lane was probably watching. And probably laughing.

"Rejected?" a light voice called.

I twisted, mouth parting at the sight of the Kota look-alike. The strobe lights from the dance floor were lighting up her face every ten or so seconds, and each time it did, the more and more I envisioned it being Kota standing in front of me.

There were a lot of differences though. Like the curve of their lips. Kota's were much more defined, having a perfect cupid's bow sitting atop her upper lip. Whereas this girl had much thinner, straighter lips.

Kota carried herself with more of a *don't fucking mess with me,* badass attitude. This girl seemed confident but wouldn't have the same ability to rip someone's heart out with her hands.

There were other small differences, but I was currently overwhelmed with the similarities.

"Not quite," I responded.

"Oh really?"

"I promise."

With a quick look-over, she responded, "You sound quite confident."

It was kind of blowing my mind that my excitement had skyrocketed by talking to someone who looked like the girl I hated with the heat of a million and one suns.

I gave a light shrug. "Confidence is key," I said jokingly.

Her voice spilled out musically like a sweet, soft lullaby. Another stark difference to Kota.

"If confidence is key," she grinned benevolently, "would it be overly confident of me if I asked what you were doing after this?"

There was no way to smother the massive grin overcoming my face. "Not at all."

***

"You know," Lane whispered beside me, "she kinda looks like—"

"Don't," I cut him off.

Isla, the Kota look-alike, trailed a few steps behind us up to the Airbnb.

When she took initiative earlier and asked to spend the night together, I was fucking astounded. This girl had bigger balls on her than I originally thought. Most girls waited for me to be the one to ask, so her asking made her even more attractive to me.

Her friends didn't seem to have a problem with her leaving early. They drilled Lane and I pretty hard before letting her leave with us, but we promised we'd get her an Uber whenever she wanted to leave, and we meant it.

I might've been a dick sometimes, but I wasn't the type of guy to put a girl in a helpless or dangerous situation. Obviously, I wasn't from around here, but I'd walk her home if it came down to it.

Once we got inside the Airbnb, Lane went straight to his room with no more than a "Goodnight" and a yawn.

I shut my bedroom door behind Isla and me quietly and carefully, practically in slow motion to bother Lane the least amount possible.

It was almost two in the morning, and while the rest of the world was asleep, my night was just getting started.

It didn't take long before our lips were meshing, legs tangling under the covers. I took things how I normally did, as if it were a routine that I knew by heart. Hands wandering across her skin, I explored her most sensitive regions as she did the same to me.

The heat between us grew, and I took things to the next step, helping her out of her clothes before taking off my own, grabbing a condom and slipping it on.

She laid below me, allowing me to hover above her and slide inside her.

All my frustration I'd been feeling earlier in the night was slowly fading, and I closed my eyes, allowing my mind to wander and my body to relax.

A gentle, desperate moan echoed around the room, coming from her small mouth as I sank deeper into her, squeezing my eyes shut. Two hands found their way around my biceps, clutching tightly.

"God," I groaned, "Kota."

The cold air hit my skin as one of her hands left my arm and planted firmly in the center of my chest. "What?"

My eyes shot open, immediately realizing my mistake. *Fuck.*

Chapter Forty-Five

Kota

"That was fucking weird," I said.

"Very," Crew responded from the kitchen.

It was only our second day back from winter break, and we'd just watched Bridget and Lane scurry out of the apartment together like they were Bonnie and Clyde about to commit a crime.

"You think they're... sneaking around?" I asked, putting my air pods back in their case.

His eyes remained on the bagel he was putting cream cheese onto, but his tone still had that spark it always had, his mouth pulling into a crooked half-smile. "You mean secretly hooking up like we have? No shot."

I was less upset about Lane and Bridget rushing out strangely than I was about them leaving me alone with Crew.

We'd already had two hookups, two massive mistakes that I was set on taking to my grave, and we didn't need any more. Plus, I didn't have alcohol as an excuse right now if I were to walk over and rip his clothes off.

"We agreed we wouldn't talk about it ever," I said, mentally gluing myself to the couch so that I didn't have the chance to do one more stupid thing to add to the list.

Crew let out a single chuckle. "Is that why you texted me the other day?"

There was that cocky side of him again. The one I loathed with every inch of my being. "I texted you because I hate you."

"That seems a little contradicting."

In order to ward off the heat rising in my cheeks, I had a few options here. One, I could've run into the bathroom and stuck my head in some ice water. Two, I could've shoved my air pods back in and pretended like he wasn't there. Or three, I could've flipped the switch and embarrassed him just as hard.

Out of all the options, number three was my favorite.

"How was your trip, by the way?" I asked.

He shrugged nonchalantly. "Fine."

"Get any girls?"

Crew's chin stayed towards his chest, but his eyes popped up to glare at me. "Why do you care?"

I let the words roll off my tongue with no emotion behind them, managing to add an innocent shrug. "Just wondering."

His jaw twitched beneath his skin as he dropped the butterknife he'd been holding. "Why? Did Lane say something to you?"

A devilish grin crept across my face at his sudden discomfort. "No. Was he supposed to?"

"No."

"Maybe I'll ask him."

Every time he glanced at me, the heat in his eyes grew hotter, every last bit of it aimed directly at me. But the best part was that we were at a point where I knew it was no longer just hatred. Lust was now involved.

"Hey, uh," I said, standing, "don't you have a rule about not fucking a girl twice?"

Crew remained still, even as I stepped towards him. His hands found their way to the countertop, leaning into them to expose his arms, those muscles that I loved digging my nails into.

His voice dropped to a seductive note, becoming the same moment I knew I might've fucked up, because this game was a bit more dangerous than I realized.

"What kind of game are you playing, Kota?" he asked.

I crossed my arms, my confidence wavering for the first time since this conversation started.

"This is just really fucking annoying," I admitted, refusing to look at him like the coward I suddenly was.

"What is?"

On one hand, it felt like the words were reluctantly getting ripped out of my throat, yet on the other hand, it felt so nice to just say it.

"How you're stuck in my head every second of the day."

The ego boost couldn't have been clearer had he tattooed it across his forehead. Two dimples popped up, sinking deeply into his cheeks as he gave that outrageously beautiful grin, nearly knocking me off my feet.

The amount of satisfaction in his voice was sickening. "Am I now?"

"Yes," I hissed. "And I need you to get the fuck out of it."

I was expecting laughter. Or for him to sprint out of the room.

But instead, the floor creaked under his weight as he rushed towards me, shamelessly grabbing the sides of my head with both hands and letting our lips collide.

Within moments, I was pushed against the nearest wall, becoming trapped.

My mouth separated from his, creating just enough distance to speak. "I thought you hated me."

His fingertips traced across my skin all the way up to my throat where his grip tightened and loosened, tightened and loosened. He pulled back to get a full view of my face, probably more than content knowing I was about to combust under his touch.

There was this sort of uncontrollable cloud of lust surrounding us. The more we experimented with the strange, intoxicating connection between us, the deeper we'd sink into this dangerous hole, and the harder it would eventually be to get out of it.

Whatever was going on here was bound to get messy. And we both knew it.

But that still didn't stop us.

The gruff timbre of his voice ripped straight through me, and there was absolutely no way he couldn't feel my erratic pulse slamming against his fingertips right now.

"Do you want me to show you how much I hate you?"

It felt like it was impossible to form a sentence, or even get a single word out for that matter. All I could do was give a trace of a nod.

A dimple slowly appeared as one corner of Crew's mouth lifted into a sinful smirk. He planted a hand beside my head on the wall, towering over me as his other hand found its way to the button of my black jeans, toying with it.

He cocked a brow. "May I?"

Oh my.

I gulped as I gave another weak nod.

With a quick flick, the button was undone, and both my jeans and panties were on the floor in seconds.

Along with Crew.

He gripped the back of my calf and threw my leg over his shoulder, not hesitating to bury his face between my legs.

With my head tipped back against the wall, my hands ran through his hair, eyes clenched shut. I let out a whimper, one after another as Crew's mouth explored my most sensitive parts.

I stole a glance, and I hated to admit that I loved seeing him there, my leg draped over his shoulder, hair a mess from my touch, head buried right where it should be.

As the minutes ticked by, I could feel the build in my stomach, my body temperature spiking drastically. My lungs were on the brink of gasping for air, and when Crew moaned, sending a vibration through my core, breathing became even harder.

My nails dug into his shoulders, legs shaking as my muscles became like jelly All at once, I could feel my body release, and knowing Crew was tasting it sent me into an entire new kind of frenzy.

If Crew hadn't grabbed me and held me up, I would've slid down the wall, incapable of holding up my own body weight.

"Crew," I spoke urgently through a strained breath.

He pulled away and looked up at me with bedroom eyes, the ring of his mouth wet and glistening under the lights. He kept our gaze locked as he slowly brought two fingers to my opening, and in one sudden movement, pushed them inside me. He gave a few pumps before taking them out and shooting them into his mouth, watching my reaction as he sucked every drop of me off.

A loud, desperate moan left my mouth. "Crew," I begged, "please."

Flashing a sexy grin, he stood, bringing his hands under my ass, effortlessly lifting me and carrying me into his bedroom.

Fuck. Here goes another mistake.

Chapter Forty-Six

Crew

I couldn't fucking focus.

I was a mess at practice this morning, playing sloppier than I have in a long ass time.

Class was going even worse. I wasn't retaining a single bit of information. Physically, I was sitting in my seat. Mentally, I was bending Kota over the desk in my bedroom.

Yesterday was too good.

Having her pinned against the wall, begging for my touch.

The only times she'd ever brought her guard down for me was when I was touching her. It may have sounded fucked up, but I wanted to see just how much control she would give me. She'd always seemed to have the upper hand, and now it felt like maybe I had an upper hand of my own.

I was tempted to leave class early, but I managed to hang on for the final twenty minutes to make sure I had all the directions I needed for my homework assignment.

After yesterday, there was a physical understanding between us. We hadn't said it aloud, but it was clear that we weren't going to stop what was going on.

There was no more worry about what would happen if one of us made a move. I mean, she outright admitted that I was in her head; that was truly all I needed to hear to let me know that she didn't want this to stop.

The second I slid into my car, I shot her a text.

Crew: Be ready for me when I get home.

This was a bad idea. Nothing good could come from any of this, but I was in too deep.

The mistakes were adding up, and at this rate, it didn't seem like they were anywhere close to stopping.

Double checking Lane and Bridget's location, I made sure they weren't home before rushing up to our apartment.

Pausing in the doorway, I raised a brow at the sight of Kota seated at the kitchen island, papers scattered around.

I gave a light tsk. "I see you didn't listen," I said.

She forced a scoff, keeping her eyes on her work. "Since when do I listen to you?"

With a wicked smile, I walked up behind her, my hands planting atop the granite on either side of her. My chest brushed against her back, and I leaned over her shoulder, conviction in my voice.

"Since now."

Silently, she stiffened to stone. For a moment, I waited for a bold remark or any sort of warning that I was about to get my ass beat, but she remained quiet, as if she was waiting for my next move.

"My room," I demanded. "Now."

I moved out of her way as she dashed off her stool, awkwardly waiting in the center of my room as I followed her in and locked the door behind me.

With lust coating her, Kota looked rather nervous. And I was loving it.

She was always so hard-headed. Always owned every room she ever walked into. She never got nervous about anything, yet I was somehow cracking her.

Dakota Darling was bad. But here she was, waiting for directions like a good fucking girl would.

"On the bed," I ordered.

With no questions asked, she sat on the edge of the bed like we were playing a game of Simon Says.

Meanwhile, I leaned against the wall, arms crossed, ready to test just how far I could take this. "Take your shirt off."

I could make out the gulp she gave as her hands found their way to the hem of her black t-shirt, wrists crossing as she lifted the shirt over her head in one, quick motion.

Her tits poured out of her bra, and I could immediately feel my dick hardening in my pants. I swallowed hard, forcing myself to stay in place instead of rushing over to touch her.

"Pants," I dared, my voice gruff.

The thin fabric of her leggings illuminated every inch and curve as she shimmied them off.

Heart immediately racing at the view of her matching red set, I nearly collapsed. I'd seen her naked numerous times now, but I'd never just stood and admired her like this.

She was *beautiful.*

I wanted to touch her, every bit of her, but I didn't even know where to start.

The mental control I'd been holding onto was wavering at the trust and certainty looming in her eyes. She wasn't looking at me like she hated me or wanted to strangle me in my sleep. She was looking at me like she *wanted* me.

And why did that turn me on even more?

Our eyes locked in on each other like a predator and its prey. I'd never held such long and intimate eye contact with a girl before. It was making my stomach do some weird flips.

In slow motion, my gaze dropped to her chest, noting how her breaths became more and more shallow by the second. Her tits were rising and falling steadily, making my mouth water.

I watched feverishly as Kota stood there, waiting.

My voice dropped low, a hurricane of greed cloaking it. "Do you want me to touch you?"

Kota's eyes ignited, and I swore I could smell her arousal wafting towards me. It was becoming harder and harder to hold this distance between us. I held my ground, trying to mask every thought and desire swirling through my mind, but I couldn't tell if she saw straight through me like a broken mirror.

"Yes," she whispered shyly, giving a nod.

I stalked forward, the predator finally pouncing on its prey. The second my fingers grazed over the warm skin on her bare stomach, I was under her spell.

And I didn't mind at all.

Chapter Forty-Seven

Crew

I was deep in a heist mission on Grand Theft Auto, racing through Vice City to steal a million dollars from some bank on the other side of the city.

I didn't play Xbox by myself often. I used to play a lot with the guys when we still lived in the house, but I'd only played a handful of times since we moved into our apartment.

However, it was currently one of the only distractions I had.

Sitting in the common areas, all four of us, was extremely painful. It felt like I couldn't act normal with Kota. We were stuck with acting like we still hated each other— if acting was what we were doing.

But I was finding it hard to remind myself to keep my hands off her, and every time I looked at her for too long, I was afraid Lane and Bridget would notice.

"B," Kota spoke, "we should get some wine tonight."

My jaw tightened, her voice immediately pulling me away from the "distraction" I'd been feeding myself. With my head forward, I kept quiet, unable to see Bridget's reaction.

"It's already eight, and I still need to clean my room and shower."

A sigh rang loudly throughout the room, and I knew without looking that it came from Kota, seated on the far side of the couch.

"Wine sucks anyway," I blurted out.

"*You* suck," she said, harsh glare burning a hole in the side of my head.

Amusement slashed across my face, my mind immediately grabbing memories of her mouth on my dick. *You wanna talk about who sucks?* I wanted to say but held it back.

Choking through laughter, I smirked at the TV.

Whether she was blatantly trying to ignore me or simply brush over the encounter so that we didn't look suspicious, she turned to Lane in the kitchen. "Do you guys have practice in the morning?"

"Yeah," he said.

"We can have a wine night tomorrow?" Bridget suggested.

Fingers pressing the buttons on the console harder than intended, I butted in, "I just said I hated wine."

Out of my peripherals, I could see Kota swing around faster than light traveled. "No one invited you."

"Wow."

"I'll have a wine night," Lane spoke.

"Cool!" Kota shrieked.

I knew we weren't disclosing our current arrangement with Lane and Bridget, but *goddamn*. If every minute we'd spent together over the last few weeks wasn't practically branded permanently in my brain, I would've thought it had all been some crazy, steamy dream.

She was being brutal, the same brutal that she was when we met.

"Oh," I complained towards the TV, "so Lane is invited and not me?"

"Exactly."

Bridget sighed, probably rolling her eyes. "Would it kill you two to be nice to each other for five seconds?"

"Yes," Kota said. "Yes, it would, actually."

"I can be nice. It's her," I said, gesturing to Kota with my head.

I could've sworn I heard a small growl from beside me, a stark difference to the blushing girl standing naked in my bedroom just a few days ago.

"Don't even," Kota snapped.

"Mom," I called out, "she's being mean again!"

"Ew!" Bridget immediately let out, lightly shivering when I glanced over. "Don't call me that." My laughter mixed with Lane's. "On second thought, I will down some wine right now. You all drove me to it."

"Yes!" Kota shot up, running over to the door to grab her purse and jacket. "Let's go grab some!"

As if second nature, I paused my game and stood to follow her. "I'll go," I said as nonchalantly as I could manage. "I'm getting myself beer."

Kota and I avoided looking at each other, just glanced at our roommates carefully to see if they were going to follow.

Bridget bobbed up and down on her toes. "I, uh, I'm gonna hop in the shower actually while you guys are gone. Get that done so that I can drink, you know?"

We gave her half a nod, and the lack of disgust from Kota as we rushed out side by side was leading me to believe that maybe she didn't mind being stuck in a car with me for ten minutes.

Maybe she wanted to be stuck near me, the same way I'd been wishing we were the only two in the room earlier.

"Do you think we were convincing enough?" I asked, slicing away the silence as I pulled out of our parking lot and headed off towards the liquor store.

Walls back up around her heart, Kota scoffed. "Did you think I was putting on a show back there?"

I can't fucking tell, I thought.

I wanted to say yes, but the lines were blurring so much, practically interlaced like one huge knot that was impossible to undo.

Going with my gut instinct, I called her bluff. Keeping one hand on the wheel, my other shot down to her crotch, rubbing tenderly. She let out a breathy note, chest hitching.

"That's what I thought," I declared, pulling away, causing her to give the lightest whimper.

254

Whether she still hated me or not, she wanted me, so at least I had that.

I didn't know what else to say though.

We both fell quiet, and the car was overtaken by some song on the radio.

Halfway through the song, Kota muttered, "Go to Target instead."

"Why?"

"Bridget needs tampons."

"Ew," I blurted.

"Oh sorry," she groaned through an eye roll, "I forgot about your *phobia.*"

"I do not have a *phobia.*"

My comment led to Kota forcing me to carry the tampon box throughout the store.

We headed to the liquor section, and I stood there for ten minutes, holding tampons and annoyed, teeth grinding as I watched Kota pace up and down the aisle as she tapped her chin, unsure of which wine to get because "they all looked so good."

Finally, she grabbed two bottles of Moscato. Gross.

I twisted towards the beer aisle, but Kota caught my arm. "You're trying wine."

"I don't like wine."

"Too bad," she insisted, scurrying off, leaving me with no choice but to follow her because no way in hell was I going to lose her in the store.

I groaned all the way to self-checkout, still groaning by the time we got into the car. When I parked, I gave one final groan.

"Oh, stop whining," Kota said. "You're gonna love it." She reached for the handle, and instinctively, my hand shot out, stopping her. As she turned around, I met her lips, content when she melted against me.

I'd been waiting for this all fucking night. It felt like a relief to just have her close, to not have to tiptoe around our roommates. "Do we have to go inside?" I whispered against her mouth.

She sighed. "Yes."

Truthfully, I wanted to stay in the car and mess around. Cloaked with disappointment, I followed her upstairs, and the second we both crossed the threshold into the apartment, our masks were on. Back to being enemies.

The girls brought out board game after board game, and it was taking everything in me not to glance at Kota every other minute. She changed when we got back, and her tiny frame was now swallowed up in an oversized, gray sweatshirt from high school, matched with black, sparkly pajama pants. Her hair was in pigtail braids, and she looked like the cutest, most innocent thing.

I wanted to grab her, squeeze her, pull her close and kiss the hell out of her.

But instead, I was pretending like I hated her.

It wasn't too hard though when arguing came so naturally to us. It seemed like she found something about me to complain about during every game we played.

I'd gotten accused of cheating. Accused of not knowing the proper rules. Accused of lying about hating the wine we were drinking. Although, I'd admit, the wine *was* kind of good. I refused to say it aloud though and give the girls that satisfaction that they were so desperately looking for. Instead, I'd rather be accused of lying.

Kota kept scowling in my direction, scoffing each time I spoke. She could play this game all night long, but the second I had her alone later, she'd be begging me to put my hands on her.

And that was fine with me.

Chapter Forty-Eight

Kota

My New Year's resolution was to start becoming active again. I used to do yoga three times a week during freshman and sophomore year. During junior year, when school got more demanding, I wasn't going as often, and eventually, I stopped going altogether.

When the weather had been nice last year, I'd go on walks at a nearby forest preserve, and Bridget would usually accompany me. But with how harsh Minnesota weather could be, and with how long winters tended to last here, there were months where I wasn't doing much physical activity outside of walking to class.

A few months ago, I realized just how out of shape I was when it started becoming exhausting to just walk up and down the stairs. I tried signing back up for yoga, but the class was full, so I told myself I'd start going to the gym instead. The first few weeks of the year had already passed, so I finally decided to hold myself accountable and sign up for a gym membership.

There was a gym inside the student center at Cedar, which all students were eligible to go to for free, but considering the boys went there almost daily, I wasn't trying to run into them. Or anyone else I knew, if I was being honest.

I wanted to get active again and to make it a priority in my life by incorporating it into my weekly routine, but I most definitely didn't want people I knew to watch me workout.

So, I chose the gym that was on the farthest side of town.

After class, I threw on a gray racerback tank and some black leggings before burying myself underneath my winter jacket and dashing out of the apartment.

I was a bit intimidated the second I walked in. There was so much equipment that it was almost overwhelming.

Mirrors took up the entire wall to my right, stretching far too long to the opposite end of the room. There was a decent amount of people there, but I didn't recognize any faces, which was a good sign.

I scanned the equipment, noting the endless rows of machines that I was assuming were to work out your arms and legs.

But I decided to start off simple and headed towards one of the only machines I did know how to use— the treadmill.

I set my water bottle in the cup holder attached to the machine, then popped my air pods in and set the treadmill to a steady pace, slowly settling in.

Alright, no one's looking at me. This is good.

Maybe if I built up enough confidence, I'd test out the ellipticals.

As the minutes went by, I got more comfortable, and I became motivated enough to increase the speed to a nice jog.

I stuck with it until I was breaking a sweat, and after a few more songs, I reduced the speed back down to what it originally was.

With a small jump, my feet landed on the outsides of the treadmill to give myself a breather. I couldn't hear my heavy breathing through the music blasting in my ears, but I didn't need to— I could *feel* it. My lungs were riding the struggle bus.

My water bottle was to my mouth in seconds, and I chugged it like I hadn't had water in days. I didn't think I'd downed any drink like that since it was my birthday freshman year and Bridget was screaming at me to chug more Fireball.

258

By the time I was done, the bottle was over halfway empty, and I hung my head to continue catching my breath.

As my eyes trailed back upwards, my stomach quivered at the familiar sight of the back of a head.

Uh oh. I knew that head of hair. I had my fingers running through it just yesterday.

Catching a glimpse of the side of Crew's face, I stiffened. His jawline was facing me, looking as sharp as glass.

Fuck, fuck, fuck. I need to sneak out of here.

What the hell was he even doing here?

As if I just drank ten cups of coffee, I moved at an inhuman pace, turning the treadmill off and grabbing all my belongings. I ducked my head down as I passed Crew, who was letting out a slight grunt as he used the chest press machine.

"Hey."

Wincing, I halted, head reluctantly lifting. "Oh," I said nonchalantly, "hey. What are you doing here?"

Crew lifted a brow, standing. The first thing I noticed was the sweat glistening on his skin, and my mind envisioned the dirtiest fantasies of licking that sweat right off him before my face twisted.

Did I really just have thoughts of licking him? His sweat? *What the fuck was wrong with me?*

"What does it look like I'm doing here?" he asked, snagging his towel resting on the back of the machine and wiping his face off.

Had he been here this entire time? How did I not notice him before?

"I thought you go to the gym on campus."

"I do."

"Then why are you here?" I questioned.

"Because I have a membership for here too."

"That makes no sense," I said, noticing the guy that was waiting nearby to use the chest press.

Crew gave him a nod in acknowledgement before wiping the machine down for him and stepping off to the side.

I had no idea why, but instead of running like I originally was going to, I slid over beside him, keeping a safe distance, which also made no sense considering our hands were all over each other less than twenty-four hours ago.

"Where's Lane?" I spit out.

"He doesn't come here."

"Oh," I said, fighting a devious smile, "I see."

Those dark brown eyes of his bore into me with suspicion, making me uneasy. "What?"

I crossed my arms lightly over my chest. "You come here to escape Lane," I accused.

"I do not come here to escape Lane," Crew said firmly, tossing his towel over his shoulder. "I come here when Lane's busy."

"Why?"

He trekked over to another machine, and I felt compelled to follow before silently chiding myself for it.

Speaking between reps, he said, "Because I hate going to the other gym without him. There's always people I know, and I feel awkward."

"Like who? Past hookups?" I snorted.

But based on the side eye I earned from Crew, along with the strange new cloud of embarrassment that seemed to settle over him, I realized there was seemingly some truth to my joke.

"Yikes," I murmured. Pretending like he hadn't heard me, Crew hit a few more reps before taking a rest.

Darkness loomed in his eyes, but it wasn't that lust-filled fog I'd gotten used to over the last few weeks. It was a glimpse of the past, of the remaining bit of animosity between us, regardless of the fact that his hands skimmed my skin yesterday like I was the best thing he'd ever laid a finger on.

"Don't look at me like that," I whirred.

"Like what?" he dared, darkness still roaming.

"Like you didn't have your dick in me yesterday."

Crew froze for a moment, the darkness lifting to starry-eyed. Mouth parting in surprise before the corners ticked upwards, he gave the smallest nod. "You want it in you again?"

Suddenly, I couldn't help the sting of embarrassment staining my cheeks. My head dipped, mouth dry. The lines were blurring again between hatred and lust, two emotions I never knew could be connected until I met Nicholas Crew.

"Are you blushing?" he smiled wider.

The edge in my voice could slit a throat. "No. I don't blush."

"Sure," he teased, wandering past me.

I scoffed before stomping out.

So much for starting to come to the gym.

***

I'd admit, I actually felt pretty good physically and mentally after going to the gym today. I somehow felt like I'd had a more productive day.

I was annoyed after my run-in with Crew, but I refused to let him ruin my New Years resolution. I was going to go to the gym as often as I wanted without worrying about whether he'd be there or not.

Bridget and I had debated going out, but we were both exhausted, so a movie night sounded much better.

We'd both chosen a rom com to watch as a double feature, but shortly after I had turned mine on, she'd gotten a Facetime call from her parents, and she'd been locked away in her room for the past fifteen minutes.

I was bundled up in my navy blue snuggie, a glass of wine beside me while my feet rested on the coffee table.

The couch dipped on the opposite half, and I nearly rolled into the incline. Crew got comfortable, shimmying against the couch like he was there to stay.

"What're you watching?" he wondered aloud.

"*How to Lose a Guy in 10 Days*," I muttered.

"I've never seen it."

I swung around, blinking rapidly at him. "You've never seen *How to Lose a Guy in 10 Days*?"

"No," he shrugged. "It looks like a girl movie."

My eyes rolled so hard they nearly got stuck in the back of my head. "It is not a *girl movie*. It's called a rom com." His nasty hand dug into the bowl of popcorn beside me, and I swatted it away. "Hey! Get your own."

Crew looked at me like I'd just killed his puppy. He gave the smallest scoff. "You can share."

"I only share with Bridget."

With the most subtle tick of his jaw, his eyes skimmed both hallways, checking that Lane was still in the shower and Bridget was still in her room. Crew leaned towards me in the slightest before his glare dropped to the bowl between us. My heartbeat sped as he placed it on the coffee table and leaned nearer, forcing me on my back and caging me in.

He towered over me, and the closer his mouth got, the more the pressure in my chest built. With his mouth settled inches away, the rasp in his voice was enough to make me surrender to him like some sort of sex potion.

"You can share."

I held my breath until my lungs burned, watching his chocolate brown eyes bore into mine like he was waiting for an answer.

My teeth cut into my bottom lip as I nodded, trying not to notice his heat seeping through my snuggie or the smell of mint on his breath.

"Good," he suddenly smirked, eyes dropping to my lips before ever-so-*slowly* touching mine with a startling softness, one that I didn't think he was capable of.

The tenderness of it left a small, uncomfortable swirl in my stomach. Butterflies.

Um, what the fuck was happening to me?

When he hopped back onto his side of the couch, he grabbed the bowl of popcorn and tossed handfuls into his mouth like nothing happened.

I was tempted to dart into the kitchen and find a bottle of vodka to drown the beautiful, traitorous insects flying around in my belly because apparently the wine was just egging them on.

For the next thirty minutes while Bridget was still on the phone, I didn't even pay attention to the movie. I was too busy trying to ignore the evil little voice in my head that was whispering to scoot closer to him. At one point, I even grabbed a decorative pillow and tried to create a border between us with it, but one tiny, measly pillow wasn't enough.

I wasn't sure if anything would've been enough.

Chapter Forty-Nine

Crew

It had been two days since I crashed Kota's movie night and I was antsy as fuck for some reason.

My life would've been so much easier if I just had Kota's location.

But considering we barely spoke a word for our first two months of living together, we never ended up sharing ours.

The temptation to scream at TJ and tell him to drive faster was tearing through me, and the only thing holding me back from doing it was the scorching anger that was aimed towards myself.

TJ was a coffee addict. If he didn't get his daily fix, he was an asshole for the day. Not to mention, his addiction was so bad that he played hockey at a ten-year-old level if he didn't have it. I wasn't sure how that science worked, and TJ had tried explaining it many times to us, but the conversation always ended with the guys telling him he was a dumbass.

Regardless of the ridiculous amount of money he spent weekly at Starbucks, he'd somehow conned me into joining him on his run this morning before practice, meaning I was at his mercy on the way home since his foot was the one on the gas.

I wasn't even sure why I was in such a rush. And that's what made me annoyed with myself.

I'd grown used to having conscious, wet dreams of throwing Kota on her back and shoving my face between her thighs, but for the first time, that wasn't on the forefront of my mind. Don't get me wrong— all those dirty fantasies were still on a loop in my head, the same way the girls had Taylor Swift's new album on repeat full blast throughout the apartment for the past week. Up until this point, every time I'd wanted to be alone with her, it was because I wanted to touch her, taste her, tease her.

But ever since the other night, I just felt like being around her in a non-sexual way. Which felt ridiculous given the way I'd done everything in my power to not breathe the same air as her for so long.

"What's wrong with you?" TJ blurted.

"What do you mean?"

I refused to glance his way, even though I knew he was fixated on the road. "You're being weird."

"What do you mean?" I repeated.

The slight acceleration of the car made me hold back a sigh of relief, and I drowned the knot of nerves in my throat with a chug of the coffee that I didn't even want, which had sat untouched in the car during practice, now cold.

"I haven't seen you with a girl in I don't even know how long. You haven't even *mentioned* any recent hookups either. And now you've been shaking your leg like a leaf for the past five minutes."

Fuck.

"The coffee makes me jittery."

"Alriiiightttt," he warily accepted, "that doesn't explain the rest."

The lie came out far easier than it should've.

"I guess I've just been taking a break from hookups."

"You? Taking a break?" he scoffed in disbelief.

Apparently, I should've come up with a better lie. "I don't know," I said.

"Why?"

I nearly spit out that I'd been busy with a five-four fireball of a girl, with long, dark hair, and sinfully sweet lips.

But I knew that answer wouldn't satisfy him. He'd push until he knew who it was. And if I was going to tell anyone about this disastrous, rule-breaking mess that Kota and I had going on, it sure as hell wouldn't be TJ. He had the biggest mouth of anyone I knew. The kid never thought before speaking. The whole thing would spread like wildfire throughout the team until it found its way straight to the one person that I sure as shit didn't want to find out.

Lane would beat my ass if he knew.

I'd given him so much shit about his crush on Bridget.

"Lane, it's a bad idea."

"She's our roommate. It's against the rules."

"You're gonna have to get over it, Lane. It can't happen."

And look at me now. I was the biggest hypocrite I knew. If Lane found out what had been going on between Kota and me, he'd lose his shit, and I wouldn't blame him.

"Alright. I have been hooking up with someone," I admitted, keeping it at that.

"Oh," TJ smirked. "Who?"

"You don't know her."

"Bullshit," he called.

"What do you mean, *bullshit*?"

"I mean exactly what I said — *bullshit*. If that was really all there was to it, then you would've said that in the beginning."

Hand clenching around my cup, my jaw tensed, and I stared out the window like I'd find my way out of this somehow written in the sky.

For how much of an idiot TJ was, I hated when he had moments of being smart.

TJ's smirk turned insidious, a husky laugh bellowing out. "You fucked someone you shouldn't have, didn't you?" There wasn't enough time in the world to come up with a good enough lie and I wanted nothing more than to smack that strangely entertained look off his goddamn face. I should've just jumped out of the moving car, honestly. "Who was it? Your roommate? El? Oh Jesus Christ, I hope for your own sake that it wasn't El."

"No! I didn't fuck El."

"Are you sure?"

"I'm sure," I hissed. "And I swear to God if I wind up dead because you babbled some bullshit to Matt, I'm gonna find a way to kill you from the afterlife."

"Alright, alright," he grinned. "So, what I'm hearing is that it was your roommate."

"No, TJ. Fuck."

"Which one was it? Kota or Bridget? Damn, if it was Bridget, Lane's gonna be pissed. I think everyone on the planet besides her knows that he's into her."

"*Neither of them*," I spat like poison. "Can you just drop it? I told you that you don't know her.

With a huff of disappointment, he finally pulled up to our apartment complex. "I'll find out eventually."

"Mhm, alright." I climbed out of the car and slung my bag over my shoulder, gripping my coffee so hard that I was surprised the cup didn't crumple in my hand.

"Hey, wait."

"What?" I snapped.

"Are you coming to the gym with us?"

My dark glare didn't seem to affect TJ at all, no trace of intimidation on his face. Then again, he was one of the best defensemen in the country. Of course, he wasn't afraid of me.

"No," I said, forcing myself to keep my eyes on him instead of scanning the lot for Kota's car. "I'm gonna nap before class."

"Fucking lame."

Eyes rolling, I said, "Suck my dick."

"You know I'm not into that," he joked.

My middle finger shot up. "Bye."

Taking the stairs two at a time up to our apartment, I was uncomfortable by my own excitement at the thought of seeing Kota lying on the couch, curled up in her snuggie.

Maybe she'd have another rom-com on that I could join her for. Maybe I'd get close enough to make her heart beat sporadically like the other night, when I was able to hear it thumping against her perfect chest over the sound of Matthew McConaughey's voice. Maybe this time, I'd sit a little closer.

But all those ludicrous thoughts weren't enough to successfully manifest it. All I found on the other side of the door was Bridget lying in the same spot Kota had been the

266

other night, her face practically smushed into the pages of a
book.

"Hey."

"Hey," she greeted me, eyes not lifting in the slightest.
When she realized that I was alone, her curiosity grew enough
to acknowledge me with a glance. "Where's Lane?"

"Uh, he had a meeting with our coach."

"About what?"

There had been a few times where I thought that maybe
Bridget was into Lane too, that maybe I shouldn't have made
him hold back when it came to being with her. If I had kept my
mouth shut in the beginning, then we both wouldn't be in
messes right now. Very different messes but messes all the
same.

"Our coach wanted his opinion on who should take his
spot as captain next year when we're gone."

Her shoulders caved in slightly, innocent eyes
saddening like a storm cloud was hovering over her. "Oh," she
nodded.

I was horrible at comforting people, especially
considering I could hardly comfort myself when I was upset
about something. I wasn't sure what had made her vibe shift to
somber, but since I did consider her as a friend at this point, I
felt the need to say *something*.

"Are you... okay?"

"Yep," she sat up. And just as quickly as that
thunderstorm had appeared above her, it disappeared, all
sunshine and smiles coming back.

"Alright..." I said. "Where's Kota at?"

"She's at the gym, I think."

Guess I was going to the gym after all.

***

My eyes caught her ponytail the second I walked in.
Even if I hadn't been looking for her though, she would've
been far too easy to spot, being the only person in the gym

whose eyes were flitting around like she had no idea how she got there.

With a single glance over her skintight purple leggings that clung scrupulously to her round ass, filthy images came to me like a flashback.

My pulse quickened as I walked up behind her, slowly approaching like a lion creeping up on an injured antelope.

"You look lost," I said, causing her to jump. I'd meant to say it casually, but the second the words rolled off my tongue, the intensity in my voice became clear.

Kota's surprise was unmistakable as she turned, brows furrowing with a bitter glare. "I'm not lost."

"Alright," I offered a nod, "not lost. Just confused."

A groan caught in her throat as her hand dug into her hip, and as easy as it was for me to lie to TJ earlier, I didn't have the same ability to lie to myself.

I was a bit turned on.

"I'm not confused," she griped.

"Not confused, huh?" Gesturing to the nearest machine, which just so happened to be a Lat machine, intended to help work out your back muscles, I said, "After you then."

Kota stared at me like she could strangle me if there weren't witnesses around to see, and I stared back with amusement, wondering if she'd admit she had no idea how to use it or if her stubborn side would win.

Ultimately, her stubborn side won.

She sat down on the bench seat— backwards, might I add. I crossed my arms, biting my lower lip to hold back laughter while she struggled to reach the handle. As she pulled it in the completely wrong motion, I spoke, "You're gonna hurt yourself."

"I know what I'm doing."

I shook my head, one hand gripping the handle to stop her mid-rep. My other hand found its way to her wrist, guiding her off the bench seat. The velvet touch of her skin was enough to give me a dopamine hit.

Her voice came out sounding disgusted, as if she hadn't been begging for my touch days ago. "What are you doing?!"

"Oh, so now I can't touch you?"

"No."

"Don't even," I dared.

She huffed. "Don't even what?"

Leaning in until my breath was skating across her neck, my voice dropped low. "Don't even pretend like if I bent you over this bench right now that you wouldn't happily take it and scream my name in front of everyone."

Giving a light tremble, she didn't express another rebuttal. I turned her around and pressed down lightly on her shoulders so that she was sitting the right way.

"What are you doing?" she asked again, this time much quieter.

"Helping you."

"I don't need help," she insisted.

Pausing, I looked right at her. "Kota."

"What?"

"Can you quit being stubborn for one damn second?"

With another groan, she crossed her arms, giving a pout. I took that as her accepting my offer and explained to her how to properly use the machine.

Surprisingly, Kota listened to my explanation without interrupting, before quietly grabbing the handle the way I'd just taught her.

As she pulled it down correctly this time, I smiled lightly. "There ya go."

A familiar sight caught the corner of my eye and a chuckle rippled through me before my fist shot up to shield it.

Immediately, a deep scowl was sent my way, so sharp that I could feel it tearing at me like a cat digging its claws in.

"Are you *laughing* at me?" Kota growled.

"No, no!" I panicked, fearful of the growing rage in her eyes. I jumped forward, squatting beside her. "You see that guy over there by the leg press?"

"Yeah."

I kept my voice low. "He has his back to us right now but just wait for him to turn around. He's here all the time and I swear he has that same shirt in at least five different colors."

With thin patience, she curiously watched.

The guy chugged his water before wiping down the machine, and the moment he spun around, Kota's small hand hovered over her mouth, shoulders bouncing with a giggle.

His bright blue t-shirt read "Milfs love me" on the front, and you could tell who in the gym was a newcomer or a regular based on if they were staring or not.

The group of guys nearby him didn't bat an eye at the sight, yet a girl on a treadmill was gawking so hard that I was impressed she didn't lose her footing and slide right off the thing.

"Now, I don't know about you," I said quietly, "but I'm pretty confident in saying there's probably not a single milf that loves him."

Kota laughed, a full belly laugh. The sound penetrated straight through me, and I gaped at her, awestruck. It wasn't until she looked back at me with a trace of confusion that I realized I'd been smirking like an idiot.

"What?" she asked with a delicate, lazy smile.

I nearly forgot my train of thought. "I made you laugh."

Making her laugh was almost more satisfying than making her blow smoke out her ears or making her moan my name.

As quickly as I could snap my fingers, her smile was gone, that mask of hers returning. "Well, you said something funny."

I stood back up straight. "Are you hungry?"

"Eh," she shrugged. "Why?"

"Do you wanna go eat?"

Kota blinked at me like I just spoke gibberish. "Eat?"

"Yeah," I said. "As in... *consume food.*"

Her eyes narrowed, and I nearly got heat stroke from the flames suddenly radiating off her, regardless of how much she resembled a cute teddy bear just minutes ago.

"I understand what the word *eat* means."

"Okay, so..." I trailed off, waiting for an answer.

"I'm confused."

"By?"

"You wanting to be seen in public together," she said.

"We're in public together right now," I pointed out.

"Not by choice," she responded, strutting past me. "For all I know, you followed me here."

Fuck.

I stood silently, worried that any response would give away the fact that I kind of did follow her here. I caught up to her, struggling to do so even though her legs were nearly half the length of mine.

Suddenly, Kota swung around, causing me to abruptly halt.

"So, are you going to be paying for this food?"

My brows knitted, unable to read her expression. I had no idea what answer she was looking for.

"Yes?" I guessed.

Her eyes widened in fear, sending every brain cell I had left into panic mode.

"No?" I corrected myself.

"Good," Kota sighed a breath of relief, walking away again. "Because this isn't a date," she barked over her shoulder.

<u>Chapter Fifty</u>

Kota

"**C**'mon," Crew smiled, "you've gotta admit the tinfoil one was pretty good."

"I'll give you props for the dedication. That's all you're getting from me," I said.

The small diner we were in reminded me of Betty's, which made me more convinced that I was having some weird dream right now where I'd been kidnapped and brought here with Crew against my will.

But the reality kept sinking in over and over.

I *agreed* to this.

Jesus. I'd officially come unhinged.

Shifting uncomfortably in my dirty gym clothes, I longed for a shower. I could feel his relentless eyes on me, and the second I met his gaze, I regretted it, visions of us showering together lurking up on me.

A jaunty grin greeted me from across the table as if he could read my thoughts.

"What're you thinking about?" he teased.

I pulled my mind out of the gutter, giving the iciest smile I could currently manage. "You crying over tampons on your ceiling."

That shrewd grin disappeared like a sandcastle getting washed away. Sitting back, he crossed his arms.

272

And here we were again. Playing this hate game.

"I had good pranks too," he whined.

"Mhm," I hummed. "Speaking of which, can you stop it with the sex boxes?"

He laughed once. Twice. Before a full laughing fit rolled out. Attempting to smother my grin, I tried my best not to allow the sound to affect me.

"Oh gosh," he wheezed. "Yeah, sorry. I didn't realize I never canceled that. Why didn't you say something earlier?"

The inside of my cheek fell victim to my sudden unease, my teeth gnawing at it until I was about to draw blood.

A devilish grin crept up on Crew's face, and I immediately knew I'd been caught. His eyes creased with delight, burning into me.

"You kept some of it, didn't you?" he said.

"No," I muttered a lie.

"You did," he smiled wider.

I couldn't look at him, not while knowing that the same objects he'd purchased to express his hatred for me were the same ones I used on myself while his face was stuck in my head the whole time.

Crew's forefinger trailed around the edge of his glass of water, still beaming. With the way the light casted through the window beside us, he was glowing like a Greek God. Hair perfectly messy, jawline dangerously sharp, charming smirk radiating to the point where I was nearly blinded.

"Well," he started, "were you ever planning on showing me what you've got?"

I sat back, doing my best to seem relaxed even though my growing attraction to him was making me want to flee the country. "Nope."

"Why not?" he taunted. "I mean, I did pay for it."

My phone vibrated on the booth beside me, and I held it at my side as I peeked, speaking, "Not happening, but you can keep dreaming."

El: Apparently Crew has been hooking up with some mystery girl and TJ just gave me a whole interrogation because he thinks it's me!! Can you believe that?!

My grip on the phone tightened, throat constricting with immediate worry as I stared at it.

"Why do you have that look on your face?"

"Did you tell anybody about us?" I panicked.

His brows crinkled. "Us?"

"Yes. Us. As in, your *P* in my *V*," I said sharply.

"God no," he said. "Why?"

I placed my phone on the table and slid it over. Crew eyed me for a long moment before touching it, although I wasn't sure if it was from a lack of trust that it wouldn't explode in his hand or if he was just too scared to look.

I watched his eyes skim across the screen, every feature of his falling before reappearing as rage, like the sun peeking out during a thunderstorm before a tornado hit.

Dropping my phone as if it was lava in his hand, Crew dug his own phone out of his pocket. It was up to his ear in seconds.

"Speaker," I whispered.

With a light groan, he complied, just in time to hear TJ casually say, "Hello?" on the other end.

"What the fuck is wrong with you?" Crew let out.

"A lot of things."

"Clearly," Crew spurred. "I told you not to tell anyone about what we talked about earlier. Why would you tell El?"

"I didn't tell Matt," TJ was quick to assure.

I wanted more than anything to butt into the conversation, but I couldn't give myself up. Meanwhile, our waitress was headed our way, probably with an update on our food, but as she got closer, something seemed to change her mind, because she halted in her tracks, mouth popping open before switching directions.

Suddenly, the root of her alarm became clear. She could tell it was a bad time. The prominent tick in Crew's jaw was hard to miss. And the closer I paid attention, the easier it was to note the smoke radiating off him like he just walked out of a burning building.

But unlike our waitress, I wasn't spooked. I'd seen this sort of anger in him many times; it's just never made me feel this odd attraction to him before.

Crew was a certified sex God around Cedar U, and the more time I spent with him, the easier it was to see why. Everything he did was somehow sexual, tempting. He could be doing the most casual things— breathing, eating, *being pissed off.* And it was somehow still enough to make women drool at the sight of him.

I used to be disgusted by those girls that would practically orgasm just by glancing his way.

Now I was becoming one of them.

Shit.

"O-kay," Crew said. "So, you took everything I said about telling no one and just applied it to Matt? Who else did you tell?"

"No one else," TJ responded, sounding like he didn't have a care in the world. "I was just doing some investigative work."

"Well knock it off," Crew warned fiercely. "Shouldn't you be buying Taylor Swift tickets right now or something?"

My face distorted back and forth between confused and amused, and I found myself choking back a howl of laughter.

Apparently, Crew struck a nerve, because TJ's nonchalance spiraled, wild chagrin echoing through the speaker. "I already told you they're sold out! Why would you say that to me? Now I'm upset!"

Giving an oily smile, Crew bobbed side to side, keeping his tone sharp. "Tell someone my business again and I'll remind you five hundred more times that you'll never see her live."

"You're an asshole," TJ muttered before the call went dead.

Although our side of the diner was empty, it suddenly sounded like it was full. Between the two of us, our laughter was loud enough to fill every crevice of the room.

It was bizarre that we were laughing together instead of at each other, and what was more bizarre was how much I sort of liked it.

"I didn't know he was a Swiftie," I chuckled.

"The biggest," Crew smiled, dimples so deep I could swim in them. "He's obsessed with her."

"Respect."

Acting as if she hadn't run away from a war zone minutes prior, our waitress returned, bright and friendly with plates stacked impressively in her hands and along the backs of her forearms.

"Omelets with sausage and hash browns," she announced, sliding Crew's food in front of him.

"Thank you," he said.

"And blueberry pancakes with a side of bacon."

"Thanks," I grinned at her.

With dark brown hair that sat along her shoulders and bangs that I could never pull off, she was gorgeous. I'd be surprised if her looks didn't get her extra tips.

Glancing briskly at her nametag that read *Bethany*, I watched her eyes land on Crew for what I swore was the hundredth time since we stepped into this diner. With none other than a sunshine smirk, she gave a light sway. Her voice came out slow and seductive, making it hard not to laugh at her.

"Anything else I can get for you?"

I was convinced the question was only meant for Crew.

It would've been so easy for him to feed into it, to do the thing he did best— flirt. To ooze that heavenly sex appeal he was full of. To make her fall at his feet and beg him to love her. Or fuck her. Or both.

But all he did was turn to me, not giving her an ounce of further attention. "Do you need anything else?"

"No," I shook my head.

"We're all set," he said with a friendly ring to it.

Failing to hide her disappointment behind a weak smile that looked almost painful, she gave a single nod before wandering off.

I dove straight for my bacon. "She was so trying to flirt with you."

"Yeah, so?" Crew mumbled between bites.

"So," I paused, "why didn't you do anything about it? She's pretty."

His eyes fell to his plate, a spark of discomfort storming in. Speaking low and hollow, he said, "I didn't feel like it."

"Why?"

276

He shrugged. "Just didn't want to," he said quietly, focused only on his food.

There was a pang in my heart, a dip in my tummy as if I was on the huge drop of a rollercoaster. My initial thought was that maybe it had something to do with me.

But I shoved that thought away, along with all the strangely unique and pleasing emotions shooting through my bloodstream.

He doesn't like me. I shouldn't even entertain the thought.

Chapter Fifty-One

Kota

Memes.

One of humanity's greatest creations, in my opinion.

I could scroll through that shit all day long, but I always did my best to hardly touch my phone during the day, knowing that doing so would make me susceptible to falling down a rabbit hole of memes and not being productive at all.

So, I saved the scrolling for nighttime.

The only light glowing in my room was from my phone as I laid in bed, snuggled in a mess of blankets like I was wrapped in a burrito.

The boys refused to turn the heat up any more even though it was still freezing outside, which meant Bridget and I were usually dressed for arctic weather.

Rob K was curled up, sleeping soundly at the end of my bed like he did every other night when he wasn't sleeping in Bridget's room. I tried to pet him but couldn't reach, giving up after the cold air hit my skin for too long.

For the fourth time in a row, I watched an Instagram Reel of a raccoon trying to open a door, and I shoved my mouth under my comforter to mute my laughter, doing my best not to wake Bridget through the wall that separated us.

We retreated to our rooms at about the same time, twenty minutes ago, but that girl's consciousness was like a

278

light switch. She could fall asleep in minutes. It was kind of impressive.

We'd been friends for so long though that I'd grown to know when she was passed out or not based off her lack of responses to the memes I would send her at night. It had already been ten minutes since I sent her a Twilight themed meme that she still hadn't opened, which told me she was sleeping.

Going back to scrolling, a banner notification popped up and I squinted at it in the darkness.

Crew: Come to my room

I had to stop myself from hopping out of bed and running down the hall.

That familiar battle seeped into my skin again, tugging me back and forth between reason and want.

I didn't see this situation between us ending in any way other than *horribly*.

In my past, I'd grown attached to people, to things, that always ended up screwing me over in the end. Which was why I preferred to keep my feelings bottled up, or better yet, to avoid them altogether.

And with the record that Crew had, the odds of not getting hurt weren't in my favor.

For a second, I thought maybe I should just not answer his text and pretend to be asleep, but there was a good chance Crew would see that I was just active on Instagram.

I typed out a short text telling him no, then shook my head and hit the backspace, typing up something else.

But ultimately, that message got deleted too.

With a sigh, I finally settled on one.

Me: umm... but everyone's home?????

Crew: So?
We'll be quiet

Me: yeah right

Crew: (;

**Just come to my room
And bring your toys**

I let out a sigh, *a fake sigh*, because we all knew I
wanted to go. At the same time, it was more so laced with
disappointment in myself, because I knew it was a bad idea, but
I couldn't stay away. Not when he was my roommate.

The saying went, *"Out of sight, out of mind,"* but how
do you keep someone out of your thoughts when you're forced
to live with them?

I accepted the fact that I was screwed, and if I was
truly doomed, then I might as well make the most of it.

Ever so carefully slipping out of the blankets without
disturbing Rob K, I grabbed my box of toys from under my
bed. The box was black with a lock latch in front, and a jitter of
nerves shot through me when my fingers skimmed along the
top. My eyes darted down both directions of the hall before the
pads of my toes met the hardwood floor, tiptoeing carefully.

I clutched my box like it was my lifeline, scuffling
across the floor in my penguin pajamas through the darkness
like a loser.

Sucking in a gulp of frozen air when I got to Crew's
door, I wasn't sure if knocking was risky; I didn't want to wake
anyone up. Instead, I just tested the waters and went straight for
the doorknob, surprised when it turned.

As if it were summertime rather than the dead of
winter, Crew was lying atop his blankets instead of under them,
wearing nothing but gray sweatpants that did a fantastic job of
showcasing the outline of his dick.

There was a stream of light from his small TV that was
mounted on the far wall, casting a glow across his top half.

With an arm propping up his head, hair perfectly messy
and taut muscles on full display, he looked like every girl's
fantasy come to life.

His voice came out like some deep, lyrical note. "Hi,"
he whispered. The sound nearly carved *NC* into my heart, and it
felt like a butterfly with razor-sharp wings was trying to claw
its way out of my stomach.

If I had had any last trace of self-control, it was surely gone now. Arms wrapping tighter around my box, I responded, "Hi."

I could make out his dark brows pulling together for a moment. "Are those penguins?"

Was he expecting me to wear something sexier?

I gave a sassy huff. "Yeah, so?"

Pearly whites lighting up the dark room, Crew shot me a smile before giving a nod. "Whatcha got in your box?"

"Voodoo dolls," I joked. "All of you."

"That would explain a lot."

Lust was bursting in his eyes like fireworks in the night sky, and he sat up, patting the bed beside him. Then there was that magically angelic voice again, pulling me right into a trance. "C'mere."

I couldn't say no.

Like a magnet, I was drawn into Crew, sitting close enough for our legs to meet. Without a word, the box was taken from me, although I hadn't fought it.

He popped the lid off, inspecting every item one by one, eyes lighting up as he did so.

Ninety percent of the items in this box came from Crew's sex toy prank. A lot of the things were stuff I'd heard about or had seen online before. So not going to lie, Crew saved me a lot of money.

There was a butterfly shaped vibrator, a mint green bullet vibrator, strawberry flavored lube, blue furry handcuffs, a hot pink rabbit, and more.

When Crew got to the rabbit, hidden at the bottom, his brow raised, and he gave a sinful half-smirk.

"Well, this looks interesting," he said.

Suddenly, my mouth went dry, blood pumping through my veins at an inhuman rate.

Crew tapped the on button and as we both fell silent, the only noise was the light vibration from the toy. Fingertips digging into my shoulder, Crew pushed me onto my back. With the toy thrown aside, he used both hands to shimmy my pants off, following with my shirt.

He'd seen me naked a handful of times already, but it still made me nervous every time. It was like I was afraid of what he would think.

Running his hands along my sides, from my ribcage all the way down to my hips, his touch was so warm, so electric. He made me feel like a virgin, as if I was getting touched for the first time.

Staring at me like a starving animal, Crew took all of me in. "You're so fucking perfect."

Stealing a peek at the prominent ridges in his abs, it felt like my mouth was starting to water.

"Are you ready for this?" he held up the toy and I nodded. I wasn't sure if I'd have to explain to him how it worked, but it seemed like he already had it figured out, not hesitating in the slightest. Tracing his thumb along my clit, he groaned. "Jesus, Kota. You're so fucking wet already and I've barely touched you."

Every time he spoke, my heart surged faster, harder, pounding against my ribcage like it was trying to escape. A whimper clogged my throat, and Crew slowly pumped the bottom part of the rabbit into me. Right as the vibrating top sat on my clit, the sensation skyrocketed down my legs like I'd just been electrocuted.

Crew was lying comfortably between my legs, his tongue tracing circles along my inner thigh. Every few moments, he'd look over to catch a glimpse of my face before he'd watch my opening intently as he continued drawing the rabbit in and out of me.

Inevitably, my eyes rolled back, and I moaned loudly.

A hot palm slammed against my mouth, my eyes shooting open in response. "Shh," Crew hushed me, heated brown eyes trailing over my face. "You wouldn't want our roommates to hear, would you?" Shaking my head against his hand, I watched his teeth sink into his bottom lip. "Good girl," he murmured.

Cautiously releasing his hand to allow me to breathe, Crew worked the toy until an orgasm shattered through me so hard that I shook beneath him. My satisfied cries couldn't be contained, and Crew shut me up by covering my mouth with his own.

Pulling away just enough to speak, his hot and sizzling breath rolled out as he muttered into my mouth, "Just moan against me, baby."

Moan after moan rippled out and Crew swallowed every single one. Using the rabbit, he applied the perfect amount of pressure to my clit, and he didn't stop even when I was letting out an array of whimpers against him, legs shaking like I'd just ran ten miles.

Each orgasm was stronger than the last, and by the third, Crew no longer cared for the rabbit. He wanted to be inside me instead.

Fucking me with the stamina, strength, and adrenaline of a D1 athlete, we both rode out our orgasms at the same time, lips quivering against each other.

With a final thrust, Crew collapsed beside me, gasping for air. It took minutes for me to catch my breath and for my body to stop convulsing.

Like the very first time I'd found myself in this bed, I laid with my back to Crew. But whereas that time was to create distance to keep his stupidity and heightened confidence from rubbing off on me during our sleep, this time, the purpose was to keep myself from *touching* him in our sleep.

My body was exhausted, craving rest, but my mind wasn't complying. There were too many thoughts and not enough all at once, and I found myself laying there with my eyes open, studying every part of his room that I could make out.

A Chicago Blackhawks poster hung, repping every Stanley Cup win they'd ever had.

The framed photo of Crew and Lane on his desk, arms slung around each other's shoulders, although I couldn't tell where or when the photo was taken.

The laptop that sat opened, black screen beside the photo frame, as if Crew had been interrupted while he was doing homework and never went back to finish.

The smallest pile of what I assumed were dirty clothes, pushed into the far corner.

Remind me to tell this kid to get better at using his hamper.

The hooks above his closet, each holding a different snapback. Cedar, Blackhawks, Nike. I couldn't make out the farthest one, granted it was all black. Although I tried not to pay any attention to him for the first few months of knowing him, I didn't remember seeing Crew wear a snapback ever, or any hat for that matter.

"Are you awake?"

Heartbeat surging at the sound, I was relieved I was facing the opposite way. I didn't want him to see the look on my face, to see how much the sound of his voice was starting to affect me.

"No," I replied.

"I didn't ask for any sarcasm."

A sadistic smile took over. "Well, you got some for free." Peeking over my shoulder at him, I said, "You wanna rub my back?"

His own grin danced in the darkness as he readjusted himself, lifted jawline so sharp that I was surprised it didn't cut his pillowcase open when it met the fabric. "Hm, that's funny."

"What?"

"I don't remember signing up to be your masseuse."

"Hmm," I hummed, shifting onto my back and closing my eyes after a moment of studying his ceiling.

Five seconds of silence passed, turning to ten. Broken once again by my enemy whose sigh even sounded heavenly.

"Do you want me to rub your back?" he asked.

Did I want him to? Yes.

Did I want him to know that I wanted him to? No.

"No," I murmured.

"Alright," he said quietly.

Back to silence.

But it didn't last.

"When's your birthday?" he suddenly asked.

I needed him to shut up. Every sound that came out of his mouth was making that razor-sharp butterfly more and more frantic inside me, and if I didn't find some sort of control soon, it was going to tear me right open.

"Why?" my voice cracked like thunder.

"I thought I heard Bridget say something the other day about it."

"Oh," I mumbled. "It's in a few weeks."

"Oh." The bed dipped in the slightest, nearly rolling me inwards as Crew inched closer to me. Close enough to graze me with his arm. I could feel his heat radiating towards me, as if daring me to touch him in a way that wasn't sexual.

"Are you excited?" he asked.

"Yeah," I admitted.

"Do you like your birthday?"

"Usually," I said, blinking rapidly at the ceiling.

"Why just usually?"

"Why do you keep asking me questions about myself?" I wondered aloud.

I knew he was facing me; his breath was trailing across my skin and if I were to turn, he'd only be inches away. My cheek was burning where he was staring at it. As the seconds ticked by, and the longer he stayed this way, the more I was convinced that maybe he *wanted* me to turn towards him.

Or maybe I was just delusional.

Only one way to find out.

Biting the bullet, I made the shift, placing my hands underneath my cheek, and although Crew and I had technically been this close before, we'd never been this close in an emotionally intimate manner.

The second I was able to focus on his face, I held back a gasp. I'd never studied him so closely before, never noticed the tiny freckle under his eye, never noticed how long his lashes were, never noticed how one side of his mouth tended to pull upwards before the other.

All the details, I memorized as well as I possibly could so that I'd have something to think about when we were no longer in this moment.

The rasp in his voice pushed my soul back into my body, snapping me to reality. "Maybe I'm just trying to find out what your weakness is."

"Is that so?"

"Maybe," he smirked slightly. The more his eyes bounced across my face, glittering, the more the lines blurred.

Jesus. I need to stop this borderline lovey dovey shit.

"Do I get to figure out your weakness too then?" I asked.

His breath fell against my lips as he let out a light sigh, so light that if the rest of the apartment wasn't so quiet, I wouldn't have heard it.

"I guess," he finally agreed.

"Alright," I said, exhaling deeply out my nose. "Rapid fire questions then."

"Fine."

"Fine," I said.

He spoke softly, sounding like some sort of sacred prayer. "You go first."

"Biggest fear?"

"Clowns," he responded. I raised a brow, but he didn't explain further. "You?"

"Small spaces. I'm claustrophobic."

"Something you hate?" he asked.

"You," I responded, the lightest grin dancing across my lips as I waited to hear his answer.

"You," he answered gingerly, a certain fire catching in his eyes.

There was that dangerous butterfly again, both beautiful and nauseating.

"Favorite movie?" I asked.

"The Terminator. What's yours?"

"Of all-time? Monster's Inc."

He gave a husky chuckle. "That's a classic. Can't go wrong with that."

"I know," I grinned. "I love Disney movies."

"Somewhere you've always wanted to travel to?"

I stared off in thought through the darkness. "There are a lot, but my top answer is pretty basic— Hawaii."

"That's on my list too. I wanna go there in the next few years," Crew said. "I think Spain is probably my top though."

"Spain is cool," I nodded against the pillow.

"You've been?"

Snuggling up into a ball with two fistfuls of the comforter, I responded, "I have actually. I went senior year of high school on a class trip."

"Was the food good?" he wondered.

"*So* good."

A lighthearted smile flashed across his face for just a moment before he asked, "Favorite season?"

"Spring. You?"

"Winter. I prefer the cold."

"That's the most hockey player answer," I rolled my eyes.

Crew's irises dug deeper into me as one dimple appeared through the darkness, the other hidden beneath his pillow.

I wondered if he did this with all his hookups— acted curious to get to know them before kicking them to the curb. And just from that thought alone, in the time it would've taken me to snap my fingers, all my lovey dovey bullshit thoughts were replaced with reminders of every reason why I hated him in the first place.

"Well, I am a hockey player," he murmured through his grin.

"Yes," I sighed. "You are."

Turning onto my back once more, I shut my eyes, waiting for tragedy to strike, for him to kick me out and tell me to go back to my own room.

But silence was all that hung in the air, and as I got closer and closer to passing out, I could've sworn I felt the warmth of his lips stain my forehead.

Chapter Fifty-Two

Crew

"**Y**ou ready?" Lane asked, tapping me on the shoulder.

"More than ever."

But the truth was that I wasn't sure if I was ready.

Because I wasn't focused.

All I could think about was Kota and it was driving me fucking nuts. Even more nuts than when she was pretending like we never hooked up.

I couldn't decode her. And I sure as hell couldn't decode myself.

I'd never cuddled a girl in my life.

But as I was lying there and I peeked my eyes open, there she was, so small and so warm. The most fragile, stunning thing I'd ever seen in my life.

And I couldn't resist.

I just wanted to touch her, to feel her soft skin pushed against mine.

As carefully as I could've managed, I bundled her up and held her to me. I'd never forget the tiny, peaceful breath she let out against my chest, how sweet it sounded, soothing me to sleep.

But when I awoke, she was gone, and my disappointment sank so deep into my DNA that it seemed to overpower everything else.

What the hell was happening to me?

My hockey stick was already taped and sitting on the rack in the corner, and just like every game before this one, I checked on it periodically.

With five minutes left until warmups, all the guys were running through their own pre-game rituals.

Lane popped his headphones in, listening to his late brother's favorite song.

Cody and Matt were doing their weird handshake that everyone usually made fun of them for.

Jett already did his— all left side articles of equipment had to go on first.

And TJ was chugging coffee like the freak he was.

After warmups, Lane and Coach Palmer both gave us a pep talk, and we set out for the ice.

Tonight, we were playing Providence. They weren't even ranked in the top ten right now, so it should've been an easy win, but Jett always wailed on me whenever I'd say shit like that aloud. He insisted that it was bad luck and that I'd jinx us.

But within the first seven minutes, we already had two goals— one by TJ and one by Jonah, who happened to score one of the best slapshots I'd seen all season while his line was on the ice.

After the second goal, things started to get ugly. To compensate for their shitty passes and lack of ability to shoot the puck into the goal, Providence started playing dirty.

And unfortunately for me, they had the upper hand.

Because I was distracted as fuck.

Kota was still at the forefront of my mind. At most of our other home games, she and Bridget would get here early to snag seats in the front row of the student section, right up against the glass. I had no idea where they were sitting right now, and that was the issue.

When the puck was hurdling my way, passed over by Matt, I nearly missed it. Rounding the curve behind the net and flying by Cody as I recovered and stick handled the puck, my gaze wasn't on the one thing I was supposed to be guarding with my life. It wasn't even in front of me. I was scanning the audience for Kota.

I was daydreaming, imagining her in my jersey again. This time, I would've liked it. And after the game, she would've been waiting for me by the front doors, smiling and glowing as I appeared before jumping into my arms.

The second I turned my head away from the glass, looking back ahead of me, I was met with a shoulder to the chest, knocking the wind out of me and sending me straight onto my back.

The high-pitched whistle blew, but I didn't budge, lungs burning as I heaved through cold air. Lane was the first one there, kneeling beside me.

"Crew," Lane panted. "Crew, can you hear me?"

"Y—yeah," I mumbled back, shaking my helmet back and forth against the ice. "Yeah, I'm good."

"You don't look good. Can you stand?"

My ears rang, and I groaned, pushing myself up. Lane's hand clutched mine, TJ appearing on the other side and grabbing my left hand. They helped me to stand, and the arena burst with cheers when I was back on my feet. Shaking off the hit, I skated a few feet to regain my composure and grab my stick. I was surprised it hadn't snapped in half amidst the chaos.

It wasn't rare for me to take a nasty hit, but that one was definitely a bit more jarring than most. The good news was that I felt fine other than the ache in my back that was bound to turn into a gnarly bruise tomorrow.

The student section was chanting "See ya bitch!" on repeat as Henry Logen was escorted into the penalty box. He glared at me while Cedar U students were already surrounding him, screaming at him through the glass. His hostility was tangible; it felt like a rope he was trying to launch my way and wrap around my neck.

But instead of feeding into it, I went straight to the bench for a break. My time on the bench wasn't used to watch the game, not really. Once again, I was inspecting the crowd, stopping on the face of every single brunette that I had the ability to see.

Since we were up already, coach let me sit out until the last three minutes of the period, throwing Keith into my place on our line. He proved himself, scoring a goal with the help of Lane.

I took three more rough hits during the remainder of the game. None were as bad as the first, but they were bad enough to get penalties called for each.

I wasn't the only one either. Lane took a few hits, along with Jett. TJ and Matt were relatively fine, granted they were both gigantic defenseman and were never targeted so aggressively.

Overall, the game was brutal, and what sucked the most was that my earlier vision was entirely all in my head.

Kota wasn't wearing my jersey. And she wasn't there waiting for me after the game.

Chapter Fifty-Three

Crew

Stallions was packed shoulder to shoulder after our win tonight, and I kept finding myself glancing around to make sure Kota was still in sight.

Some Drake song was blasting, and I was already on my fifth beer of the night, eyes skimming over Kota's ponytail that was so tight she could've whipped someone with it. Her red top looked like it was clinging onto her chest for dear life, her black skirt short enough that I could probably grab a handful of her ass in a split second.

Which also meant I was checking around to make sure no horny guys were eyeing her.

A stiff yank pulled me over, and a small panic overtook me when I could no longer see Kota's smiling face, laughing it up with Bridget.

"I think I figured it out," TJ said, all smug with confidence dripping from him.

Uh oh.

"What?" I huffed.

All seriousness in his tone, he said, "Are you hooking up with a guy?"

"Jesus Christ. What the fu— No!" I shook my head rapidly.

I truly thought TJ had been slowly catching on, but clearly, I was dead wrong.

He gave a pout, rubbing the back of his neck in defeat. "Really? I'm not right?"

"No!"

"Oh," his shoulders slumped, leaving me genuinely surprised as to how he could've possibly been so confident going into this conversation. "Well, there's nothing wrong with it if you were."

"I know that," I said, calmer. "But no, I'm not hooking up with a guy."

"Alright," TJ sighed, accepting defeat. "Well, I'll figure it out eventually." His eyes stopped not-so-innocently on a small blonde that was eye-fucking him a few tables over. "Mind if I ditch you?"

"Please do," I grumbled, watching his face light up before his gaze locked in on his target, pushing through the crowd to reach her.

But when I returned to my spot between Cody and Matt, Kota was still out of sight.

Fire burned through my chest, and I circled around myself frantically, wishing she had been a few inches taller. Or simply that there weren't so many short brunettes wandering around.

I couldn't see Bridget either, couldn't spot Lane. My panic was practically tattooed on my forehead, catching the attention of my teammates.

"You good?"

I jumped at the sound of Lane's voice coming from behind me, nearly collapsing. "Yeah..." I muttered, catching my breath. "Yeah, where are the girls?"

"Bridget's waiting by the door for me. We're both gonna go home and head to bed. We're really tired."

I don't care what you and Bridget are doing.

Keeping my voice as cold-blooded as possible, I asked, "And Kota?"

I studied every feature of Lane's, searching for any sign of suspicion. My face remained stoic even through my deafening heartbeat, praying that Lane couldn't hear it over the music.

He pointed across the bar. "She went that way."

Transfixed on the corner he gestured to, I still couldn't see her.

Lane spoke through a sigh. "Please make sure she gets home alive."

"I will."

"I mean it," he said sharply.

So do I.

"Alright, yeah, yes, I know. Good night, Captain," I waved him off, earning a mutter of expletives as he walked away.

The second he rounded the corner and out the door, I was on the move like a stalker. I had not a single clue where this protectiveness was coming from, but my heart was going to burst of anxiety if I went another minute without her standing right in front of me.

But everyone was in my goddamn way.

I was doing my best not to bulldoze all the girls in my path, beer raised high above their heads to avoid another scenario like the one that occurred on the night I met the brazen girl I was currently after.

I felt deranged; everything that was happening was way out of character for me.

I didn't cuddle with girls after having sex with them.

I didn't care to have their attention afterwards, especially if I was out with my friends celebrating a win.

I didn't lose it whenever they were out of sight.

Everybody around me was laughing, having a good time, completely oblivious to me trying to push past them with the softness and patience of a teacher but the mind of a manic.

When a small tug rattled through my arm, I swung around with the hope that it was her, but whoever the girl was was someone I didn't recognize

However, she recognized me.

"Crew," she smiled, long brown curls cascading down her chest, eyes so brightly blue that they were almost translucent.

"Hey," I casually said, pretending like I knew exactly who she was. But truthfully, I had no idea if she was a past hookup or just someone that knew who I was.

294

"You guys played really great tonight!"

Other than me getting knocked on my ass, yeah.

Her hand was still clutched around mine, and I wanted to rip myself away. "Thanks," I said, voice passive, eyes impulsively flitting past her.

"Are you busy after this?" Her lashes fluttered, thick and dark, pink lips curling upwards.

This was exactly how I would've wanted my night to go months ago. With a random girl throwing herself at me. With my arm clutched around her slim waist, leading her into my bedroom to make her scream my name loud enough that it could be heard across the ocean. Then slyly find a way to kick her out in the morning and go about my day.

But that wasn't how tonight was going to end.

"I am," I nodded, carefully releasing myself from her grip. "Excuse me," I trotted past her.

Seemingly, Heaven finally decided to answer my prayers, bringing Kota into view.

But as if Hell wanted to rain on my damn parade, she wasn't alone.

A guy in a blue flannel had his back to me, blocking and unblocking her face each time he swayed side to side.

They were alone, isolated in a corner. Who knows how long they'd been there? Talking and laughing while I was practically choking on air in her absence?

Tension rocketed down my spine as I stood, feet glued to the floor. I waited to get a glimpse of who the guy was, free hand already drawn into a fist.

I didn't give a fuck that I was standing in other people's way. Their light, yet no-so-subtle shoves barely moved me out of place.

My dark glare pinned the back of his head, wishing it had been enough to make him disintegrate to ashes.

However, it *was* enough to make him spin, standing beside her rather than in front of her.

Oh, fuck no.

My plastic cup was in pieces in my palm, beer drizzling down my arm to join the puddle I'd just made on the floor. The remnants of the cup were abandoned somewhere along the line as I neared them, eyes blazing with a vendetta. Poison was already sitting on my tongue, waiting to be spewed.

Bobby's head was lulled towards her, a sleazy and lovesick smirk painted on his face like he was sure Kota would end up in his bed tonight.

I'd burn down this whole fucking town before I'd let that happen.

With no remorse, I situated myself right between them, cutting Bobby off. "Are you ready to go home?"

As if she wasn't half naked in my bed less than twenty-four hours ago, clutching onto me tightly in her sleep like a baby koala, Kota's eyes were as frigid as Arctic waters. Any bit of warmth that I'd been able to bring into those beautiful irises was gone. The ice queen had me nearly convinced that I'd made up everything that happened last night.

Nearly convinced.

Teeth gnawing at the inside of my cheek, I watched as she took a tiny step backwards, acting startled, staring at me with those empty eyes. "Crew?!" she exclaimed. She might as well had just screamed *Where the fuck did you come from?!*

It only made the fire inside of me grow a little hotter, simmer a little brighter, because it made me insinuate that I actually *had* interrupted something.

"Ready?" I asked softly.

Slim shoulders rising and falling with a deep breath, she let her head drop for a moment. "Alright," she said, barely audible over the Taylor Swift song that was turned up so loud that it sounded like she was screeching through the speakers. I was a hundred percent sure TJ was embarrassing himself somewhere in this bar right now, and usually, I would've been the first one there to laugh my ass off at him, but it was impossible for me to take my eyes off Kota right now. "Let me just go to the bathroom," she said.

Before I could offer to wait for her by the bathroom or the back door, she was gone, leaving me with no choice but to wait for her here. Moving would've subjected me to losing her in the crowd.

With a casual tap on my shoulder, Bobby seemed too comfortable next to me, too confident. I wasn't sure if it was the liquor coursing through him or if he was just that fucking arrogant.

"Hey," he slurred. "Can we just be cool from now on? I'm trying to get back with Kota and—"

"Yeah, that's not fucking happening." And there was the poison that had been patiently waiting, finally falling out.

He seemed taken aback, giving a light scoff. "Excuse me?"

"Oh, did you not hear me the first time? I said that's not fucking happening."

Bobby's eyes turned hollow, unstable, which only made me want to keep him away from Kota more. He was absolutely sloshed; no wonder he wasn't able to stand straight when I was watching him from behind.

With a tight jaw, he said, "Well, it's not up to you."

I shook my head. "No. It's not," I agreed. "But if you were smart, you'd listen anyway."

Bobby was acting like he had no idea where this was coming from, as if we never had a similar conversation to this before. He was trying to stab me with a hostile scowl, but it felt more like a pinprick than a knife wound. "Is that a threat?" he seethed.

My words came out like a gunshot, thundering and dangerous. "Fuck yeah, it is."

"I'm not afraid of you."

I could feel my face twist into a snarl as I spoke, towering a few inches over him as I leaned forward. "You should be."

I didn't own Kota. That, I was fully aware of. She was completely capable of making her own decisions, but no way in hell was I letting her leave here with this scumbag who had already fucked up. For God sakes he made her *cry* when I had been convinced that she was unbreakable.

Also, the fact that he *thought* he had this in the bag and that he'd walk away unscathed in a fight, with Kota on his arm, was beyond me.

This kid was a solid four inches shorter than me, sitting below six-foot, at least thirty pounds lighter than me. A single punch probably would've had him on his ass, and with the backup I had in the room tonight, he *definitely* would've been fucked.

Either way, I wasn't here to fight. I was here to take Kota home. And to make sure this fuckface didn't bother her anymore.

But there was a fear eroding me away, slowly yet surely, that maybe he *wasn't* bothering her. Maybe she wanted to be talking to him.

Some of my anger seemed to dissipate when Kota appeared at my side, seeming just as flustered as she did when she wandered off.

"Alright," she muttered.

"Alright," I muttered back.

Eyeing me like I was stupid, I got another flashback to how things were before we were doing whatever it was that we were doing now.

"So, are we going?" she huffed.

I pushed off the wall I'd been leaning against. "Yeah."

With a grim, "Bye, Bobby," she led the way out, weaving through people so fast that I was nearly left behind.

"Kota!" I desperately called after her, but she either couldn't hear me or didn't give a fuck. I let out a set of swears under my breath, repeatedly reaching forward to grab her wrist but missing every time.

When the sea of people finally parted, and she slammed the door open, releasing us into the bitter winter air, she still didn't turn, not even once to make sure I was behind her. Her steps remained brisk, and I wasn't sure how two legs that were so short could manage to glide so far in front of me.

"Damnit Kota, can you slow down?" I roared, my voice echoing off the buildings surrounding us.

She swung around, arms crossed tightly, hiding her red top that I'd been admiring earlier. "What was that?"

"What was what?"

"Why were you acting jealous?"

I'd been wanting to stare at her all night, but suddenly, I couldn't look at her. Eyes whipping around from parked cars to broken trees to the thin layer of snow beneath my feet, I mumbled, "I... wasn't..."

"Oh really?" Kota's glare could've melted the snow; it sure as hell was close to melting me. But peering up to steal a glance, I felt nothing but a strange mix of insecurity, embarrassment, and lust.

She was kind of hot when she was mad.

"What did you say to him when I walked away?" she questioned.

Starting with "I..." and trailing off, nothing followed for a moment besides a deep sigh. As I shifted my weight uncomfortably, I wondered if lying was a good idea or not. Ultimately, I decided to face the consequences of the truth. "I told him to stay away from you."

"Why?"

"Because, I... didn't like seeing him talk to you."

"Why?"

"I don't want you talking to other guys."

This was it. She was either going to tell me to piss off, or she would accept what I said and go with it. Either way, it was her decision, regardless of how I felt about it.

"Why?" she practically screeched. "I'm sure you've been talking to dozens of other girls and hooking up with them too."

"I haven't," I said, but her eyes rolled, and she turned to stomp away in that same audacious, Kota-like fashion I was used to. I reached for her small wrist and caught it this time. When her head circled back to me, her eyes were much softer, as if my touch was enough to bring that side back to her. I kept my tone steady and as soft as velvet. "I swear to God, I haven't touched another girl since the first time I touched you."

Isla popped into my head. *Oh, fuck.*

"Wait, shit. I'm sorry, that was a lie."

Her face fell and a tiny shard of my heart split off and tumbled straight into my lung, nicking it open. "There was *one* girl," I admitted. "But in my defense, it was only because she looked like you."

I watched as her face skewed from despair to anger to confusion. "What?"

Still holding onto her, I squeezed a little tighter in an attempt to bring her closer, but she wouldn't budge. My head shook in embarrassment knowing that this honesty hour was about to get even more brutal.

"When Lane and I went on our trip, I couldn't stop thinking about you. And then there was this girl that looked a lot like you, and I ended up bringing her home."

I'd thought the confession would've been a compliment, even a fucked-up one, but her face twisted into sadness like I could physically see her icy heart breaking inside of her chest.

I groaned, closing my eyes. "And then I said your name in bed."

When all I heard was a choking sound, my eyes popped open. The smile on her face said it all and her laughter rang so loud in my ears that I probably could've gone deaf.

Kota bent over, snagging her wrist out of my grip just for the sake of holding her own stomach. "You *what?!*"

I hadn't heard her laugh this hard since we saw the "Milfs love me" guy at the gym. The sound was soothing, and all unease was gone, relief settling into my bones. "I'm not repeating it," I said with a tiny smile.

"That is gold!" she said, clapping her hands together. "You really shouldn't have told me that. I'm making fun of you until the day you die."

"Well, you looked sad," I said, settling into step beside her when she started off towards home.

"Maybe I was faking it."

"No, you weren't." Hand brushing against hers, I stepped in front of her, wrapping my arms around her small frame. She didn't hug me back right away, as if unsure if it was safe or not, but I held onto her until she did, her tiny arms barely reaching around me.

"You're hugging me," she muttered, face smushed against my chest. "Why are you hugging me?"

"Because I wanted to."

"We've never hugged before."

"I know."

"It's weird," she said.

"I know," I laughed. "Well, I could tell you were cold."

Easily, she called my bluff, and even through the sassy ring to her accusation, she still didn't let go. "That's not why you're hugging me."

"No," I admitted. "It's not."

"Okay," she squeaked quietly. "And hey, are you okay after the game? I never got the chance to ask you earlier."

I already gave her one embarrassing confession tonight— I couldn't give her two and admit that she was the reason I got distracted and thrown around like a ragdoll.

I pulled out of our hug but kept her hands in mine. "Yeah, I'm alright. Prolly just have to ice when we go in."

Kota nodded. "Should we go inside then?"

"Yeah," I murmured. "Let's go inside."

Chapter Fifty-Four

Crew

"You wanna go to the gym with me?" I asked Kota the second she walked through the door.

With the tiniest smile, she shook her head lightly towards the floor. "I just got home."

"I see that." I wanted her to say yes, granted I ditched going to the student gym with the guys in hopes that Kota would go with me instead to our secret gym.

Even though it obviously wasn't a *secret* gym, it felt that way. None of the other guys went there, because why would they when they could go to the student one for free?

But something I'd never admit aloud was that Kota was right when she accused me of going to a different gym to avoid running into people I knew.

I felt awkward seeing past hookups. When I was there with the guys, it was much more manageable. Less of them would approach me than when I was alone. Or the ones that stared were much easier to shrug off when I had the guys to distract me.

It became unbearable at one point, and that's when I made the decision last year to get a membership at the second gym for when I had to make the trek alone.

Embarrassingly, I'd been waiting on one of the kitchen stools, practically staring at the front door like a freak, waiting for Kota to get home. Truthfully, this obsessive behavior on my part was starting to scare the hell out of me, but I couldn't stop; I couldn't separate my thoughts away from her. If I wasn't doing something that required a hundred and ten percent of my attention, then there was room for my thoughts to circle right back to her.

I just wasn't sure why it was happening.

"So, you wanna go?" I asked again.

Kota shook off her jacket, hanging it on the front coat rack. "I don't know if I'm up for it today."

The sigh I let out was much louder than I'd meant for it to be.

Kota stopped mid-step, a motionless frown and perplexed glare aimed at me. "Don't you have other friends you can go with?"

"Other friends." Was that her way of friendzoning me?

"They already left without me," I said.

"Can't you just meet them there?"

"Can't you just go with me instead?" I challenged.

A scoff and minor eye roll later, she had me questioning what exactly was going through her head right now. Was she trying to not act eager, or did she truly not want to go with me?

"What's in it for me?" Kota asked.

With my naturally dirty mind, the first thing I thought of offering was a sexual favor, but I knew we were past that. As satisfying as it was to hear her throaty moans and breath hitch, I was longing for a much different sound at the moment.

Keeping my voice as serious as possible, I responded, "You get to see Milf Guy."

I watched the small twitch of Kota's lips as she fought a smile, but she lost the battle, and that addicting laugh of hers filled the room, the exact sound that I'd been looking for.

I leaned into the counter in her direction, just for the sake of getting closer to her orbit, and before I could chide myself for doing yet another thing that was out of character, I was smiling helplessly.

I used to loathe the sound of her laughter, because it used to be targeted at me, used to make me nearly self-implode.

Now, it was slowly becoming one of my favorite sounds.

Eyeing her like a kid asking their parent for a new toy, I asked, "So, is that a yes?"

She let out one last giggle. "Alright, yeah, fine. Let me change."

When she came back out from her room, the first thing my eyes shot to were her blue leggings, accompanied with a black racerback shirt that wasn't shy about showcasing her tits. Her hair was in a ponytail, hanging out the back of a Cedar U baseball cap.

Without a word, she strutted past me, plucking her keys off the key holder near the door.

"What are you doing?" I let out.

Kota scrutinized me with a brow raised, fingers still looped through her keychain. I was starting to get whiplash from the constant back and forth between her callous glares and starry-eyed gaze. It seemed like every time she caught herself slightly opening up in some kind of way, she did a one-eighty, throwing her guard up as high as she could.

"What does it look like I'm doing? I'm grabbing my keys."

I swayed unsteadily, a hint of doubt casting over my confident persona. "I figured we'd ride together," I said, holding my own keys up.

She gave a light tsk with her tongue, along with a cautious glance over before putting her own keys back on the holder and reaching for her jacket instead.

I followed her out, and other than the music I had playing, the car ride was spent in silence, as if we were right back to ignoring each other.

I was trying to figure her out, but the more time I spent with her, the more confused I got. There had to be a reason as to why she was as stone-cold and closed-off as she was. I wanted to ask, to dig a little deeper and truly get an understanding of how her beautifully apathetic brain worked, but I knew she didn't trust me enough for that yet. Chances were, she'd throw her guard up as high as it could go, tell me to fuck off and mind my own business, and then end whatever it was that we had going on.

304

If I was going to ask for a piece of her, I'd have to give her a piece of me, and now definitely wasn't the time to do it, but eventually, I'd get there.

When we got to the gym, the first thing she told me was that she was going for a quick jog on the treadmill. Before I could agree or rebut it, she was shoving her air pods in and roaming off.

I sighed to myself, heading to the power rack. The treadmills were behind me, but as I was doing my squats, all I could wonder was if Kota's eyes were on me or not. I was paying extra close attention, trying to pinpoint that stabbing feeling I'd get whenever she was glaring.

But I didn't feel anything.

After my first set of reps, I bumped the weight up to three-seventy-five, and after that set, bumped it up to four hundred.

When I was done, my legs disobeyed me by beginning to walk towards Kota on the treadmill, but luckily, the tiny sliver of self-control that I had stopped me in my tracks.

I wanted to wait for her to come by me.

Either she was having the same thought process, or she didn't care to be by me at all, because five minutes turned to ten, and ten turned to twenty, and I was about to lose my damn mind.

I wanted to shake her, to ask what the hell was going through her mind. I couldn't tell if this was some sort of huge, elaborate game she was playing.

Finally, I decided that my pride wasn't even worth it and went to go disturb her jog, which at this point, was just a slow walk.

Sneaking up behind her, my hand dove straight to the treadmill's power button, turning it off.

Kota popped an air pod out of her ear, snarling. "Hey! Why'd you do that?!"

Folding my forearms on the treadmill's frame, I was trying far too hard to keep my expression unfazed. "You know, if you're going to come to the gym, you shouldn't just run on the treadmill the whole time. You could do that outside."

All she gave was a hollow glare. "It's winter."

My lips puckered from stupidity, and I shifted. "Right... Well, anyways, do you wanna try something else?"

"Like what?"

"Why don't you try benching?" I suggested. "I'll spot you."

Sharp and cruel, she gave a scoff. "Um, no! You'd probably let it fall on me on purpose."

With a record-breaking frown, I shot, "Take that back. You know I wouldn't do that."

As her eyes rolled and she snagged her powder blue water bottle that had been sitting snugly in a cupholder, I got the insane urge to lean forward and kiss her.

Self-control. Self-control. Self-control.

"Fine," she agreed sternly. "But I'm watching you do it first."

"Fine," I muttered, leading the way.

Call me crazy, but a rush of adrenaline was bursting into my veins knowing that Kota was about to watch me. I tried to pretend like she wasn't there as I threw a hundred pounds onto each side of the bar. But the second I laid on the bench, the only thing I could see was her crossed arms out of the corner of my eye, her blue leggings so tight that my mouth would've been watering if it wasn't so dry. She was leaning into one hip, a sassy stance that my mind was taking down an erotic road.

If I didn't zone in on the bar right this second, I may have dropped it on myself from being so damn distracted.

A few reps later, which thankfully, didn't end in my lungs getting crushed from dropping the freaking bar on myself, I sat back up, slightly out of breath.

"Your turn," I said.

"Hmm," she hummed, turning over her own shoulder to inspect the weight options.

Mindlessly, my gaze shot to her ass, and I knew that if she caught me staring, I was at risk of getting set on fire, but the thought didn't stop me.

Light me on fire, Kota. I don't care, I thought to myself.

When she bent over to grab her water bottle, I choked on my own spit, giving a cough.

Kota whipped around, and I sat there, slightly slumped on the bench, paralyzed as I stared up at her.

"Were you checking out my ass?" she accused, the ghost of a smirk tracing her lips.

My head shook rapidly at the floor.

"You were," she said, matter-of-factly. "You were checking me out."

"It was a glance," I admitted.

"It was a *stare,*" she grinned.

"Your leggings are..." I cleared my throat, "*tight.*"

As if we were the only two in the room, she leaned in a little, and I could only hope her eyes didn't drop, because my gym shorts were not at all good at hiding the rock in my pants.

"Well," she murmured, standing over me, "leggings are supposed to be tight."

Fuck.

Rising to my feet, we switched roles, and now I was the one towering over her.

She'd been snippy with me all morning, and I knew exactly how to bring out that more vulnerable, softer side of her.

Luckily, there weren't that many people in the gym right now, and everyone that was there seemed to mind their own business as my voice dropped low, tumbling out. "You know, there's a closet down the hall."

Somewhat losing herself in surprise or lust or both, she eyed me from under her lashes, giving a heavy exhale. "You wanna do it in public? Doesn't that seem a little risky?"

A smile painted with pure greed came over my face, and it took everything in me to refrain from touching her. "I thought you didn't care about the rules." Watching as her eyes shot to the slim hallway in the corner of the room, I whispered, "I'll meet you there in two minutes."

I didn't wait for her to respond, just turned and wandered off towards the hall. Hopefully she didn't blow me off.

The only thing that would've been more embarrassing than getting caught together in a closet would be getting caught in there by myself.

Glancing both ways *twice*, I snuck into the darkness of the closet, waiting for my queen of ice to join me.

Chapter Fifty-Five

Kota

"Crew?" I whispered into the closet.

A scream nearly popped out when two hands clutched onto my hips, fingers digging deeply into my waist like I was a lifeline.

"I'm right here," he said, deep and enticing.

My eyes were hardly adjusted to the darkness when I felt his lips brush against mine. Arms folding behind his neck, we tugged each other closer at the same time.

Crew's curls tickled my skin as his lips made a home out of my neck, licking and nibbling. "No hickeys," I reminded him quietly.

That wouldn't go over very well if our roommates noticed.

"Mhm," he hummed in response, his tongue trailing up and down my neck.

Blinking through the darkness, there were shelves behind Crew. I was leaning backwards, nearly bent in half and struggling to handle his weight. My feet replaced themselves, and with each step, I could feel what I believed to be boxes scattered around us.

Crew's large frame backed me up against a wall, his hands snaking around to my backside, taking two handfuls of my ass.

When he gave a forceful squeeze, I whimpered, and he shut me up by kissing me. "Shh," he moaned, but I could feel him grinning against my mouth, "you're always so loud."

"Sorry," I giggled quietly. My hands fell from his neck, gliding down the back of his t-shirt and looping around to the front of his shorts.

He pulled away just enough to shake his head. "Mmm-mmm."

"No?"

"We don't have that kind of time."

Before I could even respond, his hand was down my pants, two fingers sliding my thong over and seamlessly gliding into me.

I snapped my mouth shut, silencing the satisfied moan that nearly escaped.

His touch was becoming so familiar to me, so comfortable. It felt natural to be this close to him now, to have part of him inside me.

Whatever connection had been slowly building between us was becoming tangible, because all our intimate happenings were getting intensified by it.

Everything was slowly starting to feel even better, deeper.

My hips pushed forward against his fingers, causing him to groan in encouragement. Hand shooting to the center of his gym shorts, my small, throaty whine filled the closet from feeling how hard he was. There was a circle of wetness on the fabric, damp from the tip of his dick.

I couldn't help myself, thumb hooking between the waistband of Crew's shorts and the hardness of his lower abdomen. Reaching in, my hand closed around him, stroking his dick to earn a groan that he released into my mouth.

Warmth and pleasure coursing through both of us, we didn't stop touching each other until both our bodies were shaking, and we clutched onto one another for stability.

Our mouths were intertwined to encapsulate the robust noises we couldn't contain, and we rode the high until we were each panting.

Crew's calloused hand cupped the side of my face, nearly taking up the whole thing. He came forward, leaving the

310

lightest kiss on my lips before separating himself and backing up.

Immediately, I missed his closeness, but I'd never say it.

"I'll head out first?" he suggested, catching his breath.

"Okay."

A crack of light shone through the closet as he slipped out into the hallway, and I waited a few minutes before doing the same.

Crew was waiting for me near the front entrance, and we both gave friendly smiles to the college kids running the front desk as we beelined past them.

Laughter crackled through the quiet car as we hopped in, subsiding as Crew began driving. He reached for the volume dial and turned it up.

My voice cracked through surprise. "Country music?"

"Yep," Crew smiled. I wasn't a big country fan myself. There were a few songs I liked, but I didn't know many.

"I didn't know you were a country kind of guy."

In the worst southern accent I'd ever heard, he said, "Well, ma'am, now ya know."

I chuckled, staring at the endless array of dead trees that were flying by out the window. "Yeah, I don't think your southern accent is one of the things you're good at."

"What *am* I good at?" he asked.

I could hear the smile shining through his voice. He wanted me to feed that ego, and even though a long list of things came to mind that he actually *was* good at, I wasn't planning on admitting any of them.

"Nothing," I grinned to myself.

"Mhm, alright." The song came to an end and within three beats of the next song, Crew turned the volume down in the slightest, just so he could speak over it. "This song reminds me of you."

Head whipping to the small screen in the center of his dashboard, I read *Last Night* by Morgan Wallen.

Never heard it before.

"Why's that?" I asked.

"Just listen to the lyrics," he simpered, staring ahead as he raised the volume back up.

I'd never been so zoned in on a song before, especially one that I'd never heard. The worst part was that if he hadn't just said it reminded him of me, I wouldn't have cared in the slightest about the goddamn song.

But there I was, trying to hear every word, fighting a relentless grin.

A couple that gets drunk, argues, then makes up.

Huh. Interesting.

Everything about it seemed accurate minus the couple part. But why was I kind of flattered nonetheless?

Crew started singing along in that terrible accent of his, and my heart betrayed me by skipping a tiny beat. I couldn't rip my eyes away from him, couldn't tame the surge of butterflies that were making yet another appearance in my stomach.

I almost wished I knew the song so I could sing along with him.

Oh no, and now he's dancing in the driver's seat.

And God, why did I like the view so much?

On the part that said *"Baby, baby,"* Crew's pointer finger dug into my side and a small giggle escaped my lips. If I hadn't been watching him so closely, I probably wouldn't have noticed the way his mouth ticked up higher at the sound.

For a song that I didn't care to hear five minutes ago, I suddenly never wanted it to end.

The sun had been hiding behind winter clouds, but it peered out, causing Crew to glow again in the same stunning way he had when we got dinner.

Crew's warm hand found its way onto my thigh. He gave the lightest squeeze, and the strong palpitation of my heart probably should've killed me.

To my chagrin, the song came to an end, but Crew's hand stayed, and that brought me some relief.

"Do you have a song for every girl you've hooked up with?" I spit out quietly.

Eyes shifting between the road and me, his grin slowly fell, leaving nothing but seriousness as he spoke. "No."

I wasn't sure what to make of that. I wanted to believe that I was starting to mean something to him if I didn't already, but I'd never been so scared of becoming attached to someone.

My phone buzzed on my lap, and Crew must've felt the vibration beside his hand, because he gave a quick glance. Seeming like he didn't make anything of it, he looked away.

But it buzzed again, and again, and again, and by the fifth time, Crew's glance had shifted to a glare.

The air got hotter when he spoke, as if he was breathing out fire. "Is it him?"

The blood was slowly and inevitably draining from my face. "Yes," I admitted. Chin dipping towards my chest, I peeked over at Crew, gauging his reaction.

It seemed like he'd done a complete one-eighty in the last two minutes, going from a singing and dancing child to a bitter man.

He was solely staring at the road now, jaw ticking as if he was moments away from stepping on the ice for a game. Keeping his voice calm but troubled all the same, he spoke, "I thought you weren't going to talk to other guys."

"I'm not," I was quick to assure. "He just hasn't stopped texting me since the other night."

The car skidded to the curb, jolting me, and my hands shot out to the door and the center console to steady myself as Crew parked us on the side of the road, just blocks away from our apartment.

"What are you doing?" I panicked.

His whole body turned towards me. "Do you want him to be contacting you?"

I blinked at him, mouth slightly agape. *What the fuck?*

"I mean," I paused, my shoulders rising to my ears, "no?"

"Do you want me to make him stop?"

A million and one responses flashed through my head as I stared at him like a doe in headlights.

What are you going to do?

Why do you care so much if he talks to me?

I can handle things on my own.

But the only thing I got out was, "What?"

Crew's hand tapped along his own thigh, voice still on edge like he'd burn down the world right now if he was pushed a little further. "If he's bothering you, then I'll make sure he stops."

"Why?"

"Because I don't want him bothering you."

I didn't need a savior, and I especially didn't need a liar. One second, it was about me talking to other guys, and the next, it was about protecting me?

My own voice was carefully rising, building up like waves. "Do you really not want him bothering me or is this about you not wanting me to talk to other guys?"

At that, Crew seemed to dial it back a little. "Both," he croaked.

There was a fine line between being protective and being possessive, and for whatever reason, Crew was straddling that line.

With a soft scoff, I rubbed my forehead. "So, what are you gonna do?"

"I'll get rid of him," he shrugged.

I raised a brow, only half-joking, "You're gonna kill him?"

"No," Crew chuckled. "Of course not."

"Then what? Beat him up?"

His head tipped towards his shoulder with a sly smirk. "I mean, if that's what you're suggesting."

"No!" I shrieked. "I'm not giving you permission to beat him up. I'm perfectly capable of telling him to fuck off."

His brown irises caught fire, falling from my face to my chest to my lap and back up. Coming forward, he propped an elbow on the center console. "Yeah? Do it," he dared.

I wasn't sure if I wanted to kiss him or smack him.

He was so close, less than a foot away. It would've been so easy to grab a fistful of his Cedar U hockey shirt and pull him to me.

Yet my jaw was also tight, and if he came closer, there was no telling if my lips would've met his or if I'd bite his damn head off.

All the tension laced into the air would've evaporated if I just picked up my phone and texted Bobby, ordering him to leave me alone.

But I didn't want Crew telling me what to do. And out of defiance, I shook my head. "I will when *I* feel like doing it. Not when you tell me to do it," I said.

As his eyes bounced all around my face, I focused on nothing other than keeping my expression stern and deadly. He needed to know how serious I was being.

I would never let a man tell me what to do.

But the dark intensity in his eyes weakened with each passing second, and all at once, it disappeared as a lazy grin greeted me.

"You're so damn stubborn," Crew shook his head. A calloused, rough finger met my chin, tipping it upward as he stained my lips with the heat of his own. Graceful, slow, and chaste, like the antidote I'd been searching for my whole life. The arteries in my heart were about to burst at the feeling.

There was no denying it anymore.

I was in way over my head.

Chapter Fifty-Six

Kota

I wasn't entirely sure what the purpose was for why women had to have periods.

As a biology student, I'd studied the human body down to every individual cell, so sure, I understood the real scientific reasonings, but bleeding for nearly a week seemed a bit excessive and unnecessary. My opinion? One to two days would have sufficed.

I wasn't even there yet this month and I was already dreading it. I was, however, already moody as hell and guilty of eating everything in the kitchen. I even broke my own rule yesterday and ate someone else's snacks. Pretty sure the chips were Lane's, but oh well.

Sorry, Lane. When the cravings called, there's no turning back.

Speaking of which, if I didn't get some sort of sweet food in my mouth within five minutes, I'd kill the first person in sight.

Unless it was Bridget. Then I'd kill the second person in sight.

Sitting at my desk, I was surrounded in drawings of flowers, panda bears, and Rob K. I'd been drawing a lot recently, using it as a new stress reliever and a way to relax my mind when I needed a break from school. I wouldn't say I was good at it, but oh well.

Abandoning my current work-in-progress of a drawing of a mountain, I speed-walked into the kitchen, on the hunt for something sweet to eat.

I shuffled past Crew, who sat on a stool, shoulders shaking through laughter as he scrolled through TikTok.

Normally, I would've made a comment about how his muscle tee made him look like a douche or I would've wrapped my small hands as far around his exposed, bulging biceps as they could go before showering him with an array of heated kisses. But I was currently on a mission— no time for funny business.

The first place I checked was the fridge, which unfortunately, contained nothing I was interested in. Nothing in the pantry enticed me either. The freezer though, was promising.

There was a tub of vanilla ice cream that was practically screaming my name.

When a box of waffle cones and an ice cream scooper accompanied the tub on the counter, I felt like I could breathe.

A deep, husky laugh rattled from behind me, reminding me that I wasn't alone. I glanced over my shoulder, catching a view of the swirling rainbow in Crew's bowl.

Fruity pebbles? At seven pm?

"What's up with you always having some sort of breakfast food?" I thought aloud.

"What do you mean?" he mumbled. "I don't."

"Bagels, eggs, toast," I named a few. "You're eating cereal right now. And you picked a breakfast place for us to go to that one time."

Only giving him a view of my back, I was left with having to imagine what his facial expression looked like right now.

He was either giving a full grimace or a cheeky grin if I had to guess.

That was one of the many strange things that had been slowly changing in the apartment.

It wasn't all dynamite and ill-behaved games whenever we'd see each other anymore. When we first started hooking up, we'd usually still groan at the sight of each other if we found ourselves in the same room, then eventually, the encounter would end with us naked.

Now, those groans were becoming less and less frequent, replaced with small smiles and mellow heart eyes. This was all just the plot twist of the century, I guess.

"Are you judging my choice of food?" he griped.

Definitely grimacing. Which only made me smile.

"I'm just saying, it's clear what your favorite meal of the day is."

Heat crept up behind me, driving my senses wild. Stealing a whiff of that sandalwood cologne I'd grown to love, I brought my ice cream cone to my mouth, waiting for Crew's next move.

"And what are you having?" he hummed, pushing himself against my ass. "Ooh, an ice cream cone."

I hid my smirk behind the cone. "Mhm."

"Gimme a lick."

"No!" I refused. "There's stuff right there. You can make your own."

"Nooooo," he dragged out. "I don't want a full one. I just want a lick."

I allowed myself to melt slightly into him, my back meeting his chest. "I don't want your germs all over my ice cream cone," I teased.

Crew's fiery touch burned my lovely skin as his fingertips trailed back and forth along my arms. But his tender caresses didn't match his brusque tone. "Oh," he said, "so it's alright if my germs get all over your pussy but not on your ice cream cone?"

I nearly choked.

Sighing, I turned, holding my cone up to Crew's mouth.

He planted his hands on my hips and gave it a quick lick. "Pretty good," he nodded. "Gimme another one."

My eyes rolled, and this time, when I held the cone up, I waited until he got close before ramming it into the corner of his mouth.

Crew stumbled back a few steps as if I'd shot him, palm wiping his face. "Okay," he grinned, full of sin. "I see how it is."

Before I could blink, his hand was encased around my wrist, using my own weapon against me to smash the cone into my chin.

A single drop of ice cream dripped off my face and onto the floor, and I stood there dumbfounded for a moment. "You should know better. Than to mess. With my snacks," I heaved.

Crew put his arms up in front of him to surrender, chuckling. "Alright. We're even."

But the "ceasefire" went right over my head, and the second he turned, thinking he was safe, my ice cream was no longer on the cone— it was a mushy, melting mess sitting in a ball in my hand.

I launched it across the room, striking Crew square in the back, causing him to jump from the cold impact. Realizing what I'd done, I sank back a little.

Crew's scoff echoed, bouncing around the kitchen. "Did you just cannonball your ice cream at me?"

My teeth gnawed at my bottom lip, eyes flitting around like an anxious child. Unfortunately, there was no reversal after throwing gasoline onto a flame.

If this were months ago, I'd probably flaunt a wicked smile, nodding my head with content as I proudly said, *"Hell yeah, I did."*

But Crew had been slowly thawing my heart of ice, little by little, and instead of standing confidently with a crown on my head, my chin dropped slightly, and I responded with a sheepish, "No."

"No? What's that then?" he pointed at the floor.

There was a small puddle of ice cream, slowly getting fed by the melting ball I'd launched.

"It... fell."

"It just," he shrugged, "jumped five feet off its cone?"

I held the empty cone tightly with both hands against my belly. "Yes."

Hand resting on his lower hip, he nodded at me. "Alright then."

I breathed a sigh of relief when he turned with no further response.

The relief didn't last long though, my reaction time being too short to dodge the rainbow hurdling my way.

Cold and colored milk drenched me, and I shrieked. "Crew!" I held my head down, watching rainbow droplets of milk fall one by one from the ends of my hair.

"I'm sorry," Crew laughed, bent over. He held a hand up. "I shouldn't have done that."

My jaw became taut as a growl rippled from my throat. "I'm going to kill you!" I hollered, reaching for the tub of ice cream.

"No, no, no." Crew's strong arms scooped me up, tossing me over his shoulder. "No more," he said.

As I took in the view of his tight ass from upside down, I let out another yelp. "Where are we going!"

"The shower."

"I don't wanna shower with you. I'm mad at you."

"C'mon now. We both know you started this," he said, setting me down on my feet in the boy's bathroom.

"Did not," I pouted quietly, crossing my arms.

The pipes cried out, screeching steadily as he flipped the shower valve on. "Did too."

"Whatever."

Like the other day, the rough pads of his fingertips found their way under my chin, and he lifted it, leaving me with no choice but to look at his beautifully crooked grin. "Stubborn *and* dramatic."

"Stubborn, maybe, but I am *not* dramatic."

The truth was that I knew I was dramatic, but I was far too stubborn to admit it.

Quicker than I could blink, Crew had a thumb hooked between my blue pajama bottoms and my skin, his eyes lit, voice coming out as rough as sandpaper. "I beg to differ."

The only sounds in the bathroom were my heavy breaths and the water rushing as Crew undressed me, sliding each article of clothing off my body before doing the same with his own and tossing it all into a pile on the floor.

He cocked a brow, motioning towards the shower. "After you."

320

We'd been naked dozens of times together, but there was something nerve wracking about showering together. I'd never showered with someone that I was just hooking up with; it had always been with guys I was actually seeing.

In my opinion, showers were intimate. Water. Soap. Naked bodies. Not to mention, there was light; it wasn't the same as hooking up in a semi-dark room. You could see *everything.*

I let out a huff as I stepped past him and into the steam. The hot water hit my chest, and I didn't realize how sticky my hands were until I raised them into the stream, watching the light-yellow residue of ice cream wash off my skin.

Right as Crew walked in, his hands were squeezing my hips and just as I thought he was about to pull my ass against him, he surprised me by leaving the lightest trace of a kiss on my shoulder.

I turned my head slightly, peeking over at him. It almost felt like the water was somehow pounding harder, matching my heartbeat as I took in his subtle grin, but I knew the sensation was all in my head.

"Sorry about your hair," he said unapologetically.

"It's fine," I murmured, shifting so that my back was towards the water. Tilting my head, I got my hair wet, hoping the cereal and milk were slowly washing out.

"C'mere," Crew insisted quietly, grabbing my hand to spin me back around.

"Why? What are you doing?"

"I'm gonna wash your hair."

Hearing the snap of a bottle opening, my eyes widened, and I swung around to look. "With your boy shampoo? Yeah, I don't think so."

His eyes rolled. "Well, this is the only option currently available."

My shoulders sank. "I don't wanna smell like a guy!"

His sigh was far louder than the water shooting past my ears. "You want me to go run and grab your shampoo?"

I pulled my mouth over to one side, hiding a smile. "Was that just a question or an actual offer?"

He ran a hand through his damp hair. "An actual offer, I guess."

Now, *I* was the one sighing. "It's fine. I'll just use water."

"No, it's alright. I'll be right back." With a kiss on my cheek, he hopped out, leaving me with another nagging round of butterflies inside me. *This shit was getting annoying.*

There were a few guys throughout my life that had given me intense butterflies before— including Bobby— but it was never like this. I usually just got butterflies if a guy complimented me or maybe as he was leaning in for our first kiss. It had never been this frequent, had never been from the smallest occurrences, like from barely touching me or from simply looking at me.

When Crew came back in, I peeked down at the Bumble and Bumble bottle in his hands. "Congrats," I teased. "You grabbed the right one."

He didn't bother looking up at me as he shrugged, too focused on the shampoo he was currently pouring into his hand. "I wasn't totally sure at first which one was yours, but I figured it out."

"You figured it out?" I asked.

Another shrug. "I know what you smell like," Crew said.

More butterflies. God fucking dammit.

"Switch spots with me," he muttered.

Blowing a heavy breath out my nose, I did what was asked of me, turning so that my back was facing both Crew and the water. I tipped my head backwards, and Crew's hands practically took up my whole head as he massaged the shampoo into my hair, slow and fragile.

The only sound was the pitter patter of the water as it hit the tile around us, and I closed my eyes, relaxing to the princess treatment I was getting.

There was an overwhelming feeling of wanting to ask Crew what the hell was going on between us. I wasn't sure if it was my fear of his response or my fear of ruining the moment that kept me from doing it.

Crew worked carefully and meticulously rinsing the shampoo out of my hair, using one hand to shield my forehead to ensure none of it got in my eyes.

322

"I think it's all out," he murmured, voice nearly getting drowned out by the water.

"There are no fruity pebbles left?"

"Nah, I don't think so."

"Okay," I said, watching him shut the water off.

Honestly, right when he'd mentioned showering, I'd been expecting some sort of sexual shenanigans to happen. I guess it had just become an assumption now, granted that's what usually happened whenever we were alone.

Peeking out the shower curtain, I eyed the two towels hung on the towel rack. There was a gray towel that was perfectly folded, taking up half the space, while the black one was hung in some unorganized knot.

"I'm assuming yours is the black one?" I taunted, stepping onto the shower mat on the floor.

"Yeah, you can use it if you want."

"Um, no thanks." Grabbing Lane's, which I assumed was clean, I wrapped it around me. Crew gave me a dirty side eye before ripping his own towel off the rack. I slyly watched as his dick disappeared when he closed it around his waist before my eyes landed on myself in the mirror, and a flash of disgust overtook my face at the sight of my reflection.

There was conviction in Crew's voice, almost sounding like a threat. "Don't look at yourself like that." I eyed him in the mirror quietly. "As if you don't like how you look," he explained further.

My heart raced, hands finding the edge of the countertop and planting themselves there, gripping onto it as I rocked unsteadily. "Sometimes, I don't," I admitted.

Crew stood there, hair damp and head tipped to expose his cutting jawline. His sharp abs were on full display, towel hung low and eyes angry at my words. And of course, he looked like a breathing wet dream while he did it.

Whereas I was ice, he was stone. And although he'd been slowly thawing me over the last few weeks, unfortunately for me, *stone doesn't melt.*

He gave me maddening butterflies, but for all I knew, I didn't make him feel a single thing.

"That's ridiculous," he finally said, voice gruff. With a tiny step, he came forward. "You're gorgeous and you know it."

My knuckles were white at this point, and I gulped. "You think I'm gorgeous?"

He laughed once like I was crazy. "Of course, I do."

There was a pulsing electricity flying through the air. I couldn't take my eyes off him as he blinked at me, looking like a masterpiece, my dream drug come to life.

Gradually, his mouth raised into a smile. "You're blushing again."

My sigh came out rough and heavy. "I told you I don't blush."

It was taking a conscious effort not to swing around and slam my lips against his. But as each millisecond passed, I was closer and closer to doing it. I probably would've had I not heard the apartment door open and close, followed by Bridget and Lane's laughter, which came to a sudden halt.

"Watch out," Lane said. "There's stuff all over the floor."

"What the hell?" Bridget let out.

Meanwhile, Crew's and my eyes were so wide that it looked like we were on drugs. We stared at each other in the mirror silently, both holding our breath as if we'd get caught if we breathed.

Finally, I spoke, swiveling around and yelling in a whisper, "What do we do!"

Crew's gaze zipped around as his hand securely gripped my waist, trying to calm me. I wished for a moment that there wasn't a towel between us. "I'm gonna sneak into my room," he spoke softly. "You showered in here after the food fight."

I nodded, watching him peek down the hall before disappearing into it.

I jumped when my phone rang against the countertop, sending the sound echoing around the bathroom. "Hello?"

"Hey, uh, what happened in the kitchen? It looks like a fucking war zone in here," Bridget said.

Nibbling on my lower lip, I focused on keeping my voice steady. "Yeah. Crew and I had a food fight."

"A food fight? Why?"

"He pissed me off," I paused, "duh."

"Of course," she murmured. "Where are you now?"

"The bathroom."

Silence. Followed by voices muttering throughout the apartment.

"Our bathroom is empty," Bridget suddenly said.

"Yeah, I'm... I showered in the boy's bathroom."

"Why?"

I spit out, "I had food all over me and I didn't wanna make our bathroom a mess."

I gave myself a mental pat on the back for the lie. Believable? Yeah, I'd say so. Sounded like something I'd do? Definitely.

"Oh!" Bridget agreed. "Good thinking."

"Yeah," I nodded to myself. "I'll be out soon to clean up the kitchen."

"Kay," she said before hanging up.

Ten minutes later, Crew and I were scrubbing the kitchen floor, not speaking, not acknowledging each other outside of an occasional glance.

But I could tell by the way his hand subtly brushed over mine when our roommates weren't looking, and I was sure *he* could tell by the look in my eyes, that pretending we still hated each other was becoming more of a challenge.

Chapter Fifty-Seven

Crew

"**O**h! I almost forgot!" Kota tapped me on the chest before shooting off my bed.

We'd been lying in my bed, not even fooling around, just napping. The more interactions like this that we had, the more and more comfortable I became with it, which was weird to me.

I knew I enjoyed spending time with her, and I sure as hell knew I liked fucking her, but my mind kept circling back to the question of *Am I ready to commit myself to her?*

We hadn't had the conversation, and I was relieved about that, but it felt like the question was slowly and inevitably on its way to being asked aloud.

I never believed in commitment growing up. My parents crushed that for me. Their individual marriages may have still been intact right now, but hell, I wouldn't have been surprised if those marriages fell apart tomorrow. I mean, my stepmother was obsessed with my best friend for crying out loud.

Was I ready to subject myself to every bad thing that could come out of commitment?

"What is it?" I asked, slyly smiling as I watched her hop up and down like Tigger from Winnie the Pooh.

Without a response, she squealed and ran out of the room.

I wasn't sure if she wanted me to follow her. I sat up, and before I could even swing my legs around the side of my bed, she was back, her smile taking up half her face, hands hiding behind her back.

"You know how I've been drawing lately?" she asked.

You mean, attempting to draw? I responded in my head. "Yes," I replied.

Kota climbed onto the bed, her voice sweet like honey. "I drew something for you."

She handed the paper over, and immediately, I had no idea what the hell I was looking at. "Oh," I smiled, "it's a..."

A growl rippled from her throat, sounding like a lioness. "It's *you*," she explained, pointing a stern finger at the silver and black blob in the middle. "See, that's you skating and that's your hockey stick and that's the net that you're about to put the puck into."

"Ah," I grinned, "I see it now."

Sorta.

Her eyes narrowed. "Do you?"

"Yeah," I lied.

With a sigh, she stood. "Alright, well I've gotta go change out of my sweats for class."

"Okay," I responded quietly, fingers sliding along the edge of the paper as I took in every detail. "Thanks for my drawing." When she left the room, I hopped out of bed and hung the picture on the small bulletin board beside my desk.

Kota's birthday was in two days, and we were planning on doing a group dinner at a nicer restaurant in town. I'd been wanting to get her a gift, but truthfully, I had no idea what.

I'd never shopped for a girl before other than my little sister who was a decade younger than me. My mind had reeled the last few days on what a good gift would be. Each time I stopped and thought of some of her favorite things, it didn't give me too many great options.

Comfy clothes. Taylor Swift. Snacks. Liquor posters. Smutty books.

There weren't many opportunities there that were good enough for the standards I wanted to meet.

I got dressed before wandering down the girl's hall to say goodbye to Kota.

Her door was shut but I could hear the ethereal tone of her voice, singing along to "Last Night."

Immediately overtaken by a smile so strong that my face hurt, I refrained from knocking, not wanting to disturb her even though I'd pay a monstrous amount of money to see the private concert she was currently putting on.

It felt right to put "Last Night" on when I got into the car, and I listened to it three times on the way to the mall.

Chapter Fifty-Eight

Kota

I hadn't expected Crew to get me a birthday present.

It made me feel even worse knowing that the only gift I had gotten him for his birthday was a pool for a bed and a fight.

My day started with a nice birthday text from Crew, followed by a billion emojis. Immediately, I wanted to hop out of bed, run into his room, and hug the fuck out of him, but Lane and Bridget were in the kitchen.

I couldn't even be mad at them though because they were making me pancakes. So, I had no choice but to save a hug for Crew for later.

When I grabbed lunch with my mom, I wasn't sure what it was about my aura that gave me away. She kept telling me I was glowing, and after numerous times of denying that there was a reason for it other than the fact that it was my birthday, she kindly called me out on my bullshit and demanded an answer.

Long story short, she knew all about Crew and me now. Other than all the spicy details, of course.

To sum up our roomie's group dinner— *it dragged.*

I appreciated Lane and Bridget so much for celebrating my birthday with me and taking me out to dinner, but every time Crew's hand squeezed my thigh underneath the table, it brought me closer and closer to exploding from too much sexual frustration mustering up inside me. It felt like it was tearing through me with the force of an EF5 tornado.

I'd been wearing my pink and white polka dot dress too, which gave him far too easy access to push the line of safety.

At one point, it was so much that I needed to step away from the table and pretend like I had to use the bathroom.

Luckily for me, Crew followed me and relieved some of the issue with his tongue. And fingers.

I didn't hesitate to quickly return the favor before we went back to the table one at a time to a giggling Lane and Bridget.

Now, it was eleven pm, and I'd snuck into Crew's room, per usual. I sat criss-crossed applesauce on his bed, eyes closed like he'd insisted even though the room was practically dark.

"Ready?" he asked.

"Yes," I smiled, feeling like a kid on Christmas morning.

My hands nearly fell to the comforter when he dropped the gift into my hands. Eyes popping open, I scanned over a white, sparkly bag and light blue tissue paper sticking out the top.

"Can you turn your desk lamp on?" I asked. "I wanna see."

My eyes couldn't help following him as he wandered over to the desk, shirtless. Muscles pulled taut as he reached down and turned the lamp on, I nearly salivated before shaking it off.

The room illuminated brighter with both the lamp and TV on, and I was able to see much better, catching a glimpse of the drawing hung on Crew's bulletin board. I smiled.

Pinching the tissue paper between my thumb and forefinger, I plucked it out and tossed it aside. My hand dug around in the bag, first grabbing a container of Oreos.

I giggled. "These are my favorites."

"I know," Crew smiled.

My grin flipped and I shot him a scowl. "These don't have toothpaste in them, do they?"

330

"No," Crew shook his head, still simpering. When my brows lifted in suspicion, he chuckled. "I promise."

My face relaxed into a hint of a smile. The card in the bag had my name written on the front.

Out of instinct, I nearly spit out a remark about Crew's child-like handwriting, but I bit my tongue because he'd done it as a kind gesture.

A Barnes & Noble gift card fell out when I opened it. "Oh!" I squealed quietly.

"I figured you could get some new smutty books."

"How thoughtful of you."

"I know," he jokingly responded.

With a playful eye roll, I set the items aside, peeking into the bag to see if anything was left. There was a small box sitting at the bottom.

I was almost scared to see what was inside, although I wasn't sure why. Gulping, I popped it open and was immediately frozen, paralyzed by shock.

"Crew..." I whispered.

The tennis bracelet was shimmering. My fingertips ran over the silver with the same gentleness and caution that would be used to touch a newborn baby.

Between every ten or so small studs, there was a star, each one glittering, the type of glitter that could blind you in the sun.

"Do you like it?" he asked.

"It's gorgeous."

Right away, I wondered how much money he spent on this. It couldn't have been cheap. But I knew that wasn't the most polite question to ask, so I didn't.

I could feel my eyes getting a little glassy, overwhelmed by a heap of emotions.

"Can you put it on me?" I shyly asked, holding my wrist out.

His voice was soft. "Sure, birthday girl."

My tummy dipped at his response. If part of my heart hadn't been draped over his shoulder yet, it was now. And for the first time, I didn't completely chide myself for it.

Any doubt that he had feelings for me was gone as he so carefully brought the bracelet around my wrist.

I practically tackled him, kissing him hard, because how could I not?

Nearly the next hour was spent with our hands all over each other, but this time was a bit different. It didn't feel like he was just fucking me; it felt like more than that. This time stood out.

His gaze hadn't roamed around my body so much. They'd stayed on my face the whole time, piercing into me like he was trying to read my soul.

He hadn't brought my hands behind my back. Instead, his fingertips repeatedly brushed over the bracelet on my wrist, and he kept my arms beside my head, his fingers intertwined in mine.

Crew was gentle with me, loving. Each thrust was slow and intentional, taking his time like he wanted to feel every second of it.

When we were done, Crew's arm snaked underneath me, tucking me against his side. He exhaled deeply and I did the same, our heartbeats gradually slowing to a steady pace.

As quiet as a mouse, I spoke, "Wanna play rapid fire questions?"

"Sure."

If his arms weren't so tight around me right now, I would've been shaking. "Do you still hate me?" I asked softly.

It felt like a lifetime before he spoke, even though I knew it had only been seconds. "No," he murmured, my head rising and falling with his chest as he breathed. "Do you still hate me?"

"No." It felt like I could throw up. I never got nervous like this, especially not when it came to a guy. "Why haven't you ever had a girlfriend?"

My head was carried higher as Crew took a lengthy inhale, and I could hear the discomfort in his voice. "I... never really had a great example of relationships growing up, so I've kind of just avoided them."

I knew I'd just asked a question, and that technically, it was no longer my turn, but I wanted to dig for more. "Do you want to explain?"

Part of me was expecting him to shut down, to tell me that he didn't want to explain and that it wasn't really my business, but he gave another deep sigh, his arm tensing around me before relaxing again.

"I was an only child when I was younger. My parents didn't have the best marriage and were both having affairs at the same time when I was about ten. It turned into a whole shitshow with them fighting all the time, and eventually, they divorced, both remarried within a year, and then both had another kid at about the same time. So, they didn't really give too much of a fuck about me for the next few years after that."

Oh.

This... explained a lot actually.

I knew Crew had issues with his parents. That was clear after the reaction on his birthday, but I had no idea that it went this deep.

There was a pang in my chest, and a sliver of guilt washed over me from all the times I judged Crew's lifestyle without knowing the backstory of *why.*

"So," he added, running his free hand over his face, "I guess I just never really found the idea of commitment to be up my alley."

"I'm sorry," I muttered. "I had no idea."

"It's alright."

I had so many follow-up questions running through my head.

Have you ever found a girl that you almost committed to?

Do you still feel the same way about commitment?

Would you ever commit to me or is that out of the question?

"Do you think..." I paused, breath hitching, "that you'll ever be okay with commitment?"

The troubled inhale he took was frightening, and I immediately regretted the words that had clawed their way out of my mouth. I was so afraid to hear his answer that I almost covered my ears.

"If it was for the right person, maybe," Crew responded. "I mean... if you're asking about the possibility of something happening between us in the future," he paused, "I wouldn't rule it out."

"Good to know," I whispered shakily.

A beat of silence passed, and I used it as a shitty attempt to prepare myself for whatever he was about to ask next. He had just given me a piece of him, and now, it was his turn to ask whatever had been lingering in his mind for the last six months of knowing each other.

Crew's voice gave a small crack. "My turn?"

"Yeah," I nuzzled my cheek against his chest.

"Why are you so hard-headed? Especially with guys?" Crew sputtered.

I internally cringed at the question. My first impulse was to spit out a rude response, to push him away, stand up, and walk out of the room. *Even though I was still naked.*

A trace of regret sat in a lump in my throat. Maybe this game wasn't the best idea...

But I surprised myself by my strength as I spoke. "I've never met my father," I said, matter-of-factly. "He and my mom were only dating for a few months in college when she got pregnant. He wanted her to get rid of me and she refused, so he disappeared."

Crew's fingertips grazed my upper back, sending a bolt of electricity through me. "I'm sorry," he uttered. "That's awful."

"I know."

"I would never do that to you. Or our kid if we ever had one."

His words dragged me out of the self-pity-party happening in my head. Hand planting in the center of his chest, I pushed myself up to look at him.

Crew's eyes gave a small sparkle, the same beautiful glimmer as the bracelet on my wrist.

"You'd have a kid with me?" I blurted out loudly before thinking, thankful that the TV was still on to drown out the noise. My chest lightened when Crew's radiant smile appeared.

He chuckled lightly. "I mean, it wouldn't be the worst thing in the world," he said. "But if it ever did happen, everyone better watch out, because I don't know if a mix of our personalities would be safe for the common public."

334

When all I did was stare at him in awe, he pulled me back down to him, holding me even closer than he originally had.

For someone that I used to want to run over with my car, it sure was strange how perfectly we seemed to fit when laying together.

Chapter Fifty-Nine

Crew

Kota never had a father, never had a male figure in her life to trust. Raised by no one besides a strong woman, she had no choice but to grow up and be the same.

I finally had that last missing piece to the puzzle, and everything made sense as to why she hated me in the first place.

I always figured there had been something about her past that made her so cruel and cold-hearted towards men. The fact that she even opened up to me said a lot. She trusted me, and as good as that made me feel, I felt terrified all the same.

Because it meant there was more at stake here.

It seemed to be unsaid between us that we were no longer just fucking, but I was completely petrified to say the words aloud. I was scared enough thinking the words to myself.

I'd never felt this way before. Looking back, I was pretty sure I'd never caught feelings for anyone *ever*.

It was part of the reason why I never hooked up with a girl twice— out of precaution. If I never hungout with a girl more than once, never allowed myself to get close her, then no feelings could be caught, and no one, including them, would end up more hurt than if I just broke things off after one night.

Now, I had shot myself in the foot.

The five-four girl who spat fire was no longer my greatest enemy. She was the person I wanted to see at the end of each long day, the person who could calm me down just by sitting next to me.

The little things about her that used to irk me no longer did. Now, I was curious about every move she made, curious as to what was going through her mind every second.

Not to mention how fucking stunning she was. I'd always thought she was attractive, ever since that first night when she glared at me with deadly malice, hands folded against her chest as she stood there, pissed-off in a skin-tight dress and sky-high heels.

So much had changed since then, and now, she wasn't just attractive. Lots of girls were attractive. But I'd seen her up-close dozens of times, had studied her fragile features as she slept, had memorized every inch of her body.

Kota was stunning. And I didn't want anyone else looking at her. It felt like I needed to hide her from every other guy on earth, to shield her so that they didn't have the chance to see the tiny pieces of her that I'd been blessed with seeing.

We were past catching feelings. Way past it.

I mean, for fucks sake, I just bought her a two-hundred-dollar bracelet without thinking twice about it.

And the look on her face when she saw it was worth every dime.

***

Kota and I had gotten good at our routine. We had it all laid out, based on Lane and Bridget's routine. They were too predictable, sticking to their precise schedules that they never stepped outside of.

Today had been a little different than a normal Saturday though. We had a game, which we won, keeping our record pretty solid with only four losses this season, all to top five teams. It was very likely that we'd move up from third in the nation to second by next week. If we were lucky and the University of Michigan lost their game tonight, then we might even move up to first.

Other than having a game today, it definitely wasn't like a normal Saturday given my fuckup.

I played fine. Actually, I played *more* than fine, getting a hat trick, my second of the season. My fuckup didn't come on the ice though— it came afterward at the apartment when I accidentally called Kota "babe" in front of our roommates and had to play it off like I meant for the comment to be towards Lane.

Which brought the embarrassment to a whole new level.

Now, we were conned into going to the celebratory party at the hockey house when all I really wanted to do was lay in bed with Kota beside me while I iced the fuck out of my whole body. I took some brutal hits tonight, same as Lane.

I had never been one to sit out of a party before, so it was already weird that I wasn't feeling up to it tonight, but I guess we were going anyway.

I wanted a bit of time alone with Kota before we were thrown into a house full of people. Either she felt the same way, or she simply read my mind because we both gave excuses as to why we were going to head to the party a bit late.

I told Lane that I had to run to the liquor store.

Kota told Bridget that she needed to hop in the shower.

We knew it wouldn't buy us a lot of time, but if there was enough time for me to grab her and kiss the fuck out of her without rushing it, then I'd be content.

Our half hour of free time was spent with me kissing her neck while she attempted to do her makeup, giggling at the wet kisses and questionable hickeys my lips were leaving in their wake. Then, getting yelled at for said questionable hickeys and watching Kota try to cover them up with makeup and complain about having to wear her hair down when she was originally going to put it up.

I watched Kota slip into a denim skirt and tiny black shirt and immediately had thoughts of ripping it all off.

Sliding her lip gloss back and forth across her lips, I wrestled my gaze away from her, knowing that I shouldn't start something that we didn't have time to finish.

Either way, my common sense seemed to fly out the window. Regardless of how hard I'd been trying to control myself, I couldn't, grabbing Kota's wrist and bringing those lush, wet lips to mine.

I hummed against her at the taste. *Cherry.* My favorite lip gloss of hers.

"You taste so fucking good," I mumbled against her.

Her mouth ticked upwards into a smile, lips still on mine before she pulled away with just enough space to respond in a breathy tone. "You usually only say that when your head is between my thighs."

Was that an invitation?

Either way, I took it as one, hands gliding beneath Kota's skirt and planting themselves on her ass before lifting her and tossing her onto the bed.

My head was between her thighs in seconds, kissing and licking and sucking in all the ways I knew were her favorites.

Her sinfully satisfied moans saturated the room, reminding me of how much I loved when our roommates were gone.

I didn't stop until she came on my tongue, and it was almost instantly the moment after that my phone rang in my back pocket. I would've ignored the call had it not been Lane.

"Hello?" I gulped, catching my breath.

"Hey, uh, where you at?"

Kota and I were one step ahead and had already turned our locations off. "I'm at the liquor store with Cody," I said, wiping my mouth off with the back of my hand.

The suspicion in his voice was tangible through the phone. "Uh, Cody's here."

Panicking, my eyes shot to Kota, who was staring with her lips unsurely puckered, a nervous gleam in her eye. "Oh, did I say Cody? I meant Keith."

"Right... Well hurry up."

"Will do."

Kota and I hauled our asses to the hockey house, arriving a half hour later than we'd originally planned to.

It was the beginning of March and still pretty cold out, especially at night, so I had Kota go inside first to avoid having her stand out in the cold. Plus, there was no way in hell I'd let her stand outside at night by herself anyway.

After waiting ten minutes, I went in, and it didn't take long to find Lane and Bridget, standing off around the bathroom. Jett weirdly dropped his head and scurried off as I approached. "Hey," I nodded to my roommates.

Lane smiled, but his response fell out through a sigh. "Hey."

"There's a lot of people here," I crossed my arms, glancing around.

"I know. It's fucking ridiculous."

I could've sworn I caught Bridget's hand clutch onto Lane's forearm as a group of people squeezed passed.

I ignored it, because there were a lot of people here and she was probably just trying to steady herself on someone that wasn't a stranger.

Then the thought went through my head again— *there were a lot of people here.*

Where was Kota?

Panic-stricken, I circled around myself like a dog chasing its own tail. That protective side was coming out of me again— or maybe it was a possessive side. Who knows?

"You good?" Lane asked, raising a brow.

"Yeah... yeah, I just... don't know where Keith went with my beer," I sputtered a lie.

"Ah," he gave a nod, but it seemed like he wasn't convinced.

I didn't currently care.

"I'll catch you guys later," I yelled over my shoulder, already on my way towards the kitchen.

I knew Kota and I wouldn't be able to talk much or hangout like we would when no one was around, but I'd feel better at least being able to see her and make sure she was okay.

There were too many people present that I didn't know. I didn't even think anyone on the team really knew who any of these people were. This wasn't a rare occurrence though. Whenever we had major, important wins and a party followed, random people always showed up like they'd been invited. But with that, came a load of issues.

Spills. Broken furniture. *Lots* of fights. Random guys trying to pull girls they had no business pulling— especially girls that were walking around by themselves, unclaimed.

Which was exactly what Kota was right now.

I didn't trust a single guy in this house that I didn't personally know. Not that my teammates wouldn't hit on her, but they wouldn't pass any boundaries. They had morals and respect. I couldn't say the same for all the strangers.

Kota was leaning against the kitchen counter, chatting with a girl that I didn't recognize at first glance. But after a minute, I realized it was Patricia, the friend Kota introduced me to on the night we hooked up for the first time.

Kota didn't spot me, but I breathed out a sigh of relief anyway. Patricia said something that made her laugh, and she flashed a smile so beautiful that I thought I might pass out on the floor.

I was tempted to go to her, but TJ and Cody were in view, and I didn't want them to get any ideas. Especially TJ, who was still determined to figure out who I'd been sleeping with.

I thought about New Year's when TJ was asking for permission to hook up with Kota. It bothered me then; it infuriated me now. I could've stomped over and clocked him in the jaw just from the thought.

And maybe I would've if I didn't spot the red solo cup in Kota's hand.

Before I knew it, I was trampling through everyone in my way.

"Where'd you get that?" I barked frantically.

Her brows furrowed, nearly touching as she glanced down at her cup. "Jett. Why?"

Another sigh of relief.

"There's just a lot of random people here. I wanted to make sure it didn't come from a stranger."

Her annoyed expression melted, and her shoulders rose and fell with a deep breath. "I'd hope you know I'm smart enough not to take drinks from strangers."

"I— I do, I just... was worried," I admitted.

"Hello," Patricia smiled, butting in.

"Hi," I said heavily, acknowledging her before turning back to Kota. "You need anything, you come grab me immediately."

She rose a brow, hiding behind her cup as she took a questionably long gulp. "Okay, Dad."

I shook my head through a smile. "Ew. Don't."

She giggled and dropped her head, her straightened hair creating a curtain between us as I reluctantly left her.

For the next hour or two, I maintained a safe distance, doing my best to not let the guys catch on to what was going through my head.

The time was spent getting interrogated once again by TJ, listening to Cody recap some fight that happened between Matt and a random spectator, and watching Jett hand off vodka lemonades to pretty girls, his typical MO.

But the second all the guys had wandered off, leaving me alone, there was a tap on my shoulder.

The girl standing before me was around Kota's height, beach blonde hair cascading past her shoulders. Judging by her sparkling blue eyes and perfectly white smile, there was no indication that she was closed-off or vicious like the girl I'd somehow become obsessed with.

"Hi, I'm Sloane."

"Hi," was all I greeted her with.

"You're Nicholas, right? Or do you go by Nick?" she asked.

"I go by Crew actually."

"Oh, sorry," she grinned again, slightly sheepish.

"You're good," I replied.

Sloane was dressed like it was July. Her red tank top was suffocating her skin, black jean shorts snug on her thighs like they were giving them a hug. She seemed outgoing, easy to talk to. She was the kind of girl I used to pick out in a bar.

As she started talking and talking, I wasn't sure if she'd ever shut up. I probably would've been into it if this happened six months ago, but regardless of how pretty she was, there was somehow no attraction to her, no urge to jump into her game of flirtation. I didn't want to be a dick and tell her outright that I wasn't interested, especially since she was just making small talk and not making an actual move.

Sloane's brows drew together, and she turned, realizing she'd been tapped on the shoulder. As she swung around, I caught sight of Kota and my jaw fell open.

Kota's hand was up, her fingers wiggling, waving in a condescending manner, matching her condescending, snarky smile. "Hello," she greeted Sloane.

Unsurely, Sloane took a small step backwards, nearly bumping into me. "Hi..."

Kota's tone remained calm, but the threat was clear. "I'm sorry, but I'm gonna need you to fuck off."

"What?" Sloane scoffed, face twisting into anger.

Kota gestured to me. "This one is kinda off-limits."

I wasn't sure if Sloane was blind to the predator she was taunting or if she just preferred danger, because all she did was cross her arms and say, "Is that so?"

Kota's brown eyes darkened, practically turning black. *Uh oh.*

With a villainous grin, Kota responded, "Yes, that is so, *Blondie*. Now please fuck off before those pretty blonde locks end up in my fist rather than on your head."

At that, Sloane ran off, and my hand was clutched around Kota's bicep in seconds, leading her through the crowd.

"What are you doing? Where are we going?" she snapped.

"Home," I said.

"Why?"

"Because I'm so turned on, my vision is blurring."

She didn't stop me as I rummaged through the sea of people flooding the house. I didn't care if any of my teammates saw us right now. Hell, I didn't even care if Lane and Bridget saw us.

I was so jealous last time I saw her talking to Bobby, and now that her jealousy was shining through, it verified that she felt the same way about me that I did about her. She didn't want me talking to other women. She wanted me all to herself, and that was hot as hell.

I pushed the front door open, and we dashed home.

Chapter Sixty

Crew

I'd been coaxed into hanging out at the hockey house, bribed with beer, pizza, and Xbox.

Every hockey player's weaknesses.

Matt called me up and told me that if I didn't get my ass over to the house *right now*, that the guys were going to come key my car.

Of course, he had me on speakerphone, and of course, the other guys chimed in, yelling that I hadn't been over to hangout in far too long.

I'd asked Lane if he was going to go. He said it was his dad's birthday and that he was going to go have dinner with him. He'd come stop by the house afterwards if we were all still there.

Kota was scrambling to finish some bio project and wanted me to leave her the fuck alone anyway, which was another reason why I figured I'd head over to the house.

I left a kiss on her cheek, which she had no reaction to because she was scribbling some drawing of a DNA strand onto notebook paper. Her tennis bracelet jangled on her wrist as she did it, and I smiled at it while backing out of the room quietly before she had the chance to lose her mind.

The guys were all exactly as I pictured them when I walked in— sitting on their asses, spread out throughout the living room and loud as hell.

The house was still semi-trashed from the party last weekend. Beer cans and garbage were overflowing the nearest trash can and random shit was scattered along the floor— half-empty liquor bottles, a spilled bag of chips, articles of clothing left by strangers.

I tiptoed through the mess. Matt and Jett were locked in on their GTA mission with cops on their tails as they both screamed at each other to get their shit together.

"What a lovely welcome," I declared, collapsing onto the adjacent couch where I'd found room beside Cody, who was scrolling through TikTok and laughing to himself. TJ was nowhere to be found.

"Hello, shithead," Jett called out and I immediately knew the comment was meant for me and not Matt.

"Asshole," Matt tipped his head, greeting me.

"Wow, such great hospitality," I said.

Matt didn't bother looking away from the TV as he spoke. "You used to live here. You don't get hospitality."

I laughed once before diving into the box of fresh pizza on the coffee table in the center of the room. "Where are the others?" I asked between bites.

"TJ ran upstairs. Probably jerking off or something, I don't know," Matt replied. "Keith and Jonah are on a double date."

I raised a brow. "A double date?"

"Well, Jonah saw it as a double date. Keith probably saw it as a creative way to get laid."

It was comical how much Keith and Jonah resembled Lane and me. Keith, my replacement in the house and soon to be my replacement on the starting line once I left, embodied all the qualities that I carried with me throughout college— nonchalant playboy that didn't care much about anything other than his boys, his game, and his own future.

Whereas Jonah was a smart and caring natural talent, who dabbled in hookups but didn't care for them all that much. Mr. Rule Follower and future team leader. He was practically Lane 2.0.

"Interesting," I said, wiping my hands together to rid myself of pizza crust crumbs.

"Crew," Jett spoke sharply, "can you please shut up? You're distracting Matt and making him suck more."

"You're the one that fucking sucks," Matt barked back.

"I didn't come over to listen to you guys bitch at each other," I chimed in.

They just responded with sighs and groans.

I watched their game go on for another ten minutes before Jett accidentally cut Matt off on a sharp turn, sending the two flying off the road and getting arrested.

"Goddamnit, Jett!" Matt shot up off the couch as Jett tossed the remote on the couch beside him. "I'm never playing with you again."

I loved Matt, but he was like a ticking bomb with no time warning; you never knew when he'd explode.

On the ice, Matt played fucking dirty. And my prayers went out to every player who ever pissed him off out there because he showed no mercy, becoming a complete animal with no regard for safety.

Same went for off the ice. He'd gotten pissed off at us before, but he never got physical with us. Thank God.

I considered myself to be a damn good fighter; I'd never backed down from a fight. But if Matt ever tried to swing on me, you'd bet your ass I'd be running.

I wasn't at all surprised hearing the details of his fight from the party last weekend, where he'd allegedly destroyed the guy's face and given him a bruised rib or two. It took Lane, Jett, and Cody to get him off the guy. I never understood why any dude ever thought it was a good idea to walk into the hockey house and start a fight anyway.

After Matt threw his small tantrum and disappeared for a few minutes, he came back with an ice-cold beer, acting chipper as if nothing happened.

I don't understand this kid, I thought.

"I told TJ to get his ass down here," Matt said, taking his spot back on the couch.

"What was he doing?" I asked.

"He was fucking sleeping," he scoffed, holding his beer halfway to his mouth before he brought it home.

I held my hands out. "You didn't get me a beer?"

"Again," Matt raised an annoyed brow, "you used to live here. You know where we keep the beer. Go get your damn own."

"Fucking assholes," I murmured under my breath as I stumbled into the kitchen and grabbed a beer out of the fridge. When I got back, Jett had now disappeared and TJ had turned up shirtless, yawning and stretching after his interrupted beauty sleep.

"Oh, Crew," Matt nodded towards me. "Did you see the thing Rave 'N' Roll posted on Instagram this morning?"

"Nah, what was it?"

"They're having like a half-off drinks night on Wednesday so we're all gonna go get drinks and bowl."

"Like, just us, or the whole team?" I asked, setting my beer beside my feet on the floor.

"Whole team, probably. And whoever everyone wants to invite."

TJ sat on the armrest of the couch, opposite the side Matt was seated on. His brows furrowed, voice coming out strained like he was stressed out. "How come I didn't know about this?"

"You've been sleeping on and off all goddamn day," Matt answered, holding his beer out to the side.

"Whatever," TJ ruffled his dirty blonde hair. "I'll find a girl to bring."

Cody sounded bored, still scrolling aimlessly on his phone. "Good for you."

With an eye roll, the corners of TJ's lips climbed upwards as he repositioned himself on the armrest. "Are the lovebirds gonna go?"

I took a swig of beer. "Who are the lovebirds?"

My first thought was that the stars had aligned for Matt and that he'd finally hooked up with El.

But apparently, I was way off.

TJ looked at me like I was an idiot. "Lane and Bridget."

My beer shot down the wrong tube as I started laughing, sounding like I was delirious. I think the entire planet was fully aware that Lane had been pining for Bridget since night one. "He wishes," I joked.

For whatever reason, the other guys had their eyes locked on TJ like snakes waiting to strike. But still, they kept quiet, on standby for TJ's response.

He gave a light chuckle, rubbing the light stubble along his jaw. "I mean, I don't think he's gotta."

"TJ," Matt growled, burying his head in his hands.

"What?"

For the first time since I'd arrived, Cody was paying full attention. He shook his head at TJ. "You're a fucking idiot."

"What the hell do you mean?!" TJ whirred, twisting around as his eyes jumped from Cody to Matt to me. "I was just asking a question!"

There was obviously something I didn't know, something that Matt and Cody were fully aware of, but I couldn't tell TJ's part in it all.

"Well, now I'm confused," TJ confessed.

"Yeah," I said sharply, "so am I."

Matt turned towards TJ, bringing a hand up to block his mouth. "He doesn't know."

Jaw twitching, my teeth clenched. It felt like there was an inferno currently blazing around my body, set alight by my surging ire. "I can still *fucking* hear you," I seethed. "What don't I know? What the hell is going on!"

Cody made a face before sitting back against the couch. "Now you gotta tell him."

Whatever twisted game they were playing right now needed to stop. I didn't like to be left in the dark, and they better speak up now because I sure as hell wasn't leaving this house without answers.

The look on Matt's face said, *Um, what the fuck, no?*

"Well, I'm not telling him," Cody said. "I don't want this shit pinned on me."

"Me neither," Matt finally spoke.

My brows had been wrinkled for so long that they might stay that way permanently. I couldn't figure out whatever the fuck was going on. "What shit?!" I yelled.

Eventually, Cody sat forward and sighed. When he finally found his voice, it came out soft and slow, like he was afraid the news would give me a heart attack if he wasn't careful. "Jett caught Lane and Bridget coming out of the bathroom together at the party last weekend."

My stomach collapsed as reality caught up to me, slowly and painfully. "What?" I let out.

Cody bit his lip. Matt aimlessly glanced around the room like he was lost and not part of the conversation. And TJ had finally realized that he fucked up, sitting there slumped over, shoulders rounded as his expression twisted into that of a sheepish child.

Just to make matters worse, TJ added, "According to Jett, they've been dating for a while. I just didn't realize you didn't know."

I knew from the get-go that Lane had a thing for Bridget. He wore his emotions all over his face, practically rocking heart eyes every time she walked into the room. But he never mentioned any sort of growing relationship to me. I felt like a hypocritical dick for being mad, granted Kota and I had been sneaking around too, but I couldn't even count on one hand the number of times that Lane lied to my face.

Everything was clicking in my head. Every time they were "going to the library to do homework or study" or "running to the grocery store" or "both going to have dinner with their families" just conveniently on the same day at the same time, they were going on secret dates.

All those times that I asked what he was up to, he fucking lied to my face. I may have left out what was going on between Kota and me, but at least I didn't outright lie about anything. If Lane hadn't been so busy in his own secrets and had put two and two together, I probably would've told him the truth if he'd confronted me.

But I couldn't say the same for him.

Squeezing my beer can until it caved in, I chugged what was left of it and stood.

"Where are you going?" Cody asked.

"Home."

"Make sure you don't pin this shit on us! It was all TJ's fault!" Matt called after me.

"Hey!" TJ started, his voice becoming muffled as I walked out the front door and slammed it behind me.

Chapter Sixty-One

Kota

The second I heard Crew's tone through the phone, I knew something was wrong. He was practically growling, sounding so disturbed that I could feel it rattling my bones.

I had no idea what was going on. Didn't have a single clue. I'd be lying if I said I wasn't a little scared.

When I first picked up the phone and heard the words, "We need to talk," I nearly crumpled to the floor sobbing. Whenever someone heard those words from the person they'd been falling for, it usually never ended well. My lungs had immediately halted, and I held my breath until it burned. Ten minutes was enough time to cry over Bobby, but it sure as hell wouldn't have been enough for Crew.

But Crew assured me that it had nothing to do with us, or with me, I should say.

Which didn't leave me with much to guess on— maybe something about his parents? Hockey? Did his teammates piss him off when he went to go hangout?

Crew barged into my bedroom with so much force that I was surprised my door didn't fall off its hinges.

"Listen to this!" he exclaimed.

I sat on the edge of my bed, speaking indifferently. "Listening."

He began pacing back and forth, making me a bit unsettled. Brows furrowing, I slowly lifted my legs onto the bed and scooted backwards.

"Our roommates... our *best friends*," he spat like poison, "have been lying to us."

"How so?"

"They're dating."

I stared at him silently, watching him pace, steam rolling off his body. Finally, I gave a laugh. "There's no way. Bridget would've told me."

"Well, apparently she wouldn't because she didn't."

I held my hands up, shaking my head. "Where did you get this information from?"

"TJ."

Another laugh. "You're gonna trust what TJ says?"

"All the other guys backed it up."

"I'm going to need a little bit more information," I said skeptically.

"At the last party, Jett caught Lane and Bridget sneaking out of the bathroom together. I don't know if Jett started asking questions or what, but according to Jett, they're a couple."

I crossed my arms, staring off in thought. If this information was coming from TJ, I doubted every little bit of it. No offense to TJ but he wasn't the most reliable source, in my opinion. Half the time he was clueless, and the other half, he was saying something stupid.

But, if this was coming from Jett, then we had an issue. Jett had a good head on his shoulders. He was smart, put-together, and responsible. His only true flaw that I was aware of was that he used vodka lemonades as a ploy to get girls to talk to him but other than that, he was probably the second-most reliable person on the hockey team.

Second to Lane, of course.

Eventually, I shrugged, letting my hands drop to my comforter. "Do you really believe this?"

Crew stepped close enough to place a hand on the bed and lean towards me. "Think about it," he said quietly. "All those times they went off to 'study' for hours and hours on end, numerous times a week? All the times they conveniently had to go to the same places at the same time?"

I thought about what Bridget had been like since her and Mitch split up. It was a stark difference to how she'd been when she broke up with her freshman year boyfriend, Ethan.

There was a solid month after Ethan where she basically had me handcuffed to her, counting on me for comfort and stability. She was a complete wreck for a while, turning to a puddle of strawberry blonde tears whenever she was alone. It took a lot to get her out of that mindset and back to a good place.

Bridget was strong. She was independent. But in times of sadness and stress, she leaned on people she loved the most.

On the day that her and Mitch ended things, she hadn't even called me. She texted me, which was unlike her when she had something important to tell me. And I came home to Lane consoling her in her bedroom, sitting dubiously close to one another, heads tipped like they were about to kiss if I hadn't barged in.

Oh my God. She didn't call me because she called Lane.

In the months following the breakup, she wasn't attached to my hip. She was attached to Lane's. It was when she and Lane started to get close.

She didn't need me because she had Lane.

"Oh my gosh!" I screeched, jumping up on my bed. "They're dating!"

"I know!" Crew shouted back.

I plopped back down on my ass, feeling the bed bounce from the weight. "Do you think they know about us?"

Crew chewed on his lip for a moment, stuck in thought. Finally, he slowly shook his head. "Nah, I think they would've said something if they suspected it."

"Yeah... you're probably right."

"So, what do we do now?"

"We're gonna have to say something," I said. "You know I won't be able to keep my mouth shut."

"Alright," he nodded, slipping his phone out of his pocket. I watched him tap it a few times and pull up their locations on Find My Friends. "Looks like they're leaving Starbucks right now."

I gave a slow nod, staring mindlessly at my comforter. "Are they heading home?"

"I think so..."

"Alright. I guess we'll wait then."

Chapter Sixty-Two

Crew

Like stalkers, Kota and I watched their locations as they pulled into the apartment complex parking lot.

We didn't have a plan on what we were going to say or do, but we were equally pissed.

It was hypocritical, for sure. Did I think it was fucking dumb of me to break a rule that I set in the first place? Yeah, of course. But for a while now, I wanted to figure out my own thoughts and feelings before sharing them with anyone else. Kota and I hadn't even had that conversation ourselves. I knew how strongly I felt about Kota, but I was still easing into accepting relationship territory.

Lane always had shit figured out. He always knew exactly what he was doing, always had a clear head, whereas I was the opposite. And I always knew it, but it was actually starting to bother me a little bit now.

I was jealous of him for it.

Kota and I could hear Lane and Bridget laughing from down the hall. My heartrate sped with anticipation when I watched the lock on the door turn, and as Kota crossed her arms, I did the same.

Bridget slightly jumped at the sight of us, caught off guard. Lane's laughter slowly faded until he was cloaked with unease, brows pulled down and eyeing us like they just walked into a trap.

They kind of did.

"Hello?" Lane cautiously spoke. "Can we help you?"

Ire was slowly searing my bones. My scorned gaze flickered back and forth between them. "How was your date?"

Lane hardly seemed on edge, standing stiff, unintimidated. "What?" he bellowed.

But Bridget's face said it all. The rosy pink rush to her cheeks was as bright as a neon sign, and I could visibly see the way her tiny hand tightened around her Starbucks cup.

Finally, Kota stepped in, and the dark animosity in her voice reminded me of how she used to speak to me so long ago. "We know." Neither of them responded, but I could see Lane ease back a bit, shoulders falling. "How long have you two been secretly dating?"

I couldn't stop staring at Lane. With every second that passed, it felt like the knife in my heart was getting drilled deeper and deeper.

My best friend lied to me.

My *brother* lied to me.

Lane hung his head low, accepting defeat. "Almost two months."

"Two months?" Kota roared. "You've been lying to us for two months?"

Bridget's face skewed from looking like she'd been punched in the gut to looking like she wanted to punch *us* in the gut. "Yeah, well..." she paused unsteadily, "we know that you two have been fucking!"

Kota gasped, sounding like she just got her first breath of air after drowning for minutes on end. Her voice rumbled, "We have not..."

I made a face, undoubtedly cringing and giving us away. Lane's hand swiped through the air, and he spoke in the same tone he used when we were in between periods of a game and playing like trash. "Oh, don't give us that shit. We've heard you guys loud and clear."

Fuck. When?!

My guess had to be at some point in the middle of the night. We were usually so careful otherwise, only messing around when our roommates weren't home. We were also typically quiet at night— well, as quiet as possible— but there was always room for error, I guess.

"Alright," I said, taking in a puff of stale air and nearly choking on it, "so we've hooked up once or twice."

Droplets of Bridget's coffee flew into the air when she slammed it down on the counter beside her, bringing her hand to her hip. "Once or twice, *my ass.* We know you guys have a whole routine going. You were probably going at it before we walked in."

I could feel my muscles constricting, teeth clenching as I shook my head, overtaken by far too many emotions all at once. "This isn't about us."

"Then what's it about? Us?" Lane motioned to Bridget and himself. "Because that hardly seems fair."

The room went quiet, and it felt like the floor was falling through, but honestly, I would've been okay with it if it had.

There was an odd, sour taste in my mouth— the taste of betrayal. Bitter and cold, hollow and deadly, it was radiating throughout the apartment, contaminating us all.

Kota and I sat with frowns, mirroring the two people we loved most in front of us. If disappointment were tangible, it would be filling the room up to my throat right now.

Lane stalked forward, and my shoulder rammed back as he bumped into me, but I managed to stay on my feet. "Let's go talk."

For a moment, I didn't move; I couldn't at first. The fury simmering inside me was fading back to hurt, and I finally headed towards my room, chin to the floor the entire time.

But when I walked inside and closed the door, all I could do was stand there, back turned towards Lane, hands planted on my hips as I tried to catch my breath.

However this conversation were to go, I needed *one* thing from Lane.

For him to not speak to me as my roommate. Or my friend. I didn't want him to speak to me as my teammate. Or my captain.

I needed him to speak to me as my brother.

I fostered the courage to look at him. I could hear the ache in my own voice as it came out, low and rasped. "I really hope you're not going to blame this on that stupid rule."

Lane was always so calm and collected. It was a rarity to see him genuinely torn up.

Yet here he was, standing before me with eyes just as glossy as my own, a haunted expression overtaking his face.

"I don't care about the rule, Lane," I let out. "I care that you lied to me."

He pointed to the center of his chest, and instantly, I realized he was pointing to the bullet hole I'd just left. "And *you* didn't lie to *me*?"

And just like that, my hand shot up to my own chest, covering my own wound now. I rubbed right over my heart.

"Sure, I left part of the truth out, but you knew how I felt about her! I'm not the one that's been going around for however long pretending to hate her. Putting on a show *just* to deceive you." He stumbled back a little. "How long has it been going on for anyway?"

Longer than two months, I remembered, gulping through the thought.

"How long, Crew?"

"A few months," I replied quietly, ashamed.

Shaking his head, he said, "You have no right to give me any shit."

"Lane—"

"No," he cut me off. "I didn't lie to your face like you lied to mine."

Anger was resurfacing, and it seemed like we'd both be dead on the floor, covered in bullet holes by the time this conversation was over. "That's bullshit. That's such bullshit."

"Name a lie that I told you to your face."

"What about every time I asked what you were up to, and you always responded saying that you were just hanging out with Bridget? When in reality, you were sneaking around behind my back, going on secret dates?"

At that, he backed down a bit, grabbing the back of his neck. "Technically, I wasn't lying. I was hanging out with Bridget like I said."

"Don't try to get me on a goddamn technicality, Lane!"
I hurled. "The bottom line is that you fucking lied."

You lied. I lied. The girls both lied. Everybody in this house was just a fucking liar apparently.

Hurt was running through me, soaring through my bloodstream, alongside guilt. Lane wasn't the only one that needed to be held accountable. I knew that half of this mess was my fault, and that reality only added more pain.

I spoke through shaking and cracked words, my strong and confident persona vanishing— what was left of it, at least. "I had to find out from fucking TJ! Fucking TJ! Instead of from you. It seems like everyone on the damn planet knew before I did. Do you know how fucking upsetting that is? We're supposed to tell each other shit! Brothers are not supposed to lie to each other!"

Lane cringed, wounded. He blew out a strained breath, eyes bright with pain. "Crew..."

"I'm serious."

"I know," he croaked. "I'm sorry." Silently, I stared at him, unsure if I just heard him correctly. "I am. I'm sorry."

Eyes glancing up to meet his, the weight felt like it was lifting off my chest in slow-motion. I gave a shaky exhale. "I'm sorry too... Can we please never do this shit again?"

"Yeah," he nodded quietly.

Immediately, my arms were open, and he mirrored me. We met halfway, embracing for a hug that brought ease back to me.

Lane and I didn't hug often, if ever. If it wasn't hockey induced, then it usually wasn't happening.

It did feel nice to hug my brother though.

"Alright," I pulled back after it felt like it was getting weird. "Long enough."

He smiled and rolled his eyes, letting me know that things were going to be okay.

"You think the girls are fine?" I asked.

"Probably," he shrugged.

"I mean... you know how Kota can be."

"I know. But Bridget can handle her own," he grinned.

Chapter Sixty-Three

Kota

Bridget looked lost, standing in the middle of my room like it was her first time ever walking into it.

I sat against the headboard of my bed, unprepared and uncomfortable.

Didn't think we'd be doing this *today. Definitely wasn't on my daily to-do list.*

I'd considered telling Bridget what was going on a handful of times over the last few months, but every time, I bit it back.

There were too many facets of the truth that I hadn't fully grasped or accepted, if I was being honest.

First and foremost, how the hell could I have fallen for someone who symbolized qualities that I hated so much? Sure, Crew had softened and opened up, so I knew a different side of him now, but at first glance, he was still that cocky, playboy hockey player that I met back in August.

Second, we still weren't official. I was embarrassed enough expressing the situation to my mom; I didn't want to feel the wave of all those emotions by expressing it to Bridget too. After what I went through with Bobby and now where I was at with Crew, I'd almost been feeling like I couldn't get a guy to commit to me?

When Bridget sat at the edge of my bed, I wanted to look at her, but I was finding it difficult to. So, I stared at my purple comforter instead. I nearly just spit out the truth to get it over with, but like a coward, I zoned in on her side of the story first. "Why didn't you tell me, B?"

"Why didn't you tell *me*?"

My throat burned as the words reluctantly rolled out. "Because I was embarrassed."

The slight snappiness that she'd just had dulled, and she became the soft-spoken, sweet Bridget that I knew. "Why would you be embarrassed?"

Shaking through a sigh, I squeezed my eyes shut. "Because Crew encompasses everything in a man that I hate. Everything I promised myself I would never go for." I sighed, my voice dropping to a whisper, "Yet here I am."

From the second she entered the room, it felt like we were strangers given the space between us, both physically and emotionally. But finally, she scooted closer to me, brows pulled in with sympathy. "Kota, you don't need to beat yourself up over hooking up with someone."

Oh no. She still hasn't fully gotten it. I must not have been clear enough.

My mouth formed a tight line, and I had to force myself to say the words. "Well, it's a little bit more than that."

"Oh."

"We aren't together, but we've talked about that being a future possibility."

"Oh."

I shrugged, focusing far too hard on keeping my face as expressionless as possible. Even though B was my best friend in the entire universe, I still didn't have it in me to be candid about my feelings, with her or with anyone. I was used to bottling it up and choking it down, burying it so deep until it disappeared altogether.

Acknowledging my feelings was hard enough for me to do internally. It was a whole different ball game to do it aloud.

B's voice came out softer than velvet, but there was a rigid layer behind the words that forced me to pay close attention. "Kota, you don't have to keep acting like you're invincible. It's okay to talk about your feelings, or to *have* feelings for that matter." She gestured around, "I'm the only one in the room anyway."

My nails dug harshly into my palms, leaving me surprised that I didn't draw blood. Bringing my guard down just enough to be honest, I spoke unsteadily, "I guess I was just in denial that..."

"That you have feelings for him?" she finished for me, and instinctively, I shot her a glare. "It's okay to admit it."

A raspy sigh came out, and I stared at the ceiling. "Okay, yes. No matter how much I hate it and *loathe* myself for it, I do have feelings for him."

"It's alright that you do. There's nothing wrong with that."

"I figured you'd find out eventually," I sighed again. "I just thought it would be from me."

"Trust me, it *was* from you," she choked on her own laughter.

I somehow cringed and laughed at the same time, then playfully nudged her in the shoulder. "Shut up!"

Once our laughter subsided and the room grew quiet again, Bridget's vibe shifted right back to the nervousness she embodied when she first walked in.

"Honestly though, I feel kinda bad."

"Why?"

Her eyes turned solemn and dropped, and she sat there as if she was basking in shame. "Because you just gave me a legitimate reason of why you didn't tell me, and truthfully, the only reasons I have are that we didn't want to piss you guys off about breaking the rule and we also became too stubborn to fess up first."

I soaked in her words, trying to gather my own thoughts. The rule was honestly the last thing on my mind. I never cared much about that dumb rule anyway. It was kind of the most unnecessary rule we'd put in place, but at the time, I didn't think much of it because I never would've guessed that our living arrangement would lead to all this. It was no secret though that Lane and Bridget were the biggest rule followers in history, so I wasn't surprised they didn't want to be caught.

In regard to the stubborn comment, I *was* a little surprised about that one. If I was asked to list the top, most

362

relevant qualities of Lane and Bridget, stubborn wouldn't have even been in the top hundred, whereas Crew and I were notorious for being stubborn.

Ultimately, I shrugged, rather carelessly at the thought of my two friends sparking up some sort of forbidden romance under our shared roof. "You and Lane being together doesn't bother me. I always kinda knew you guys had a thing for each other, but you never mentioned it, not even once, so I figured I had to have been wrong."

"I'm sorry," was all she said, biting her lower lip.

"So am I. And I'm also sorry if I made you feel like you couldn't tell me."

B's strawberry blonde locks bobbed as shook her head lightly, eyes softened and brows slanted. I could feel her guilt circling through the air like campfire smoke and I hoped she didn't think she was the only one that felt that way. "There were so many times where I wanted to tell you. Really, I did. At first, I didn't say anything because I wasn't sure where things with Lane would go, and I didn't want everything in the apartment to be thrown off if everyone knew. But as we got a bit deeper into our relationship..." she shrugged, "I still couldn't do it. And I don't know why. I know for Lane, he most definitely didn't want *Crew* knowing but..." she trailed off.

Not going to lie, it did make me feel better knowing that B's silence was probably rooted from Lane's wish to keep Crew in the dark, and that it had less to do with me. I scoffed lightly. "I don't blame him. Crew's the biggest hypocrite. He probably would've lit the apartment on fire."

"Exactly," she chuckled.

I never got mushy, almost ever. There were only a few people in the world that I ever showed true emotion towards, and Bridget was one of them. I'd never had a friend like her before, and I loved her on another level. "And I mean, yeah, it sucks that I got to miss the beginning with all the most exciting parts of you guys getting together, but if you're happy with him, then I'm happy for you." Placing my hand gingerly atop hers, I asked, "Are you happy with him, B?"

"I am."

"That's what I care about most."

"Are you happy with Crew?" she asked.

I couldn't help but let out a snort. "Most of the time."

She laughed, a true, full, Bridget Bell laugh, and the sound calmed me after the heaviness of this whole conversation— really, of this whole *day*.

With a hopeful smile, she asked, "So, you forgive me?"

"Of course, I do," I nodded. "Do you forgive me?"

"Yes," her smile grew, and she offered her pinky finger. "No more secrets?"

My pinky grabbed onto hers like I was making the most important promise of my life. "No more secrets."

The next twenty minutes were spent with us spilling all the juicy details of our relationships. I told her everything, every detail between our first hookup to now. I even got questionably graphic and spilled some spicy memories to her, which led her to stare at me silently with her mouth agape, looking slightly disgusted, but she was my best friend, so she ended up high fiving me anyway.

My confession caused her to open up about some of her spicy encounters too, and I was pleasantly surprised— *not in a weird way*— to hear that Lane insisted she put his jersey on and then fucked her over her bedroom desk.

Regardless of how vulgar this conversation had ended, I somehow felt as light as air, like a weight had been lifted that I hadn't even realized existed.

Chapter Sixty-Four

Crew

It was the conference championship against our rivals, St. Cloud State, and I was feeling more pressure than when we were in the NCAA tournament last year.

By the middle of the second period, we were up by two, but it wasn't without difficulty.

St. Cloud was playing fucking dirty. *And they were getting away with it.*

Number fifty-nine on the opposing team, Ethan Silas, was playing the filthiest of all. Our schools had bad blood dating back for decades, but he wasn't just playing dirty— he was playing *personal,* specifically targeting Lane.

A lot of teams targeted Lane since he was our best player and the hardest to maintain, but goddamn, this was another level.

Lane had been tripped, rammed against the glass more times than I could count, elbowed, pushed to the ice... The list went on and on.

I wasn't safe from any of it either. There were a few hits that I took that knocked me on my ass too, and when the refs didn't call it, the crowd lost their shit.

I was pissed, knowing they'd just gotten away with dirty hits, but I didn't have the time to sit there and cry about it. In the middle of a game, you had little to no reaction time.

Everything and every*one* moved at the speed of light, and if you didn't keep up, you were in fucking trouble.

Thankfully, even with how immoral St. Cloud was, we still managed not to reciprocate, playing clean enough to set a new record for our team, only receiving two minor penalties throughout the whole game. On top of that, we won. Coach was ecstatic.

It wasn't over yet though.

Conference championships were best of three, which meant we had another game tomorrow. If we could clinch the win, we'd be conference champs. If not, we'd have to play a third game.

My favorite part about today though? Seeing Kota wear my jersey.

The first time she ever wore my jersey, I wanted to walk into the stands and rip it off her, then soak it in bleach to make sure all her germs were off it.

Now, the sight was branded into my mind like a core memory.

Every time the whistle had blown, I used it as my opportunity to get a glimpse of her in the crowd. I wished she'd jump up, wave at me, show off my jersey like she was proud to be wearing my name and number. In a perfect world, Bobby would've been nearby to see it. I'd admit, I was a jealous and petty prick for that part, but I wanted him to know how fucking off-limits she was.

But unfortunately, none of those things in my fantasy happened.

Kota had been sitting in a flock of all our moms, including mine, and my mother had absolutely no idea what was going on between us.

But having introduced themselves as my roommates, and with Bridget wearing Lane's jersey, my mom didn't think anything of it other than a few of our friends coming to support us.

Going to the bar a night before a game, especially one as major as tomorrow's, was typically a big no-no.

The exception? *Lane requested it.*

Long story short, he had some deeply rooted issues with his mom, and after the conversation I overheard post-game outside the locker room, a drink was in store.

So, like every other day of my teammate's and my life, Lane made the rules tonight.

Rule number one: no one was allowed to get hammered. Buzzed, fine. But nothing more.

Rule number two: only our starting line was able to go, because the underclassmen weren't trusted to not get obliterated.

My post-game request? I asked Kota to wear my jersey to the bar. But apparently, I wasn't as smooth as I thought because she laughed in my face.

I couldn't tell what expression I'd been holding, but whatever it was, my disappointment must've shone through, because her compromise was that she'd put it back on later for me.

A thousand and one obscene visions flew through my mind, but I buried them down, trying to be on my best behavior to spend some quality time with all the people I cared about most— my teammates, Lane, Bridget, and Kota.

Currently, I was trapped between Cody and Matt as they screamed at each other, giving me déjà vu. Unlike New Year's, this fight wasn't about bigfoot or the Lochness monster. It was about the fucking Bermuda Triangle.

Cody was arguing that all the disappearances and mysteries of the Bermuda Triangle were due to some magical magnetic forcefield.

Matt claimed it was aliens.

Who the fuck let these two come out with us?

It felt like I was getting stupider and stupider by listening to the conversation, but it was too entertaining to walk away from.

Until my bullshit radar started going off.

The bar was pretty packed. Clearly, most people came straight from the game, surrounding us in a sea of Cedar U gear.

Even through the crowd, I was able to spot Bobby, and I followed his eyesight all the way to where it was focused on Kota.

I fucking swear to God.

This kid was relentless. Not to mention careless. Was he trying to get himself killed? After all the threats and warnings I'd given him?

I pushed right through Cody and Matt, holding my beer high as I beelined towards Kota. Well, as fast as one could beeline through a mob of people.

"Hey," I said.

"Hi," she smiled at me, and the flutter in my stomach nearly knocked me to the ground.

"Stay by me, yeah?" I requested, grabbing her small hand and rubbing my thumb over it.

Her smile didn't waver. "What for?" she asked sweetly.

"I just wanna—"

"Kota."

She swung around at the sound of her name, and the temptation to guide her behind me and protect the fuck out of her was overpowering all reason within me.

I didn't hesitate to do it, but she fought me on it, giving a slight scoff. "Crew."

Bobby stiffened, growing an inch, but still not tall enough to even come close to my height.

In that moment, I turned cold-blooded and bloodthirsty, ready to fight any second.

Pretending like I wasn't there, Bobby gave a slight lean so that he had a clear view of Kota from behind me. "Can we talk?"

I responded, "Uh, no," at the same time that Kota said, "Alright."

My jaw hit the floor and I stared at her like she just grew a second head. What could she possibly be thinking right now? Was she trying to make me jealous?

Because if so, watching him whisk her out of my reach was working.

I stayed in place, my feet practically cemented to the floor. Every move Bobby made, I watched with malicious intent, waiting for him to do something— anything— out of line.

Get too close to her. Touch her. Smile at her.

368

I didn't care. If he overstepped any boundary, he'd be waking up in the hospital.

Unfortunately, I sucked at lip reading, and it was far too loud to make out what they were saying from six feet away. But thankfully, he was maintaining his distance, definitely not as intoxicated as he was the last time we ran into him.

"Hey," Lane tapped me.

I didn't turn to look at him, didn't budge. Didn't do anything other than acknowledge him with a hollow, "Hey."

He stepped beside me when he realized I wasn't going to face him. "Ah," he expressed with a small nod, following my eyesight, "trouble in paradise?"

I folded my arms stiffly across my chest. "Everything's fine." *Hopefully.*

He rested an arm on my shoulder. "Alriiight, well, when you're done with... whatever's going on here... George wants to interview us."

Everybody on campus knew who George was. He was practically a campus celebrity. He was a bigger, African American guy with a heart of absolute gold. He illuminated teddy bear vibes and was someone that everyone wanted to be friends with.

George was also a huge sports fan, especially hockey. He attended every home game and had a sports blog where he wrote all sports-related content. There were a handful of times where he would ask to interview some guys on the team, and no one ever had the heart to say no to him; he was too nice.

George was truly one of the nicest guys I'd ever met, but goddamn, I didn't have the time or mental capacity right now.

My first priority in this very moment was Kota. I needed to make sure she was okay, and that Bobby didn't try to pull any shit either. Because I swore to God if she left this bar with anyone other than me, I'd lose my fucking mind and burn this city down until it was nothing but a pile of dust.

I still didn't bother looking at Lane as I spoke. Quite frankly, it seemed impossible for me to look anywhere other than at Kota and Bobby. "Can't he interview somebody else?" I sharply replied.

"He said, and I quote, that he wanted to 'interview the dynamic duo'."

My brows faltered and I huffed. "Why the hell did he call us that?"

"I dunno," Lane shrugged.

"Well, he might be waiting awhile."

"Alright," he gave a friendly pat on my back. "Let me know if you need any backup."

"Mhm."

There were a few times where Kota caught my gaze, just for a millisecond each time, but it was enough for me to notice. I didn't really give a fuck if I was giving stalker vibes. I was stubborn. I was protective. And I was feeling a strange knot in my core at the sight of her with *him*.

Kota lightly placed her hand on his arm. It felt like my world was being so swiftly torn apart, and all I did was stand there and endure the damage. But just as quickly as she had touched him, she walked away, and the tornado that had been ripping me to bits vanished.

I was dragged out of my own disastrous thoughts as she stopped a mere foot away. "So?" I asked.

Her scornful glare was giving me slight whiplash after how sweet she'd been before Bobby came over and ruined it all. "So, what?" she cocked a brow, arms crossing.

As if I wasn't getting burned from the dark fire in her eyes, I asked, "What did he want?"

Kota sighed, breaking eye contact. "He said he was sorry. And that he wants to try things again and actually be together this time."

Holding back a growl, my voice turned low. "And what did you say?"

"I told him no."

I had to focus on holding back a smile. I could sing and dance right now if there weren't people around. "Why?" I asked, longing to hear the words.

A tiny smile stained Kota's lips, and I took a mental screenshot to replay this moment over and over again in my head later. With a stiff finger, she poked my shoulder. "You know why."

I had an assumption of why, but I wanted her to say it.

"No, I don't," I grinned, shaking my head. "Tell me."

But of course, once again, she refused to give me what I wanted. "You know why," she repeated. "I gotta go over by B."

"Kota, I—"

Gone.

Compelled to follow her but forcing myself the opposite way, I joined Lane and George over in the corner.

George smiled so brightly at Lane and me that it made me feel bad for ever dreading these interviews. With his phone camera pointed at us in one hand and a microphone that didn't actually work in the other, he asked question after question about our game tonight, our thoughts about it, and how we felt going into tomorrow's game.

The microphone was shoved in my face, practically sitting atop my mouth when Kota ran straight to me, squeezing my hand so hard that she probably could've ripped it right off my body if she pulled. I held a finger up to George and with a worried nod, he backed away.

Frantically, Kota's gaze bounced back and forth between Lane and me, and the fear caught in her features was causing my fight or flight to kick in like no other.

"What? What is it?" I panicked, looking her up and down to make sure she was unscathed.

"It's Bridget," she answered, causing Lane to step forward, matching my distress.

"What happened? Where is she?" he let out breathlessly. After knowing Lane for years, I'd never heard that level of concern in his voice before. Over anything.

I wasn't sure if it was his rampaging heartbeat or my own that was hammering in my ears.

Kota was speaking in bits and pieces, and if we were strangers that hadn't lived with her for seven months now, we would've had no fucking idea what she was trying to say.

"Ethan. Her ex. On St. Cloud. He won't leave her alone. He just followed her to the bathroom. He's—"

Lane was off before anyone could blink, rummaging through everyone as quickly and respectfully as a true gentleman could.

I was fully aware already that St. Cloud was in the building— we were all aware of it. My bullshit radar was going off the second they had walked in, all cocky and smug even though they took a major loss just a few hours ago. It was ballsy of them to walk into a bar that wasn't theirs. For them, this was enemy territory, and I had a feeling they were about to get shown how badly they'd just fucked up.

A crash drowned out the music, and over the heads of the people before us, I was able to see flashes of Jett, standing aside the bar as he warily pushed Bridget behind him.

Uh oh. Here we go.

Gripping onto Kota's hand, I pulled her along with me through too many people. I didn't even know why they allowed so many people in this fucking building.

Heads were turning from the commotion and as more people caught sight of the fight that was bound to start, they spread outwards, probably just trying to get a front row seat to the show.

Bridget stood off to the side, out of the direct crossfire, but still too close for my liking. I grabbed Bridget's wrist, holding each of the girls in one hand and leading them a little farther off to the side.

My voice was strained, rolling out as a warning so they understood how serious I was being. "Don't get any closer."

Lane and Silas were standing face to face, almost chest to chest. St. Cloud's starting lineup stood behind Silas, ready to back him up, and our players mirrored them, fists clenched and chests broadened like they were simply waiting for Lane to tell them when.

As Lane's right-hand man, it was only right for me to position myself behind him and a step off to the side, securing my spot on the front line if things got ugly.

I had no idea what words had been exchanged before my late arrival. But judging by the dark, teasing gleam in Silas's eye and the rising, boiling, uncontrollable resentment that was oozing off Lane, it couldn't have been good.

Lane was protective of our team. He was hands-down the best captain this team had ever seen and would've done anything for any of us.

Yet even though I hadn't known about him and Bridget for long, I could already tell that protective behavior was multiplied by a hundred when it came to her.

I knew the feeling.

"Don't make me tell you again, Silas," Lane hissed.

It was like I could smell their thirst for blood, specifically Silas. No wonder why it seemed like he'd had a personal vendetta against Lane on the ice. As far as I knew, Lane didn't know a single thing about him being Bridget's ex, and quite honestly, I was fucking surprised that she dated Ethan at all.

Bridget was one of the sweetest, most soft-spoken people I'd ever met in my life, and I didn't know Ethan Silas well beyond our encounters on the ice, but his persona screamed asshole. It seemed like he was the complete opposite of Lane.

At least she upgraded, I thought to myself.

Ethan flashed an insidious grin, acting untouchable. "Why do you want her anyway, Avery? I feel like you could do better."

I stepped forward, ready to shut Silas up myself, but the back of Lane's hand met my chest, and I halted instantly.

I was amped up for a fight. I wasn't sure if it was the leftover enmity that Bobby placed into my veins like an IV, or if it was hearing this son of a bitch say something so degrading about Bridget. Maybe it was a mixture of both.

Bless Lane's heart though. I could tell it was taking every little bit of control that he had to keep his cool. And my guess? He was trying to protect our team, our chance at the conference championship.

If someone on our line got hurt and had to sit out tomorrow, Lane would never forgive himself.

"If you want to be half as good as you need to be tomorrow," Lane said, "I suggest you leave and go to bed. This is our fucking bar, Silas. And we sure as hell don't have room around here for assholes trying to start shit or pussies who mess with our girls, or any girl for that matter."

This whole time, Ethan's brash grin hadn't wavered, but all at once, it disappeared, and he stared at Lane with a glare that could crack glass. But Lane stood unimpressed and impervious.

"Just a word of advice, Avery," Ethan said, bringing that shit-eating grin right back, "all you have to do is drop the L word to get her to open her legs."

There was no reaction time before Lane's hands were on him, propelling him backwards into his own teammates.

That was the green light we'd all been waiting for.

Every Stallion player had their target chosen, and no one hesitated to charge forward and strike like we were on a battlefield.

Xander Hicks was my counterpart on St. Cloud. Their right wing was more than familiar to me, having been the fifteenth pick in the second round during the same year that I was drafted. He was no stranger to me or to the league, being notorious for starting shit on the ice.

He didn't hesitate to swing first, underestimating my speed. I ducked easily and rebounded quick enough to land a left right combo, my fists meeting both of his cheeks.

Stumbling a few steps, he caught his footing and came back for more.

Before he had the chance to make a move, my hands planted in the center of his chest, pushing him full force and onto his ass.

Launching at me from halfway off the floor, Xander greeted my jaw with his fist. The ache was immediate, spreading through my face like a wildfire.

Yeah, that's gonna leave a bruise.

Head lulled off to the side, I pulled one back and let him have it, every ounce of my fury from tonight thrown into that single punch.

He dropped to the ground again, limp. A tiny pool of red appeared when he spit onto the floor, probably trying to rid his mouth of the metallic taste.

With my guard up, ready for more, I waited for Xander to pop back up, to try tackling me to the floor or get even for the possible loss of a tooth that I just caused him.

But he stayed down.

A high-pitched, obnoxious screech wailed in the distance, becoming louder and clearer as it approached, accompanied by flashing red and blue lights.

Cops. Fucking great.

The crowd that had been surrounding us was dwindling as people rushed out, pushing and tripping over each other like there was a fucking fire behind them. St. Cloud players were fleeing one by one, disappearing into the sea of chaos.

Adrenaline had already been racing through our bloodstreams, and now, it was saturating the air. Every Stallion stayed put, frantically looking at Lane and waiting for directions like kindergarteners would. For everyone else, running was second nature, even for the people that weren't involved in the fight at all. But for us, following Lane was second nature.

Veins bulging out of his neck, Lane screamed, "My place! Now!"

With an unsaid, "Yes, Captain," the boys started scurrying through people to get to the backdoor.

I was already reaching for Kota, thanking God that she was smart enough not to move from where I'd left her, even with the absolute turmoil happening around her.

Lane pointed at Bridget. "Grab her!"

With a rushed nod, each of my hands encircled around the girl's wrists, dragging them towards the back. Bridget wasn't making my life easy though. She was fighting me on it, digging her heels into the ground while she clawed at my hand to undo herself from my grasp.

I knew she was trying to stay behind, to be left with Lane and try to protect him from whatever was bound to happen next. But he'd handed her over as my responsibility, and I wouldn't go against his wishes.

I tightened my grip on Bridget, not enough to hurt her, but just enough to keep her from getting loose.

When we set foot outside into the cool March air, it looked like a prison had just accidentally left the doors open and a mob of prisoners got loose.

Dozens of people were everywhere, shouting for their friends and running around madly, which I didn't quite understand. They were acting like an underaged house party just got busted, not a fucking bar fight.

I guess drunk people ran from cops regardless of the circumstances.

Jett and Matt were waiting outside our apartment as I brought the girls and myself to a stop, heaving from the state of panic.

Resting his back against the wall outside our front door, Jett stood with his head down. The hallway lighting was shitty, but I could make out the disheveled ruffle to his jet-black hair and the lightest trace of blue along his cheek.

Matt rested beside him, looking completely unscathed. No surprise there. I wish I saw what his opponent looked like. Guess I'd see tomorrow. That was, if he was decent enough to play.

I pulled Kota and Bridget into the apartment, and the guys followed.

"You see Cody and TJ while you were out there?" Jett asked me.

"No," I murmured quietly, concern creeping in. As if Kota had just been the one in a brawl, my gaze flitted over her, inspecting for injuries as she stood in the corner of the kitchen where the countertops met.

Her skin was still that smooth, light bronze it always was, face still ethereal with a dash of unruly. She seemed perfectly fine, other than the light rub she was giving her wrists.

Did I hurt her?

Rushing to her side, my heartrate spiked again, right after it had finally begun settling down. "Are you alright?" I whispered, gently reaching for her wrists like I was picking up a newborn.

"I'm fine," Kota said sternly, eyes landing on my jaw. Her brows furrowed, and she brushed her fingers along the sore skin. A small wince left my throat, and in the moment, I forgot that Jett and Matt had absolutely no idea that we'd been messing around. I hoped they weren't watching.

"Jesus Christ," Cody announced his arrival, his breath hitching as he bent over in the doorway with TJ on his heels.

"It's fucking insane out there," TJ said.

They joined the other guys on the couches, and I studied the empty spot between Cody and TJ like Lane would appear there in a puff of smoke like a magic trick.

Filling in the space between Cody and TJ on the long couch, I sat, trying to calm down after the madness of the last twenty minutes.

Bridget was standing beside the door, staring hopelessly at it. My heart cracked a little from the sight.

Meanwhile, as if she was an old-fashioned war nurse, Kota circled around the room, handing out ice packs and examining our wounds. When she got to me, she gave another cringe when her eyes landed on my jaw. But after simply placing an ice pack in my hand, she didn't linger, moving right along to TJ.

The cold compact hit my skin, immediately soothing the ache that was still pounding along my jaw. Minutes of silence ticked by, until I finally stood, asking the question aloud that everyone was thinking to themselves. "Where the hell is Lane?" I tossed my ice pack behind me, onto the couch.

"I don't know," Matt said, "but if he's not back soon, we need to go find him."

Cody shook his head. "I say we go find him now."

Agreed.

Feet digging into the ground, TJ pushed himself back against the couch. An icy scowl settled over his face, jaw twitching. "You guys think they went back for him?"

Tightening and loosening his fists repeatedly, Matt leaned forward. The skin on his knuckles was broken, split apart and branded with drying blood. "They're dead if they tried."

My mind was spinning, and it felt like I was detached from my body as I wandered over into the foyer by Bridget. Voice echoing in a scratchy, pained note, I muttered, "I'm more concerned about the cops."

"Way to bring that up," Jett grumbled behind me.

"Just being realistic."

"Does anyone need water?" Kota asked. In any other circumstance, I would've smiled at how exceptionally warmhearted she was being. If this bar fight happened six months ago, she probably would've been high fiving St. Cloud and treating their wounds instead.

A chilled water bottle was placed in everyone's hand, aside from Bridget, who still hadn't moved an inch from her spot beside the door.

In an attempt to give her some sort of comfort, I reached for her shoulder, but she lunged forward, out of my grasp as Lane burst through the door.

"Lane!" she screeched, but he groaned in pain as he caught her, rolling his shoulder once she eased back.

My rampaging heart was finally able to still, and the relief in the air tasted sweet like honey, filling everyone's lungs.

The guys stood, eyes resting solely on Lane, same as me. As he consoled Bridget for a moment, we waited quietly for an update or an order or really anything at all.

The second Kota pulled Bridget aside, I swept in, arms around Lane like he'd been missing for twenty years, rather than twenty minutes.

Lane hadn't said it aloud, but he just sacrificed himself for us. He stayed to make sure we got out. I could see it all over his face, could read his mind like a book as he viewed us one by one, checking over us like a concerned dad.

"It's getting late..." Matt spoke. "We need to go home and get to bed. We've got morning skate."

"No one's leaving," Lane announced, face stoic like a talking sculpture. Eyes droopy with exhaustion but layered with urgency, he made sure every single one of us felt the weight of his words. "There are cops all around us right now, and on the off chance that they see a group of slightly bruised and bloodied hockey players after getting called about a bar fight, we'd be screwed."

No denying that.

We already dodged a bullet tonight that no one got significantly hurt. We may have been a little bruised up, and it sure as hell would feel sore tomorrow, promising to ache and burn with every hit we each received on the ice, but we were still good enough to play. This was a valuable victory, and it would be stupid to gamble that now.

378

If anyone got caught by the cops, we would be in deep shit. They'd probably have their ass taken to the station and coach would probably whip the rest of our asses with our own hockey sticks.

Cody nodded to Lane, respectfully asking, "Are you locking us in, captain?"

"Team sleepover!" TJ exclaimed, securing seven eye rolls from the rest of us.

Ignoring him, Lane spoke again, a cutting edge of authority in his tone. "We've got plenty of room for everyone here. Crew and I will drop everyone off at the house in the morning so you guys can grab your shit before morning skate." When no one gave a response, Lane's tone hardened further. "Got it?"

"Got it, captain!" we responded as one.

"Good," he nodded.

"Um," Bridget squeaked, leaning closer to Lane, "someone could take my bed tonight."

"Oh, me!" Jett's hand shot up.

The floor shook as Matt stepped forward, giving Jett a playful swat on the shoulder. "I want the bed," he whined, sounding like a toddler trapped in the body of a six-foot-five man.

"Not unless you wanna share it."

With a visible shudder, Matt griped, "Hell no! You'd probably try to spoon me in the middle of the night."

To outsiders, the brotherly bickering that often occurred between all of us was probably entertaining. Some girls had even overheard Cody and Jett argue over who was an uglier baby and the girls thought the argument was "cute."

But to us, we thought our useless arguments were extremely annoying in the most endearing way.

Crossing his arms, Jett gave Matt an ornery side eye. "Oh, please."

When Kota's hand raised inch by inch, I thought she was about to tell them to shut the fuck up. But I couldn't have been more wrong.

Teeth nibbling at her bottom lip, her eyes found their way over to me, looking self-conscious in a way I'd never seen in her before. "Someone can have my bed too."

"Mine!" Matt screamed, before reading the room and sinking backwards as much as a human giant could. Everyone else, with the exception of Lane and Bridget, were gaping at us. "Wait..." Matt said. "You two too?"

Tipping my head side to side, I admitted, "Sorta."

"I knew it!" TJ yelled.

"Shut up, TJ," I squinted at him. "You didn't know shit."

Jett pointed a lousy, accusatory finger between Kota and me. "What, so... you two have been fucking?"

Get me out of here.

Talking about my feelings made me uncomfortable. Hell, *feeling* my feelings made me uncomfortable. And it was especially torturous being open and honest with the group of people who knew me for being notoriously unemotional.

"It's not just like that. We actually... sort of care about each other," I said.

"Ew!" the guys hollered altogether.

"It's not gross." Kota scoffed.

"I'm sorry," Cody shook his head, "but Crew having feelings is a little gross."

All I could do was scratch the back of my head, wincing through the awkwardness of this conversation. Truthfully, it had nothing to do with Kota. I'd shout from the rooftops proudly that she was the one I'd been sneaking around with. The embarrassment stemmed solely from my own discomfort of being mushy.

"Welcome to my world," Lane said.

Jett made a face. "I gotta side with them on this one." A heartless glare plowed over Jett as Kota stood like a soldier on the frontlines, ready for war. Immediately, Jett knew he fucked up, and if she went berserk on him, I'd just sit back and watch. I'd probably cheer her on, honestly. "It's nothing against you, I promise!" he assured.

"Mhmm," Kota hummed.

In a panic, Jett brought his hands up, surrendering. "I promise I didn't mean it like that. Please don't dye my underwear pink or hurt me in my sleep."

"Mhmm," she repeated, grabbing my hand and dragging me through the guys.

We made sure everyone was situated with plenty of pillows, blankets, and water for the night. I watched Bridget tuck the boys in on the couches before we all retreated to our sleeping arrangements, the apartment falling silent.

Tonight may have been a whirlwind from start to finish but our thoughts all went to the same place when our heads hit the pillow.

We had a fucking game to win tomorrow.

Chapter Sixty-Five

Crew

After yesterday's game and the fight last night, I had half a dozen bruises on my body.

That's doubled since the puck dropped.

St. Cloud wasn't just out for blood. They were out for broken bones and concussions.

That's what it seemed like at least, given the brutality of this game tonight.

The conference title was on the line, but it seemed like the cohesiveness and dexterity of our line was falling apart.

After last night, every single one of us had a target on our back, and it showed. This wasn't just a hockey game anymore. It wasn't just a trophy. It was fucking personal.

In the first period, we just took it, all of us getting pummeled while St. Cloud's players were getting rotated in and out of the penalty box.

But we weren't so gracious in the second period. After twenty-five minutes of us getting checked, tripped, pushed, and charged, we'd fucking had it.

TJ, Matt, and I were playing dirty, and we knew it. I didn't care anymore if I spent a few minutes in the penalty box. I was tired of being a personal punching bag.

By the start of the third, I'd managed to find myself in the sin bin for charging. Again. Only this time, I wasn't alone.

Xander Hicks sat as far from me as the bench allowed, getting tossed in here for tripping Lane. *Again.*

While the rest of us were taking savage hits, Lane was getting fucking massacred. They might as well have pinned him down and beat him with his own hockey stick.

But in honorable Lane fashion, he didn't bother engaging in the dirty plays; he was too smart for that, too classy.

I sat there catching my breath in the penalty box, caged in. Surrounded by the student section on three sides, this was most definitely the loudest seat in the arena.

On my half, guys were chanting my name and girls were hollering at me.

On Hicks' half, everyone was screaming at him to go fuck himself.

Ah, the joys of a home game.

Blocking out the raucous the best I could, I stayed focused on the game of four on four happening in front of me. Stick held tight, I gulped in dry, freezing air as I glanced up at the scoreboard.

Three-to-three. Eleven minutes left of the game.

Lane had the puck in his possession, and he zoomed across the ice like he had rockets on his feet instead of skates. He trickled through the maze of jerseys with no problem, taking the puck just outside the crease before getting met by Silas's shoulder.

As Lane flew through the air and onto his back, I swore I could feel the blow. I stood to get a better look, cringing through it.

I'd taken a similar hit earlier in the season, when I'd gotten distracted from trying to find Kota in the crowd. Lane had been the first one by my side, and it pained me that I couldn't be the first one there for him now.

Matt lifted Lane effortlessly, helping him to his feet before leaning in to whisper something to him.

Even from fifteen feet away, I could see the surge of fury blossoming in Matt's eyes. Gulping, I plopped my ass down. I recognized that look.

Someone was about to get their fucking ass beat.

I was appalled when the whistle wasn't blown, feeling my stomach drop as Lane skated off slowly, free hand holding his back.

That hit should've been called. Not that I wanted to sit next to Silas for my final minute in this torture box, but it would've been better than having him out there with Lane.

When the puck was back in play, Matt didn't seem to give a fuck where it was at. Like the cunning and vicious psycho that he was, he waited for the puck to be passed to Silas, and right when it made contact with Silas's stick, Matt charged him.

Coach threw his hands in the air, veins visibly bulging out of his neck while he screamed at Matt, who was getting led our way by two refs.

Matt was already reaching for his helmet before the glass was shut behind him. He casually popped it off and shook his head like a dog, sweat flying off him.

"Ew, what the hell, Matt!" I shouted.

"Sorry," he said, bumping me over to take the seat beside the glass. He angled towards me, "I was trying just to aim for Hicks."

Pretending like he hadn't heard Matt's comment, Hicks stood, ready to be let out.

And now it was three on five. Fantastic. *Great fucking timing, Matt.*

Luckily, it was only for twenty seconds, and the guys managed to keep St. Cloud at bay. Stepping in front of the door, I blew out a heavy breath and glanced back at Matt.

He smiled. "See you in two minutes."

I dashed onto the ice, ready to play. For those two minutes of Matt being locked up, it was the same old shit. Hard hits, aggressive steals, and shit talk, which was mostly directed towards Lane.

I could see his patience wearing down, and I hoped he had the control left to hold all the pent-up anger in for just seven more minutes while we tried to get one more goal.

The play ended, and everyone caught their breath, skating around themselves. Head low, I studied the glazed ice. I wanted this game series to be over; I sure as hell did not want to play another game like this tomorrow.

384

I felt like one giant, breathing bruise. My lip was busted open, and my muscles were a strange, contradicting combination of both stiff and jelly-like.

Even if we did win this game, I wasn't sure how enjoyable our celebration would be afterwards.

Catching brisk movement out of the corner of my eye, I glanced up as whistles were blown, one after another.

Lane was atop Silas, gloves abandoned as he wailed on him over and over.

So much for holding in his anger.

Instead of pulling them apart, everyone took it as a thumbs up to have their own round two. Sticks and gloves were scattered around the ice, silver jerseys paired with red ones as fists flew.

Turning around myself, only to see refs struggling to control the fights and small puddles of red beginning to stain the ice, I couldn't even tell where Hicks was.

Until I caught him speeding in Lane's direction.

I put everything I had into catching up to him, which wasn't much with my waning energy, but I managed, launching into him shortly before he could reach Lane.

There weren't enough refs to control the situation, and one by one, each fight was getting broken up.

A fistful of my jersey was tugged upwards, pulling me with it. I didn't fight the ref on it, letting him escort me back to the penalty box for the fourth time.

More and more players were getting added to the box, squeezing us in like a can of sardines. As I stood there for a faint moment, my ears ringing from the roar of three-thousand people, I waited for them to bring Lane.

Pushing through two St. Cloud players to get a view of the ice, all the blood drained from my face. They were forcing him the other way.

He'd been ejected from the game.

Chapter Sixty-Six

Kota

I'd been gripping onto the bottom of Crew's jersey for the entire third period of the game, clutching it so tightly that my hands were sweating.

Or maybe my hands were sweating from anxiety.

Last night was fucking rough. After Lane's ejection, he didn't speak to anyone.

Not me. Not Crew. Not even Bridget.

He just locked himself away in his room, probably drenching himself in guilt and regret.

Meanwhile, Crew and I had done our best to console Bridget, wiping away her tears and dismissing her countless apologies to Crew because she felt like she was somehow to blame for their loss.

He'd scooped her up into a hug, promising her that no one was to blame besides Silas. And he assured her that their final game in this series wouldn't end any other way besides with that trophy in their hands.

Seeing Crew be so fragile with someone I cared about was so heartening.

Now, as the clock approached zero, we could only hope that St. Cloud didn't make another goal and tie the game to send us into overtime.

Crew's line had played for an insane amount of time tonight, and I didn't know how their bodies were handling it. All the callous hits. All the nonstop movement. All the *pressure.*

Honestly, I was impressed with how well they'd managed the stress that they were probably under during every second of this game. The fate of this game would determine if they would reign conference champions or not. In addition to that, if they did win, they'd get an automatic bid into the NCAA tournament.

I knew how hard the boys had worked for another shot at the national title. They deserved it more than anything.

With two minutes left, each Cedar player held the same expression— stoic, focused, and determined. Through their exhaustion, they were playing at such a high level.

After nearly a full game, the boys were still moving at the speed of light, and if I hadn't kept my eyes directly on Crew since the play started, I would've lost him in the chaos.

Crew skated so effortlessly, like this was what he was made for. I was amazed by how gracefully he glided across the ice, how naturally it was for him.

He'd told me during one of our night talks that he started skating when he was only three. And standing there watching him, I had visions of what life would be like if somewhere down the line, we did have a kid together.

I could envision Crew tying his little skates up, patiently teaching him how to skate, picking him up when he'd fall, and eventually, handing him a tiny hockey stick and a puck.

I think I might want to be a boy mom?

My heart throbbed inside my chest, and I wrapped my arms around myself, hugging myself tight.

I'd gone my whole life hating men, but now, I'd found one that might've changed my mind.

The roar of the student section snapped me back to reality, sounding louder than a mob of crazed fans chasing Justin Bieber. My ears were ringing painfully, but I was so zoned into the game that I ignored it.

Bridget and I hadn't spoken in a solid ten minutes. The air in the arena was thick with tension and we were religiously puffing it in and out like chain-smokers.

As the final ten seconds hit, Bridget grabbed my hand and squeezed the life out of it. If I wasn't so damn distracted, I would've yelled at her for crumbling my bones to dust.

Everyone counted down with the clock and when the shrill buzzer went off, the entire arena exploded in a heap of madness, cheering and jumping and crashing into each other.

All the boys threw their sticks and abandoned their helmets, revealing how sweaty they were underneath their gear. But still, they tackled each other with pride and excitement.

Lane accepted the trophy on behalf of the team and of course, Crew was the first one to greet him. The first thing Lane did was put the trophy down and wrap his arms around Crew, and Bridget was on it, phone out, taking pictures to make sure this moment was captured.

"Send those to me," I smiled at her, and she nodded.

Lane and Crew each took a side of the trophy and brought it to the rest of the team, and we watched with sheer awe until the rest of the arena had cleared out.

Chapter Sixty-Seven

Crew

It felt like nothing more than a subtle prick, maybe the equivalent of a minor bee sting.

Getting a tattoo wasn't something I necessarily saw myself ever doing. I guess I was never entirely opposed to the idea, but it seemed like some people grew up knowing the exact tattoo they wanted, and I just simply wasn't one of those people.

Waking up this morning, violently hungover and feeling like I'd been hit by a truck after playing three games this weekend, a tattoo hadn't really been on my agenda for the day.

Everyone had been out until two in the morning, celebrating our championship win. So of course, no one woke up on time for class, but we did wake up fighting over who got to stick their head in the toilets first.

A lot of Pedialyte and Tylenol later, the girls decided to treat us to lunch to celebrate our win, and it was then that they told us about their tattoo appointment.

Now, Lane and I had somehow ended up in the parlor chairs, getting tattoos of our own.

I watched the needle glide across my skin, branding me with the number that would forever be part of me.

1.

Lane's number.

I glanced at his wrist as he stood beside my chair, noticing the red, irritated skin surrounding the *18*, and I couldn't fucking believe he loved me enough to permanently stamp me onto him.

The idea of matching tattoos may have been a little cliché, but it was entirely unplanned, and we hadn't had the idea until we walked in.

Lane hadn't decided what team he would be committing to, and I didn't want to pressure him further about coming to Chicago, but if I lost him to the Minnesota Wild, at least I'd have part of him with me.

The girls, however, had their tattoos planned out for weeks, having kept it a secret from us. Theirs were so tiny that it only took the guy ten minutes each.

Kota had half a heart on her pinky, the other half etched into Bridget's pinky. *Definitely cliché.* They probably got the idea off Pinterest or something, but Kota was excited about it, and I didn't have a death wish, so I kept my thoughts to myself.

When we first moved into our apartment, I thought it was a fucking disaster. And all I could do at the time was curse myself for whatever I'd done in a past life *or this current life* to deserve such horrible karma.

But some tragedies really were just blessings in disguise.

The universe worked in weird ass ways, and it felt like Kota coming into my life was what I needed to become more mature.

She didn't deal with my shit. It was like she was immune to it all, and I'd become so obsessed with her that I'd shed all those horrible parts of me to fit the image of what she deserved.

I was more emotionally aware overall, less interested in surrounding myself in one-night stands or meaningless interactions with girls.

Kota was as real and as strong as a girl could be, and I hated that she had to go through everything she did, but I was fucking grateful that it made her who she is.

As the tattoo artist finished up, a dull sting spread throughout my wrist, and all I could do to numb the pain was watch Kota across the room while she took pictures with Bridget of their tattoos.

Her smile was radiant, pulling me deeper into the trance that she'd had me in for months now.

I couldn't wait to hop out of this chair and kiss that fucking smile.

Chapter Sixty-Eight

Kota

My pinky was doused with Aquaphor and wrapped in saran wrap, and I rocked that shit when we went out for round two of celebrating the championship win.

I still couldn't believe Bridget and I had gotten matching tattoos. The idea first came about when we were drunk sophomore year and I got naked to show Bridget the tiny flower tattoo on my pelvic bone that I'd gotten on my eighteenth birthday.

I'd always wanted a tattoo growing up, but my mom had never been fond of them, so like the young teenage idiot that I was, I got one somewhere that she'd never see.

I vividly remember Bridget laying on the floor of our dorm, laughing at the ceiling while I told her the story. When I laid beside her, the idea came naturally. We went over countless ideas, and at the end of the night, we agreed that if we were still best friends by the end of senior year, then we'd get matching tattoos.

And that's exactly what we did.

Now she was *really* stuck with me for life.

I hadn't been expecting the boys to join us for our tattoos, and I definitely didn't think they'd get tattoos of their own.

392

It was sweet though that they did. For two people that weren't actually related, they treated each other like their other half. I knew Bridget and I were best friends; we did everything together. But Crew and Lane were some next level shit.

It was a Monday, and the only people at Stallions were the hockey team and our friend group. The rest of campus was sane, probably at a night class or sitting at home, doing homework and getting their life together.

Whereas the hockey team was acting like it was spring break.

I'd already seen Matt crush three cans against his forehead. I even sent a video to El, and all she responded was, "Ew."

Jett and Cody were sloshed, leading a conga line with the rest of the hockey team attached.

And TJ had been dancing in the corner by himself for fifteen minutes to Taylor Swift. No one knew why Taylor Swift had been playing back-to-back for so long, but we assumed TJ had been the one requesting all the songs.

I smiled, watching Lane spin Bridget and waltz around with her. They were adorable. After everything she'd been through, I was thankful that Lane came in and showed her what she truly deserved. He was like Prince Charming in the flesh.

Meanwhile, Crew was leaned back into his bar stool, an arm extended across the countertop, clutching his beer while his other hand was snaked around my waist. We were practically the same height now, nearly eye level.

Taking in the scene before me, I shook my head. "I knew you guys were crazy," I said, "but I didn't realize you were *this* crazy."

Crew's lazy, drunken smile cut straight through to my heart. He was so captivating without even trying. "You haven't seen anything yet."

"No?" I questioned.

"Nah. Just wait for Bender Week."

My face twisted at the name. "What the hell is Bender Week?"

With a light lick of his lips, he slipped his hand into my back pocket. "When the season ends, we go on a week-long bender. Drinking night and day for a week straight."

Brows nearly touching, I blinked at him. "Aren't you just hungover the whole time?"

"Yep, the whole time," he stated, matter-of-factly.

"Then how is that enjoyable?"

Crew shrugged. "It's not about being drunk. It's about being together and celebrating."

"Then why do you have to be drunk at all?"

He smiled at the snappy attitude in my tone. "Because it makes it more fun."

My eyes rolled, head lulling with it until my mouth reached my straw. Taking a swig of my long island, I nearly spit it all out and onto the floor when Crew leaned into my ear and listed every single thing he wanted to do to me right that second.

Naturally, I gulped, sending my long island down the wrong tube. Shoving my face into my elbow, I coughed uncontrollably.

"Are you okay?" Crew chuckled, lightly grabbing my wrist.

Nodding, I kept coughing. *Geez, I'm sure my coughing is really setting the mood.*

Next thing I knew, Crew was holding a water up to my face. "Thanks," I muttered once I could breathe again. "I'm alright."

As Crew's lips met my cheek, my brain released an unimaginable amount of dopamine and oxytocin that probably should've left me dead on the floor from overdosing.

I knew we didn't have to hide anymore since everybody knew we had a thing going on, but it was still such a switch up being touchy in public.

Change was scary sometimes, even when it was a good change.

I loved Crew's playful and sweet side, but it was confusing me more, and that was what scared me. For someone who hated the thought of commitment, why act like my boyfriend?

When Matt chugged the rest of his beer and took his phone out to give a drunk call to who I assumed was El, Crew took that as our cue to leave, whispering that we didn't want to be around to see the shit show of drunk Matt in his feels.

During our short walk to our apartment, I could tell Crew was excited to be alone. He couldn't keep his hands off me the whole time, looping his thick fingers into the belt loops of my jeans, squeezing the life out of my hand, brushing my hair over to the side.

But the second he closed his bedroom door and threw his hands on my waist, I covered them with my own, squeezing.

"Wait."

Concern sliced across his face and his grip immediately loosened on me. "What's wrong?" he softly asked. "Did you not want to? We don't have to."

My heart stuttered within my ribcage at his gentleness. I could feel my face soften as I toughened my grip on his hands, making sure they stayed in place. "No, no, it's not that," I assured him. "I'm just... I haven't finished my period yet."

"Oh," Crew murmured, finally understanding before he just stayed there for a few moments, beats of silence flying by. Then suddenly, the lustful blaze in his eyes relit and he shook his head, his thumbs slipping into the waistband of my jeans. "I don't care."

"You don't care?"

"No."

I made a face, still unsure. "I don't wanna gross you out."

He flashed a dimple, and my tummy dipped. "You could never gross me out."

Another rebuttal was about to slip out, but he shut me up with his mouth, kissing me hard. It was the type of kiss that was full of passion and heat and feeling, the type that left you in need of air.

My tampon came out, a towel went down, and he fucked me like he couldn't care any damn less that I was still on my period.

After we showered and got ready for bed, he pulled me to him, clutching onto me like you would with a teddy bear.

The same thoughts were repeating over and over in my mind, nagging me until I had to bite my bottom lip to keep them from spilling out.

What are we?

I'd been as patient as I could be for a few months now and considering Crew would be leaving for Chicago in less than two months, time was ticking away.

I needed answers, but I was scared of them.

My thoughts were getting drowned out by the deafening roar of my pulse, and right as I festered up the bravery to force the words out, I heard the peaceful and even snoozes that Crew was letting out.

He'd fallen asleep.

Chapter Sixty-Nine

Crew

Last night before falling asleep, I kept thinking about how grateful I was to have another conference championship under my belt, earned alongside my best friends. And my very last thought before passing out entirely? How lucky I was to have Kota lying beside me, snuggled up against me like I was the most comfortable pillow she'd ever laid on.

But I woke up to Kota tossing and turning, and after catching a glimpse of her face, it looked like she hadn't slept much.

I slept like a fucking rock.

I rubbed her back when she was facing away from me, and when she shifted again, giving a small, exhausted grumble, I rubbed her stomach. Maybe she had cramps or something?

The possibility reminded me of last night, and honestly, period sex wasn't that bad. It wasn't as messy as I thought it would be. Would I have ever done it with a random girl I hooked up with? Definitely fucking not. But Kota was different. She wasn't just some random girl; she was *the* girl. The only girl.

I didn't have eyes for anyone else, and I'd never been so submersed in anyone's world like this. It was a new feeling, at times, a scary feeling because it was so unknown, but it was also one of the best feelings.

"Hey," I finally whispered, my thumb running across the bare skin above her belly button.

All she did was sigh with her eyes closed.

"You okay?"

"Mhm."

I'm gonna take that as a no.

"What's wrong?"

Her eyes popped open, small bags sitting beneath them. "What are we doing?"

I blinked at her, a little confused by the lack of clarity in her question. "We're... laying down?"

"No," she sighed again, sitting up. "Like what's going on between us? Because we still haven't talked about it and you're leaving soon and if this isn't going anywhere, then we should just end it now, because—"

"Kota," I stopped her, sudden adrenaline spinning through my veins from the exasperation eased into her words. I sat up beside her. "Don't talk about ending it. That scares me," I admitted before I could stop myself.

"Well, *I'm* scared." We wallowed in silence for a moment until she spoke again, keeping her head down. "I just know how you feel about relationships and I'm not sure I can keep going on like this unless I know where it's heading."

She was trying to be firm, to keep her voice steady, but I could hear the fear and restlessness that had been keeping her awake all night, causing her words to shake.

Stuttering, I inched closer to her, "I... I'm not saying no, or that it will never happen. I just... I just need a little bit more time."

I knew how I felt about her, and I knew I wanted her to stay in my life. But my upbringing molded me into being afraid of anything and everything that resembled love and commitment, and I wasn't sure if I was ready to push myself past that fear.

Kota's head snapped up, a sudden sharpness entering her tone. "How much time?"

"I—I don't know," I admitted.

"Because you're leaving soon," she pointed out, jumping off the bed like she no longer wanted to be near me. That glowing aura of hers that I'd gotten used to as we drew closer was rusting like metal submerged in a flood, and suddenly, I was revolted by myself. "We act like a couple, yet we're not one. This is all starting to feel like déjà vu after everything that happened with Bobby. We've been doing this weird, in-between thing for months now, and if you can't commit to me by now, then I'm not sure if you're ever gonna."

I knew this conversation was bound to happen, but I hadn't been expecting it to *hurt*, and I wasn't sure why it was. Maybe because I could feel her pulling away from me? Rebuilding the stone wall that used to sit between us?

I wanted to give her what she wanted, to say the words she was longing to hear. But they were jammed in my throat, and all I could do was stare at her with my lungs shaking, mouth hung open, heartbeat dangerously slow like it was about to halt altogether.

The huff she let out was tainted with emotion, and with crossed arms, she walked out of my room, leaving me sitting there trying to unravel the clusterfuck in my head.

It couldn't have been longer than two minutes before I heard the front door open and close, and I sprang out of bed, not bothering to put clothes on before I was running down the hall in my boxers, only to find her room empty.

Fuck.

Charging out of the apartment, I could hear the elevator door close. I beelined for the stairs, taking two at a time and praying I didn't trip and tumble down them.

I'd never chased after a girl before.

Until now.

Kota was walking to her car, a small bag slung over her shoulder, chin tipped up like she was forcing herself to keep it there.

She was walking away from me. From *us*.

"Kota! Where are you going?"

Her breath hitched as she swung around, not expecting me to have followed her out here. Her eyes skimmed over my bare skin and boxers, but she didn't comment on it.

"Where are you going?" I repeated when she didn't answer as fast as I needed her to.

"My mom's."

"Why?"

With a lengthy exhale, she gripped the strap of her bag as if it would give her some stability. "I don't feel like being at the apartment right now."

She didn't wait to give me a chance to respond before she was approaching her car and I ran over, ready to sacrifice everything I thought I wanted, and ready to fight for everything I thought I *didn't* want. "Kota, *stop*! Please don't go."

"Why not?" she seethed, full of vitriol. But it was the haunting pain in her eyes that scraped into my heart.

"Because I'll lose my fucking mind if I have to watch you drive away. I want you to stay," I said firmly.

"That's not a good enough reason."

The pressure in my chest was complicating my lungs, forcing my words to come out breathlessly. My shoulders weighed down, heavy, but refusing to stop fighting. "Because watching you walk away made me realize that I don't like watching you walk away. I *need* you to stay."

I kept my eyes on hers, hoping that she'd see the misery shining through mine and give in. This was feeling like my personal doomsday, and I hadn't been expecting it when I opened my eyes just thirty minutes ago, but it felt like I was fighting for my life now. She held my heart in her hands, and if she drove off right now, there would be nothing left to keep me alive.

Kota's teeth dug into her bottom lip, and she shivered, looking like she was doing her damn best not to show me how broken she was feeling. "That's still not good enough."

The beep of her car unlocking sent me past panic mode. Hands finding the back of my head, I buried them into my hair, jaw tightening, mind reeling. She reached for her door handle, and the next thing I knew, I was screaming. "Because I love you!"

Kota froze with eerie stillness, soaking in my words until she finally turned in slow motion, her voice barely audible. "What?"

Shyly, I stared at my bare feet, kicking small pebbles away. "I'm not saying it again," I mumbled, suddenly embarrassed.

Her bag slid off her shoulder, meeting the ground. "You love me? Do you mean it?"

"Yeah, I—I think so."

"You *think* so?"

"I—I've never been in love before. I'm not entirely sure what it's supposed to feel like but I'm pretty confident that it's supposed to feel the way I feel about you." The skepticism she'd been hiding behind faded away. Tipping her head, she melted, and I felt like it was safe for me to take a step closer. I motioned to our building, "Fuck everything I said inside. *I want you.* Every little bit of you. Even the part of you that's a pain in the ass sometimes. And if being in a relationship is what you want and need, then you've got it." She just stared at me in awe, and if I had one fucking wish right now, it would be for the ability to read her damn mind. "I'll do anything," I added desperately. "Stay. And I'm all yours."

Her tears were about to roll over, and I feared that I'd failed. "Only if you say it again," she rasped.

"Stay?"

Kota shook her head, and I realized what she meant.

The first time I'd said it, she was facing the other way, but now, her gaze was fixed on me, waiting. I should've felt more pressure, more terror, more of every bad emotion that I'd just managed to rummage through since stepping outside.

But I didn't feel anything besides calmness.

"I love you," I said, the words unwavering.

She smiled wide and let out a strange, high-pitched shriek, hopping back and forth on her feet like the ground was on fire. I caught her as she dove into me, squeezing her arms around the back of my neck and sighing against my skin. "I love you too."

This might've been my new favorite moment.

I held her tight, afraid that she'd vanish in my arms. "Come to Chicago with me," I let out against her hair.

"What?"

Setting her on her feet, I grabbed both her hands. "I want you to come to Chicago with me."

The only answer I wanted was yes, but I was expecting some sort of stumble, for her to outright say no or tell me she would have to think about it.

But with the most beautiful, tiny smile, she nodded. "Okay."

"Yeah?" I beamed.
"Yeah."
And I kissed the fucking hell out of her.

Chapter Seventy

Crew

Kota was practically still clinging onto me when we walked in, with both her arms wrapped around one of mine as if she was about to climb me like a tree.

The aroma of burnt toast and eggs hit my nose, making my stomach growl. Memories rushed back to Kota accusing me of breakfast being "my favorite meal of the day."

I couldn't really deny it honestly. I fucking loved breakfast food.

Lane's chilling blue eyes slid over to us while he stood at the stove, flipping scrambled eggs around. An array of colors was taking up the kitchen island, all different kinds of chopped up fruit— strawberries, kiwi, bananas, mango.

How the fuck did Lane manage to make an entire breakfast buffet in the last ten minutes since I chased Kota out of the house?

Kota threw her arms around me again, and I nuzzled my face into the crook of her neck, rocking us back and forth as I hugged her.

She squealed when she pulled away, running off towards her room. "I gotta go call my mom!"

Lane stared at me with a crease in his brows, looking disgusted but not surprised as his gaze raked over me. "Why are you naked?"

I swallowed, throwing a lazy thumb towards the girl's hallway. "We're dating now."

I guess that wasn't as hard to say aloud as I thought it would be.

I'm in a relationship. I'm committed to someone.

Kota and I are dating.

I repeated the thoughts over and over to myself, becoming oddly comfortable with it much quicker than I would've expected myself to.

"Okay," Lane said blankly. "That doesn't explain why you're fucking naked."

Arms held out to the side, I looked down at myself. "I have boxers on."

The indifference in his voice lingered. "Alright. We'll just act like it's not fucking weird."

"Thank you," I said, taking a step closer to get a better look at everything he was making. "What are you doing anyway?"

"Bringing breakfast to Bridget in bed."

Well, that's a tongue twister.

"Why?" I asked.

"Because that's what you do for your *girlfriend*," he said scornfully, giving a teasing grin afterwards. "You should probably take notes."

Shit. I felt so oblivious. I was probably going to be the worst boyfriend ever.

Lane was good at this stuff. He'd never had an official girlfriend before Bridget, but he'd dated around. Plus, he was a natural gentleman. It was practically coded into his DNA.

I, on the other hand, didn't have a single clue as to what all the boyfriend rules were. Was I supposed to be making her breakfast right now? Would it count if I stole some of Lane's food and brought it to her in a gourmet fashion on a silver platter?

"Yeah, yeah," I muttered. "Whatever."

"So," Lane glanced at me suspiciously out of the corner of his eye, giving a light click with his tongue, "I see Kota's already telling her mom. Are you gonna tell *your* parents?"

"Ah, I don't know," I cringed. "They're both gonna wanna meet her."

Lane shrugged. "Your mom's already met her," he pointed out.

That was true, however, she met Kota as my roommate, not as my girlfriend. Not that it was a huge difference, but at the same time, it sort of *was* a huge difference. I'd never brought a girl home. Point, blank, period.

"You want my opinion?" Lane said, tossing eggs onto a plate.

"Yeah, I guess."

"I think you should nip all this in the ass once and for all."

"What do you mean?"

When he looked back at me, he threw a hand up, shielding his view. "Can you please go put fucking clothes on? I don't wanna have this conversation while you're standing there naked."

I scoffed. "Ugh, fine." Returning with a plain black t-shirt and gray sweats on, I leaned against the island, arms crossed while I waited for whatever explanation Lane had to give.

"Thank you," he sighed when he saw me. "Anyway, what I was saying was that I think it's time for you to say something to your parents. You're an adult now. You have the right to stand up for yourself and to tell them when shit is bothering you."

"And what am I supposed to say?"

Lane looked like a chef Picasso right now, carefully orchestrating a plate of food like he was a contestant on Hell's Kitchen. Shrugging, he said, "If they want to meet her, then tell them they can but under your conditions. Put 'em in the same room together and make them act like adults."

I wasn't following. My first instinct was that I'd just heard him wrong. Speaking in fragments, I tried wrapping my mind around it all. "You. Want me. To throw my parents. In the same room?"

Another shrug. "Maybe it'll help."

"*Or* we'll be sitting in a courtroom listening to a murder trial in six months."

Lane was bent over the island, inspecting every inch of the plate to make sure nothing was out of place. He glanced up at me only as he spoke. "Nothing will get out of hand if you don't let it."

My hands flew up over my face, clawing at it. "Ugh, I don't know."

"I finally stood up to my mom after all these years and it hasn't been long obviously, but I think things are slowly getting better."

Lane's rocky relationship with his mom went back to the age of fifteen. Shortly after we first met, he'd confided in me about his cruel and neglectful mother, and I did the same, explaining my own experiences and trauma that had to do with my parents. It was a big turning point in our friendship, drawing us closer right off the bat. I didn't feel very comfortable talking about my parents with many people, but I knew Lane understood me. He could listen with nothing but support and love, no judgement at all.

I was proud of him for finally saying all the things he needed to say to his mom. It hadn't even been a whole week, but I could already tell he seemed freer. He even brought his mom up the other day before our final conference game, which was something he never used to do. He used to avoid talking about her at all.

Rubbing my hand along the light stubble on my chin, I sighed. "Alright. I guess I'll... tell them," was all I agreed to for the moment.

He poured a glass of OJ, holding it in one hand while grabbing the plate in his other. "And just know," he said, taking a few steps towards the girl's hall and cocking his head that way, "if you don't put an end to all this shit with your parents, then you're subjecting *her* to it now."

Fuck.

When Lane disappeared, I retreated to my room, typing out identical texts to my parents.

I didn't want to pull Kota into all this. She'd been through enough; she didn't need my family bullshit added to the mix.

Me: I have a girlfriend

Mom: Oh my goodness!! This is so exciting!! What's her name? I want to meet her!

Me: You've already met her

Mom: Is it Kota?

Damn, how'd she know? Was it that obvious? My fingernails were down to the edge of my fingertips, but I shoved them in my mouth anyway, biting away my anxiety.

Before I could even respond, my dad finally answered.

Dad: Wow, Nick! That's great. You should bring her over for dinner. We want to meet her.

The saddest part was that they were both insisting on meeting her right away, which wouldn't have been a problem if I didn't know in the back of my mind that part of the motive had to do with *meeting her before the other.*

I answered my mom first.

Me: Yes

Mom: Oh! I like her. She seems to have a little sass to her, which I think you need.

Rolled my eyes at that one.

Mom: I want to get to know her better though. And I haven't seen you guys together yet! Do you want to do dinner soon?

Once again, I typed out an identical text, biting the bullet. It was hard to gather the courage to do this for myself but doing it for Kota was much easier. It was like some secondary force from deep within me that compelled me to speak up, to protect her from the chaos of my past.

I changed the wording of the text to fit the person, swapping "Mom" or "Dad" out where necessary, then read it back to myself three times.

You can meet her, but Mom/Dad wants to meet her too. You guys have been fighting over me for my whole life, and you're not going to do that to Kota too. If you want to come out to dinner with us this week, that's fine but Mom/Dad may also be there, and I expect you guys to be cordial.

Thumb hovering over the send button, I paused, staring at it. My mind was swirling like a whirlpool, but I couldn't keep running from my problems. I'd spent half my life doing so and it was exhausting. I was sick of being emotionally drained every time I spent time with my parents.

Guess I was overcoming two fears today, I thought to myself, hitting the send button.

A strange sense of relief washed over me, almost like it was washing all the hurt out of my body. The air was clear and tasted sweet as it entered my lungs, and I sat on the edge of my bed, relishing in the feeling as I waited for my phone to buzz once again.

Mom: Okay. I will come to dinner.

Dad: Alright, Nick. If that's what you want.

Holy shit, I did it.

I wanted to give myself a big old pat on the back and throw myself a party for finally speaking up.

Until I realized what I'd just signed myself up for.

And what I signed Kota up for.

Maybe I just fucked up.

Chapter Seventy-One

Kota

I was surprised by how much my mom ended up liking Crew.

I didn't necessarily think she would *dislike* him, but with what she'd heard at the beginning of our living arrangement, I was prepared for the worst.

I used to call her ranting about Crew, giving her every reason as to why he was the worst person on the planet. And now we were *dating*.

My mom assured me that she would go into lunch with an open mind, and she surely kept her promise. Crew hadn't admitted it, but I think he was nervous. When I first told him that my mom wanted to meet him immediately, he froze like an icicle, eyes wide, breath stalled. It took him a few minutes to ease up, and a few days later, we spent our Saturday afternoon at Stella's, and of course, Crew ordered breakfast food even though it was one o'clock in the afternoon.

Waking up on Sunday, my stomach was already in nervous knots. The day felt like one long countdown to dinner with Crew's parents, and the closer we got to five o'clock, the more anxious I became.

I'd already met Crew's mom, and she was an angel, but I had yet to meet his dad. Honestly, I think most of my anxiety was stemming from knowing that *Crew* was anxious.

He hadn't sat still since he woke up, fidgeting and pacing like an animal at the zoo.

Now, smoothing out my baby blue dress in the passenger seat, my eyes jumped back and forth between the road and Crew. His chest was visibly rising and falling so heavily that it was quite alarming. I could hear the strained exhale he let out, breathing uncertainty into the air.

Reaching for his hand, I said, "You okay?"

He gave my hand a squeeze, but it wasn't very reassuring. "Yeah."

"Nervous?"

Another deep breath, his voice falling off. "Yeah..."

The Italian restaurant we were going to was called *Francesca's,* and it was supposed to be really nice, located right in the middle of town. Bridget had actually been here once on a date with Mitch way back when she was seeing him, and she said the food was amazing.

As we walked in, it felt like entering a cave. The sunshine from outside disappeared, replaced with dim lighting. Paintings of Italian landscapes adorned the walls, along with fancy lamps that looked like the same candelabras from Beauty and the Beast.

With each step, Crew's grip on my hand tightened, and as we turned the corner, catching a glimpse of his parents seated at a table across the room, he stopped in his tracks.

"Okay," he breathed with a light shiver. "My parents haven't been in the same room in years. I'm gonna apologize ahead of time for their behavior."

"Crew," I shook my head, "it's okay. Everything is going to be fine."

"Yeah, I hope so," he murmured, hardly audible over the instrumental music playing overhead.

Closing the gap to their table, it felt like I was dragging Crew along. He was resisting so much that I wasn't sure if he was about to turn around and book it.

Crew's dad was sitting on his phone while his mom faced the opposite way, crossing her arms. Clearly, they hadn't spoken more than five words to each other. Even though their chairs were seated next to one another, they had separated their seats further, practically each settled at the corners of the table.

410

Already disapproving of their behavior, Crew gave a stern announcement to our arrival. "Hey."

"Oh!" his mom beamed, jumping up and embracing me for a hug. "Kota! It's so nice to see you again, sweetheart."

"You too," I smiled. Crew's dad stood, shaking my hand with a warming smile.

"It's nice to meet you," he said.

"You too," I repeated, taking a seat across from his mom.

"Have you guys been here long?" Crew sat.

"Nah," his dad said. "I got here five or so minutes ago."

"Me too," his mom said, but there was an edge to her tone, a stark difference from the vibrant persona we'd seen just moments prior.

Going into this dinner, I'd gone through a checklist in my head of things to do and not to do, revolving around manners and making a good impression.

But sitting here now, feeling the light shake of Crew's bobbing leg beside me and catching the petrified gleam in his eye, all I could think about was comforting him.

I laid my black napkin on my lap, then reached for Crew, resting my hand on his shaking knee. Immediately, he relaxed under my touch, placing his hand over mine. His warmth soaked into my skin, and I knew the squeeze he gave was the closest thing to a "Thank you" that he could currently give.

"I wasn't sure what you both wanted to drink, but our waitress should be back shortly," Crew's dad said.

I barely had time to nod before his mom was speaking, pretending like her ex-husband wasn't there.

"So, Kota, I remember last time I saw you that you mentioned you were starting to prep for finals. How's that going?"

"It's going well, actually. I still have two weeks to study, but I'm feeling prepared."

"That's great! What was your major again?"

"Biology," I answered. I was trying to make eye contact with both of them, to make it feel like one, cohesive conversation. But there was an invisible line drawn between them, and I got the feeling this was going to be a much messier dinner than I thought.

"Right," she smiled. "That seems like a really difficult and elevated major."

"It definitely hasn't been easy," I chuckled, shaking my head.

"I bet," she agreed. "Do you know what you want to do?"

"Definitely some sort of lab work, but I haven't quite figured out the specifics. I just recently started looking though."

Smile brightening with hope, she placed her elbows on the table, chin resting in her hands. "Where at?"

"Um, Chicago," I admitted.

"Oh!" she squealed.

"That's great," his dad said. "You'll be close to Nick."

I opened my mouth to respond, but his mom was back at it.

"Do you guys think you'll live together again?"

Crew and I glanced at each other. "Probably," I said.

"You'll be able to go to all his home games!" his dad beamed.

It seemed like every time they were looking at Crew and me, they were the happiest, most awestruck people in the world. But when they caught a glance of each other, only hostility remained.

Crew stayed quiet as his mom continued asking questions, hijacking the conversation as if we were the only two in the room. Each time I glanced at his dad, he seemed to become more and more frustrated, opening his mouth numerous times to speak before getting cut off by his ex-wife. His jaw clenched, eyes rolling as he angled his body the opposite way just to let out a huff.

Getting interrupted by our waitress didn't help as much as I hoped it would. The air eased for just a moment as she took our orders and brought wine for Crew and me.

It felt like our table was surrounded by a bubble of bitter resentment, blocking out the tables around us. We were in our own world over here, and as awkward as I was feeling, I couldn't imagine what was circling through Crew's head.

412

Turning to his ex-wife for the first time since we arrived, Crew's dad snapped. "Do you ever stop talking?"

"Here we fucking go," Crew muttered under his breath.

My mouth popped open, and I shut it quick, holding my breath.

The stars in his mom's eyes morphed into an inferno. "Hmm..." she gave a condescending laugh. "That's interesting coming from you."

"Oh really?" he seethed. "What's that supposed to mean?"

"Oh nothing," she grinned maliciously.

"I don't know why you feel the need to try to make me look bad in front of our son and his new girlfriend."

"Me?" her voice cracked. "You were the one who started this."

"Yes, because you never know when to shut up and let other people talk."

She growled, "You're acting like a child."

Crew tossed his napkin on the table as he stood, stomping out without a word.

Unsurely rising to my feet, I nervously muttered, "Excuse me," before racing towards the door, nearly knocking over a waiter carrying three plates.

With his hands placed on his hips, head tipped upwards, Crew stood with his back towards me. My white heels tapped against the pavement with each step, erasing the space between us. If he heard me coming, he didn't turn. My arms barely reached around him as I hugged him from behind, smushing my face against his back and hoping that I didn't get any makeup on his white button-up.

Inhaling the husky aroma of sandalwood, I sighed through the sudden burst of alleviation that overwhelmed me just from the smell.

"Are you alright?" I spoke.

"I knew this was a bad idea," he sighed.

"Hey," I quietly said, spinning him around.

Beneath his beautiful brown irises, there were years of pain shining through. Golden hour had set in, and usually, at this time of the day specifically, Crew resembled what every girl dreamed their future husband would look like— stunning and strong, like a real prince.

But he was currently a shell of that god-like man I'd encountered. The sun wasn't illuminating every gorgeous feature of his; it was only amplifying the glossiness of his eyes, the crumbling of his spine.

Chin dipping, I could see the apology plastered on his face.

"I'm sorry," I said, cupping his jaw in my hands.

"No, *I'm* sorry," he replied. "We should just go." Shaking his head, he stepped backwards, out of my grasp.

"No!" I caught his wrist. "Why don't you go back in there and tell them how you really feel?"

"Ah," he made a face, "I don't know."

"C'mon. I know they're your parents, but you don't have to keep going on like this. I can tell how much it's been hurting you for a long time. Go in there and tell them off." Giving a light sway, I smirked with encouragement, "You've done it to me plenty of times."

The flicker of a smile that I caught made my heart speed, a nice reminder that it was still working after this mess of a dinner. If you could even call it a dinner. I mean, goddamn, we hadn't even gotten to our appetizers yet.

"I don't even know what to say."

"You don't have to plan it," I shrugged. "Just say whatever comes to mind. That's usually when the most powerful parts of the truth come out."

Quickly nodding, Crew grabbed both sides of my face, syncing our lips for a searing kiss. He tasted pungent like Italian wine, and even though I preferred my wine sweet, I kissed him like he was the most delicious thing I'd ever tasted.

Still holding my cheeks between his calloused hands, his eyes bounced around my face. "I love you."

Not only was my heart speeding, but now it was swelling, doubling in size like the Grinch. "I love you too."

He smiled that infamous, striking smile of his, touching our lips once more before leading the way back inside.

Chapter Seventy-Two

Crew

Even from across the restaurant, I could tell they were still fighting. If I had to guess, the argument had skewed from the original root cause, now probably trying to cast the blame on each other for running me out of the place.

As Kota and I approached, they both shut up, spinning around in their chairs, spines straightening like they were pretending they hadn't been quarreling the whole time we were gone.

Sitting, I gave the dirtiest look to both of them, and they sank back.

"You alright, Nick?" my dad cringed as my mother nervously tucked her hair behind her ears, her shameful eyes dipping.

Voice eerily calm, I said, "Am I alright? No, not really." With a massive inhale, I froze for a second, unsure if I should continue speaking. But when Kota's hand found mine again, I found the courage. "Honestly? You're my parents, and I love you, but I hate spending time with you. Both of you." Eyes ricocheting back and forth between them, I threw everything off my chest that I'd been holding in for the last decade of my life. "All you guys do is fight over me and talk shit about the other one. I never get quality time with either of you. It's annoying and emotionally draining, and you've ruined a lot of things for me because neither of you are emotionally mature enough to put decade-old shit aside for your own kid." I wheezed, realizing I hadn't taken a single breath through that entire thing.

"Not to mention," I added, "Kota is obviously my first girlfriend, and I wanted this evening to go smoothly but you managed to ruin it after less than twenty minutes of us being here."

Silence gripped the four of us, and I looked everywhere other than at my parents, too afraid to see their reactions. Pushing my lips into a hard line, I waited for someone to speak. It would've been great if our waitress came by right now.

My mother's fragile hand shielded her face, and my stomach knotted. *Please don't be crying. I'll feel like the biggest dick if I just made my own mother cry.*

"No, you're right," Mom shook. "Our behavior isn't okay."

"It's not," my dad agreed, head hung low. "This was an important night for you, and we wrecked it."

I didn't even sugar coat my answer. "Yeah. You guys did."

"I'm so sorry, honey," Mom said, reaching across the table for my hand.

"We've let our own issues get in the way of our relationship with you, and that was wrong. I'm sorry," Dad said.

Crossing my arms, I pushed my chair back until it was balancing on two legs. "Good. Now apologize to each other."

Dad's face twisted like he'd just smelled something rotten, but when he caught my stern and dangerous expression, he retorted. They let out matching sighs, swallowing their own pride as they turned towards each other.

Mom choked through her words, fidgeting uncomfortably. "Neil, I'm sorry for being rude earlier, and... for being uncivil for," she cleared her throat, "the last however many years."

Dad winced like the words were getting reluctantly ripped out of his throat. "Jane, I'm sorry for everything I have done or said in the past that has been hurtful and unjust."

God, I could tell this was fucking killing them. Was I a psychopath if I admitted that I was enjoying it?

Looking at me at the same time for approval, I nodded. "Don't you guys feel better now?"

"Well..."

"Eh, I—"

"Don't answer that," I held up a hand. "Baby steps, I guess. Now can we please get through the rest of dinner without any arguments?"

"Yes," they nodded.

"Does it count if *we* argue?" Kota joked. The playful smile she gave was breathtaking.

"No," I teased. "That wouldn't count."

Chapter Seventy-Three

Crew

Ever since last week, things seemed to be moving in the right direction with my parents. They both texted me after dinner, offering another apology and assuring me that from now on, they'd not only stop shit-talking each other, but they'd play nice so that we could do things altogether sometimes.

My dad had been going on for fifteen minutes about the NCAA tournament starting this weekend and about the end of my brother's hockey season. His youth hockey team apparently lost in the championship for their league, and Nate was heartbroken. I felt bad for the kid. I knew what losing a trophy felt like; it sucked. But it was better that he learned young that winning wasn't always guaranteed. It was going to take hard work and years of commitment if he was going to reach all the milestones he longed for.

I was currently in the middle of that dream now.

With six days until the start of the tournament, I'd never been so focused on anything in my life. I came to Cedar University with the goal of winning an NCAA title and if I left this school without one, I'd be wrecked.

"He just keeps on crying," my dad said through speakerphone while I folded my laundry in stacks on my bed. "I don't know how to cheer him up."

"Nate will get over it. He'll probably be back to normal in a few days."

Sighing, he said, "Yeah, hopefully."

Whatever he said afterwards, I wasn't sure. I zoned out, hearing the gruff timbre of Lane's voice, accompanied with the sweet ring of Kota's.

My two favorite people were hanging out in the living room without me? Immediately getting a rush of *fomo*, I stuttered, cutting my dad off. "D—dad? I, uh, can I call you back later? I've gotta run."

"Oh, sure. Love you, Nick."

"Love you too."

"No," Lane said as I wandered in, "Crew."

"Did I hear my name?" I smirked, arms widened like the cocky son of a bitch I was.

But Kota's wince broke my smile. She was sitting beside Lane on the couch, a soothing hand rested on his back. His shoulders were weighed down, head buried into his hands between his legs.

When he looked up, all I saw was a haunted expression, causing a pang in my heart. Eyes glossy, he let out a shaky breath.

"Is everything alright? Am I interrupting something?"

"Actually, uh," Kota stood, "I think you guys should talk."

"Okay..." I shifted my weight nervously side to side. "You wanna come talk in my room?"

"Yeah," Lane softly agreed.

I closed the door behind us. "What's going on?"

He stared at me for a moment, those gears in his head turning like he had no idea what to say. My heart was practically spasming inside my ribcage as I waited for an answer. I was about to grab Lane by the shoulders and shake him.

"I wanna sign with the Blackhawks," he spit out.

I could feel my face light up, and I hopped up and down like a kangaroo. "Are you serious? Holy shit! I knew you'd come around! I knew—"

"Wait," he stopped me, shoulders visibly shaking. After taking in my excitement and watching it disappear just as quickly, Lane's skin paled. He looked like he could vomit. "Bridget wants to stay here."

I gasped lightly for air, giving a small claw to my chest to feel for the knife wound. My disappointment was running through the air, thick like smoke. I stepped over to my desk, planting a hand on it to steady myself before sitting in my desk chair. "So..." I paused, soaking in the news, "you're not coming with me?"

"I don't know."

"Why can't Bridget just come with? I'm sure Kota—"

"I tried that. She wants to stay here to be closer to her mom."

Bridget was adopted, and after a lifelong search for her birth mom, she finally found her a few months ago. I didn't blame her for not wanting to leave now.

I was torn between telling Lane to stay with Bridget and begging him to come to Chicago with me.

My voice cracked, "Lane... you know I'd follow you anywhere. I'd stay in Minnesota just to make your life easier, but," I shrugged, "I'm already signed. My hands are tied."

He stared at the floor. "I know."

I flipped my wrist over, staring at the *1* that was forever etched into my skin. "But I want you to know I'll understand if you choose Bridget."

Practically whispering, Lane asked, "If this were flipped, would you choose Kota?"

"No," I immediately answered. "Over anyone else, I'd choose her. But not you."

I didn't even have to think about it. My heart was with Kota, every bit of it. And that was why I put my fears aside to keep her in my life. Having her as part of my future was more important than remaining caught up in my past. She's brought a lot into my life— love, happiness, patience, resilience.

But my soul was with Lane. We hadn't spent longer than a few days apart in almost five years, and the thought of being nearly five hundred miles away from him was harrowing.

"You don't have to rush this, Lane," I said, watching him tug at his own chest, eyes still glassy. "You still have a little bit of time."

"Barely."

420

"Stop looking at it like the countdown to a bomb explosion. Try not to think about it anymore tonight. Sleep on it." All he did was nod.

I was struggling to envision Chicago without Lane, but at the same time, what kind of brother would I be if I didn't support whatever decision he made? Clearly, this was hard enough for him already.

"And just know that either way, I'm on your side," I assured him. Offering a ghost of a smile, Lane opened his arms, gesturing for me to do the same, but I waved him off. "We've been hugging too much lately."

He smiled wider. "Fine, didn't want to anyway."

Chapter Seventy-Four

Kota

Lane chose Chicago.

I wasn't sure why Bridget thought he would choose otherwise.

Five days ago, Crew and I sat on the hardwood floor beside his bedroom door, with it slightly ajar to hear the entire conversation spiraling out of control between Lane and Bridget.

I'd seen and heard Bridget cry plenty of times, but I'd never heard her like *that*. Her pain was tangible, lingering through the apartment until it found us hiding away in Crew's room, eavesdropping.

Each response Bridget gave only broke Lane down further, forcing the almighty Stallions caption to crumble. I could see the torment on Crew's face as he bit into his hand like someone just poured salt into an open wound of his.

It was scary, honestly, how a couple that had been so solid since the start of their relationship could disintegrate to a pile of dust in minutes.

We never actually heard the word "breakup," so there was hope, at least.

However, Bridget fled the apartment, and none of us had seen her since. According to Lane, she said she was heading home. She turned her location off and still wasn't answering her phone.

422

She wasn't even answering me.

Based on the conversation we had on the phone just hours after she left, I wasn't surprised. I'd given her my true opinion, which was that she was being hypocritical about the situation.

She didn't like that very much.

I knew she was just hurt and that she would come around eventually. I just didn't think it would take this long.

Last night, Crew and I had our own little date night at home. With the tournament starting today, we knew we couldn't do anything crazy. We also didn't want to be having an affectionate date night in front of Lane, so we stayed in my room.

We ordered Chinese food and played games, and I even got the incredible honor of watching Crew try to draw a portrait of me.

It was a stick figure of course, with one single strand of hair on each side of my face. He didn't draw me any fingers, but I was somehow holding an ice cream cone, smiling with an absurd amount of teeth that took up half my face.

The picture was hanging up beside my desk now.

Since the boys had the tournament starting today, I was doing all the dishes from the last two or so days even though it wasn't my turn to do them. I wanted the boys completely focused, without having anything to worry about other than their game later.

That was easier said than done though for Lane. He still wasn't himself, still moped through the apartment, broken.

I woke up at seven when the boys did. They had morning skate, and now, Crew was taking his usual pre-game nap.

El was supposed to be coming to watch their game, so I was excited to finally meet her.

My phone was resting on the island behind me, lowly playing Taylor Swift while I muttered the lyrics to myself, hands deep in water and dish soap.

"Still no Bridget?"

Water flew up as I gave a small jump, catching a glimpse of Lane over my shoulder. Usually, I'd curse him out for nearly making me piss my pants, but he was having a hard enough time already. "No."

"Have you heard from her at all?"

"No," I sighed.

There was already such an ache in his voice alone that I was afraid of turning around to see the look on his face.

"This is just..." he breathed heavily. "This is ridiculous. She needs to come home."

"I've tried, Lane," my voice weakened. "She'll come home when she's ready." Lane stomped over to the door, shoving his feet into gym shoes. "What are you doing?"

"When Crew wakes up," he grabbed his keys off the hook, "ask him to pack my bag for me."

My blood chilled, and I frantically dried my hands on the nearest hand towel. "Lane... where are you going?"

"To go get her," he responded dryly.

Jaw dropping, I wasn't sure if I should try to talk him out of it myself or scream for Crew to get up and get his ass out here. "You're going to make the three-hour drive to Sumner right now?"

"Yeah."

"Um, are you forgetting you have a game tonight? A very important game, might I add? And might I also add the fact that it's nearly an hour away?"

"I need to do this," he insisted, reaching for the door handle.

"Why?" I panicked.

"Because she needs to know how much I love her."

Just like that, he disappeared out the door, and I knew I needed to do something, but I was so in shock that I couldn't move.

Was I supposed to chase after him? Was I supposed to run to Crew? Was I supposed to contact Bridget and warn her?

Probably all three, honestly.

"Fuck!" I screamed, throwing my hands up and booking it out the door, not bothering to put shoes on.

Scouring the parking lot, I didn't see Lane's car anywhere. I ran back and forth through the lot like a madwoman, cursing every time I stepped on a rock.

Onto Plan B, I guess.

Wasting no time, I took the stairs, charging up them two at a time. I busted into Crew's room.

"Crew! Crew! Wake up *now!*"

He flung himself up, hair ruffled wearing nothing but his boxers. Spinning around himself like he was looking for danger, he huffed. "What?!"

"Lane is gone."

"What?"

"Lane is gone. He just left to go find Bridget."

Crew rubbed his eyes, confused. "Doesn't she live like hours away?"

"Yes. Why else do you think I'm freaking out?"

Bringing his fingertips to his chin, he stared at me calmly. "So, you're saying," he paused, "that Lane, the most responsible person I've ever met, just left to go drive around the state when we have one of the most important games of our lives today?"

My voice turned stern, teeth clenching. Apparently, I needed to spell it out for him. *"Yes."*

"Fuck!" he shouted, tearing through his pillow and comforters in search of his phone. "Alright, I'm gonna call him. Try to get a hold of Bridget. Maybe she can call him and convince him to turn around."

"Alright," I nodded, dashing out of his room to find my phone on the countertop, playing "my tears ricochet".

Well, that certainly fit the vibe today.

Chapter Seventy-Five

Crew

Coach Palmer was a scary dude when he was mad. I'd seen that unforgiving, savage side of him plenty of times over the last few years.

But when he was *panicking*, he was fucking terrifying.

We weren't dressed in our uniforms yet, but it was almost that time. What would usually be music playing and conversations going while we stretched and started warming up our muscles, was instead the opposite.

The locker room was entirely silent, other than the mutters and expletives coming from coach as we watched him pace back and forth. He'd been doing this for ten minutes straight.

When we boarded the bus without Lane, I instantly had hundreds of questions chucked my way. I had my fair share of low anxiety throughout my life, but this level of stress was nothing like I'd ever experienced before.

Everyone was turning to me, waiting for an explanation while their own anxiety slowly began settling into their bones. I didn't have an explanation to give them though.

I answered every single person the same.

"Lane had a quick emergency to tend to, and he's going to meet us there."

That was the best I could do at the moment.

At first, Coach had studied me, staring into my soul like that would provide him with more answers. If this was any other player besides Lane, this probably wouldn't be allowed. The school's rules were that we were all supposed to travel together to away games. But since St. Paul was only an hour away, and this was the star player we were talking about, Coach accepted it.

It didn't seem like he was accepting it now though.

Ever since we'd gotten set up in the locker room, Coach had asked me at least five times where Lane was. And every time he asked, the pressure only increased.

Hiding my phone in my hand, I snuck out, dialing Lane's number for the hundredth time today. He'd been ignoring all my calls, and I was fed the fuck up. I'd been covering for him all day, and he couldn't even answer my calls? Couldn't even send me an update as to what the hell was going on?

"Hello?"

"Where the actual fuck are you!" I screamed. Great, now *I* was pacing.

"I'm almost there."

If it was possible to overdose on anger, I'd probably be rushed to the hospital right now for carrying a lethal dose in my veins. I wished Lane could see the uncontrollable trepidation that he was causing his team right now.

This was the worst headspace for us to be in going into this tournament.

The roar of my voice echoed through the tunnel outside of the locker room. "'Almost there' isn't fucking good enough, Lane! I've got everybody asking about you. Coach is about to have a fucking aneurysm and is breathing down my neck, and—"

"Did you tell him?" Lane panicked.

"No," I growled through clenched teeth. "I've been covering for your dumbass this entire time!"

"I'm sorry."

"Just get here," I hissed, grip tightening around my phone. "How far are you? We're forty minutes away from warmup."

"Forty minutes," he replied.

"Well, you better make it thirty," I threatened.

"Alright, I'll see you soon... Oh wait!"

Letting out a heavy exhale through my nose, it felt like my eye was starting to twitch. "What?"

"Is Bridget there?"

If there was something, literally anything, around me to kick or punch or throw, I would've done it. "Are you— How the fuck am I supposed to know?"

Lane's voice was too smooth for my liking. I wanted him to be frantic, shaking, breaking a sweat like all of us here were. "Has Kota said anything to you?"

Jesus Christ. I'm going to kill him.

My scoff sounded more like the deep roar of a bear. If this conversation was happening in person, my hands very well might've been around his neck. "Lane, I've been in the locker room for God knows how long, getting ready for a *national tournament*, you fucking idiot. Do you think I've spoken to her recently?"

I could hear his sassy tenor carry through the phone. "Alright. See you shortly."

"You fucking better," I hung up.

Rubbing his hands together, Coach scanned over the room, brown eyes darkening to black when I walked back in. It was the same old shit for the next forty minutes while we got suited up for warmups, but now, it wasn't just Coach giving me dirty looks. It was *everyone*.

I'd been glancing at the door ten times a minute since I got off the phone with Lane, waiting for him to walk through it.

"Everyone start heading to warmup," Coach demanded. His finger landed on me, shooting flames in my direction. "Besides you."

Fucking great. I was about to get my ass handed to me.

I watched everyone scurry out of the locker room like they couldn't get out fast enough; I gulped.

Coach leaned forward and rested his hands on his knees, inches away from me. I was trying to focus on not wearing my fear all over my face, but it was pretty damn hard to when his expression broke into that of a beast.

Voice low and gruff, his jaw ticked. "Where is he? Where's Lane?"

Struggling to keep eye contact with him without loosening the stoic expression on my face, I responded, "I don't know, sir."

"Bullshit," he seethed with a single nod. "Where is he?"

"Coach, I don't know."

"Nicholas, I fucking swear to God."

Just take me out of the game at this point, Coach. I won't throw my brother under the bus, even with how much I wanted to kick his fucking ass right now.

Shooting me a sickened glare like he was fighting the urge to backhand me, Coach stepped back. "Get on the ice for warmup," he mumbled, walking away.

Everyone had their eyes on Jonah during warmups.

With Lane being AWOL, Jonah would have to take his spot on our line for the time being. And who the hell knew how long that would be for?

Jonah was an incredible talent, and he'd improved drastically since the start of the season from being guided by a team that was primarily filled with veterans.

But even with Jonah's speed, accuracy, and sharp passes, he still wasn't Lane.

Western Michigan defeated us in the tournament last year, and we were either going to get redemption or feel a heavy sense of déjà vu tonight.

Warmups were a bit shaky for me, I'd admit. I used the time between warmup and puck drop to try to clear my head, but it was fucking hard to without Lane here. Not to mention that not hearing him give a captain speech before the game was throwing a lot of us off. Our routine had been disturbed, and we could only hope that it didn't affect how we played.

Shifting side to side in my skates, I stood between Jett and Cody in our straight line, helmet at my hip as we stood for the national anthem.

I can't believe I'm about to play this tourney game without him.

Sliding into position to the right of Jonah, I took in a puff of air so cold that it burned the back of my throat.

We were playing at the Xcel Center, home to the Minnesota Wild, which was a little ironic with our current situation. The arena was over four times the size of ours back at Cedar, and almost every seat tonight was full. Immaculate energy swarmed from each side of the arena, and I tried to focus on that instead of focusing on the fact that Lane wasn't next to me.

To the left, an entire section was full of Stallions fans, painting the space a sea of silver and black. Even through hundreds of faces, I could spot Kota. It was like Kota's presence alone was strong enough for me to pick her out of a lineup with my eyes closed. She stood when she saw me looking at her, waving her arms frantically through the air as she repped my name and number, dulling my anxiety. I smiled and waved back.

With just over a minute left until puck drop, Coach's screaming pulled me away from the moment, and as I turned, I spotted an ashamed Lane skating forward, head down.

Our entire line, ready and waiting on the ice, breathed a sigh of relief as Lane replaced Jonah.

Even with how relieved I was, it didn't stop a scowl from taking over my face. "Look who made it."

"I'm sorry," he stared at the ice.

Stealing another glance at Kota, I sighed, softening. I couldn't even blame him. If the tables were turned, I probably would've done the same thing. "Did you at least find her?"

"I did." He was still studying the ice, still afraid to look me in the eyes and see the leftover rage that had been waiting for him all day, but I could make out the trace of a smile on his lips, letting me know that everything was going to be okay.

"Good. Now you have no excuse to suck tonight."

Lane shook his head through a chuckle, and for the first time today, I was actually excited for this game.

We'd been working all season for this moment. All our *lives* for this moment. To be one of sixteen lucky teams in the NCAA tournament.

And now here we were.

Round one of four.

We wanted that fucking title more than anything, but even if we didn't get it, at least I got to close out my college career alongside my best friend.

Chapter Seventy-Six

Kota

With an empty seat on either side of me, I held my breath as the puck was minutes away from dropping.

Miraculously, Lane had skated his way onto the ice, and considering he was across the state just a few hours ago, it felt like he teleported here.

But even with his relaxed demeanor, there was still no Bridget in sight. My texts to her wouldn't even go through because the service in this arena sucked.

I had no idea if Lane found her, if they talked, if things got worse, nothing. I knew nothing. And if we weren't moments away from my boyfriend's tournament game starting, I would've been running around trying to find signal.

Right now, it felt like I had to either figure out where Bridget was or wait and watch the start of my boyfriend's game.

Either way, I felt guilty.

"Kota!"

Turning my head, a glowing girl with a caramel-colored ponytail waved my way, and I stood.

"El!" I jumped up, greeting her as she scooted through the people in our row to meet me.

Arms flinging around each other, I smiled, taking in a whiff of her floral-smelling Juicy Couture perfume.

"Sorry I'm late," she said, setting her black clutch down as she sat beside me. "I didn't want to be rude and find my spot while they were still singing the anthem. Where's Bridget?"

"Hopefully coming soon," I sighed, leaving it at that. Eyes skimming over her, my smirk turned devious. "Just friends, huh?"

El looked down at Matt's jersey. "Yep," she muttered, but it didn't sound like she was even convinced.

"Mhm, right."

"Hey," she grinned, playfully pushing my shoulder. "We are just friends. Unlike *some* people."

"I know, I know. It's the plot twist of the century," I chuckled, my eyes following Crew as he positioned himself for puck drop.

"You still need to tell me all the details," El said. Glancing at her, I tried to follow her line of sight, and if I didn't know any better, I'd say she had her eyes glued on Matt. "Most of what I know has come from Matt."

I snorted. "So, it's probably false information then?"

"Probably," she laughed.

After Matt found out about Crew and me, I received a long array of text messages from El, demanding answers. I'd given her a shortened version of events, but she'd been begging me for the full story ever since.

I, on the other hand, was much more interested in whatever was going on with her and Matt.

It was funny to me how El and I had never met in real life, yet it felt like we had, as if I'd known her for years. Obviously, she could never replace Bridget as my best friend, but I hadn't had a lot of close girlfriends growing up, so I was thankful to have a new one now.

The second the puck hit the ice, hockey sticks were battling for it, and Lane secured it quickly. Just like countless previous games, I struggled to keep up with the pace, half the time not knowing where the puck actually was. Everything was moving in fast forward.

Ramming into an opponent, Matt sent him falling to the ice like a fly.

"Yes!" El screamed, clapping. "Let's go, Matt!"

"Mhm, just friends."

Smiling, she shook her head. "Don't tell me you're hopping on the 'El and Matt bandwagon'."

"Who says I'm just now hopping on? Maybe I've been on it for a while."

El's eyes stayed on the ice, squinting as her head snaked around, following the puck. "Hate to break it to you, sis," she said, "but I'm not gonna date Matt."

"Why not?" I groaned.

El's eyes matched her hair color, pure caramel under the fluorescent lights. "He's my best friend," her voice dipped with a wave of emotion. "It would be too complicated," she shrugged.

"But—"

"Hey!"

I turned, catching B's smiling face as she took her seat to my left.

"Oh my gosh, B!" I squealed, wrapping her up in a hug. Burying my face into her hair, I sighed. "What happened? Are you okay?"

Softness creased her features, and relief shone through her eyes. "Yeah, I'm okay."

Lightly pushing her arms out of the way, I beamed. The number *1* sat comfortably across her chest; her beautiful strawberry locks were covering it right now, but I knew *Avery* was spelled across her upper back and it overwhelmed me with joy.

"Everything's good?" I asked.

"Yeah," she nodded. "I'll tell you later."

"Okay."

"Hi!" El intervened, stretching a hand past me. "I was hoping you'd be here!"

B smiled, greeting her, and the two caught up for a few moments while I sat back and watched the game.

When Matt held off the defense well enough for Lane to successfully pass the puck off to Crew, giving him the chance to sink it into the net, all three of us leapt up.

My heart felt so full.

This was exactly where I was meant to be right now.

<u>*Epilogue*</u>

Kota

"**I** can't believe we're here," I said, mesmerized. I'd been smiling since the skyscrapers first came into view, and the closer we got to the heart of the city, the bigger my smile became.

"I can't believe we're still stuck in traffic," Crew whined.

Giggling, I watched cars inch forward in the lane beside us. Meanwhile, we'd been stuck in place for almost five minutes without moving at all. Our first taste of city life.

"I can't believe the four of us are going to be living together again."

"*I* can't believe Bridget's bio mom agreed to move to Chicago to be closer to her."

Was this some sort of new game we were starting? Seemed like it.

"I can't believe you guys are about to be in the NHL," I said.

"I can't believe you're going to be working at a fancy biology lab," Crew grinned.

I laughed again, staring out the passenger window. The city was so alive; even from our stationary place on the highway, it was like a never-ending array of movement and life around us.

434

Trains were still sailing past. Planes louder than missiles were flying overhead, preparing to land into O'Hare. Cars were cutting each other off to get to the nearest exit.

It was the perfect time to be moving— spring had arrived, each day getting gradually warmer. I wasn't quite sure how warm it would be just blocks from Lake Michigan, but it probably helped create perfect weather in the summer.

I took it all in like a child seeing Chicago for the first time. "I can't believe you're a *champion*," I teased, giving Crew a light poke in his side.

Giving me a quick, starry-eyed gaze, Crew's dimples sank deeply into his cheeks as he smiled. "I can't believe you're still bringing that up."

I was tempted to lean over and stick my finger in those pretty dimples just for the hell of it. "Are we almost there?" I chuckled.

"I think so. GPS says thirteen minutes."

The GPS failed to mention that traffic would add another fifteen minutes.

That was okay though. I didn't mind spending a few extra minutes in the car with Crew.

Based on Lane and Bridget's location, they were stuck miles behind us. It'd probably take them at least an hour to get to our new apartment.

Finally, Crew and I beat the traffic, driving through downtown and managing not to turn the wrong way down a one-way.

There was a parking garage that connected to our building. Luckily for us, we were on the top floor, the fifteenth floor, which meant we'd have the best view in the building.

I'd never actually seen the apartment in person, only in pictures. Lane and Crew had set out a few weeks ago to apartment hunt, catching a flight in the middle of the night without telling Bridget and me.

At first, we were ticked off. Obviously, we would've wanted to join, but the boys insisted on choosing the apartment, because up until then, Bridget and I had vetoed every option they'd shown.

The reasoning? They were all expensive as hell. They were all beautiful, I'd admit, but absolutely out of our price range.

For Lane and Crew though, they no longer had a price range. Their NHL contracts were in full swing, so they took it upon themselves to find the most lavish four bedroom available, telling us not to worry about the rent.

Stepping into the apartment, it was even more stunning than the photos. The floors were light-colored hardwood, accompanied with white walls, which brightened the place.

The wall on the far side of the apartment was made of floor-to-ceiling windows, and I ran over, squishing my body up against it in the shape of a star.

"Wow," I said, my hot breath leaving fog.

Whoops.

The apartment overlooked Lake Michigan. From the crystal blue hue and the endless span of water that disappeared once it met the horizon, it honestly looked like the ocean.

Boats were scattered throughout the lake, and Navy Pier was just as lively as everything else in this city; the ferris wheel was spinning peacefully, and from this height, people looked like ants running around.

It felt like I was standing in a fairytale.

"It's so beautiful," I said.

Appearing beside me, Crew smiled. "It is."

"You better not hit me with that cheesy line right now."

"What line?" he asked.

"It's beautiful, but not as beautiful as you," I said in a mocking tone, causing that full, husky laugh that I loved so much to roll through his chest.

"Noted. Alright," he nodded. "I won't call you beautiful then." Once I shot him a look, he let out a snort and shielded his grin with the back of his hand. "You're gorgeous?" he said, trying to smother away the hardness in my eyes. "I love you?"

Raising a brow, I waited silently.

"Is there something else I should say?"

I couldn't hold back my laughter, stepping over to wrap my arms around his midsection. Nuzzling my face against

436

Crew's chest, he tightened his arms around me, squeezing like this was the last time we'd see each other rather than the start of our lives.

Standing there for a moment, the only sound was our heartbeats pulsing in sync, and nothing in my life had ever seemed so perfect before.

"Well," I quietly said, treading away as Crew reluctantly let me go. He watched me head straight for my purse that I'd thrown into the empty corner; I pulled a small bag of pretzels out and took a seat on the floor.

"You have snacks?" he laughed.

"I always have snacks," I said. "Do you want one?"

Scoffing in disbelief, Crew sat in front of me. "You're offering to share your snack with me?"

"You're right. That does seem unlike me, doesn't it?" I nodded, speaking through bites. "I'll share with you, though." My own voice sounded foreign to me. It was higher-pitched, sweeter and smoother. That cruel note that used to overtake me was nowhere to be found. I dropped a few pretzels into Crew's hand.

Observing our new apartment as we ate, we were a bit clueless as to what to do next. Lane and Bridget were still far, and we weren't ready to start unpacking after the long car ride.

We obviously had no furniture or TV or even Rob K to play with. I'd lost rock, paper, scissors the other day, which meant Bridget got to take him in the car with her.

So, for now, it was just me, Crew, the floor, and our pretzels.

"You wanna play rapid fire questions?" I asked.

"Sure," he said through a mouthful. "You go first."

"Okay," I leaned back into my hands, thinking. "Do you miss your old lifestyle?"

My question seemed to catch Crew off guard. He froze, blinking at me before his eyes creased at the corners, softening. "No. I don't. I like my life how it is now."

I gave the tiniest smile, butterflies soaring around in my belly. I used to hate that feeling, but now, I welcomed it, longed for it.

"My turn," Crew said to himself. "Do, uh... do you think we'll get married someday?"

Just when I thought the butterflies couldn't flutter any more sporadically than they already were, they proved me wrong.

"If this is your way of telling me you want *me* to propose to *you*, then no," I joked, relieved to hear his laughter once again. "But honestly... yeah, I do. Maybe." My chin fell towards the floor, a shitty attempt to hide the red staining my cheeks. "Do you think we will?"

"Yeah," he rapidly said. "I do."

My grin was threatening to break my face in half. "I love you."

"I love you too," he said softly. "You're my favorite pain in the ass."

The End.

Acknowledgements

To start, thank you to each and every one of you for reading this book. I cannot express my immense gratitude for your support. Without you, I would not have the same passion to write. If you enjoyed this book, please consider leaving a review on Goodreads and Amazon!

To my family, specifically my sisters, thank you for your unconditional love.

To all my bookish besties— you know who you are— thank you for keeping me sane during this process.

Thank you to my friends who have encouraged me as I continue my writing journey: Clarissa, Liv, Kate, Lyss, Alli, Chloe, and Kelsey.

My incredible editors, Elaine and Cierra, thank you for being superstars during the editing process and for assuring me that this manuscript wasn't as much of a wreck as I thought it was!

And lastly, thank you to all my characters for allowing me to write your story. I'm incredibly honored you chose me to do it.